DEFENDERS OF ULTHUAN

ELDAIN DREW HIS sword as they finally reached the tower, its white walls blazing with inner fire and the golden carvings blinding to look upon. He, Rhianna and Yvraine had fought their way through to the tower in stuttering fits and starts, the Sword Master cutting them a path through the magical creatures with lightning quick slashes of her sword.

Rhianna had regained her composure, each step taken that brought them closer to the tower reinvigorating her with the pure magic that flowed from it. Fierce battles raged on, with the Sword Masters linking up and fighting in disciplined phalanxes instead of the isolated struggles the initial attacks had forced upon them.

Yet even with such methodical precision, more and more of the horrific creatures were emerging from the slithering pools of magical energy shed by those that were slain. For every beast killed, more would rise to fight again and slowly, step by step, the Sword Masters were being forced back against the tower.

More Graham McNeill from the Black Library

· WARHAMMER ·

GUARDIANS OF THE FOREST
THE AMBASSADOR CHRONICLES
(Omnibus containing *The Ambassador* and *Ursun's Teeth*)

High Elf novels
Book 1 – DEFENDERS OF ULTHUAN
Book 2 – SONS OF ELLYRION

· TIME OF LEGENDS: THE LEGEND OF SIGMAR ·

Book 1 – HELDENHAMMER
Book 2 – EMPIRE
Book 3 – GOD KING

· WARHAMMER 40,000 ·

THE ULTRAMARINES OMNIBUS
(Omnibus edition containing books 1-3 in the series:
Nightbringer, Warriors of Ultramar and *Dead Sky, Black Sun*)

Book 4 – THE KILLING GROUND
Book 5 – COURAGE AND HONOUR
Book 6 – THE CHAPTER'S DUE

STORM OF IRON
(An Iron Warriors novel)

· HORUS HERESY ·

FALSE GODS
FULGRIM
MECHANICUM
A THOUSAND SONS
THE OUTCAST DEAD (November 2011)

· AUDIO ·

(with Dan Abnett)
THE DARK KING/THE LIGHTNING TOWER

A WARHAMMER NOVEL

DEFENDERS OF
ULTHUAN

GRAHAM MCNEILL

BLACK LIBRARY

For Adam Troke, probably the most decent man I've ever met. An invaluable helper and good friend.

A BLACK LIBRARY PUBLICATION

First published in Great Britain in 2007 by
The Black Library,
Games Workshop Ltd.,
Willow Road, Nottingham,
NG7 2WS, UK.

10 9 8 7 6 5 4 3 2 1

Cover illustration by Marek Okon
Map by Nuala Kinrade and Karl Kopinski

A CIP record for this book is available from the British Library.

UK ISBN: 978 1 84970 157 0
US ISBN: 978 1 84416 558 2

See the Black Library on the internet at
www.blacklibrary.com

Find out more about Games Workshop
and the world of Warhammer at
www.games-workshop.com

Printed and bound in the UK by CPI Mackays, Chatham ME5 8TD

THIS IS A DARK age, a bloody age, an age of daemons and of sorcery. It is an age of battle and death, and of the world's ending. Amidst all of the fire, flame and fury it is a time, too, of mighty heroes, of bold deeds and great courage.

AN ANCIENT AND proud race, the high elves hail from Ulthuan, a mystical island of rolling plains, rugged mountains and glittering cities. Ruled over by the noble Phoenix King, Finubar, and the Everqueen, Alarielle, Ulthuan is a land steeped in magic, renowned for its mages and fraught with blighted history. Great seafarers, artisans and warriors the high elves protect their ancestral homeland from enemies near and far. None more so than from their wicked kin, the dark elves, against whom they are locked in a bitter war that has lasted for centuries.

THESE ARE BLEAK times. Across the length and breadth of the Old World, from the heartlands of the human Empire, and the knightly palaces of Bretonnia to ice-bound Kislev in the far north, come rumblings of war. In the towering Worlds Edge Mountains, the orc tribes are gathering for another assault. Bandits and renegades harry the wild southern lands of the Border Princes. There are rumours of rat-things, the skaven, emerging from the sewers and swamps across the land. And from the northern wildernesses there is the ever-present threat of Chaos, of daemons and beastmen corrupted by the foul powers of the Dark Gods. As the time of battle draws ever nearer, Ulthuan, and all of the civilised lands, need heroes like never before.

Naggaroth

Blighted Isle

Shrine of Khaine

Chrace

Shadowlands

Phoenix
Gate

Anlec

Dragon Gate

Unicorn Gate

Ellyrion

The Sunken Lands

Griffon Gate

Eagle Gate

Gaen
Vale

Tor Elyr

Sea of Dusk

Tor Anroc

The Sunken City

The Inner Sea

Tiranoc

Shrine of
Asuryan

The Dragon Spire

Vaul's
Anvil

150 Miles

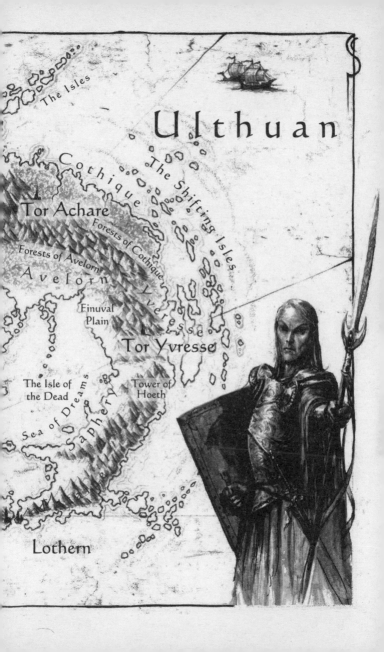

The Isles

Ulthuan

Cothique

The Shifting Isles

Tor Achare

Forests of Cothique

Forests of Avelorn

Avelorn

Yvresse

Finuval
Plain

Tor Yvresse

The Isle of
the Dead

Saphery

Tower of
Hoeth

Sea of Dreams

Lothern

BOOK ONE
NEPENTHE

Chapter One

Survivors

Thunderous booms echoed from the cliffs as the surf crashed against the rock and exploded upwards in sprays of pure white. The icy, emerald sea surged through the channels between the rocky archipelagos to the east in great swells, rising and falling in foam-topped waves that finally washed onto the distant shores of a mist-shrouded island.

Amid the great green waves, a splintered shard of wreckage was carried westward towards the island, the last remnants of a ship that had fallen foul of the obscuring mists and shifting isles that protected the eastern approaches to the island. Clinging to the debris was a lone figure whose golden hair was plastered to his skull and tapered ears, and whose clothes were torn and bloodied.

He clung desperately to the wreckage, barely able to see as salt spray stung his eyes and the hammer-blows of the waves threatened to tear him from the wood and

11

drag him to his doom beneath the water. The flesh of his fingers and palms was torn as he gripped tightly to all that remained of the ship he had sailed in.

Clinging to the hope that the sea would bear him to the island's beaches before his strength gave out and water claimed him for its own, he kicked feebly as he was pitched about like a rider on an unbroken colt. His every muscle burned with fire and blood streamed from a swollen gash on his forehead, the dizziness and nausea threatening to part him from the wreckage as surely as the waves. The sea was carrying him towards the island, though the glittering mists that shrouded its cliffs seemed to distort the distance between him and his salvation; one minute promising imminent landfall, the next dashing those hopes as the land appeared to recede.

Not only did the mists confound his sight, but also, it appeared, his hearing. Even amid the tumult of the waves, he fancied he could hear the slap of water on the hull of a ship behind him as it plied the treacherous channels. He turned his head this way and that, seeking the source of the sound, but he could see nothing save the endless expanse of ghostly mists that clung to the sea like a lover and the tantalising sight of the white cliffs.

He swallowed a mouthful of sea and coughed saltwater as his body shook with exhaustion and cold. A dreadful lethargy cocooned his limbs and he could feel the strength ebbing from his body as surely as if drawn by a spell. His eyelids felt as though lead weights had been attached to them, drooping over his sapphire blue eyes and promising oblivion if he would just close them and give up. He shook off the sleep he knew would kill him and ground his torn palms into the splintered edges of the wood, the pain welcome and necessary even as he threw back his head and screamed.

He screamed for pain and for loss and for an anguish he did not yet understand.

How long he had been in the water, he did not know. Nor could he remember the ship he had sailed on or what role he had fulfilled as part of its crew. His memory was as insubstantial as the mists, fragmentary images scudding across the surface of his mind without meaning, and all he could remember was the cruel sea battering him with unthinking power.

The ocean lifted him up, high atop a roaring curve of water before slamming him back down into yet another bottle-green trough, but in the instant he had crested the wave, he spied the landscape of the island through salt-encrusted eyes once more.

Tall cliffs of pearl-white stone crowned with achingly beautiful greenery were closer than ever before, the echoes of powerful waves splintering to crystal shards at their base now deafening. Fresh hope surged in his blood as the mists parted and he saw a golden curve of beach beyond a spur of marble rock.

Hysterical laughter bubbled up inside him and he kicked desperately as he struggled against the tide to reach the soil of his home. He gritted his teeth and struggled with the last of his strength to reach the salvation of the shore. Angry at being denied its prize, the sea fought to retain him, but he plumbed the depths of his desperation and courage to break its embrace.

Slowly the bow of beach grew larger, sweeping around the edges of a rocky bay upon which numerous watchtowers and lighthouses were perched. He felt his strength fade as he passed into the more sheltered waters of the bay and pulled himself further onto the timbers of his lost ship as the currents carried him onwards.

His vision dimmed. He knew he had pushed his tortured body too far and he had nothing more to give. He lay his head down on the smooth surface of the timber and felt his limbs relax as consciousness began to fade. He smiled as he watched the coastline of his homeland draw nearer, tall poplars and hardy grasses marching down to the shoreline from the cliff tops high above.

Winged shapes pinwheeled in the sky above him and he smiled as the sea birds filled the air with their cries, as though welcoming him home once more – though he could not recall why or for how long he had been gone. His mind drifted as the current carried him towards the beach and it took him several minutes to register the soft impact of his makeshift raft against the shore.

He lifted his head to spit saltwater as his eyes filled with tears of joy at the thought that he had returned home. He wept and pulled himself from the timbers that had carried him through the cold green waters of the sea and rolled into the shallow surf.

To feel the soft sand beneath him was ecstasy and he gouged great handfuls in his bloodied fists as he clawed his way to dry land. Inch by tortuous inch, he dragged his sodden frame onto the beach, each herculean effort punctuated with wracking sobs and gasps of exhaustion.

Finally, he was clear of the ocean and collapsed onto his side, the breath heaving in his lungs and his tears cutting clear paths through the grime on his face. He rolled onto his back, staring up at a heartbreakingly beautiful blue sky as his eyes fluttered shut.

'I am home,' he whispered as he drifted into darkness. 'Ulthuan…'

* * *

ELLYR-CHAROI, THE GREAT villa of the Éadaoin family, shone as though aflame, early afternoon sunlight reflecting dazzlingly from gemstones set within its walls and the coloured glass that filled the high windows of its many azure-capped towers. Built around a central courtyard, the villa's architecture had been designed to render it as much a part of the landscape as the natural features that surrounded it. Its builders had employed the natural topography in its design so that it appeared that the villa had arisen naturally from its surroundings rather than having been raised by the artifice of craftsmen.

Set amid a wide stand of trees, the villa was bounded on two sides by a pair of foaming white waterfalls that had their origin high on the eastern slopes of the Annulii Mountains. The waters of both joined beyond the villa, flowing fast and cold to a wide river that glittered on the horizon. An overgrown pathway led from the gates of the villa to a sweeping bridge of arched timbers that curved over the rushing waters and followed the course of the river through the eternal summer of Ellyrion to the mighty city of Tor Elyr.

Autumn leaves lay thick and still against the smooth stone of the villa and climbing vines curled like snakes across the cracked walls, unchecked and wild. A soft breeze blew through the open gates like a sigh of regret and whistled through cracked panes of glass on the tallest towers. Where once warriors had stood sentinel by the portal that led within and surveyed Lord Éadaoin's realm from the watchtowers, all that remained now was the memory of those faithful retainers.

Within the walls of the villa, golden leaves danced in the ghostly breaths of wind that soughed through echoing and empty rooms. No water gurgled in the fountain and no laughter or warmth filled its deserted halls. The only sound to break the silence was that of hesitant footsteps as they made their way along a marble-tiled cloister towards elegantly curved stairs that led from the courtyard to the master of this villa's chambers.

RHIANNA LOOKED UP from her book as Valeina emerged from the shadow of the leaf-strewn cloister and stepped down into the Summer Courtyard, though such a name seemed now to be at odds with the autumnal air that hung over the open space. The young elf maid carried a silver tray upon which sat a crystal goblet of wine and a platter of fresh fruits, bread, cheese and cold cuts of meat. Dressed in the livery of the household, Valeina had served the lords of the Éadaoin for almost a decade now and Rhianna smiled in welcome as the young girl passed the silent fountain at the courtyard's centre.

In the year and a half since she had lived in the Éadaoin villa, Rhianna had grown fond of Valeina and valued the times they were able to speak. Inwardly, she knew that she would never have considered such a friendship back in her father's estates… but a lot had happened since she had left Saphery.

'My lady,' said Valeina, setting the tray down beside her. 'Lord Éadaoin's food. You said you wished to take it to him yourself.'

'Yes, I did,' replied Rhianna. 'Thank you.'

The girl inclined her head in a gesture of respect, the boundaries between noble born elf and common citizen still strong despite their growing friendship, and Rhianna needed no mage sight to sense that it sat ill with Valeina in bringing this repast to her instead of directly to the master of the house. Etiquette demanded that no highborn elf of Ulthuan should carry out such mundane tasks as serving food, but Rhianna had politely requested that this meal be brought to her first.

'Will you be requiring anything else, my lady?' asked Valeina.

Rhianna shook her head and said, 'No, I'm fine. Won't you sit awhile?'

Valeina hesitated and Rhianna's smile faltered, knowing that she was simply using the girl as an excuse to delay taking the meal to its intended recipient.

'I know this is... unorthodox, Valeina,' said Rhianna, 'but it is something I need to do.'

'But it's not right, my lady,' said the elf maid. 'A lady of your standing doing the work of the household, I mean.'

Rhianna reasserted her smile and reached out to take Valeina's hand in hers. 'I'm just carrying some food upstairs to my husband, that's all.'

The elf maid cast a glance towards the stairs that curled upwards into the Hippocrene Tower. Once, a portion of the crashing waterfalls beyond the villa had been channelled down grooves fashioned into the sides of the tower to feed the fountain at the centre of the Summer Courtyard, but now cracked leaves filled the cascading marble and silver bowls instead of glittering crystal waters.

'How is Lord Éadaoin?' asked Valeina, clearly nervous at such an intrusive question.

Rhianna sighed and chewed her bottom lip before answering. 'He is the same as always, my dear Valeina. The death of Cae... his brother is a splinter of ice in his heart and it cools his blood to those around him.'

'We all miss Caelir, my lady,' said Valeina, squeezing

Rhianna's hand and naming the grief that had settled upon the Éadaoin household like a shroud. 'He brought this house to life.'

'He did that,' agreed Rhianna, struggling to hold back a sudden wave of sadness that threatened to overwhelm her. A strangled sob escaped her, but she angrily caged the sorrow within and reasserted control on her emotions.

'I'm sorry! I didn't mean to–'

'It's all right, my dear,' said Rhianna. 'Really.'

She knew she had not convinced the elf maid and wondered if she'd convinced herself.

Two years had passed since Caelir's death in Naggaroth and though the sadness was still a bright pain in her heart, chains of duty that were stronger than death bound her to her fate.

She remembered the day she had watched the Eagle ships returning to Lothern after the raid on the land of the dark elves, the hated druchii, the gleaming silver of the Sapphire Gate shining like fire in the setting sun behind them. No sooner had she looked into the haunted eyes of Eldain as he had stepped onto the quayside than she knew that Caelir was lost, the visions of Moraiheg that had filled her dreams with dark premonitions suddenly brought to horrid life.

The druchii had slain Caelir, explained Eldain, and the all-consuming grief he felt at his brother's loss was as hot and painful as hers. Together they had wept and held each other close, allowing their shared loss to bring them closer that they might heal themselves.

She shook off the memory of that dark day and looked down at the pledge ring on her finger, a silver band with a swirling cobalt coloured gem set amid a pair of entwined hands. Soon after, Eldain had spoken of the promise he had made to his younger brother upon their departure for the Land of Chill; a promise that he would take care of Rhianna should anything happen to Caelir.

They had been wed the following year and the elven nobility of Ulthuan all agreed that it was a good match.

As well they might, thought Rhianna, for she and Eldain had all but been betrothed to one another before she had lost her heart to Caelir after he had saved her from death at the hands of druchii raiders a year previously.

But dreams of love were long gone and she was now the wife of Eldain, lord of the Éadaoin family and master of this villa.

Rhianna slid her hand from Valeina's and lifted the silver tray. She stood smoothly and said, 'I should take this to Eldain.'

Valeina stood with her and said, 'He has a good soul, my lady. Just give him some time.'

Rhianna nodded stiffly and turned away, making her way to the stairs and her husband who brooded alone with his grief in the tallest tower of Ellyr-charoi.

ELDAIN GRIPPED THE edges of the window tightly as he stood before the tall lancet that looked out over the rolling greensward of Ellyrion and listened to the voices drifting up from the Summer Courtyard. Every word was a dagger in his heart and he closed his eyes as he felt the pain of them stabbing home. He let out a deep breath and tried to calm his racing heartbeat by reciting the vow of the Sword Masters of Hoeth.

Though he had never journeyed to the White Tower,

where the legendary warrior mystics trained, he still found their mantra soothed him in times of trial, the rhythmic cadences of the words sounding like music in his ears.

Eldain opened his eyes and, taking a deep, calming breath he raised his eyes to the soaring mountains that lay to the west. The Annulii Mountains towered over the grasslands of Ellyrion, stark and white against the pale blue of the sky, their summits lost in the swirling mists of raw magic that flowed between the outer and inner kingdoms of Ulthuan. The reassuring permanence of the mountains was a balm on his soul, and his eyes roamed over their craggy peaks and tree-swathed slopes, picking out paths and sacred groves amongst the great spires of rock.

In their youth, both he and Caelir had roamed the land of Ellyrion on the back of steeds they had raised from foals and who had become their boon companions since first they had ridden together, but now Caelir was dead and Eldain's steps barely carried him from Ellyr-charoi.

'He has a good soul,' he had heard Valeina say, and he did not know whether to laugh or cry at the words. He turned from the window and paced the circumference of the Hippocrene Tower, his long cloak of sky-blue cloth trailing behind him as a cold wind scattered leaves and papers across an exquisitely carved desk of walnut.

The inner walls of the tower were lined with bookshelves and pierced by tall windows at each of the eight compass points, allowing the Lord of Ellyr-charoi to survey his domain and keep watch on the mighty herds of Ellyrion steeds as they thundered across the plains.

Eldain slumped behind his desk and gathered the

papers the wind had scattered. Amongst the reports of Shadow Warriors from the western coasts and missives from the garrison of the Eagle Gate high in the mountains were numerous invitations to dine at the homes of nobles of Tor Elyr, entreaties to the latest spectacle of wonder of Saphery and word from his agents in the port of Lothern concerning his trade investments.

He could focus on none of it for more than a moment and he looked up to face the portrait that hung on the wall opposite his desk. For all the difference between the portrait's subject and Eldain, he might as well have been looking into a mirror and only more careful study would reveal the differences between the two.

Both wore their platinum blond hair long and confined by a golden circlet and both had the strong, handsome bone structure common to the Ellyrion nobility – a rugged windswept countenance that spoke of a lifetime spent in the open air atop the greatest steeds in Ulthuan. Their eyes were both a crisp blue, flecked with ocean grey, but where the face in the portrait displayed a well-fed, roguish insouciance, Eldain's features were gaunt and serious. The artist had captured the boyish mischief that always glimmered in his younger brother's eyes as well as the quality of dashing adventure that always seemed to surround Caelir like a mystical aura. Eldain knew well enough that he possessed none of these qualities.

His eyes locked with those of Caelir and he felt the familiar guilt stir within, welcoming it like an old friend. He knew it was perverse to keep the portrait of his dead brother – and his wife's former betrothed – hanging before him where he would be forced to see it every day, but ever since his 'triumphant' return from the land of the druchii, he had forced himself to confront the reality of what had happened on Naggaroth.

Every day it ate away at him, but he could no more deny himself the guilty torment than he could stop the beat of his heart.

Eldain looked up as he heard Rhianna's footfalls on the steps leading up to his chambers. Even had he not heard the conversation below, he would have recognised her tread. He forced a smile to his full lips as she came into view, holding a silver tray laden with sweet smelling morsels.

He took a sharp intake of breath at her beauty, each time finding some aspect of her to savour anew. Her waist length hair spilled around her shoulders like a run of honey and her delicate oval features were sculpted more perfectly than any artist could hope to capture with the finest Tiranoc marble. Her long blue dress was threaded with silver loops and spirals and her soft eyes flickered with hints of magical gold.

She was beautiful and her beauty was yet another punishment.

'You should let Valeina do this,' he said as she set the tray down before him.

'I like coming here,' said Rhianna with a smile, and he could hear the lie in her words.

'Really?'

'Really,' she said, moving towards the window and staring into the distance. 'I like the view. You can practically see all the way to the forest of Avelorn.'

Eldain tore his gaze from Rhianna and looked down at the tray of food she had brought and reluctantly lifted a piece of bread. He had no appetite and dropped it back onto the tray as Rhianna turned from the window and said, 'Why don't we go riding today, Eldain? There's still plenty of light left in the day and it's been too long since you rode Lotharin.'

The mention of his faithful steed made Eldain smile and though the midnight black horse roamed the plains with the wild herds that ran free throughout the kingdom of Ellyrion, the merest thought would summon him back to Ellyr-charoi at a gallop, such was the bond they shared.

He shook his head and waved his hand at the scattered papers upon the desk. 'I cannot. I have work to finish.'

Rhianna's face flushed and he could see her anger manifest itself in the soft glow that built behind her golden eyes. A daughter of Saphery, the power of magic coursed in her veins and Eldain could feel the actinic tang of it in the air.

'Please, Eldain,' said Rhianna. 'This is not healthy. You spend every day cooped up in this tower with nothing but books and papers and… Caelir for company. It is morbid.'

'Morbid? It is morbid now to remember the dead?'

'No, it is not morbid to mourn the dead, but to live life in their shadow is wrong.'

'I live in no shadow,' said Eldain, lowering his head.

'Do not lie to me, Eldain,' warned Rhianna. 'I am your wife!'

'And I am your husband!' he said, rising from behind the desk and sweeping the silver tray onto the floor. The plates clattered noisily and the crystal goblet shattered into a thousand fragments. 'I am the master of this household and I have business to attend to that does not allow me time for frivolous pursuits.'

'Frivolous pursuits…? Is that what I am to you now?'

He could see the tears gathering in her eyes and softened his tone. 'No, of course not, that's not what I meant, it's just…'

'Just what?' demanded Rhianna. 'Don't you remember how you lost me before? When the druchii almost killed me, it was Caelir that saved me because you were spending all your time locked up in this tower "attending to business".'

'Someone had to…' said Eldain. 'My father was dying, poisoned by the druchii and who was there to look after him and keep Ellyr-charoi safe? Caelir? I hardly think so.'

Rhianna stepped towards him and he felt his resolve crumbling in the face of her words. 'Caelir is dead, Eldain. But we are not and we still have lives to lead.'

She lifted a sheaf of papers from the desk and said, 'There is still a world beyond Ellyr-charoi, Eldain, a living, breathing world that we ought to be part of. But we pay no visits to our fellow nobles, nor do we dine in the halls of the great and good or dance at the masquerades of Tor Elyr…'

'Dance?' said Eldain. 'What is there to dance about, Rhianna? We are a dying people and no dance or masquerade can conceal that. You would have me plaster on a fake smile and dance at our race's funeral? The very thought sickens me to my stomach.'

The vehemence of his words surprised even him, but Rhianna shook her head, moving close to him and taking his hands in hers. 'Do you remember that you promised your brother you would take care of me?'

'I remember,' said Eldain, picturing the handsome Caelir as he confessed the fear he had for his survival on Naggaroth as their ship had passed the Glittering Tower at the mouth of the Straits of Lothern.

'Then take care of me, Eldain,' she said. 'Others can help look after Ellyr-charoi. Look out the window, Eldain, the world is still here and it is beautiful. Yes, the dark kin across the water prey upon us and yes, there are foul daemons that seek to destroy all that is good and wondrous, but if we live our lives in constant terror of such things then we might as well take a blade to our throats now.'

'But there are things I must do, things that–'

'They can wait,' said Rhianna, pulling his hands around her waist and drawing him close. The scent of summer orchards was in her hair and he took a breath of it, feeling his cares lighten even as he savoured the scent.

Eldain smiled and relaxed into her embrace, feeling her hands slide up his back.

He opened his eyes and stiffened as he looked into the eyes of his brother.

You killed me...

CHAPTER TWO

NEW BLOOD

A RED GLOW lit the dusky horizon behind the three Eagle ships as they patrolled the south-western coastline of Ulthuan, their silver hulls like knife blades as they cut through the green waters. Captain Finlain of *Finubar's Pride* watched the craggy peaks of the Dragonspine Mountains and the smoke-wreathed Vaul's Anvil recede as his small flotilla made its way towards its evening berthing upon the sandy shores of Tiranoc.

The thin strip of coastline of this rugged kingdom had once reached out beyond where his ships now sailed, but ancient malice and powerful magic had destroyed this once fair realm. Monstrous tides had swept over the plains of Tiranoc in ages past, sweeping thousands to their deaths and submerging its ripened fields and glorious cities forever beneath the waves. Only the mountains and the bleak haunches of land that huddled at their feet remained above the water now and Finlain knew navigating this close to the shore was always fraught with danger.

'Sounding,' said Finlain, his voice muffled by the low mist that hugged the surface of the water and slithered over his vessel's hull.

'All's well, captain,' came the reply from Meruval, the *Pride's* navigator. Finlain glanced over to the prow of his ship, where the mage Daelis sat in a high backed chair of ivory coloured timber, his eyes closed as he probed the waters and mists ahead with his magical sight for any dangerous rocks that might pierce the hull.

His crew were on edge and Finlain shared their unease. The red sky above Vaul's Anvil bled into the clouds like a bloodstain and the air had a foulness to it that was more than simply the sulphurous reek of the volcano.

'I'll be glad when we reach the beach for the night,' said Meruval, moving from the gunwale to stand next to his captain.

Finlain nodded, peering through the purple dusk towards the other vessels in his command. *Glory of Eataine* was riding a little low in the water and *Asuryan's Fire* lagged behind, her captain keeping a little too much distance between his ship and her sister vessels.

'Indeed,' said Finlain. 'The sea has an ill-aspect to it this evening.'

Meruval followed his captain's gaze and nodded in agreement. 'I know. I've had to steer us around rock formations I've never seen before. It's worse than sailing east of Yvresse.'

'Have you known this stretch of water to be this inconsistent before?'

'Not in my memory,' said Meruval, 'but in my

grandfather's time, he spoke of Tiranoc rising to the surface with great heaves that threw up bleak islands that sank almost as soon as they breached the surface.'

'As though the land sought to return to the light.'

'Something like that, yes. He said that when Vaul was angry, he would strike his anvil and the land around would heave with fire and earthquakes.'

Finlain glanced over his shoulder at the smoking peak of Vaul's Anvil and sent a quick prayer to the smith god that he would spare them such anger this night, since the light was fading fast and a brooding fog was rapidly closing in. Strange noises and flickering lights danced at the edge of perception, and though such things were not unheard of in the magical mists that obscured the isle of Ulthuan from predatory eyes, they were still unsettling.

Only the keen hearing of his crew and the mage sight of Daelis would see them safely to the shoreline and the feeling that he could do nothing more was anathema to him.

No sooner had he thought of the mage than his sonorous voice sounded from the prow.

'Captain! Land ahead, we must slow our progress.'

'Hold us here!' ordered Finlain, gripping the smooth timbers of the gunwale as the vessel came to a smooth halt.

'Come on,' he said and set off towards the mage, not waiting to see if Meruval followed him or not. He marched down the length of the ship, passing sailors eager to be on dry land for the evening. The ship was allowing the current to carry her to the shore, the crew ready to make any adjustments necessary to keep them on course.

'Almost at the beach,' he said as he passed the crew,

radiating a confidence he did not yet feel. He climbed the curved steps to the elaborate eagle prow and the mage who guided them slowly through the mist.

Daelis sat rigid on his chair, his cream and sapphire robes glittering with magical hoarfrost and a soft glow limning the edges of his eyes.

Without looking up, the mage said, 'We are close to land, captain. The shore is less than two boat lengths away.'

The mage's voice was distant, as though he spoke from within a great, echoing cave and Finlain could feel the ripple of magic work its way up his spine, a fleeting image of a dark, undersea world flickering behind his eyes.

'Two boat lengths?' said Meruval. 'Impossible. We haven't sailed far enough to be that close to land. You are mistaken.'

Daelis inclined his head towards the navigator, but did not open his eyes. 'I am not.'

'Captain,' said Meruval, indignant that his piloting skills were being called into question, 'we cannot be that close. He must be wrong.'

Finlain had sailed with both Daelis and Meruval for long enough to know that both were highly skilled at what they did and he trusted their judgment implicitly. However, in this case, one of them had to be wrong.

'I'm telling you, captain,' said Meruval. 'We can't be that close to the shore.'

'I believe you, my friend, but what if Daelis is correct also?'

'I *am* correct,' said Daelis, lifting his arm and pointing into the mist. 'Look.'

Finlain followed the mage's outstretched hand and

narrowed his eyes as he sought to identify what he was being shown. Scraps of mist floated like gossamer thin cloth and at first he was inclined to agree with Meruval that the mage was mistaken, but as the wisps of fog parted for a moment, he caught sight of a towering wall of glistening black rock rearing up before his ship.

Meruval saw it too and said, 'Isha preserve me if he wasn't right after all...'

'You said it yourself, Meruval, the sea was unsettled this night.'

'You have my humble apology, captain,' said his navigator. 'As do you, Mage Daelis.'

The mage smiled and Finlain shook his head as he marched back to his crew and issued the orders that would see them sail along the cliff until they reached a bay with a beach large enough to land all three ships.

'Guide us along the coast, Meruval,' said Finlain as a sudden whipcrack sound echoed behind him, followed by a trio of rapid thuds. He turned in surprise, seeing bright red runnels of blood streaming down the white back of the mage's chair and the barbed points of three crossbow bolts of dark iron that had punched through his chest.

Daelis gurgled in pain, pinned to his prow chair by the bolts, and it took a second for Captain Finlain to realise what had happened. He looked out into the mist, knowing now that Meruval had been right after all, they hadn't been close to land, and that great black cliff was not part of Ulthuan at all... it was...

The mists parted as a great crack of groaning rock echoed from the murky depths and the mighty cliff seemed to *twist* and rise from the ocean. Seawater poured from fanged portals and great idols of armoured warriors carved into the rock as they rose from the sea and a great beacon of flame bloomed high above him.

'To arms!' shouted Finlain, as a flurry of dark cross-bow bolts flashed through the air from somewhere high above him. Screams tore the air as many found homes in elven flesh and the stink of blood filled his senses. He staggered as a bolt tore across the side of his calf and embedded itself in the deck. He gritted his teeth against the pain, blood pooling in his boot, and looked up as a great flaming missile arced from the black cliff to engulf the *Glory of Eataine*. Her sail erupted in fire and flaming brands scattered all across her deck.

Its deception unmasked by the attack, the tall cliff of sheer rock cast off its mantle of poisonous mist and Finlain was rooted to the spot in terror as he saw the monstrous, unbelievable size of their attacker.

No mere ship was this, but a mountainous castle of incredible bulk set adrift on the sea and kept afloat by the most powerful enchantments. One of the dreaded Black Arks of the dark elves, this was a sinister floating fortress, tower upon tower and spire upon spire of living rock that had been sundered from the isle of Ulthuan over five thousand years ago.

Crewed by an entire army of deadly corsairs and dismal home to thousands of slaves, the Black Arks were the most feared seagoing vessels in the world and dwarfed even the might of Finlain's Eagle ships. Finlain had heard it said that the bulk they displayed above the surface of the water was but a fraction of their true size, with great vaulted caverns below the waterline that were home to terrible monsters, slaves and all manner of foul witchcraft.

Even as he recognised the identity of their attackers, a

brazen gate of rusted iron shrieked open in the side of the ark and a long boarding ramp crashed down over the gunwale, jagged spikes splintering the deck and wedging it fast into its prey.

Finlain pushed himself to his feet and swept his sword from its sheath, a glittering silver steel blade forged by his father and enchanted by the archmages of Hoeth.

Dark shapes gathered in the shadow of the gateway in the rock and a volley of white-shafted arrows slashed past Finlain's head to fell them with lethal accuracy. Another volley followed within seconds of the first and this time it was their enemies that were screaming.

He threw a glance over his shoulder to see that Meruval had formed several ranks of archers, their bone-white bows loosing arrow after arrow into the dark portal.

In answer, a scything spray of crossbow bolts spat from the mouth of the ark and Finlain heard the screams of his warriors as they died in the fusillade. Elven archers were the best in the world, but even they could not compete with the rate of fire the infernal weapons of their enemies could manage.

Keeping low, Finlain darted forwards as the deadly crossbow bolts thinned the defending elves long enough for the boarders to dash across the lowered ramp. Screaming druchii corsairs clad in dark robes and swathed in glittering cloaks formed from overlapping scales charged from the depths of the Ark, their twin swords gleaming red in the ruddy glow of Vaul's Anvil.

Finlain rose to meet them, his sword slashing through the first warrior's neck and pitching him into the sea. He stabbed the next enemy warrior through the groin and desperately blocked a deadly riposte to his own neck. It had been many years since Finlain had fought the dark kin of his race, slender ivory-skinned elves with long hair the colour of night. Their faces were twisted in hatred and their movements as swift and deadly as his own.

So like us... he thought sadly as he parried another blow and despatched his foe with a roll of his wrist that plunged the tip of his blade through the corsair's eye and into his brain. Blue-fletched arrows flashed past his head and sent more druchii screaming into the sea, most passing less than a foot from Finlain's head, but he feared no injury from his own warriors.

Another blade joined his and he smiled in welcome to see Meruval, armed with his twin, moonlight-bladed swords leap into the fray. With the aid of his faithful navigator, he was finally able to take more stock of the battle and risked glances left and right to see how the other ships in his command fared.

Glory of Eataine burned from stem to stern and Finlain knew she was lost. *Asuryan's Fire* was invisible in the dark and mist, but he feared the worst as he heard the raucous victory chants of the druchii and the screams of the dying.

Only *Finubar's Pride* fought on and he knew they had to break the hold the Black Ark had on them if they were to stand any chance of survival. Finlain stepped back from the desperate fighting and shouted, 'Meruval! Can you hold them?'

The navigator plunged his blades into the chest of a druchii warrior and kicked another into the sea, spinning on his heel and opening the belly of a third.

'For a time,' he said, as a pair of iron bolts smacked into the deck beside him.

Finlain nodded and limped away from the desperate

fight, shouting, 'Axes! Bring up axes, we need to cut ourselves free!'

Fire erupted from nearby and his heart sank as he saw *Glory of Eataine* break apart and sink beneath the waves along with her crew.

Finlain vowed that such would not be *their* fate…

'MY LADY,' SAID the warrior in the tall helm who carried a long, leaf-bladed spear. 'It is getting late and we should be heading back to the villa.'

Kyrielle Greenkin smiled as she heard the note of exasperation in the warrior's voice and put on her best pouting expression of innocence. Her auburn hair was woven in long plaits, held tight to her skull by silver cord that framed a beautiful face with shimmering jade eyes and a full-lipped mouth that could charm even the hardest heart.

A simple warrior had no chance.

'Not yet, silly,' she said, and there was beguiling magic in her voice. 'It is in the gloaming that some of the most wondrous plants flower. You wouldn't want me to return without something wondrous to present to my father, would you?'

The warrior glanced helplessly at his comrade, pinned like a butterfly by her captivating gaze and knowing he could not deny her, even had he desired to.

'No, my lady,' he said, defeated.

It was unfair of her to use magic on the guards her father had provided her with, but she had not lied when she spoke of the beauty of the night blooming flowers; the pearl-leafed Torrelain, the singing blooms of the magical Anurion (named for her father and its creator) and the beautifully aromatic Moon Rose.

She picked her way down the cliff top path that led to the beach, one guard before her and another behind as they made their way down to the shore. Kyrielle went barefoot, her keen eyes easily picking out sharp rocks and thorny brush before they could injure her.

Her long dress was fashioned from green silk and clung seductively to her slender form, its fabric woven with looping anthemion patterns. In one hand she carried a delicate reticule of tightly woven cloth and in the other a small knife with a silver blade – for night blooms should only ever be pruned with a silver blade.

The scent of the night filled her senses and she could smell the perfumes of the local flora as well as the powerful fragrances dragged from the depths of the ocean and borne upon the air. When the shifting isles on the eastern coast of Ulthuan renewed themselves, the darkness of the deep sea was disturbed and all manner of strange plant life was washed ashore as well as unknown aromas that scented the night air – the chief reason her father had sited one of his terraced garden-villas on this largely deserted peninsula of rock on the coast of Yvresse.

The pale crescent of the rising moon bathed the beach in ghostly radiance and turned the white cliffs into softly glowing walls of light as the surf crashed against them further out to sea and the waves rolled up the sand with soft sighs.

She loved this time of night, often seeking the peace and tranquillity that the sound of the waves brought her. To be out on a night like this, with the evening blooms spreading their petals and the light of the moon caressing her skin was heaven for Kyrielle, a time where she could forget the troubles of the world around her and simply enjoy its beauty.

'Isn't this magical?' she asked as she danced onto the beach, pirouetting beneath the moon like one of the naked dancers at the court of the Everqueen. Neither of the guards answered her, both aware when her questions were rhetorical. She laughed and ran down the beach along the line of the cliffs with long, graceful strides. Even this high on the beach, the sand was wet beneath her feet and she knew that the shifting isles must have undergone a violent transformation indeed to stir the oceans this strongly.

She stopped beside a particularly vivid Moon Rose, its petals slowly uncurling to reveal its romantically dark interior. The dusky scent of the plant sent a shiver of pleasure through her and she reached down to snip one of the pollen-producing anther before placing it in her reticule.

The soft clink of metal announced the arrival of her bodyguards, their armour slowing their pace and she laughed as she imagined their consternation as she had run down the beach and left them in her wake. She moved on, taking cuttings from a dozen different plants before she stiffened as she caught the bitter scent of something else, something that didn't belong.

'Can you smell that?' she asked, turning to her guards.

'Smell what, my lady?' replied the guard she had bewitched on the way down to the shore.

'Blood,' she said.

'Blood? Are you sure that's what you smell, my lady? Might it not be some kind of flower?'

She shook her head. 'No, silly. You're right that there are some plants that carry the scent of blood, but none that are native to Ulthuan. The druchii ferment a brew called blood wine and the vine the grapes come from is said to smell like congealed blood, but that's not what this is.'

At the mention of the druchii, both guards moved to stand beside her, their movements tense and martial as Kyrielle sampled the air once more and said, 'Yes, very definitely blood.'

Without waiting for her guards to follow her, she set off towards the shoreline where the waves tumbled to the sand in cursive lines of foam. She skipped lightly across the sand, leaving almost no marks where she trod as she followed the scent of blood across the beach.

Kyrielle halted as she saw the figure at the water's edge, lying spread-eagled on his back and looking for all the world like a corpse.

'There!' she said, pointing towards the body. 'I told you I could smell blood.'

Before she could set off once more, the nearest guard said, 'Wait here, my lady. Please.'

Reluctantly she acceded to the warrior's request; after all, there *was* a chance that this person might still be dangerous. Nevertheless, she followed behind the two guards as they cautiously advanced towards the body. As she drew nearer, she saw that it was a young and handsome elf dressed in a torn tunic of the Lothern Sea Guard. Even from behind her guards, she could see the slight rise and fall of his chest.

'He's alive,' she said, stepping towards him.

'Don't, my lady,' said one guard as the other knelt beside the figure and checked him for weapons. She watched as he removed the figure's cracked leather belt, upon which hung a knife sheathed in a metal scabbard of black and gold, and passed it back to his comrade.

'He's alive, all right.'

'Well, I told you that already,' said Kyrielle, pushing past the guard now holding the knife belt to kneel beside the unconscious elf. His hands were torn open and there was a nasty gash on his forehead, but he was breathing and that was something. His lips were moving as though he muttered to himself and she lowered her head to better hear what he was saying.

'Be careful, my lady!' said her guard.

She ignored his warning and held her ear to the young elf's mouth as he continued to whisper faintly.

'...must... told... I need... tell... Teclis. Needs to know... Teclis!'

'Please, my lady!' said her guard. 'We don't know who he is.'

'Don't be silly,' said Kyrielle, lifting her head from the unconscious figure's fevered ramblings. 'He's clearly one of our people, isn't he? Look!'

'We don't know anything about him. Who knows where he came from?'

Kyrielle sighed. 'Honestly! Look at his tunic. Whoever he is, he's clearly come from Lothern. Obviously his ship sank and he was able to swim ashore.'

'I've never heard of any Lothern ships falling foul of the Shifting Isles,' said one guard. 'Certainly not one of Lord Aislin's.'

'Lord Aislin?' said Kyrielle. 'How do you know he is one of Lord Aislin's sailors?'

The guard pointed to the partially obscured eagle claw emblem on the figure's tunic and said, 'That's Lord Aislin's family symbol.'

'Well that settles it then,' said Kyrielle. 'It's our duty to help him. Come on, lift him up and carry him back to the villa. My father will be able to help him.'

Seeing no other choice, the guards knelt beside the supine figure, hooked his arms over their shoulders and lifted him between them.

Kyrielle followed them as they carried him from the beach, smiling happily at this mystery that had washed up on her doorstep.

CAPTAIN FINLAIN AND three of his crew who had loosed all their arrows fought their way through the hail of iron bolts back towards the prow of *Finubar's Pride*, each warrior bearing a long-hafted shore axe. Searing tongues of magical flame streaked the dark sky, but none came near Finlain's ship, the arcing missiles all slamming into the hull of *Asuryan's Fire* and punishing her terribly.

A desperate exchange of arrows and crossbow bolts slashed back and forth between his ship and unseen enemies concealed high on the jagged, rocky battlements of the Black Ark, his warriors forced to conserve their arrows until their keen eyes spotted a definite kill shot. The druchii showed no such restraint and showered the deck of the *Pride* with deadly bolts at will, such that her deck and the roofs of her cabins resembled the hide of a porcupine.

The sporadically lit darkness and swirling smoke from the burning wreckage of the *Glory of Eataine* that still floated hampered the druchii marksmen and Finlain used its cover to move towards the sound of shouting and clashing blades, where Meruval fought the corsairs trying to board his ship.

Blood streamed from numerous cuts on Meruval's arms and chest and Finlain wondered how he could still be fighting, such was the amount of red on his tunic. Meruval fought with speed and grace, his pale blades killing with every stroke. Finlain wanted to shout to him, but knew that to break his concentration would be fatal. Instead, he turned to the warriors who accompanied him and said, 'That boarding ramp is embedded in the deck and gunwale, so you need to cut it free. Go, and no matter what happens, don't stop until it's done. Understood?'

Their grim expressions were all the answer he needed and Finlain simply nodded and said, 'Asuryan be with you.'

The four of them rose from their cover and charged towards Meruval, Finlain lagging behind as the wound in his calf flared painfully. One of the axemen was immediately pierced through the top of the skull by a crossbow bolt and fell to the deck, but the others reached the side of the ship and swung their axes in great overhead sweeps. Finely crafted timber splintered under their blades and Finlain winced at the damage being done to his faithful vessel, even as he knew it was necessary to save her.

Finlain swung his own blade at a corsair readying a killing blow against Meruval, but the blade slid across the warrior's scale cloak without penetrating. The druchii spun to face him and slashed with a pair of wickedly curved daggers that dripped black venom. Finlain ducked under the first dagger and blocked the second, hammering his fist into the corsair's jaw and pitching him from the ramp.

'Withdraw!' shouted Finlain and Meruval stepped back from the fight as the captain of *Finubar's Pride* took his place at the head of the ramp. More bolts thudded around him, but he paid them no mind as he raised his sword to meet a fresh wave of corsairs. Before they charged, he turned to Meruval and said, 'When the ramp is cut free, get us out of here!'

Meruval nodded, too breathless and exhausted to speak, and staggered back along the deck. Finlain returned his attention to the approaching corsairs and bellowed a cry of defiance as they came at him with their cruel eyes and deadly blades.

He fought in a trance, his sword moving as though of its own accord as it opened throats and bellies with each graceful cut. He felt blades cut his own flesh, but he felt no pain as he killed his dark kin with relentless precision.

Dimly he could hear their screams of pain and hatred, mingled with the solid chopping of axe blades, but everything felt muted, as though the battle were being fought underwater. A druchii blade seemed to float past his head as he turned it aside then brought the blade back in a decapitating sweep. From the corner of his eye, he saw a cloaked warrior thrusting with a long, dark-bladed sword, his green eyes bright with centuries of malice, and knew he would not be able to block the strike.

Even as he realised that this was the blow that would kill him, the boarding ramp lurched as his axemen finally chopped it free of the deck. The druchii on the ramp staggered and the green-eyed swordsman slipped as the ground slid out from beneath him. Finlain plunged his bloody sword between the corsair's ribs and kicked him from the ramp.

'Captain!' cried one of the axemen. 'We're free!'

Finlain took a backwards step and shouted, 'Meruval! Now!'

No sooner had the words left his mouth than *Finubar's*

Pride surged back from the Black Ark. With nothing to support it, the boarding ramp tipped a dozen druchii corsairs into the churning sea as it fell against the side of the cliff with a resounding clang of metal.

Finlain lowered his sword and placed a steadying hand on the torn sides of his ship as a wave of pain and dizziness threatened to overcome him. More of his warriors rushed to help the ship into getting as much distance between them and the Black Ark as possible. He let out a deep breath and turned to the breathless axemen.

'Well done,' he said, as the great, dark cliff began to recede, the Eagle ship's superior speed and manoeuvrability getting her clear with great rapidity. 'You saved the ship.'

Both warriors bowed at the captain's compliment as Meruval bellowed orders to get the sails raised.

As the mist closed in around them, Finlain knew that they were by no means out of danger. He made his way along the length of the deck, offering words of praise and congratulations to his warriors until he reached Meruval, who sat slumped beside at the stern at the tiller.

'The others?' said Meruval.

'Lost. I saw *Glory of Eataine* sink and heard nothing but slaughter from *Asuryan's Fire*. I fear that only we escaped, my friend.'

'We're not clear yet, captain,' said Meruval.

'No,' agreed Finlain. 'I know nothing of how quickly a Black Ark can get underway, but I do not plan on waiting to find out. Get us to Lothern by the swiftest route and then have those wounds seen to. We have to take word to Lord Aislin that a Black Ark sails the waters of Ulthuan.'

'How in the name of Isha did a Black Ark get this far south?' said Meruval.

'I don't know,' said Finlain. 'But there's only one reason for it to be here.'

'And what's that?'

Finlain gripped his sword tightly. 'Invasion.'

ELLYRION POSSESSED SOME of the most beautiful countryside in Ulthuan, decided Yvraine Hawkblade as she crested a rise and looked over the wide expanse of golden plains and lush forests spread between the city of Tor Elyr and the great barrier of the Annulii Mountains. Birdsong entertained her, the sweet scent of summer was in the air – as it always was – and the midday sun warmed her pale skin.

Herds of horses dotted the plains, and here and there she could make out Ellyrion riders amongst them, looking for all the world as though they were a part of them. Perhaps they were, thought Yvraine, knowing that the bond between Ellyrian nobles and their horses was more akin to that shared by old friends than that of rider and steed. Rightly it was said that it was better to harm the brother of an Ellyrian than his horse…

She set off down a sloping path, her steps sure and measured, leaving no trace of her passing, though her head was still clouded after the journey from Saphery to Ellyrion, despite the best efforts of the shipmaster to make her journey across the inner sea as comfortable as possible. It felt good to have the sun on her face, the wind in her hair and solid ground beneath her feet. Yvraine disliked travelling by any means other than her own two feet, and though the ships of the elves rode smoothly across the seas, she had found it next to impossible to meditate during the voyage, her every attempt thwarted by the conversations of the crew or the rocking swell of the ship.

Yvraine brushed her long, cream robes and adjusted the ithilmar armour that lay beneath, the gleaming links and smooth plates contoured for her slender frame. Across her back was a huge sword, sheathed in a long scabbard of soft red velvet and fastened to her armour by a golden clasp at her breast.

She stopped and shielded her eyes from the sun as she peered into the verdant countryside, seeing the far distant gleam of sunlight on the pale stone walls of a villa at the foot of a tumble of rocks. Mitherion Silverfawn had told her that the villa of his daughter's husband nestled between two waterfalls and the sentinels at the gates of Tor Elyr had given her detailed directions on how to find the Éadaoin villa.

Sure that the villa before her was the one she sought, Yvraine lifted the sword from her back, a great, two-handed blade of exquisite workmanship and uncanny grace, as she gracefully lowered herself into a cross-legged position. She would reach her destination in the morning and desired to sweep away the lethargy of the journey before then.

And the best way to do that was to perform the cleansing ritual of the Sword Masters.

Yvraine placed the huge sword across her lap and closed her eyes, letting the natural sounds of Ellyrion ease her into her meditative trance.

Her breathing slowed and her senses spread out from her body as she slowly whispered the mantra of the Sword Masters of Hoeth as taught to her by Master Dioneth of the White Tower. Yvraine felt the softness of the grass beneath her, the warmth and fecundity of the earth below that and the raging currents of magic that pierced the very rock and kept the island of Ulthuan from vanishing beneath the waves.

The air around her sparkled as the magic carried on the wind became attuned to her subtle vibrations and a soft glow built behind her eyelids. In one smooth motion she drew her sword and held the silver, leaf-shaped blade before her, its length enormous and its weight surely extraordinary, yet Yvraine wielded it as though it were as light as a willowy sapling.

Her pale, almost white, hair reflected in the smooth sheen of the blade, the perfection of the weapon matched only by the steely concentration in her sharp, angular features. Yvraine let a breath of anticipation whisper from her lips and nodded to herself.

Her legs uncoiled like striking snakes and in the blink of an eye she was standing, the sword raised high above her and glittering in the sun. The blade spun in her hands and her grip was reversed, the sword slashing in an intricate series of manoeuvres that were almost too fast for the naked eye to follow.

Her feet were in constant motion as she lunged, parried and thrust at imaginary opponents, the mighty blade cleaving the air in an impenetrable web of ithil-mar that swooped gracefully around her body. One by one, she performed the thirty basic exercises of the Sword Masters before moving onto more advanced techniques.

Once more she brought the enormous sword upwards and held it before her face, the golden quillons level with her cheeks and her breathing crisp and even. With barely a trace of visible effort, Yvraine spun the sword in a dazzling series of manoeuvres that would have made the greatest swordsman of men weep at his own lack of skill and which was beyond all but the most gifted of warriors of Ulthuan. Only through the superlative training of the Loremasters of the White Tower could a warrior transcend mere skill and become a true master of the martial arts to perform feats of swordsmanship beyond imagining.

Mind and body in total harmony, the mighty sword became part of Yvraine, her perfect physical and spiritual qualities manifesting in swordplay that was simply sublime. With a selection of the most advanced techniques performed, she moved into a more personal series of manoeuvres, where her own soul flowed into the blade and informed its every movement.

Each Sword Master had their own particular style with a blade and each warrior bared an element of their heart when they fought, an aspect of their personality that was so unique and distinct as to be unmistakable to another practitioner of the art. Yvraine's sword reached further and faster, the tip cutting the air in dizzyingly fast sweeps that would have been impossible were it not for the decades of training and her mastery of her own body.

At last the sword ceased its motion; so suddenly that an observer might have been forgiven for thinking it had never moved at all. With a whip of silver steel it was returned to its sheath and Yvraine was cross-legged once more, her breathing returning to normal as she emerged from her meditation.

She opened her eyes, calm and refreshed after her exercises, and smiled as she felt the cobwebs that had entangled her soul during the journey from Saphery fall away from her as though cut by her blade. Yvraine rose smoothly to her feet, slinging the sword around her back and buckling the belt across her armour once more.

She adjusted her cloak over the sword and set off in the direction of the distant villa.

CHAPTER THREE

CALLS

FIRST THERE WAS light. Then came sound. He could feel the light burning through his eyelids as though someone held a bright lamp before them and kept them tightly shut as he registered more of his environment through his other senses. He lay on a soft mattress, his limbs comfortable and covered by soft bedding. The air was moist and tasted green, with an earthy scent as though he lay outdoors or within a hothouse for exotic plants.

It smelled sweet and pleasant, and he took a deep breath of the myriad scents that surrounded him. Wherever he lay, it was certainly pleasant, without any sense of danger, and he felt no need to move beyond the identification of his surroundings.

He could hear droning insects and the rustle of the leaves disturbed by a soft breeze, as well as soft puffs of what sounded like perfume dispensed from a noblewoman's atomiser. By degrees, his eyes grew more accustomed to the light, and he risked gradually opening them in stages, adjusting to each level of glare before opening them still further.

At last his eyes were fully open, though the brightness of the light still made him slightly nauseous. Above him, he could see swathes of shimmering panes that rippled like water in golden frames of wire surely too slender to support the weight of such an amount of glass.

Twisting his head, he could see that the strange ceiling stretched away to his left and right, though for how far was a mystery as it was soon obscured by the tall branches of strange trees. He now saw that his earlier suspicion that he was lying outdoors was only partially correct, for he lay within a space whose shape was formed from the trunks of the trees and rendered impermeable by the weaving of bushes and plants between them.

Through the transparent ceiling, he could see clouds chasing one another across the sky, but could feel no breath of wind where he lay. Perhaps the ceiling above him was some form of magical barrier that kept out the worst of the external environment while maintaining a constant internal temperature? As he watched, a portion of one of the shimmering panes seemed to shiver before dispensing a fine spray of water across the plants nearest it.

He tried to sit up, but pulled up short as the muscles in every one of his limbs protested and he collapsed back onto the bed with a grunt of pain. Tentatively he lifted his hands, seeing that they were bound with bandages and feeling a raw numbness in his palms.

But more surprising was the fact that he wore a silver pledge ring on his left hand.

He was married? To whom? And why did he have no memory of her?

A deep and painful ache seized his heart as he tried and failed to remember the name of the maiden that had given him this pledge ring. Was she even now searching for him, unaware that he had survived his shipwreck? He wondered if she might already be mourning him…

He had to get up and discover where he was and find some means of restoring his memory if he were to return to her. Reaching up to his forehead, he felt another bandage covering the side of his head and winced as he probed what was clearly a fresh cut.

How had he come to this place? And where in the name of Isha was it?

All he remembered was floating in the sea, clinging desperately to a fragment of wreckage; beyond that was a blank. There had been a beach and he remembered clawing handfuls of sand as he had pulled himself ashore. He realised he must have been discovered by his fellow elves and the simple fact of his survival made him want to laugh and cry.

His head had been hurt and his palms were raw, but what other wounds did he bear?

He pulled back the soft sheets that covered him and discovered that he was naked beneath them, his flesh pale and obviously starved of sunlight. Tentatively, he pushed himself upright in the bed and probed his flesh for other injuries. He found knots of scar tissue on his hip and shoulder, but they were old wounds, the skin pale and long healed. How he had come by those wounds, he could not remember, but aside from the injuries to his head and palms (and the stiffness of his muscles) he appeared to be otherwise healthy.

Marshalling his strength, he slowly eased himself into a sitting position, his every muscle aching with the effort, and swung his feet onto the floor. Standing up took an effort of will and his heart thudded against his ribs with the exertion. Suddenly very aware of his nakedness, he looked around for something to wear and saw a small table sitting behind his bed with a fresh shirt and loose leggings.

Swiftly he donned the clothes, the fabric soft and fragrant. When was the last time he had worn fresh clothing? It seemed he had forgotten the softness of silk or the comfort of clothes and, try as he might, he could still remember nothing of his life before his plight in the ocean.

Who was he and how had he come to be floating in the ocean, bloodied and near death?

These were questions he desperately needed answers to, but he had no idea how to get them. Deciding that he had better find out where he was first, he took a few hesitant steps around the verdant room, testing his strength and balance.

He was unsteady at first, but with every step, he felt stronger and more confident.

The chamber he found himself within was a long oval, its perimeter formed by the trunks of slender trees with a shimmering, oily looking bark. He reached out and pressed his fingers against the nearest tree, grimacing at the stickiness of the sap. Reaching up for a wide leaf, he wiped it from his hand, though he had to admit that the fragrance of the sap was pleasant. The more he saw, the more he felt that this place was less like Ulthuan and more like the stories he had heard of the woodland realm of Athel Loren, far to the east in the Old World.

Turning from the tree, he saw that no obvious exit presented itself, but as he approached one end of the room, the coiled vines and creepers intertwined with the trunks pulled back with a rustling hiss, like a curtain of beads parted by an invisible hand.

Startled, he hesitated before moving any closer, but peering through the gap he saw long rows of plants and seed beds stretching out before him and more of the strange, rippling ceiling above them. Cautiously he stepped through and the curtain of vines hissed closed behind him.

This space was much larger than the room he had woken in and displayed some measure of the handiwork of elves: long terraced walls and graceful columns from which hung a variety of outlandish plants – most of which he did not recognise.

The door he had passed through had brought him out midway down what appeared to be a terrace of hanging gardens built into the side of a cliff. High above him, he could just make out the outline of an imposing, plant-wreathed dwelling.

He set off down the nearest aisle of plants in search of a route upwards, the air filled with a multitude of different scents and hot with a moistness that felt good on his skin. To his left, this great garden space rose up in a series of blooming terraces to a sprawling villa, while on the right it fell away in curling paths down the cliffs. Beyond the transparent liquid wall held by the golden wire, he could see the bright light of the morning and the brilliant blue of the great ocean, its vast expanse dotted with mist-shrouded isles.

He shivered as he again felt the cold of the water's embrace and turned from the ocean.

Wandering down the aisle of strange plants, he felt the unmistakable tingle of magic washing in from the sea. That, combined with the sight of the coast and the misty isles beyond, told him that he must be in Yvresse, though what had brought him here was a mystery he hoped would be answered soon.

He paused to take a closer look at some of the plants, but he could recognise none of them, which did not surprise him, for as far as he knew he was no botanist. Some plants he approached, others he did not, as many of the larger ones had a predatory quality to them; wide, serrated petals and thorny vines that waved in the air like agile whips that appeared to be beckoning him closer.

A powerful scent suddenly filled his nostrils and he turned to see a tall plant with a collection of bright red cones set amid a thorny frill of stamen that drooped like the branches of a willow tree. Almost without conscious thought, he found himself approaching the plant, hearing a strange sound that resonated beyond the simple act of hearing, as though it reached into his mind to soothe his troubled thoughts. The scent of its bloom swelled until it was overpoweringly intoxicating, and his senses filled with its seductive promise.

His steps carried him towards the plant and he smiled dreamily as he watched the red cones slowly flare open to reveal circular mouths ringed with teeth and which leaked glistening saliva.

The sight of such an array of barbed teeth should have alarmed him, but the siren song in his mind kept such thoughts at bay and he continued to walk towards the plant. The drooping stamen slowly drew themselves erect, opening outwards as he walked willingly into their embrace.

Dimly he was aware of a shape standing at his shoulder, but he could not tear his eyes from the gaping, toothed mouths of the plant as more of the sticky saliva moistened the leaves.

Then the soothing song that filled his mind turned to a scream and he cried out as the piercing wail echoed within his skull. The haunting scent of the plant faded and was replaced with the acrid stench of burning leaves. Sparkling fire leapt from the opened mouths of the plant as they writhed in the pellucid blue flames.

Freed from the plant's bewitchment, he staggered backward, suddenly repulsed by the smell of sap and earth as he dropped to his knees and gagged on the stench. When he had recovered enough, he looked up to see a beautiful elven maid standing before the shrivelled husk of the burned plant, shimmering traces of magical flames dying at her fingertips. Auburn hair held by a woven silver cord at her temple poured across her shoulders and her piercing green eyes regarded him with an expression of faintly amused exasperation.

'Silly boy,' she said. 'Father will be most displeased.'

ELDAIN HURRIED DOWN the stairs from the Hippocrene Tower, fastening a velvet tunic over his silk undershirt as he went. Valeina had woken him just after dawn with news that a visitor had arrived at the gates of Ellyr-charoi and was asking to speak to the master of the house.

Normally, Eldain received no visitors and would have sent such a caller on their way unsatisfied, but this was no ordinary guest. When pressed for a description of the visitor, Valeina had described a warrior clad in shining ithilmar armour, a tall plumed helmet and who bore a mighty sword.

Eldain had known immediately what manner of person had arrived at his gates.

A Sword Master, one of the warrior-mystics who travelled the length and breadth of Ulthuan, gathering news and information for the Loremasters of the Tower of Hoeth. One did not refuse the visit of such an individual and thus he had ordered Valeina to prepare a morning meal of fresh bread and fruits while he dressed himself.

What could one of the Sword Masters want in Ellyr-charoi? Even as he framed the question in his mind, a cold dread settled upon him and his last steps into the Summer Courtyard were leaden and fearful. Rhianna was already waiting for him and he could see from her expression that she was similarly surprised at the arrival of this visitor, though her surprise was more of excitement than wariness.

'Have you seen our guest?' said Eldain without preamble.

Rhianna shook her head. 'No, she awaits in the Equerry's Hall.'

'She?'

'Yes, Valeina tells me her name is Yvraine Hawkblade.'

'Did she also tell you why a Sword Master comes to Ellyr-charoi?'

'No, but she must bring important news to have come all the way from Saphery.'

Eldain nodded and said, 'That's what worries me.'

Together they crossed the courtyard and followed the line of the walls to a tall door of carved ash with gold and silver banding carved into the form of horses. Eldain took a deep breath and pushed open the door, marching through the airy vestibule of white stone and emerging in to the Equerry's Hall, a wide, dimly lit chamber lined with trophies and wondrous paintings depicting scenes of previous lords of the Éadaoin family at hunt. A long table in the shape of an elongated oval filled the centre of the hall, where in times past the equerries of the noble house would carouse and sing and dance after a successful hunt.

Now, the hall was bare, no songs were sung and it had been decades since last the lord of the Éadaoin had hunted. Eldain and Rhianna's entrance scattered fallen leaves and as they passed through the vestibule, the chamber's occupant looked over from her scrutiny of a painting that showed a noble elf atop a steed of purest white, slaying a foul, mutated beast of the Annulii.

'Is this you?' said the Sword Master, her voice soft and melodic.

Eldain glanced at the picture and felt his heartbeat jump. 'No, it is my brother.'

'He is very like you.'

'Was,' said Eldain. 'He is dead.'

The Sword Master bowed deeply and Eldain saw the tremendous sword upon her back, the weapon surely almost as tall as its bearer. 'My apologies, Lord Éadaoin, I am sorry for your loss. And forgive my manners; I have not yet introduced myself. I am Yvraine Hawkblade, Sword Master of Hoeth.'

Yvraine Hawkblade was tall for a female elf, slender and seemingly ill-suited to the role of a Sword Master. Her features were sharper than most elves of Ulthuan and Eldain relaxed as he saw no guile in her young face.

'And I am Eldain Fleetmane,' he said. 'Lord of the Éadaoin family and master of the lands from here to the mountains. And this is my wife, Rhianna.'

Again the Sword Master bowed. 'It is an honour to

meet you and may the blessings of Isha be upon you both.'

'And on you,' said Rhianna. 'You are welcome in our house. Will you join us in our morning meal?'

'Thank you, I shall,' said Yvraine. 'It has been a long and, I confess, tiring journey. I would be glad of some food and water, yes.'

Yvraine took a seat at the table and Eldain caught a shadow of faint disappointment pass across her face and he could well imagine its cause. Ever since the death of his father, the ancestral home of his family had become a place of mourning instead of a place of joy. Brooding silences and ghosts of glories past filled its halls, where once laughter and song had rung from the rafters. Death had reached into the chests of the Éadaoin and stilled the wild beat of their reaver hearts.

He and Rhianna took their seats opposite Yvraine as Valeina entered carrying a wide tray bearing bread, fruit and a crystal pitcher of cold mountain water. She placed the tray in the centre of the table and Eldain nodded in thanks.

'That will be all, Valeina,' he said, reaching out to pour Yvraine and Rhianna some water before filling his own glass. Valeina withdrew and closed the doors to the Equerry's Hall behind her, leaving the three of them sitting in silence.

Yvraine sipped her water, showing no sign yet of revealing her purpose here and Eldain could barely contain his curiosity. Oft times, Sword Masters travelled with no purpose other than the gathering of knowledge, journeying to the furthest corners of Ulthuan to quiz local nobility and warriors on recent events that they might be communicated back to the White Tower, but

Eldain already knew that this was no such occasion.

Every movement of Yvraine Hawkblade told Eldain that she had come here with purpose.

'Have you travelled directly from Saphery, Mistress Hawkblade?'

'I have,' said Yvraine, helping herself to a ripened aoilym fruit.

'And to what do we owe the pleasure of your company?'

He felt the heat of Rhianna's gaze upon him, knowing he was being discourteous by being so blunt, but knowing that if this warrior brought his doom then he would sooner face it than dance around it.

Yvraine displayed no outward sign of noticing his boorish behaviour, taking a bite of the fruit and savouring its perfectly moist flesh. 'I bring a message to the daughter of Mitherion Silverfawn from her father.'

'A message for me?' said Rhianna.

Eldain's heart calmed and a beaming smile of relief spread across his face. So typical of an Archmage to resort to the pomp of sending one of the Sword Masters to deliver a message, when there were a dozen different ways to communicate by magical means.

He reached out to take a piece of fruit and said, 'Then I urge you to deliver it, Mistress Hawkblade. How fares my father-in-law?'

'Well,' said Yvraine. 'He prospers and his researches into celestial phenomena continue to meet with favour from the Loremasters. In fact his divinations are proving to be of great interest these days.'

Rhianna leaned forwards across the table. 'Please do not think me rude, but I would hear what my father has to say.'

Yvraine placed the core of the aoilym back on the platter and said, 'Of course. He simply asks that you accompany me back to the Tower of Hoeth.'

'What? To Saphery? Why?'

'I do not know,' said Yvraine and Eldain could sense that there was some other part of the message yet to be imparted. 'But it was with some urgency that I was despatched. I have taken the liberty of securing us passage on a ship from Tor Elyr and its captain has orders to await our arrival before sailing. If we leave soon, we can be in Tor Elyr before nightfall.'

'Is he ill? Is that why he sends for me?'

Yvraine shook her head, a faint smile on her lips. 'No, he is quite well, I assure you, my lady. But he was most insistent that you both accompany me back to Saphery.'

At first, Eldain thought he'd misheard, then saw the look of quiet amusement on the Sword Master's face. 'Both of us? He wants both of us to travel with you?'

'He does.'

'Without a reason?'

'I was not given a reason, simply a directive.'

'And we're supposed to pack up and go because he says so?' said Eldain.

Yvraine nodded and Eldain felt his irritation grow at her lack of elaboration. Though he held great respect for Rhianna's father, he was, like many practitioners of magic, somewhat mercurial and capricious. A trait he was more than aware existed in his daughter.

But to travel the breadth of Ulthuan with no clue as to why or what awaited them at the end of the journey seemed like an unreasonable request, even by the standards of a mage.

Rhianna seemed similarly confused by her father's

request, but the prospect of visiting her father soon won
out over any concern as to the reason.

'He gave no hint as to why he wants us to travel to the
White Tower?' said Rhianna.

'He did not.'

'Then would you mind speculating?' said Eldain. 'You
must have some idea of why he sends one of the White
Tower's guardians to retrieve his daughter.'

Yvraine shook her head. 'In life, the wisest and sound-
est people avoid speculation.'

Wonderful, thought Eldain, a warrior *and* a
philosopher...

HER NAME WAS Kyrielle Greenkin and she had saved his
life.

When the pain and discomfort of the carnivorous
plant's aromatic siren song had faded from his mind,
she helped him to his feet and tutted as she dusted off
the fresh clothes that had been laid out for him.

'Look at the state of you!' she said. 'And I went to such
trouble to find one of the guards the same size as you.'

'What...' he said, gesturing feebly at the smoking
remains of the plant, 'was that?'

'That? Oh, that was just one of father's more outlandish creations,' she said dismissively and waving
a delicate hand. 'It was a bit of an experiment really,
which, between you and I, did not work out too well,
but he does love to tinker with things from beyond this
world to see how they combine with our own native
species.'

'Is it dead?'

'I should think so,' she said and then laughed. 'Unless
my magic is becoming *very* rusty.'

'You are a mage?'

'I have a little power,' she said, 'but then who of Saphery doesn't?'

'Saphery? Is that where you are from?' he said, though he had already guessed as much.

'It is indeed.'

She smiled and said, 'You are a guest of Anurion the Green, Archmage of Saphery, and this is his winter palace in Yvresse. I, on the other hand, am his daughter, Kyrielle.'

He could feel the expectant pause after she had spoken her name, but he had nothing to tell her and said, 'I am sorry, my lady, but I have no name to give you. I can remember nothing before my time adrift in the sea.'

'Nothing? Nothing at all? Well that's unfortunate,' she said in a masterful display of understatement. 'Well I can't very well speak to you if you haven't got a name. Would you mind terribly if I thought of one for you? Just until you remember your own of course!'

Her speech was so quick he had trouble following it, especially with the fog that seemed to fill his thoughts. He shook his head and said, 'No, I suppose not.'

Kyrielle's face screwed up in a manner that suggested she was thinking hard until at last she said, 'Then I will call you Daroir. Will that do?'

He smiled and said, 'The rune for remembrance and memory.'

'It seems fitting, yes?'

'Daroir,' he said, turning the name over in his mind. He had no connection to the name and instinctually knew that it was not his real name, but it would suffice until he could recall what it truly was. 'I suppose it is fitting, yes. Maybe it will help.'

'So you don't remember anything at all?' said Kyrielle. 'Not a thing?'

He shook his head. 'No. I remember almost dying in the sea and crawling up the beach. And… that's it.'

'Such a sad tale,' she said and a tear rolled down her cheek.

The suddenness of her mood swing surprised him and he said, 'With a tear in her eye and a smile on her lips…'

Even though he heard himself speak the words, they sounded unfamiliar to his ears, yet flowed naturally from his mouth.

She smiled and she said, 'You know the works of Mecelion?'

'Who?'

'Mecelion,' said Kyrielle. 'The warrior poet of Chrace. You just quoted from *Fairest Dawn of Ulthuan*.'

'I did?' said Daroir. 'I've never heard of Mecelion, much less read any of his poems.'

'Are you sure? You might be the greatest student of poetry in Ulthuan for all we know.'

'True, but what would a student of poetry be doing at sea?'

Kyrielle looked him up and down and said, 'No, you don't look much like a student, too many muscles. And how many students carry wounds like yours on your shoulder and hip? You've been a warrior in your time.'

Daroir blushed, realising that she must have seen him naked to know of the old wounds on his body. She laughed as she saw the colour rise in his cheeks.

'Did you think you got undressed all by yourself?' she said.

He didn't answer as she took his hand and led him towards a gentle arch of palm fronds that parted at her approach to reveal stairs that rose towards the villa at the top of the cliff.

So artfully were the stairs cut into the rock, that Daroir wasn't sure that they hadn't formed naturally. Unusually for this place of wondrous flora, the steps were completely free of any trace of growth and earth, as though the plants knew to keep this ascent clear.

He followed her willingly as she led him up the steps. 'Where are we going?'

'To see my father,' she said. 'He is a powerful mage and perhaps he can restore your memory to you.'

She released his hand and began to climb the steps. Daroir felt a warm glow envelop him at her smile, as though some strange, soothing magic was worked within it.

He followed her up the steps.

FAR, FAR AWAY, in a land devoid of kind laughter or sunlight that warmed the skin, a shrill cry that spoke of spilled blood echoed from a tower of brazen darkness. About this highest and bleakest of towers were a hundred others, cold and reeking with malice, and about these were a thousand more. Black smoke coiled around the towers, which rose above a city hunched at the foot of iron mountains and which lived in the nightmares of the world.

For this was Naggarond, the Tower of Cold… the forsaken domain of the Witch King, dread ruler of the dark kin of the elves of Ulthuan.

The druchii.

Black castles and turrets ringed the mighty tower at the centre of the city, shrouded in the ashen rain of those burned upon the sacrificial fires that smouldered, red and black, in temples that ran with blood.

Walls a hundred feet high encircled the city, and from the walls rose an evil forest of dark and crooked towers, upon which flew the bloody banners of the city's infernal master. An army of severed heads and a tapestry of skins hung from the jagged battlements and the sickly ruin of their demise dripped down the black stone of the wall.

Carrion birds circled the city in an ever present pall, their cries hungry and impatient as they crossed the bleak and cheerless sky. The beating of hammers and the scrape of iron rose from the city, mingling with the cries of the anguished and the moaning of the damned into one murderous death-rattle that never ended.

The dwelling places of the dark elves; bleak and shattered ruins, windy garrets and haunted towers filled the city, each more forlorn than the last.

The scream that issued from the tallest tower at the centre of the city lingered, as though savoured by the air itself, and those below gave thanks to their gods that it was not they who suffered this day. The screaming had been going on for days, and while screams were nothing new in Naggarond, these spoke of a level of suffering beyond imagining.

But the cause of those screams was not one of the city's ivory-skinned elves, but a man, though he had forsaken all bonds with his species many years ago in the ecstasy of battle and the worship of the Dark Gods of the north.

In a shuttered room lit only by the coals of a smouldering brazier, Issyk Kul worked his dark torments upon a canvas of flesh granted to him by the Hag Sorceress. Where the youth had come from was irrelevant and what he knew was unimportant, for Kul had not begun his tortures with any purpose other than the infliction of agony. To work such wonderful ruin on a perfect body, yet keep it alive and aware of the havoc being wrought upon it was both his art and an act of worship.

Kul was broad and muscular, his body worked into iron-hardness by the harsh northern climes of the Old World and a life of war and excess. Leather coils held a patchwork of contoured plates tight to his tanned flesh, his armour glistening and undulating like raw, pink meat and his skin gleaming with scented oils. Lustrous golden hair topped the face of a libertine, full featured and handsome to the point of beauty. But where beauty ended, cruelty began and his wide eyes knew nothing of pity or compassion, only wicked indulgence and the obsession of a fetishist.

When he was done with this plaything, he would release it, eyeless, lipless and insane into the city to drool and plead for a death that would be too slow in coming. It would roam the streets a freak, cries of revulsion and admiration chasing it into the dark corners of the city where it would become a feast for the creatures of the night.

Kul straightened from his works, discarding the needles and selecting a blade so slender and fine that it would be quite useless for any purpose other than inflicting the most excruciating tortures on the most sensitive organs of the body.

More screams filled the chamber and Kul's joined those of his plaything, his growls of pleasure climaxing in an atavistic howl of pleasure as he completed his violation of what had once been a pale, bright-eyed messenger.

With his desires sated for the moment, Issyk Kul bent to kiss the mewling scraps of flesh and said, 'Your pain has pleased the great god, Shornaal, and for that I thank you.'

He turned to leave the chamber, pausing only long enough to retrieve a gloriously elaborate sword of sweeping curves and cruel spikes. Quillons of bone pricked the flesh of his hands and a razor worked into the handle scored his palm as he spun the blade into a rippling sheath across his back.

Beyond the confines of the room he used for worship, a stone-flagged passageway curved away to either side, following the shape of the tower, and he set off with a long, graceful stride towards the sounds of chanting and wailing.

The music of the tower was pressed into its structure, millennia of suffering and blood imprinted into its very bones. Kul could feel the anguish that had been unleashed in this place as surely as if it happened right before his eyes. Ghosts of murders past paraded before him and the torments that built this place were like wine from the sweetest blood vineyard.

At last the curve of the passageway terminated at a wide portal of bone and bronze that led within the core of the tower. Six cloaked warriors in long hauberks of black mail and tall helms of bronze guarded the portal, their great, black-bladed halberds reflecting the light of the torches that burned in sconces fashioned from skulls. Each warrior's face was branded with the mark of Khaine, the Bloody Handed God of murder, hatred and destruction, and Kul smiled to see such wanton deformation of flesh.

Though he was well known in Naggarond, their

weapons still clashed together to block his passage through to the ebony stairs that led to the inner sanctum of the tower.

Kul nodded in satisfaction, knowing that had they admitted him into the presence of their lord without challenge, he would have killed them himself. More than one champion of the Dark Gods had fallen foul of the treachery of a trusted comrade and Kul had not lived for three centuries by assuming that the faith of friends was eternal.

'You do your master proud,' said Kul, 'but I am expected.'

'Expected you may be, but you do not go before Lord Malekith unescorted,' said a voice behind him and Kul smiled.

'Kouran,' he said, turning to face the commander of the Black Guard of Naggarond, the elite guard of the Witch King's city. Kouran was almost a foot shorter than Issyk Kul, but was a formidable presence nonetheless, his dark armour forged from the unbreakable metal of a fallen star and his blade ensorcelled by ancient, forgotten magic.

The elf's violet eyes met Kul's and the champion of Chaos was pleased to see a total absence of fear in his gaze.

'You do not trust me?' said Kul.

'Should I?'

'No,' he admitted. 'I have killed friends and allies before when it suited me.'

'Then we will go up together, yes?' said Kouran, leaving Kul in no doubt that it was not a request. He nodded and waved the captain of the Black Guard forward. Kouran wrapped a hand around the hilt of his sword and Kul could feel the blade's malice seep into the air like sweet incense.

The gleaming blades of the Black Guard parted and Issyk Kul and Kouran passed through the portal of bone, a hazy curtain of sweet-smelling smoke arising from the floor to surround them and bear them onwards. The chamber beyond the portal was cold, a web of frost forming a patina of white across his armour. The oil chilled on his flesh and his breath feathered the air before him as Kouran led the way through the purple mists towards a spiral staircase of stained metal from which dripped a sticky residue of old blood.

Kouran climbed the stairs and Kul followed him, his bulky frame unsuited to such a narrow stairwell. He had dreamed of walking the route to the Witch King's presence a thousand times since he had brought his army to Naggarond, and felt a delicious wave of apprehension and excitement thunder through his veins as he followed Kouran upwards. Though he had killed and tortured for hundreds of years, Kul was only too aware that the darkness he had wrought upon the world was but a fraction of the shadow cast by the Witch King.

For more than five thousand years, the Witch King had reigned over Naggaroth and all the later ages of the world had known his dread power. In Ulthuan, his name was not spoken except as a curse, while in the lands of men, his power was a terrible legend that still stalked the world and plotted to bring about its ruin. To the tribes of the north, the Witch King was just another ruler of a distant kingdom, by turns a mighty tyrant to dread or an ally to fight alongside.

A red rain of spattering blood fell from high above, rendering Kul's golden hair to lank ropes of bloody crimson and he licked the congealed droplets from his lips as they ran down his face.

The creaking, iron stairs seemed to go on for an eternity, climbing higher into the aching cold and purple smoke that surrounded him. The oil on his skin cracked and his muscles began to shiver as he drew near the throne room of Malekith.

At last they reached the summit of the tower, the pinnacle of evil in Naggarond, and Kul's every sense was alive with the living quality of hatred and bitterness that flavoured every breath with its power.

The darkness of the Witch King's throne room was a force unto itself, a presence felt as palpably as that of Kouran beside him. It coated the walls like a creeping sickness, slithering across the floor and climbing the walls in defiance of the white, soulless light that struggled through the leaded windows of the tower.

Kul began to shiver, his heavily muscled frame unused to such bitter, unnatural cold and without a shred of fat to insulate him. He could see nothing beyond the faint outline of Kouran and the all-encompassing darkness that seemed to press in on him to render him blind as surely as if a hood had been placed over his head.

No, that wasn't quite right...

Kul's senses were no longer those of a mortal, enhanced and refined by Shornaal to better savour the agonies of his victims and the ecstasies of his triumphs. Even as he concentrated, he could feel a rasping iron breath in his head, as though a great engine pulsed in the depths of the tower and the echoes of its efforts were carried up its length. He could feel a presence within his mind, a clawing, scraping thing that sifted through his memories and desires to reach the very heart of him.

He knew he was being tested and welcomed the intrusion, confident that he would be found the equal of the task he had been summoned to perform. The clammy thought-touch withdrew from his mind and he relaxed as he felt the awesome power of the Witch King recede, apparently satisfied.

The darkness of the chamber appeared to diminish and Issyk Kul saw a great obsidian throne upon which sat a mighty statue of black iron, one hand resting on a skull-topped armrest while the other clasped a colossal sword, its blade burnished silver and glittering with hoarfrost. Kul knew that the magic of his own blade was powerful, but the energies bound to this terrible weapon were an order of magnitude greater and he could feel the enchantments worked upon his armour weakening just by its presence.

A great shield, taller than Kul himself, rested against one side of the great throne and upon it burned the dread rune of Shornaal – though the druchii did not use the northern names for the gods, and named his patron as Slaanesh. A circlet of iron sat upon the horned helm of the statue and at the sight of this monstrous god of murder, Kouran dropped to his knees and began babbling in the tongue of the elves.

Kul had to fight the urge to drop to his knees alongside Kouran and give praise to this effigy of Khaine, for Shornaal was a jealous god and would surely strike him down. Even in the holiest of holy places to Shornaal, Kul had never felt such awe and sheer physical presence of his own god as he felt now. The druchii were fortunate indeed to have a god of such potent physicality.

Even as he stared in awe at the magnificent and terrible idol, he felt the approach of another presence behind him and a voice, laden with lust, said, 'Do you not pay homage to my son? Is he not worthy of your obeisance?'

Pale and slender hands slipped around his neck, the nails long and sharp. They caressed his throat and he felt himself respond to their touch, a tremor of arousal and revulsion working its way down his spine. He knew who came upon him by her touch as surely as though she had whispered in his ear.

Her hands slid over the plates of armour covering his chest, sliding down to the bare flesh of his abdomen and stroking the curve of his muscles.

'Your son?' said Kul, twisting his head to the side and catching sight of her bewitching beauty. Pale skin, dark-rimmed eyes of liquid darkness and full lips that had worked their way around his body on more than one occasion.

'Yes,' said Morathi, slipping gracefully around his body to stand before him. 'My son.'

She was exquisite, as beautiful as the day she had first wed Aenarion thousands of years ago, and draped in a long gown of purple with a slash that ran from her collar to her pelvis. An amber periapt hung between the ivory curve of her breasts and Kul had to force his gaze upwards lest he be reduced to a quivering wreck of raging desire, as had countless suitors and lovers before him.

Mother and, some said, unholy lover of the Witch King, Morathi's sensuous splendour was like nothing he had ever experienced and her epithet of the Hag Sorcer- ess seemed like such a hideous misnomer to Kul, even though he knew the hellish reality behind her wondrous appearance.

'Lady Morathi,' said Kul, bowing extravagantly before

her. 'It is a pleasure to see you again.'

'Yes it is,' she said, backing away from him and toying with her amulet.

Kul took a step forward and Kouran rose to his feet, his hand reaching for the hilt of his sword. Not only was Kouran the captain of the city guard, but also bodyguard to its rulers.

'I received your summons, Lady Morathi,' said Kul. 'Is there news from the isle of mists?'

'There is,' she said, 'but first tell me of my messenger. He was to your tastes?'

Kul laughed and said. 'He was most enjoyable, my lady. He will not be returning to you.'

'I had not thought that he would.'

Kul waited for Morathi to continue, spellbound by her monstrous beauty and already picturing the violation he would wreak on her flesh if given the chance. As he stared at the Hag Sorceress, her features rippled as though in a heat haze, and a flickering image of the passage of centuries was etched upon his eyeballs, the wreckage of age and the ruin of years heaped upon flesh unable to sustain it.

Such was the dichotomy of Morathi, her beguiling beauty and her loathsome reality, one maintained at the expense of the other by the slaughter of countless innocent lives. Kul could only admire the determination and depths Morathi had plumbed to retain her allure.

'It is time for us to make war upon the Asur,' said Morathi, breaking his reverie.

'First blood has been spilled?' he said, unable to keep the relish from his voice.

'It has indeed,' said Morathi. 'The *Black Serenade* encountered a handful of their ships a few days ago.

Many lives were taken and one vessel was allowed to escape to carry word back to Lothern.'

'Fear will eat at them like a plague,' said Kul. 'They will be ripe for blooding.'

'And fire will be stoked in their hearts,' said Kouran, practically spitting each word. 'The Asur are proud.'

'As it should be,' said Morathi. 'Much depends on the fire of Asuryan's children being directed correctly. The thrust of our sword must draw our enemy's shield to enable the assassin's blade to strike home.'

'Then we must set sail,' said Kul, flexing his fists and running his tongue along his lips. 'I long to practise my arts on the flesh of the Asur.'

'As I promised you, Issyk Kul,' said Morathi. 'We will set sail with our warriors soon enough, but there are yet offerings to be made to Khaine and sport to be had before we wet our blades.'

Kul nodded towards the great iron statue behind Morathi and snapped. 'Then make your offerings to your god and be done with it, sorceress. My blade aches for the bliss of the knife's edge, the dance of blades and the pain that brings pleasure.'

Morathi frowned, then, as realisation of Kul's meaning became clear, threw back her head and laughed, a sound that chilled the soul and reached out beyond the chamber to slay a hundred carrion birds that circled the tower. She turned to the figure of iron and spoke in the harsh, beautiful language of the druchii.

Kul took a step back, reaching over his shoulder for his sword as he saw emerald coals grow behind the thin slits of the statue's helmet and felt a horrific animation build within the terrible armour, though it moved not a single inch.

No statue of Khaine was this, he now realised, but the Witch King himself...

With a speed and grace that ought to have been impossible for such a monstrous being bound within this vast armour of iron and hate, the Witch King rose from his obsidian throne. He towered above the Chaos champion, breath hissing from beneath his helmet and the light of his evil putting the paltry debaucheries of Kul to shame with the weight of suffering he had inflicted.

The great sword of the Witch King swept up and Kul felt certain that this would be his death, such was his terror of this moment.

'Mother...' came a voice so steeped in evil that Kul felt tears of blood welling in the corners of his eyes.

'My son?' said Morathi, and to Kul's amazement, her tone was awed.

'We sail for Ulthuan,' said the Witch King. 'Now.'

CHAPTER FOUR

TRAVELLERS

ANURION THE GREEN'S villa was like nothing Daroir had ever seen before. His idea of a palace was marble walls, soaring ceilings and graceful architecture that celebrated the craftsman's art while blending sympathetically with the surrounding landscape. At least on this last count, the palace more than exceeded his expectations.

The palace was a living thing, its walls seemingly grown from the rock of the cliffs, shaped and formed according to the whims of its creator – and he was a person of many whims, Daroir was to discover. Living things grew from every nook and cranny, vines creeping across walls and columns of trees forming great vaults of leaves to create grand processionals.

Not only was the natural architecture astounding, but also confounding, for no sooner had a passageway formed than it would reshape itself or be reshaped as the palace's master wandered at random through his home and caused new blooms to arise in his wake. Every open space within Anurion's palace was a place of wonder and beauty and Daroir again imagined that this must be what Athel Loren was like.

He had thought that Kyrielle was leading him straight to her father, but Anurion the Green, it appeared, followed no one's timetable but his own and when they had reached the palace at the top of the cliff, it had been to eat a meal of bread and fresh fruit and vegetables – many of which Daroir could not recognise or had outlandish names that were not elven or of any language he could recognise.

The next three days were spent regaining his strength and in discovery as he and Kyrielle explored her father's palace, the ever growing and changing internal plan as new to her as it was to him. Aside from Kyrielle, he saw only a very few servants and some spear-armed guards around the palace. Perhaps the full complement of Anurion's retainers remained in Saphery.

Each morning they would survey the magnificent landscape of Yvresse from the tallest tree-tower, savouring the beauty of the rugged coastline fringed with dense coniferous forests and long fjords that cut into the landscape from the ocean.

Deep, mist-shrouded valleys thrust inland and hardy evergreen forests tumbled down to the water's edge, where the ocean spread out towards the Shifting Isles and the Old World beyond. To the west, the foothills of the Annulii marched off to distant peaks towering dramatically into the clouds. The tang of magic from the raw energies contained within them set his teeth on edge.

Kyrielle pointed to the south and he saw the tips of

glittering mansions and towers that were all that could be seen of Tor Yvresse, the only major city of this eastern kingdom and dwelling place of the great hero, Eltharion. Daroir had to choke back his emotions at the sight of it, such was the aching beauty of its distant spires.

He would often return to the tree-towers just to see the lights of the city, knowing that soon he would need to journey to Tor Yvresse to cross the mountains and return to the inner kingdoms of Ulthuan.

Each day was spent in flitting conversation, with Kyrielle's rapid subject changes unearthing a wealth of sophistication within him he had not known he possessed.

As they spoke it soon became apparent that knowledge of poetry was not the only artistic talent of which he had hitherto been unaware. One morning Kyrielle had presented him with a lyre and asked him to play.

'I don't know how to,' he had said.

'How do you know? Try it.'

And so he had, plucking the strings as though he had been playing since birth, producing lilting melodies and wonderful tunes with the practiced grace and élan of a bard. Each note flew from his hands, though he could feel no conscious knowledge of what he was doing and had no understanding of how he could create such beautiful music when he could remember nothing of any lessons or ability.

Each day brought fresh wonders as he discovered that as well as playing music he could also create it. Now aware he could play, an unknown muse stirred within him and he composed laments of such haunting majesty that they brought tears to the eyes of all that heard them. Each discovery brought as many questions as it did answers, and Daroir's frustration grew as he awaited an audience with his unseen host.

Each piece of the puzzle of his identity that fell into place brought him no closer to the truth and each day he fretted over the silver ring on his finger. Every day spent without knowledge of his true identity was a day that someone mourned his loss: a friend, a brother, a father, a wife…

On the morning of the fourth day of his sojourn at Anurion's palace, Kyrielle entered the bright arbour in which he sat, and he looked up from the ghost of his memories and saw that she brought him a weapon.

Without a word she handed him a leather belt upon which hung a long-bladed dagger sheathed in a scabbard of what felt like a dense, heavy metal. The scabbard was banded with three rings of gold along its length, but was otherwise plain and unadorned.

'What's this?' he said. 'Do you want to see if I can fight?'

She shook her head. 'From the wounds you bear, I'd say that's a given. No, you were wearing this when I found you on the beach. Do you recognise it?'

'No,' he said. 'I don't remember seeing it before.'

'Not even when you were in the sea?'

'No, I was too busy trying to hold onto the wreckage to worry about what I was wearing. What *was* I wearing anyway?'

'You were dressed in the tunic of the Lothern Sea Guard. I'm told the heraldry on your arm was that of Lord Aislin.'

'The Sea Guard? I have no memory of serving aboard a ship, but then I've had no memory of lots of things I've been able to do since you took me in, haven't I? Maybe I should head to Lothern after I've spoken to your father?'

'If you like...' said Kyrielle. 'Though I hoped you would stay with us a little longer.'

He heard the beguiling tone of her voice and knew she was working her charms upon him. He pushed aside thoughts of remaining here and said, 'Kyrielle, I may very well have a wife and family. When my strength is returned I should get back to them.'

'I know, silly,' she said, 'but it has been so wonderful having you here and trying to help you regain your memory. I'll be sad to see you go.'

'And I'll be sad to leave, but I can't stay here.'

'I know,' she said. 'I will send a messenger to Lothern to take word to Lord Aislin that you are here. Perhaps he will know what ship you were on.'

He nodded and returned his attention to the dagger she had given him. Turning it over in his hands he was surprised at its weight. The workmanship was plain, though clearly of elven manufacture, for there was a sense of powerful magic to it. Though he spoke truthfully in saying that he did not recognise the blade, Daroir felt a connection to the weapon, knowing somehow that this weapon was *his*, but not how or why...

'I feel I *should* recognise this,' he said, 'but I don't. It's mine, I know that, but it doesn't mean anything to me, I don't remember it.'

Daroir grasped the hilt of the dagger and attempted to pull it from the scabbard, but the weapon remained firmly in its sheath and no matter how hard he pulled, he could not draw the blade.

'It's stuck,' he said. 'I think it's probably rusted into the scabbard.'

'An elven weapon rusted?' said Kyrielle. 'I hardly think so.'

'You try then,' he said, offering her the scabbard.

'No,' she said, shaking her head. 'I don't want to touch it again.'

'Why not?'

'I felt... wrong. I don't know, I just didn't like the feel of it in my hand.'

'The magic... is it dark?'

'I do not know. I cannot tell what kind of enchantment has been laid upon it. My father will have a better idea.'

Daroir stood and slipped the belt around his waist. One hole in the belt loop was particularly worn and he was not surprised when the buckle fit exactly within it. He adjusted the dagger on his hip so that it was within easy reach, though a dagger that could not be drawn was not much protection.

Kyrielle stood alongside him and straightened his tunic, brushing his shoulders and chest with her fingertips.

'There,' she said with a smile. 'Every inch the handsome warrior.'

He returned her smile and sensed a growing attraction for her that had nothing to do with her magical ability. She was beautiful and there was no doubt that he desired her, but he wore a pledge ring that suggested his heart belonged to another...

Though he knew that he should not feel such an attraction to Kyrielle, some deeper part of him didn't care and wanted her anyway. Was that part of who he really was? Was he a faithless husband or some reckless lothario who maintained the façade of family life while making sport with other women?

That felt like the first thing that made sense to him

since he had been plucked from the ocean. The idea of betrayal stirred some deep current within him, dredging up a forgotten memory of a similar cuckolding, but was it one he had perpetrated or a wrong that had been done *to* him?

He looked into Kyrielle's eyes and felt no guilt at the feelings he had for her. Reflected in her features was the same attraction and he reached up to brush his palm against her cheek.

'You are beautiful, Kyrielle,' he said.

She blushed, but he could see his words had struck home and sensed a moment of opportunity that felt deliciously familiar. He leaned forward to kiss her, her eyes closing and her lips parting slightly.

Before their mouths touched, a rustle of leaves sounded as a wall of branches parted behind them and a tall figure swathed in green robes who muttered to himself lurched into the arbour with his arms outstretched.

A flickering ball of light floated between his hands, like a million tiny fireflies caged in an invisible globe of glass.

He turned to face them and frowned, as though not recognising them for a moment, before saying, 'Ah, there you are, my dear. Would you mind helping me with these? I created a new form of honey bee this morning, but they're rather more vicious than I intended and I rather feel I'll need your help to make sure they don't do any more damage...'

Finally, thought Daroir, Anurion the Green.

ELDAIN WATCHED THE city of Tor Elyr recede as Captain Bellaeir eased the *Dragonkin* through the sculpted rocky isles of the bay and aimed her prow, freshly adorned with the Eye of Isha, through the channels that led to the Sea of Dusk.

He stood at the side of the ship, wrapped tightly in a cloak of sapphire blue, though the temperature was balmy and the wind filling the sails was fresh.

He shivered as he remembered the last time he had left shore and travelled on a ship to a distant land. Caelir had been beside him and a seed planted that was to bear bitter fruit in the land of the dark elves. On those rare days he allowed the sun to warm his skin, he could convince himself that it had been the evil influence of the Land of Chill that had caused that seed to flower, but he knew only too well that the capacity for his actions had their roots within him all along.

It had been nearly a year since he had seen Tor Elyr, but it was as beautiful as he remembered, the crystal and white spires of its island castles rising from the peaked rocks of the water like cleft shards of a glacier. A web of silver bridges linked the castles to each other and Eldain's heart ached to see it diminish behind him.

'We'll be back soon enough,' said Rhianna, slipping her arms around him and resting her chin on his shoulder as she approached from behind.

'I know.'

'It will be good for us to travel. We've spent too long cooped up in Ellyr-charoi. I've missed the sun on my face and the sea air in my lungs. I can already feel the magic of Ulthuan growing stronger all around me.'

Eldain smiled, reminded once again that his wife was a mage of no little power.

'You're right, of course,' he said, surprised to find that he actually meant it.

Perhaps it *would* be good to travel, to see cities and

places in Ulthuan he had not seen before. When this business with Rhianna's father was concluded, perhaps they might travel to Lothern and sample some of the fare from distant lands.

He turned within her grip and placed his own arms around her. 'I do love you.'

'I know you do, Eldain,' said Rhianna, and the hope in her eyes was like a ray of sunshine after a storm, full of the promise that all will be well. He held her close and together they watched the jewel of Ellyrion as it slid towards the horizon.

The journey from Ellyr-charoi had taken longer than normal, for Yvraine was not as skilled a rider as he and Rhianna. Their own steeds could carry them swift as the wind through the forests and across the plains, but Yvraine did not possess the innate skill of an Ellyrion rider. As a result, by the time they reached Tor Elyr, their progress onwards was stymied by the news that a Black Ark had attacked the ships of Lord Aislin as they patrolled the western coasts of Ulthuan. Only a single ship had survived the encounter but its captain had managed to bring warning of the druchii's attack, and now as many ships as could be mustered were being gathered in Lothern to mount a defence in the event of an attack.

As a consequence, the three travellers had been forced to await the arrival of a small sloop from Caledor to transport them across the Inner Sea to Saphery. This set-back chafed at Yvraine, who paced like a caged Chracian lion at the enforced delay, though Eldain and Rhianna had taken the opportunity to dine in Tor Elyr's exquisite eating houses and indulge in some wild riding across the grassy steppes.

In truth, Eldain had not been displeased at the delay, now relishing his time away from the stifling confines of the Hippocrene Tower and his guilt. Just being out in the open air had improved his mood immeasurably and he had laughed for what seemed like the first time in an age when he and Rhianna had first gone riding for the sheer joy of it.

As the days passed, it quickly became apparent that Yvraine had not long been in the service of the Loremasters, the subject coming up one evening while the three of them dined atop the highest spire of Tor Elyr in a crystal-walled dining room.

Rhianna had asked of the lands Yvraine had visited in her duties, only to be met by a rather embarrassed pause before the Sword Master said, 'Merely Ellyrion.'

'Is that all?' Eldain had said. 'I though you travelled all across Ulthuan?'

'I shall when I complete this mission for Mitherion Silverfawn.'

Eldain had quickly realised what that meant and said, 'Then this is your first mission?'

'It is, everyone must begin somewhere.'

'Indeed they must,' said Rhianna. 'Even those born to be kings do not become great without taking their first humble step on a long and winding road.'

Yvraine had looked gratefully at Rhianna and Eldain was struck by the realisation that, for all her outward inscrutability, Yvraine Hawkblade was desperately afraid to fail.

Thinking of the Sword Master, Eldain watched her sitting in the bow with her sword held before her as she tried to meditate. She had spoken of the difficulties in meditating while previously aboard ship, but he could only imagine how difficult it must be to achieve any sort of silent contemplation on a vessel this small.

'She's so young,' said Eldain.

Rhianna followed his gaze and said. 'Yes, she is, but she has a good heart.'

'How do you know?'

'The Loremasters do not take just anyone into the ranks of the Sword Masters. Only those who desire wisdom ever reach the White Tower; all others find their footsteps confounded until they are back where they began.'

'Where is the wisdom in using a big sword?'

Rhianna smiled and shook her head. 'Don't mock, Eldain. For some the path of wisdom lies in the exercise of physical mastery of the ways of the warrior. Yvraine will have spent many years training at the feet of the Loremasters.'

'I know,' said Eldain, 'I'm just teasing. I'm sure she is pure of heart, but it's like she's shut part of herself off from the world around her. Surely there must be more to life than meditating and practising with a sword.'

'There is, but for each of us there is a path and if hers takes her on the road to mastery of weapons, then we are fortunate indeed to have her travel with us. She may be an inexperienced traveller, but she will be a formidable warrior, have no doubt of that.'

'We are only sailing across the Inner Sea,' said Eldain. 'What could happen to us here? We are perfectly safe.'

'As I'm sure Caledor thought, right before he was attacked by assassins on his way from Chrace to become the Phoenix King all those years ago.'

'Ah, but he *was* perfectly safe,' said Eldain, 'for the hunters of Chrace saved his life.'

She sighed indulgently and said, 'But the point remains. Better to have a Sword Master and not need her help, than to need it and not have her.'

'Very true,' he said. 'But have you actually seen her do anything with that sword?'

'No, I have not, but the exercise of her art is a private thing, Eldain.'

'Well let's just hope she knows how to use it if the need arises.'

'I don't think you need worry about that,' said Rhianna.

'Hmmm... aside from the wound to the head, there is nothing that would suggest an injury severe enough to result in the loss of one's memory,' said Anurion the Green, removing a set of silver callipers from Daroir's head. The archmage checked the readings on the measuring device and nodded to himself before frowning and placing the callipers over his own skull and comparing the results.

They sat in Anurion's study, though to call it a study gave it a degree of formality it did not possess. Formed from a hybrid of marble walls and living matter, tall trees curved overhead to form a graceful arch with trailing fronds reaching to the ground like feathered ropes. Plants and parts of plants covered every surface, hanging from baskets floating in the air or suspended by streamers of magical light that bubbled upwards from silver bowls. Budding flowers climbed the legs of the chairs and tables, each of which had been grown into its current form instead of being fashioned by the hand of a craftsman.

A dense, earthy aroma hung in the air alongside a

million scents from the dizzyingly varied species of
blooms that covered almost every surface in the chamber. The scents of so many living things should have
been overpowering, but Daroir found it entirely pleasant, as though Anurion had somehow managed to find
the exact combination to ensure that the air remained
pleasingly fragrant.

Once Kyrielle and her father had contained the vicious
bees, the archmage had turned to Daroir and said, 'So
you're the one without his memory, yes?'

'I am, my lord,' said Daroir, for it was never a good
idea to show discourtesy to a powerful archmage.

Anurion waved his hand dismissively. 'Oh, stop all
this "my lord" nonsense, boy. Flattery won't help me
restore your memory. I'll either be able to do it or I
won't. Now come on, follow me to my study.'

Without another word, Anurion had stalked into the
depths of his organic palace, leading them through
great cathedrals of mighty trees and grottoes of unsur-
passed beauty. With each new and magnificent vista,
Daroir had to remind himself that this was one of the
archmage's *lesser* palaces. Though more pressing matters
occupied his thoughts as he and Kyrielle set off after her
father, he hoped that one day he would be able to visit
Anurion's great palace in Saphery.

It seemed to Daroir that their route took them
through a number of arbours and clearings of marble
and leaf they had passed before and he wondered if even
Anurion knew his way around his palace – or if such
knowledge was even possible.

At last, their journey had ended in Anurion's study
and both he and Kyrielle looked in wonder at the sheer
diversity of life that flowered here. Plants and trees that

Daroir had never seen before and had probably never existed before the tinkering of Anurion the Green surrounded them.

'Sit, sit...' Anurion had said, waving him over beside a long table strewn with ancient looking texts and a host of clear bottles containing variously coloured liquids. Daroir had been about to ask where he should sit when a twisting collection of branches erupted from the earthen floor and entwined themselves into the form of an elegant chair.

And so had begun an exhausting series of tests that Daroir could not fathom. Anurion had taken samples of his saliva and his blood before proceeding to measure his body, his height, weight and lastly the dimensions of his skull.

'Right,' said Anurion. 'I have the physical information I need, boy, but you'll need to tell me everything you remember prior to my daughter fishing you from the ocean. Omit nothing; the tiniest detail could be vital. Vital!'

'There's not much to tell,' said Daroir. 'I remember floating in the sea, holding onto a piece of wreckage... and that's it.'

'This wreckage, was it part of your ship?'

'I don't remember.'

Anurion turned to his daughter and said, 'Did your guards bring the wreckage back to the palace as well as this poor unfortunate?'

Kyrielle shook her head. 'No, we didn't think to bring it.'

'Hmmm, a shame. It could have held the key,' said Anurion. 'Still, never mind, one does what one can with the tools available, yes? Right, so we know nothing about your ship, and you say you remember nothing except being in the sea, is that correct?'

'It is. All I remember is the sea,' said Daroir.

Anurion swept up a strange, multi-pronged device that he attached to a number of coils of copper wire, which he then looped over Daroir's head, pulling the wire tight at his forehead.

'What are these for?' he said.

'Quiet, boy,' said Anurion. 'My daughter tells me that you were muttering something when she found you. What were you saying?'

'I don't know, I wish I did, but I don't,' said Daroir.

'Unfortunate,' said Anurion, adjusting the wires on his head, pulling them tight and leaving a trailing length of copper over his shoulder. 'Kyrielle, I do hope you remember what he was babbling.'

'Yes, father,' said Kyrielle. 'It was something about Teclis, about how he had to be told something. Something he needed to know.'

'And that doesn't sound familiar to you, boy?' said Anurion, turning his attention back to Daroir.

'No, not even a little.'

'Fascinating,' said Anurion. 'Frustrating, but fascinating. What information could a lowly sailor have that would be of interest to the great Loremaster of the White Tower?'

'I have no idea,' said Daroir. 'You keep asking me questions to which I have no answer.'

'Hold your ire, boy,' said Anurion. 'I am taking time from valuable research to deal with you, so spare me your biliousness and simply answer what I ask. Now... Kyrielle tells me that you possess a dagger that cannot be drawn, yes? Let me see it.'

Daroir stood from the chair of branches and unbuckled his belt, handing the scabbarded dagger to the archmage.

'Heavy,' said Anurion, closing his eyes and running his long fingers along the length of the scabbard. 'And clearly enchanted. This weapon has shed blood, a great deal of blood.'

Anurion gripped the hilt, but like Daroir, he could not force it from its sheath.

'How can it be drawn?' said Kyrielle.

'Perhaps it cannot,' said Anurion. 'At least not by us.'

'A poor kind of enchantment then,' said Daroir.

'I mean that perhaps it cannot be drawn by any other than he who crafted it or without the appropriate word of power. Only the most powerful magic can undo such enchantment.'

'More powerful than yours?' said Daroir.

'That remains to be seen,' said Anurion. 'But the question that intrigues me more is how you came to be in possession of such a weapon. You are a conundrum and no mistake, young... what was it my daughter christened you? Daroir, oh yes, how appropriate. You bear an enchanted dagger and have no memory, yet it seems you possess some knowledge that your unconscious mind deems necessary to present to Lord Teclis. Yes, most intriguing...'

Daroir felt his patience beginning to wear thin at the eccentric archmage's pronouncements and a strange heat began to build across his skull, further shortening his temper's fuse.

'Look, can you help me or not?'

'Perhaps,' said Anurion, without looking up from his desk.

'That's no answer,' said Daroir. 'Just tell me, can you restore my memory?'

'What manner of answer would you have me give, boy?' said Anurion, rounding on him and gripping his shoulders. 'You have no idea of the complexity of the living material that makes up your flesh. Even the simplest of plants is made up of millions upon millions of elements that make it a plant and allow it to function as such. Now, despite the evidence of your foolish words, your mind is infinitely more complex, so I would be obliged if you would indulge my thoroughness, as I do not want to reduce your intelligence any further by acting rashly.'

Anurion released his grip as an expression of surprise spread across his face and he once again adjusted the coils of copper wire around Daroir's head.

'What? What is it?'

'Magic…' said Anurion.

Kyrielle stood and joined her father and an expression of academic interest blossomed on her features.

Daroir frowned at their scrutiny, feeling like a butterfly pinned to the page of a collector's notebook. He glanced over at the table next to him and saw the stem and blooms of some unknown plant laid open like a corpse on an anatomist's table and felt a sudden sense of unease at whatever had piqued their sudden interest.

'What is it?' he said. 'What do you mean, "magic"?'

Anurion turned from him and lifted a golden bowl filled with a silver fluid that rippled and threw back the light like mercury. He returned to stand before Daroir and lifted the trail of copper wires that dangled at his shoulder, unravelling them and placing the ends into the golden bowl.

So faint that at first he wasn't sure what he was seeing, a nimbus of light built in the depths of the liquid, slowly intensifying until it seemed that Anurion held a miniature sun in his hands.

'I mean that whatever is causing your amnesia, it is not thanks to some blow to the head or near drowning.'

'Then what is it? What happened to my memory?'

'You have been ensorcelled, boy,' said Anurion, removing the copper wires from the bowl. 'This was done to you deliberately. Someone did not want you to remember anything before you went into the sea.'

The idea of someone tampering with his memories appalled Daroir, and the horror of such mental violation made him almost physically sick.

'Can you undo the magic?' said Kyrielle.

Anurion folded his arms and Daroir saw the reticence in his eyes.

'Please,' he said. 'You have to try. Please, I can't go on not knowing who I am or where I am from. Help me!'

'It will be dangerous,' said Anurion. 'Such magic is not employed lightly and I can offer you no guarantees that what memories you retain will survive.'

'I don't care,' he said. 'After all, what am I but the sum of my memories? Without them, I am nothing, a cipher…'

He pulled the coils of copper wire from his head and threw them onto the table, standing square before Anurion the Green.

'Do it,' he said. 'Whatever it takes, just do it. Please.'

Anurion nodded. 'As you wish. We will begin in the morning.'

CHAPTER FIVE

MEMORIES

SHIMMERING LIGHTS CHASED the *Dragonkin* as she plied the mirror smooth waters of the Inner Sea, the ship silent aside from the creak of her timbers and the occasional soft conversations of her small crew. Eldain watched these elves as they calmly went about their duties and wished a portion of their calm would pass to him. Even he could feel the magical energies of Ulthuan here, the ripple of half glimpsed shapes beneath the waves and the prickling sensation of always being watched.

Captain Bellaeir stood at the vessel's prow, standing high on the bowsprit and periodically issuing orders to his steersman.

'I am beginning to understand your reticence about travelling by ship,' he said to Yvraine as a jutting series of brightly coloured islets passed alongside.

The Sword Master looked up with a smile and he returned the gesture, glad to see a less ascetic side to her. As had become customary, she sat cross-legged on the deck with her sword across her lap as she tried to meditate.

'I am sure we are quite safe,' she said, abandoning her position and rising to her feet in a smooth motion. For all his misgivings about her youth and inexperience, Eldain could not help but be impressed by her lithe grace and poise.

'You have made this crossing once before, so do you have any idea where we are?'

'I think so,' she said, pointing to a smudge of brown and green on the northern horizon.

'What's that?' said Eldain, shielding his eyes from the sun with his hand. 'Is that the coast of Avelorn? I didn't think we would come this far north.'

'We haven't,' said Yvraine. 'That's the island of the Earth Mother.'

'The Gaen Vale?'

'Yes, a long and beautiful valley of wild flowers, apple trees and fresh mountain springs. It is a place of beauty and growth, where every elf maid is expected to visit at least once in her life.'

'Have you?'

'No,' said Yvraine. 'I have not yet had the honour of setting foot on her blessed soil, but I know that one day soon I shall visit the great cavern temple of the Mother Goddess and hear the words of her oracle.'

'It sounds like a beautiful place,'

'I am told it is, but, sadly, it is a beauty you will never know, for no males are permitted within the valley on pain of death.'

'So I have heard. Why does the Mother Goddess not allow the presence of males?'

'Birth and renewal,' said Yvraine, 'are the province of the female. The life giving cycle of the world and the rhythms of nature are secrets denied to males, whose gift to the world is destruction and death.'

'That is a harsh assessment,' said Eldain.

'Prove me wrong,' she said, and Eldain had no answer for her.

'Rhianna was to travel to the Gaen Vale,' he said, watching as the island vanished over the horizon as the captain called out more orders and the ship angled its course to starboard.

'Why did she not?'

'I would prefer not to speak of it,' said Eldain, once again picturing Caelir's face. Rhianna had planned to travel to the Gaen Vale not long after she and Caelir were to be wed, but his death had put paid to such plans. After her wedding to Eldain, the subject had never come up and he wondered why she had never again spoken of travelling to the temple of the Earth Mother.

He turned away from Yvraine, his thoughts soured, and walked towards the vessel's prow without another word. He nodded respectfully at the crew and passed the foresail, its silken fabric rippling in the fresh wind that propelled them across the sea.

Eldain watched Captain Bellaeir nod to himself as they passed the last of the rocky spikes and tiny atolls that dotted this part of the Inner Sea. Sensing his scrutiny, the captain inclined his head towards Eldain as he leapt nimbly from the bowsprit.

'How long before we reach Saphery?' said Eldain.

'Hard to say, my lord. The sea around here is unpredictable,' said Bellaeir.

'In what way?'

Bellaeir gave him a sidelong glance as though he were afraid he was being mocked, but decided he was not and said, 'We've been at sea for four days, yes?'

'Yes.'

'And, given fair seas and a trim wind, I'd expect to make Saphery in maybe another four, but out here… that's not how things work. You know that, don't you? You cannot tell me that you haven't felt the pull of the island…'

'I have felt… something, yes,' said Eldain.

'The seas have never been the same since the invasion of the fat Goblin King,' spat Bellaeir and Eldain felt his own bitterness rise at the mention of the goblin invasion that had laid waste to the eastern kingdom of Yvresse.

'Grom…'

Though Eltharion of Tor Yvresse had eventually defeated the Goblin King, a great many of the ancient watchstones that bound the mighty forces that kept Ulthuan safe had been toppled by the goblins' unthinking vandalism, and the cataclysmic forces unleashed had been felt as far away as Ellyrion.

'Indeed, though do not speak his name aloud, for the echoes of the past still cling to the ocean,' said Bellaeir. 'The Sea of Dreams is now a place of ghosts and evil memory, for the magic that once kept us safe fades and the terror of the past lives again in our dreams.'

Eldain said nothing as the captain touched the Eye of Isha pendant around his neck and made his way back to the steersman. He knew what the captain spoke of, for he too had felt the unnatural sensation of time slipping away from him, and the brooding shadow of ancient things pressing in on his thoughts.

How long they had truly been at sea and how long the remainder of their journey would take was a question not even the most experienced captain could provide an answer to. The passing of days and nights seemed to have no bearing on the senses here and it took an effort of will to even feel the motion of time, for their course was taking them close to one of the most mysterious places of Ulthuan.

The Isle of the Dead.

Eldain fought the urge to cast his gaze southwards, but the allure of the powerful magic was impossible to resist. Mist gathered at the horizon, lit from within by unearthly lights that glittered and flitted like corpse candles. Within the mist a shadow gathered, a dark outline of a forgotten land with a deathly aura that seemed to reach out and take his soul in a grip of ice.

He found his steps taking him towards the gunwale and he gripped the sides of the ship as a great weight of legend welled up within him, as though the island sought to remind him of the tragedy that had seen it sundered from the world.

In ages past, the island had been a place of great power, a lodestone of magical energies that drew the greatest mages of Ulthuan to its shores that they might bask in its power.

But at the dawning of the world, the Isle of the Dead had become much more than this: it had become a place of desperate hope, a place where the world had been saved and the fate of the elves sealed.

In the time of Aenarion, the first Phoenix King of Ulthuan, the gods of Chaos had walked the earth and fought to claim the world as their prize. Hordes of daemons and foul beasts of Chaos had destroyed all before them and the horrific followers of the Ruinous Powers had finally besieged Ulthuan. Aenarion had led his people in battle for decades to keep his lands safe, but even he could not defeat a foe that was constantly reinvigorated by the monstrously powerful magical currents surging across the face of the world from the ruptured Chaos portal in the far north. Thousands of elves died in battle, but for each twisted daemon they slew, a host of diabolical enemies arose to fight anew, and doomsayers wailed that the End Times were upon the world.

Eldain remembered his father telling him of Caledor Dragontamer, Aenarion's great companion and greatest of the high mages of old, and how he had conceived of a means by which the hordes of Chaos might be denied their power. In defiance of Aenarion's wishes, Caledor gathered a great convocation of mages upon the Isle of the Dead and a spell of great power was begun, a spell to create a mighty vortex that would drain the magic from the world. Though the mightiest daemons of Chaos sought to thwart Caledor, Aenarion fought them with the Sword of Khaine, the mightiest weapon in all the world, and held them at bay long enough for Caledor's mages to complete their spell...

Great was the destruction wrought by its completion: oceans toppled and lands sunk beneath the waves as the mages' spell took effect. Death and destruction followed in its wake, but the mages of old had triumphed, drawing the excess magic of the world to Ulthuan and denying the daemons of Chaos its sustaining power.

Like fishes stranded on dry land, the daemons were without the means to remain in the mortal world and the mortally wounded Aenarion was able to lead his warriors to victory, though he was soon to pass from the ages of the world.

Though the spell had saved Ulthuan, it was to have terrible consequences for Caledor and his mages, who were trapped forever on the Isle of the Dead.

Eldain shivered as he remembered these stories from his youth, stirring tales of sacrifice and heroism that had been told down the ages since the time of the first Phoenix Kings. None now travelled to the Isle of the Dead, for the titanic energies unleashed by Caledor had destroyed time itself there and left it adrift within the currents of the world, forever unseen and unknowable.

It was a place of ghosts and memory, legend and sorrow.

He felt a hand slide into his and he smiled as Rhianna appeared at his side, following his stare out into the haunted mists at the edges of the Isle of the Dead.

'They say that if you were able to reach the Isle of the Dead you would still see the mages of old, caught like flies in amber as they chant the ancient spells that preserve the balance of the world,' said Rhianna.

Eldain shivered at the thought, overwhelmed at the idea of elves trapped forever in time and bound by ancient duty to eternally preserve a world of men that had no knowledge of them and no understanding of the awesome sacrifice that had been made in its name.

'Why would you ever want to go to the Isle of the Dead?'

'You wouldn't,' said Rhianna. 'I'm just saying what you would see if you did.'

'I do not like passing so close to such a place,' said Eldain. 'I feel a terrible shadow envelop my soul at the very mention of its name.'

'The most powerful magic ever conceived was unleashed here,' said Rhianna. 'The sea and the air have long memories. They know what happened and they retain the knowledge of the debt we owe to those who saved our world. You can feel it with every breath you take.'

'And you?' said Eldain, well aware that her magical senses were far superior to his.

Rhianna bowed her head and Eldain was surprised to see tears glistening on her cheeks. He released her hand and put his arm around her shoulder.

'I can still feel their presence,' she said. 'I can feel the sadness all around me. The mages knew that Caledor summoned them to their doom, but they went anyway. Even as they chanted the words of the spell to create the vortex, they could feel their deaths and knew that they would be ripped from time and trapped for all eternity. I can feel it inside me and I know that doom also.'

Eldain pulled her tight and said, 'There is no doom upon you, Rhianna. While I draw breath, I give you my oath that I will let nothing happen to you.'

'I know you won't, but some things are stronger than oaths.'

'Like what?'

'Like fate,' said Rhianna, staring into the shadow-haunted mists of the Isle of the Dead.

THE RUSTLE OF the softest breeze stirred the leaves above Daroir's head, its balmy fragrances helping to soothe his fears of what was to happen here. He sat cross-legged on the warm grass, naked but for a plain loincloth and with the palms of his hands pressed to the ground. The feel of the earth beneath him and the sense of peace in this part of Anurion's palace flowed through him, as though the land of Ulthuan sought to prepare him.

He sat in the centre of a clearing (or a room, it was sometimes hard to tell the difference in Anurion's palace) that was as close to the ideal of harmony as Daroir could ever have imagined. Statues of elven gods ringed the edge of the clearing – Asuryan, Isha, Vaul, Loec, Kurnous and Morai-heg. Each was rendered in silver and gold, worked into the landscape with such skill that they appeared as hidden voyeurs rather than adornments.

Kyrielle sat next to him, her face lined with concern. She held a silver goblet worked with precious stones and a silver ewer filled with an aromatic liquid that steamed gently sat beside her.

'You are sure you want to go through with this?' she said.

'I'm sure,' he said. 'What I told your father was the truth. Without my memories I am nothing. What kind of a life is that?'

'But if something should go wrong... My father said that you might lose even the few memories you have now? Is a past life you remember nothing about worth that risk?'

'I believe it is.'

'But what if it is just pain that awaits you? What if it was *you* who used magic to bury those memories? Did you consider that?'

Daroir reached up to stroke her cheek, the silver pledge ring glinting on his finger. 'That may be the case, but if it is so, then I need to stop running and face the past. But if it was not then I need to reclaim my past to undo the wrong done to me.'

He smiled and said, 'I will be fine. I promise you.'

'And if you get your memories back… what about me? Will you forget me?'

'No, Kyrielle, I will not,' he said. 'You saved my life and no one could forget such a debt.'

She nodded and Daroir looked up as Anurion the Green entered the clearing in which they sat. The archmage was clad in a shimmering green robe tied at the waist with a golden belt and bore a sea-green pendant around his neck that shone with a magical inner light. His soft features were hardened and his hair pulled back tightly over his head. He bore a long sapling of slender, dead wood, the furthest reaches of its twig-like branches bare of leaves or growths.

The archmage approached him slowly, his eyes dancing with magic and Daroir knew that the mage had been preparing himself for this since the previous night. A crackling nimbus of power played about Anurion's head and for the first time, Daroir felt the touch of unease flutter in his stomach.

Was he ready to risk an absence of memory? If Anurion was correct and the powers binding his recollections into an impenetrable fog were too strong, what would be left of him afterwards… a drooling simpleton? An adult with no more capacity for reason than a newborn? The thought terrified him, but then the alternative was no better and his resolve hardened once more.

'Are you ready?' said Anurion, his voice sonorous with power.

Daroir nodded.

'Say the words,' said Anurion.

'I am ready.'

'There can be no turning back once we begin,' said the mage. 'It will be painful for you and you may see things you would wish you had not, but if we are to succeed, then you must be able to bear such sights. Do you understand me?'

'I understand,' said Daroir, hoping he had the strength to see this through.

Anurion nodded and lowered himself to the ground before him. He placed the sapling between them and the earth opened up to receive it. Thin roots snaked from the base of the sapling, twisting and worming their way into the dark earth.

'Give me your hands,' said Anurion. 'And close your eyes.'

Daroir did as he was bid, placing his hands in those of the mage and pressing his eyes tightly shut. Anurion pulled his hands towards the sapling and wove both their fingers along its length.

'As the branch was once dead, so too are your memories,' said the mage. 'But as the power of creation flows through it once more, a measure of the new blooming life will pass into you and I will use that energy for growth to bring your memories back into the light.'

Daroir nodded without opening his eyes and said, 'I understand. I am ready.'

They sat in silence for a measure of time that Daroir measured in the beats of his heart and just as he wondered when Anurion was going to begin, he felt a precious, fleeting sense of things moving at a speed almost too slow to be noticed.

The ground beneath him grew warm, as though a powerful current of energy moved through it, drawn to this place by Anurion's magic. A wondrous sense of peace reached up from the ground to envelop him and the harmonies of nature suffused his entire body, spreading calming waves of contentment through him.

Was this the power of creation at work?

He could feel the heartbeat of the world, a glacially slow pulse that began in the centre of everything and reached out to touch all living things, whether they knew it or not. Tendrils of white power reached up from the depths of somewhere incalculably old, the faintest wisps of its beauty brushing against the new-formed roots of the sapling.

Daroir wept as he saw the starved roots flourish at the touch of this bounteous, healing magic, cracked wood becoming green and vibrant, dried sap running like honey along the veins of the dead sapling.

Lines of power intersected here in this clearing and it was no accident that Anurion had sited his palace here. Daroir now felt the essence of Ulthuan, the titanic energies that sustained it and kept it safe from harm. To be near such power was intoxicating, and as it flowed into his hands sudden terror seized him at the thought of touching such colossal, elemental magic.

He wanted to pull away, but Anurion's warning that this ritual, once begun, could not be stopped returned to him and he summoned all his courage to hold on.

The energy flowed along his arms and he could feel the lethargy and aches that had plagued him since his awakening vanish, washed away in the healing balms of the world. It reached into him, filling his chest with such powerful forces that he gasped in astonishment as he struggled for breath.

'Hold true, boy!' said Anurion, his voice sounding as though it came from across an impossibly distant gulf of space and time. He struggled to retain his focus as the white light filled his body and reached up his chest, flowed into his neck and onwards into his head.

'Now we begin,' said Anurion.

Daroir gasped as the scent of the ocean filled his nostrils and his senses told him that his lungs were filling with water. He fought for calm as he saw the heaving expanse of dark, mist-shrouded water all around him.

'No!' he cried out in panic, but strong hands held him firm.

'You are safe!' said a strong voice. 'Where are you?'

'I am in the sea, I am drowning!'

'No, you are not,' said the voice and the name Anurion leapt to the forefront of his mind as he fought down the impulse to thrash his arms and kick his legs. The scent of the trees and plants around him reasserted themselves and though he could *feel* the water around him, he knew it was not real.

He fought to control his breathing, letting the vision of his memory carry him onwards.

'I can see the ocean,' said Anurion. 'This is a memory you already have. We must go further. Think, boy! Think back!'

Daroir let the currents of his memory carry him onwards, the deepest depths of his mind dredged for meaning and recall. Images flashed across the shallows of memory, cold faces with cruel eyes shrouded in shadow, rough hands holding him fast as he wept at being hurled deliberately into the sea.

No sooner had he tried to focus on the image than it sank from sight and he cried out in frustration.

'Let the new life take root, boy,' said Anurion, the effort of holding the magic in check telling in the tremor of his voice. 'Do not force it, let it come naturally.'

As much as he tried to take heed of the mage's words,

Daroir found it increasingly difficult not to struggle for meaning in the morass of images that danced just out of reach and meaning. A grey mare galloped past as the sea receded and he let out an anguished cry of recognition. He knew this horse, it… it had…

Aedaris…

He knew he should know this name, but its meaning eluded him and as the horse galloped away he saw that it ran free and joyous across a swathe of corn-ripened fields at the foot of a great range of white mountains. He knew this land and his heart swelled with love for… his home?

He tensed as he saw a dark shadow arise to envelop the landscape, a spreading shadow from the west that slowly passed over the fields and forests, turning them to ash as it went. Ancient malice and centuries of bitterness poisoned the rivers and rendered the land barren and he could do nothing to prevent it.

'This is no memory,' said Anurion and Daroir knew he was right.

'No,' he said, 'it is a warning.'

'It is indeed, boy, but of what?'

Daroir struggled to answer, but felt his inner vision carried off once more before he could answer. The tone of this memory changed to one of agony and he twisted in Anurion's grip, a fire building in his shoulder and hip. Though he could still feel the soft ground beneath him, hot, sharp pain stabbed into him and he looked down to see the spectral outline of dark crossbow bolts protruding from his body.

Blood ran from his body and he heard a soft voice whisper in his ear…

Goodbye, Caelir…

As though a pitcher of freezing water had been upended over him, his head snapped up and his hands tore free of Anurion's with a cry of a drowning man desperate for air.

'No!' he cried, seeing a face so like his own drift before him even as it vanished into the mists of his memories.

The images of his devastated homeland and the cross-bow bolts faded from his mind as the power that flowed through him from the sapling was withdrawn. He collapsed like a boneless fish, his back thumping onto the soft grass and his eyes misting with tears of anguish, betrayal and anger.

The pain of the phantom wounds was still strong and he reached down to place his hands where the bolts had pierced him. The skin there was unbroken, though his body was bathed in sweat and his flesh felt hot to the touch.

He felt a hand on his forehead and looked up to see Kyrielle's face above him, her eyes speaking eloquently of her worry. Her skin was cool and he felt his strength flood back into his body as the remembered pain of his wounds faded into memory.

'Are you all right?' she said. 'Do you remember me?'

He nodded slowly, pushing himself upright as fresh vigour filled his limbs like the rush of having just ridden a fine Ellyrion steed across the steppes. He smiled to himself as he realised that he remembered galloping hard with a grey mare beneath him and the wind in his hair.

'Well?' said Anurion and he looked across at the mage, not surprised to see a full-grown tree in the centre of the clearing where once had stood a dead sapling. 'Has your memory returned?'

Kyrielle's father's face was ashen, his eyes listless and hollow. The pendant that had once shone with light now lay in fragments amid the roots of the tree and the crackle of magical energy hung in the air like the aftermath of a lightning strike.

He took a deep breath and said, 'I'm not sure. I have images and parts of things that might be memory, but it's disjointed and… there are things I know are memories of mine, but I can't connect them.'

'It is as I feared,' said Anurion. 'Memory is more than simply the recall of events, it is these things connected by context and experience. Without this, they will remain like tales told to you by another. Vivid certainly, but without the connection to make them real they will never be anything more. My power has unlocked the doors to your memories, but it is not sufficient to force it open and allow that which will connect them to you to return.'

He pushed himself upright, pleased at the lithe power and youthful energy he once again felt in his limbs.

'I saw my homeland,' he said.

'As did I,' said Anurion. 'Ellyrion if I am not mistaken.'

'Yes. And I saw it destroyed,' he said. 'A creeping shadow of evil from the west swallowed it and brought about its ruin.'

'Might that be the warning you felt you had to take to Teclis?' said Kyrielle.

'I think it might be, yes.'

Anurion pulled himself to his feet, using the tree that had grown between them for support. 'Then to Teclis you must go. He is the greatest mage of Ulthuan and what I have begun, he will finish. You must journey to the White Tower of Hoeth and tell him what you have seen. An evil threat gathers against Ulthuan and we must unlock the rest of your memories to uncover the nature of that threat. Only Teclis or the Everqueen have the power to do that.'

Kyrielle reached out to help her father as he swayed unsteadily on his feet.

'Daroir,' she said. 'Help me, he's weak!'

He reached out to take hold of Anurion's arms and smiled suddenly.

'That's not my name,' he said. 'I remember now...'

'Then what is your name, boy?'

'My name is Caelir,' he said.

BOOK TWO
SAPHERY

CHAPTER SIX

THREATS

PAZHEK HAD NEVER put his faith in omens, but as the sun set behind him, bathing the bleached white stone of the mountains in blood, he smiled in anticipation of the kill he was soon to make. Though the sun was now gone, the sky was still too light to move, the hateful brightness of the day preventing him from departing his hiding place below a tumbled rock that formed a natural overhang.

He waited patiently for the light to drain from the great valley, allowing shadows to form and darkness to creep back into the world like a guilty secret. His fuliginous robes merged with the night until only the glint of malice in his eyes was visible.

Satisfied that it was dark enough for his purposes, he slid from his place of concealment. He slithered over the top of the rock on his belly, careful to hug the edge of the valley and keep himself pressed flat. It had been fourteen nights since he had swum ashore from the magically shrouded Raven ship, moving under cover of darkness and never allowing impatience to force his pace.

Such caution was essential; the slightest hint of his presence would spell his doom, for golden winged eagles watched from the skies and shadow-cloaked hunters stalked the mountains. These Shadow Warriors were the descendants of the Nagarythe and scions of the deadly Alith Anar, skilled hunters – the best the enemy had – but they were not the equal of one trained at the Temple of Khaine since birth to master the art of death.

Pazhek moved with all the skill his race possessed, but even the most graceful dancer of Ulthuan had not the poise and liquid grace of the assassin. His black-clad form moved like a shadow, moving from perch to perch as though the mountains themselves reformed themselves to match his movements and hasten him on his way.

A pair of short, stabbing swords were wrapped in cloth across his back and a curved dagger hung at his waist. These were not the assassin's only weapons, for his entire body was a weapon, fists that could seek out an enemy's vulnerable regions to incapacitate or kill with a single blow, feet that could shatter bones and an array of deadly poisons concealed within a number of small pouches on his belt.

Pazhek had killed since he had been stolen away from his crib during the insane debaucheries of Death Night, raised by the dark beauties of the temple to learn the secrets of Khaine: the martial arts, the power of poisons, how to move without sound and to slip through the night unseen. The assassins were the agents of the Witch

King, heartless killers who owned the darkness and slew his enemies without mercy.

The night closed in around Pazhek and though the land of Ulthuan was alien to him and its air reeked of magic, he slipped effortlessly over the peaks towards his destination. His passage was maddeningly slow, but so skilful was it that even a scout standing within a yard of him would have been hard pressed to discover him.

The night wore on, his shadowy form slipping through the rocks and crags of the mountains, his innate sense of spatial awareness telling him that he was almost where he needed to be. If the maps he had been shown in Naggarond were correct, it would be close to dawn when he reached his target.

For another three hours, Pazhek ghosted through the high peaks of the mountains until he could see a dim glow rising behind the craggy horizon above him. He did not let the excitement of having arrived hurry his movements. Such a moment was when an inexperienced assassin could let the thrill of the moment overwhelm him into making a mistake, but Pazhek was too skilled and detached to allow himself to make such an elementary error.

With as much patience and care as he had employed since his stealthy arrival on Ulthuan, Pazhek warily moved to the edge of the ridge above and found a cleft in the rock to peer through to avoid silhouetting himself against the skyline.

A pale white glow filled a wide valley below him, the soon to rise sun already seeping over the eastern horizon with the first golden hints of its arrival. Stretching from one side of the valley to the other, a high wall of silver-white stone reared up to block the route through the mountains. High elf warriors manned the walls of this great fortress, gathering sunlight winking from hundreds of spear tips, swords and bows and glinting upon mail shirts and plates of ithilmar armour.

But the most prominent feature of this mighty fortress was the jutting head of a great stone eagle that reared from the centre of the ramparts. The arc of its spread wings was cunningly fashioned into the structure of the wall to provide artfully curved bastions and its majesty gave the fortress its name.

The Eagle Gate.

Raised in the time of Caledor, the Eagle Gate was but one of the gateway fortresses built in the Annulii Mountains to defend the passes that led to the Inner Kingdoms. In the thousands of years since, not one of Caledor's fortresses had fallen and each was garrisoned by some of the finest warriors of Ulthuan. A single gate of azure steel was the only way through the wall, but anything that dared approach this fastness would be pierced by a thousand arrows before they had covered half the distance between the turn in the road and the gate.

Sculpted towers reared from the great wall, streaming blue pennants snapping from their finials and ringed with graceful parapets upon which sat fearsome war-machines. Pazhek knew only too well the carnage these machines could wreak, having seen such weapons hurling silver bolts the length of a lance that could punch through the heart of a dragon or sending withering hails of lighter, but no less deadly darts with terrifying rapidity.

But a fortress was more than simply weapons and warriors; it had a living, beating heart that sustained it as surely as the strength of its garrison. Tear out that heart and the fortress would die.

In the case of this fortress, Pazhek knew that the heart of the Eagle Gate was its commander, Cerion Goldwing.

Using the long shadows of the imminent dawn, Pazhek made his final approach to the fortress with murder in his heart.

THE LAND OF Yvresse was harsh and unforgiving, very different from the balmy, eternal summers of Ellyrion, though Caelir was forced to admit that the land had a rugged splendour that spoke to his adventurous soul of living in the wild and facing things head on. The folk of Yvresse were known as quiet, dignified souls touched with sadness, for their land had been ravaged by the coming of the Goblin King less than a century before.

Though the land had suffered terribly at the hands of the goblins, it was a hardy realm and its rivers now flowed clear again and new forests hugged the soaring mountain peaks once more. Only the previous day they had crossed an icy river of crystal water across a shallow ford and Kyrielle had told him that this was the Peledor Ford where elven scouts had first engaged the Goblin King's army.

The river had been choked with goblin dead, and the water polluted for years to come with their foul blood. But the land of Ulthuan was strong and sustained by powerful, cleansing magic. What had once been a tainted, evil river now flowed strong and clear to the sea, the regenerative powers of the land having washed itself free of the invaders' taint.

Here and there, they passed isolated watchtowers, but they encountered no other travellers, for Yvresse

was a land of jagged rock and sheer cliffs and mist. Few
dwelled here and though Kyrielle had told him that the
scouts of Tor Yvresse would be abroad, he saw no sign
of them.

He and Kyrielle rode on the backs of fine steeds provided from the stables of Anurion's villa, while Anurion
himself rode a winged pegasus, the magnificent beast
circling above them even now as it stretched its wings
and Anurion surveyed the landscape ahead of them.
Caelir had never seen such a magical creature, its grace,
intelligence and beauty unlike anything he could have
imagined. Even the famed steeds of his homeland could
not compare to this exquisite mount.

In addition to Kyrielle and Anurion, a dozen hand-
picked guards rode with them, their armour bright and
their long lances glittering in the sun.

Kyrielle wore a long gown of pastel green, her auburn
tresses unbound and falling to her waist. Caelir smiled
at her and she returned the smile. He felt better than he
had in days, the muscles of his limbs feeling powerful
and young; the oppressive fog clouding his mind lessened now that he knew his name.

Anurion had dressed for travel, with his billowing
robes substituted for a practical tunic of pale green
and a long cloak that appeared to be woven of autumnal leaves. He carried a staff of slender wood, its tip
crowned by intertwined thornvines.

In the time since Anurion had attempted to undo the
magic that imprisoned his memory, Caelir's vigour and
energy were restored and though he could remember no
more than his name and homeland, he felt that it was
simply a matter of time until he was restored.

They had set off later that day, making their way

southwards towards the city of Tor Yvresse and the route across the mountains.

Caelir soaked up the dramatic scenery of Yvresse, basking in its wild majesty and periodically galloping off whenever they encountered a stretch of flat ground simply for the thrill of riding hard through an unknown land. The wind in his hair, the beat of hooves on the grass and the freedom that came of being at one with a steed was as close to a homecoming as he could have wished for.

The horse he rode was a fine, snow-white beast of Saphery, its coat a shimmering dust of white and though no doubt a prince amongst steeds in its stable, it was nothing compared to the regal power, strength and agility of an Ellyrion mount.

Kyrielle and the warriors would attempt to match his incredible feats of horsemanship, but none of them had been raised in a land where the young were taught to ride as soon as they could sit in the saddle.

Whatever else he had forgotten, he had not lost his skill as a rider.

Just being on a horse again lightened Caelir's mood and he laughed as he urged his steed on to greater displays of skill.

The shadows lengthened and a sombre mood came upon the company as they drew near the ruins of an ancient citadel built into the side of the mountains. Its once slender towers were now fallen to ruin, the great mansion at its centre gutted by fire. Once impregnable walls were shattered, its stones cast down and the great basalt causeway that led to its vine-choked gateway littered with fallen rubble.

Fallen guardian statues lay toppled in the dry moat,

their sightless eyes staring with forlorn anguish at what had become of their former home. Caelir thought the scene unbearably sad and felt tears prick the corners of his eyes.

He turned to Kyrielle and said, 'What is this place? Why has it been left in such ruin?'

It was Anurion who answered him, his voice heavy with emotion. 'This is Athel Tamarha, once the keep of Lord Moranion and outpost of Tor Yvresse.'

'What happened here? Was it the Goblin King?'

Anurion nodded. 'Yes. The goblins came ashore further north, at a place called Cairn Lotherl, but it did not take them long to find a target for their wrath. No one knows how the Goblin King heard of Tor Yvresse, but hear of it he did, and his army burned and destroyed all in its path as they sought to find it. Fields of magical crops unique to Yvresse were trampled beneath ironshod feet, never to be seen again, and any settlements in the goblins' path were razed to the ground. On their way south they found Athel Tamarha and, thinking it Tor Yvresse, they attacked.'

Caelir urged his mount from the route they had been following and rode towards the cracked remains of the causeway. Understanding a measure of his sorrow, both Anurion and Kyrielle followed him, carefully directing the hooves of their steeds through the rubble.

Caelir passed beneath the broken arch of the gateway, riding into the fire-blackened courtyard where the ghosts of the Goblin King's invasion lingered. Splintered gates and doors hung on sagging hinges and everywhere he looked, Caelir could see the devastating fury of the goblin attack. Broken sword blades, snapped shafts of arrows and shattered shields lay strewn about, the detritus of war forgotten and abandoned.

'They knew not what they did,' said Anurion, surveying the wreckage from the back of his pegasus. 'When the goblins came, only boys and old men defended the walls of Athel Tamarha and they say that when Moranion saw the green horde from his tower he knew that his home was lost.'

'Where was his army?' said Caelir tearfully. 'Had he no sons to fight for him?'

'His eldest son, Eltharion, led most of his army in the north against the druchii, while his youngest studied in Tor Yvresse,' said Anurion. 'By evil fate, the goblins had attacked at the worst possible time for Athel Tamarha and its doom was sealed.'

'Eltharion the Grim...'

'The very same,' said Anurion. 'Though he was yet to earn such a sad name.'

Caelir dismounted and picked his way across the courtyard of the keep to stand within the fallen ruins of the central mansion. The ceiling had long since collapsed and piles of broken timber and fallen stone choked the once grand halls and elegant chambers.

Kyrielle followed him inside and took his hand as he wept in the lost keep of Athel Tamarha, overcome with sorrow at seeing such a magical place destroyed. Though he had never heard of Athel Tamarha before now, he could see the savage goblins running rampant through its gilded halls, tearing priceless tapestries from the walls to use as bedding, burning irreplaceable tomes of knowledge for warmth, destroying ancient works of art for their primitive amusement and swilling wines older than many human kingdoms like water.

'A palace that had endured for two millennia was

levelled in a single day by a tribe of mindless barbarians who knew not what it was they destroyed,' said Anurion, his voice little more than a whisper and redolent with the knowledge of times past.

Such barbarism was beyond Caelir's understanding and his anger towards the invaders surged hot and urgent through his veins. The battle fought here was long over, yet Caelir felt the pain of loss as surely as though he had stood upon its fallen battlements and witnessed its bloody ending. The tumbled ruins spoke to him on a level he had never before experienced, as though the memory of the violence done to it was imprinted on its very walls, the horror of its destruction passing to him and ensuring that its loss would never be forgotten.

'We should go now,' said Kyrielle, taking him gently by the arm and leading him back to his horse.

'How could anyone destroy something of such beauty?' said Caelir.

'I have no answer to give you, Caelir,' said Kyrielle, her normal sprightly vigour absent from her voice. 'The goblins are elemental creatures and live only for their own gratification.'

'I cannot understand it,' he said. 'It is just… *wrong*.'

'I know, but Moranion was avenged,' said Kyrielle. 'Eltharion's army returned from the north and led the warriors of Tor Yvresse in a great battle. You must have heard the ending of the tale?'

'I have,' said Caelir. 'Eltharion sailed his fleet into the bay and his warriors fell upon the goblins from behind. It was a slaughter.'

'Indeed it was,' said Anurion. 'But many elves fell that day and the city of Tor Yvresse was almost destroyed.

The goblin shaman almost undid the magic at the heart of the Warden's tower, magic that could have destroyed our beloved land. Though Eltharion stopped him, it was only at terrible cost.'

'What cost?' said Caelir, mounting his horse once more.

Anurion said, 'No one knows, for Eltharion will not speak of it, but it has blighted his life ever since. Together with the bravest warriors of his army, he entered the Tower of the Warden and undid the fearful damage done by the Goblin King's shaman, stabilising the vortex created by the mages of Caledor. He was hailed as a hero and became the Warden of Tor Yvresse, but the cheers of the crowd moved him not. In all the days since, it is said that no beauty touches him, no tale of heroism moves him and no light dares enter his soul. From that day forth he became known as Eltharion the Grim.'

Caelir took a last look around the achingly sad ruins of Athel Tamarha and said, 'I will remember this place.'

'Good,' said Anurion. 'It is right that we remember the past, for we shall surely rue the day we forget those who came before us. Whether for good or ill, it is they who shape us, form our thoughts and send us into the future with their memories.'

Caelir nodded and said, 'And what will I leave for those who come after me? I have no memories. What will be my legacy?'

'Your legacy is what you do from here onwards,' said Anurion. 'You are on a path, Caelir, and where it leads I do not know. You are young and the impetuous fire of youth burns in your heart, but I do not believe there is evil in you. Even if Teclis is unable to restore your memory, you have the chance to make new memories. Since your rebirth in the ocean, you have been creating new memories and *that* is the legacy you will carry with you. That and the lives you touch along the way, for we are all the sum of those whose influence touches our hearts.'

Caelir smiled in thanks to the archmage of Saphery, feeling his spirits rise at his words.

They rode out through the gates of Athel Tamarha and even though the sadness of the ancient palace's destruction was still lodged in his heart like a shard, he felt better for having seen it, as though the grief was like a cooling balance to the heat of his anger.

Once again, the company set off towards the south and Tor Yvresse.

Home of Eltharion the Grim.

A BITTER WIND was blowing from the west and Cerion Goldwing was feeling the weight of his years as he walked the length of the Eagle Gate this cold and gloomy morning. The scent of the sea air was carried on the wind, a dark, musky aroma that sent a chill down his spine as he thought of the cold, evil land that lay beyond it.

As though to dispel such morbid thoughts, he turned and cast his gaze eastwards to the land of Ellyrion. This high in the mountains, the rolling steppe of Ellyrion was a faint golden brown haze and it warmed his heart to see such a bounteous land and know that it was kept safe by the courage and heart of his warriors.

Passing the Eagle Tower, he surveyed the mountains that towered above his command, the silver peaks of the Annulii glittering with magic like a frosting of ithilmar. The magic here was so strong that even a simple warrior like him could see it and the haze of whispering energy that hung over the mountains promised more activity for his soldiers.

'Strong today,' he said to himself, feeling the magic pulse in his veins.

When the magic blew strongly, the creatures of the mountains were drawn to the rush of powerful energy that swirled around the island of Ulthuan. Such raw magic was capable of almost anything and many of the creatures drawn to such magic were unnatural monsters of Chaos.

Tall and clad in a simple tunic the colour of an autumn meadow over a thin, yet incredibly strong coat of ithilmar mail, Cerion was a stately figure of an elf. His silver helmet was tucked into the crook of his arm and he kept another hand on the hilt of his sword, a blade hammered out on the anvil by his grand sire.

His features were drawn and had once been handsome, though the passage of years had not left him unmarked. A druchii blade had taken his left eye nearly a century ago and when the blade of another had snapped, the spinning shards had left a scar that ran across his temple and over the bridge of his nose.

As he continued his morning tour of the walls, the soldiers of the Eagle Gate smiled warmly at him, though he had made no special effort to be liked in his three decades of command. The respect his warriors showed him had been earned. He was a warrior of proven courage and strategic skill, and it had been a willingness to share in the hardships endured by those who served under him that had won their respect.

He stopped beside a warrior with jet-black hair who sat cross-legged on the battlement with an unstrung

bow propped beside him on the parapet. A quiver of
arrows sat next to him and he worked industriously on
weaving a string for his bow.

'Good morning, Alathenar,' said Cerion. 'Something
wrong with your bow?'

The warrior looked up with a smile and said, 'No, my
lord, nothing wrong with it.'

'Then what are you doing?'

'Just trying something out,' said Alathenar. 'My Arenia
has been growing her hair for the last few years to weave
into my bowstring and now it's finally long enough. I
think it might help me get an extra ten or twenty yards
of range.'

Cerion knelt by the archer and watched him at work,
his fingers deftly working the thin strands of hair into
the length of his bowstring.

'An extra twenty yards?' he said. 'You're already able
to put an arrow through a druchii's eye at three hundred
yards. You really think you'll be able to coax more out
of that weapon?'

Alathenar nodded and said, 'She travelled to Avelorn
and had the strands blessed by one of the handmaids
of the Everqueen, so I'm hoping some of their skill and
magic will have passed into it.'

Cerion smiled, remembering a misspent youth in the
forests of Avelorn when he had joined the wild carous-
ing of the Everqueen Alarielle's court and partaken in
the indulgent lifestyle practised beneath the magical
boughs of her forest realm.

Consort of the Phoenix King, the Everqueen was one
of the twin rulers of Ulthuan and her court roamed like
a great carnival through the forest of Avelorn, its silken
pavilions ringing with music, poetry and laughter. He

well remembered the Everqueen's handmaids, elf maids as skilled with spear and bow as they were fair of face and lithe of body...

'Well,' he said. 'If any warrior's blessing can pass into a weapon it would be theirs. Be sure to let me know when you have put your bow together and we'll see how the magic of the handmaids holds up.'

'Of course, my lord. We'll have an archery contest when I'm off duty. Maybe wager a few coins upon the outcome...'

Cerion tapped his ruined eye and said, 'I do not think you need a blessed bow to outshoot me in an archery contest.'

'I know,' said Alathenar, 'That's why I was going to let you wager on me.'

'You are too kind,' said Cerion, pushing himself to his feet. Alathenar was already the best shot with a bow in the Eagle Gate's garrison and though Cerion doubted the addition of a maiden's hair to the bow-string would make any tangible difference, he knew well enough that the superstitions of soldiers were a law unto themselves.

Technically, Alathenar was on duty at the moment and, in disassembling his bow, was in dereliction of that duty by not having his bow at the ready, but Cerion was wise enough to know when to apply military law with an iron hand and when to let it bend like a reed in the wind. Besides, such a competition would help the morale of the garrison and strengthen the bonds between his warriors.

If only others could appreciate such things, he thought sourly as he saw his second in command, Glorien Truecrown, marching towards him from the Eagle

Tower. Alathenar caught his expression and looked over to see Glorien strutting towards them.

The younger officer wore an elaborate *ithiltaen*, the tall, conical helmet of the Silver Helms and a magnificent suit of ithilmar plate, the armour gleaming and polished. Glorien's noble status entitled him to wear the *ithiltaen*, though most nobles considered it unseemly to wear such a helmet without first having earned it by serving in a band of Silver Helm knights.

Cerion nodded briefly to Alathenar and went to meet Glorien, hoping to head him off before he reached the archer and decided to discipline him.

'Glorien,' said Cerion. 'Good morning.'

'Good morning, my lord,' said Glorien, his tones clipped and formal. 'I have transcribed the latest reports from our scouts.'

He held out a leather scroll case and Cerion took it reluctantly, already aware of what it contained, having spoken with the scouts when they had returned the previous evening.

'You know you don't have to do this, Glorien,' he said.

'But I do,' said Glorien. 'It is expected.'

Cerion sighed. 'Very well. I shall read them later this morning.'

He saw Glorien looking over his shoulder and knew exactly what he saw. As Glorien was about to speak, Cerion reached up to turn him around and march along the length of the wall with him.

'Was that Alathenar the Archer without a string to his bow?' said Glorien.

'Never mind that, Glorien,' said Cerion, leading him towards the stairs cut in the face of the mountainside that led to the Aquila Spire, a narrow projecting tower built into the southern cliff face that served as his personal sanctuary and study.

'But he is without a weapon! He has to be disciplined.'

As loyal as Cerion was to his race, he now cursed its love of intrigue and petty politicking.

Cerion knew that Glorien Truecrown had only secured his appointment to the Eagle Gate through his family connections rather than any ability as a warrior, for the Truecrown family could trace its roots to those linked with the Phoenix Kings of old. Their factional power in the court of Lothern was in the ascendant, enabling them to secure prestigious positions of authority for scions of their family members.

Glorien was simply biding his time until Cerion decided to retire and thus secure the position of Castellan of the Eagle Gate, but he knew in his heart that Glorien was simply not ready for such an important position.

'You would discipline the best archer in this fortress?'

'Of course,' said Glorien. 'No one is above the rules. Just because Alathenar can loose an arrow with some skill is no reason for him to believe he is exempt from following the rules.'

'Alathenar is more than just a skilled archer,' said Cerion. 'The warriors of this fortress respect and love him. His successes are their successes and when his name is spoken of in the barrack halls of other Guardian Gates, it reflects on them too. They look up to him, for he is a natural leader.'

'And?'

Cerion sighed. 'Discipline Alathenar and you will alienate all the warriors in this fortress. If you are one day to command the Eagle Gate, then you must learn to understand the character of those you lead in battle.'

'Command this fortress? The Eagle Gate is yours,' said Glorien, and Cerion almost laughed at his clumsy attempt at denial.

'Spare me the massage of my ego, Glorien,' said Cerion. 'I know your family tried to have me replaced in order for you to take command here. Thankfully, saner heads prevailed.'

At least Glorien had the decency to look embarrassed and Cerion felt some of his anger fade. Perhaps Glorien could yet learn how to be a soldier and a leader, though he suspected the odds were against it.

'There is more to command than simply getting warriors to follow rules and regulations,' said Cerion. 'You cannot simply apply your rules and mathematical formula to the defence of a fortress. It is in the minds of your warriors that a battle will be won or lost. Warriors will fight and die for a leader they believe in, but not for one they do not trust.'

'But discipline must be enforced.'

'Yes it must,' said Cerion. 'But not when its application would do more harm than good. Discipline Alathenar now and you risk losing the hearts of your soldiers.'

'I do not care to win the affections of the soldiery,' said Glorien.

'Nor do you need it. But without their respect, you are lost.'

Cerion glanced over his shoulder, knowing that the warriors of the Eagle Gate did not need to hear their superior officers arguing. Thankfully, the elven warriors in the courtyard were sparring with swords or practising formation spear discipline and were too intent on their labours to notice the discussion.

'I will think on what you have said,' said Glorien, but Cerion already knew that the younger elf had dismissed his words as the ramblings of an aged warrior long past his prime.

'Be sure that you do,' said Cerion, 'for if this fortress *does* become yours to command, you will be entrusted with the fate of Ulthuan. If an enemy army were to breach the walls, Ellyrion would suffer terribly before the armies of the Phoenix King could muster to fight it. Think on that before you decide to weaken the defence of this garrison by disciplining its best archer.'

Cerion brandished the scroll case Glorien had given him and said, 'Now, if you will excuse me, I think I shall retire to my chambers to read these reports.'

He had no wish to read Glorien's pedantry, but it gave him an excuse to be away from his subordinate.

'Of course, my lord,' said Glorien before saluting and turning on his heel.

Cerion watched him go and his heart sank as he pictured the Eagle Gate under his command.

IN ITS PRIME, Tor Yvresse had been considered the jewel of Ulthuan, but time and invasion had taken its toll on the once great city. Built atop nine hills, the great, spired city dominated the landscape, its mighty walls high and white and carved with protective runes. Glittering gold and bright silver shone in the afternoon sun and the titanic towers of its palaces soared above the walls, linked to one another by great bridges hundreds of feet above the ground.

Since the city had come into view, Caelir had stared, open-mouthed, at the magnificent spectacle. He had vague, disconnected memories of Tor Elyr, but nothing

that could compare to the sheer magnificence of Eltharion's city.

Tor Yvresse shone like a beacon against the dark rock
of the landscape and the green shawl of forests draped
over the mountains behind it.

'It's magnificent,' said Caelir once again and Kyrielle
smiled at his awe.

'You should have seen it a century ago,' she said. 'Its
amphitheatres were the envy of the world. Even the
Masques of Lothern would come to play in Tor Yvresse
and you know how particular they are.'

Caelir didn't, but already felt he was sounding like an
uncultured fool and simply nodded in reply.

Anurion flew above them on his pegasus and only
Kyrielle rode alongside him, the guards keeping a
respectful distance from the two of them. He could barely contain his excitement at seeing one of the great cities
of Ulthuan, though he could still feel the ache in his
heart from the ruins of Athel Tamarha. Tor Yvresse had
suffered terribly at the hands of the Goblin King and
though it had survived thanks to the heroism and sacrifice of Eltharion, he knew it had not escaped unscathed.

'Will we get to see much of Tor Yvresse, do you think?'
he said.

'That depends on father, I suppose,' said Kyrielle. 'I
know he is keen to get you to the White Tower and
Teclis.'

'I know, but surely we can take a day to explore?'

'I do hope so. There are many things I would like to
show you. The Fountain of Mist, Dethelion's Theatre,
the River of Stars…'

'Perhaps we can come back after the White Tower.'

'I'd like that,' she said. 'I'd like that a lot.'

Caelir smiled to himself and returned his attention to the city ahead, its magnificent walls looming above them as they followed the road that led to its tall gate of shimmering gold. Black banners fluttered from its towers and the spears of the warriors on its walls glittered like a thousand stars.

He looked up as he heard a beat of powerful wings and Anurion's pegasus gracefully landed behind them, its wings spread wide as it came to earth once more. The magical beast's wings folded neatly along its flanks and the archmage rode up to them without pause.

Caelir could see from his face that he bore ill-tidings and grimly awaited his pronouncement.

'Father?' said Kyrielle, also recognising the import of her father's expression.

'The currents of magic are alive with tidings and portents from all across Ulthuan,' said Anurion. 'The druchii have attacked the fleet of Lord Aislin off the coast of Tiranoc. It is said that a Black Ark sank two ships, though a third was able to escape.'

'The druchii…' said Caelir.

'We must make all haste in getting you to Teclis, boy,' said Anurion. 'If this is connected to the vision you saw of the darkness engulfing Ellyrion, then the attack of the dark elves may well be the opening moves in an invasion.'

Caelir nodded in agreement, all thoughts of exploring the city of Tor Yvresse with Kyrielle vanishing from his mind at Anurion's mention of Teclis. 'I think you are right.'

He kicked his heels into the flank of his steed.

'Let us hasten to Tor Yvresse.'

CHAPTER SEVEN

WARDEN

TOR YVRESSE, CITY of Eltharion…

From his initial awe, Caelir felt a strange mix of sadness and disappointment as they drew closer to the greatest city of Yvresse. What from afar had seemed mighty and regal looked faded and neglected when seen at close range. Though the high walls were no doubt steadfast and strong, the number of warriors manning them seemed woefully few for such a vast stretch of battlements.

The road leading to Tor Yvresse was deserted and their company was the only group of travellers abroad. The golden gate of the city remained closed and Caelir could feel the suspicious glares from the soldiers on the walls as they watched them approach.

An eerie silence clung to the landscape around the city and though he had no memory of travelling to such a metropolis before, he found it strange and not a little unsettling that he could not hear the bustle and vigour of a city the size of Tor Yvresse beyond its walls.

As they drew to within a hundred yards of the walls, the gate swung smoothly open and a disciplined regiment of spearmen emerged, marching in perfect step to take position in the middle of the road. Their spear tips shivered as they halted before the gate and a line of archers appeared at the embrasures of the white wall above them.

An officer at the centre of the spearmen stepped from the front rank and raised an open palm before him.

'In the name of Eltharion, I bid you halt, and demand your business within the city of Tor Yvresse.'

Caelir was about to reply when Anurion rode forward on his pegasus, his face thunderous and crackling, flickering arcs of power rippling along his robes.

'I am Anurion the Green, Archmage of Saphery, and I need not explain myself to the likes of a common gatekeeper. I demand entry to this city.'

The officer blanched at Anurion's obvious power, but to his credit, he did not back down. Instead he simply took another step forward and said, 'I mean no disrespect, my lord, but Lord Eltharion requires us to demand the business of everyone desiring entry to our fair city.'

'My business is my own,' said Anurion, but his tone softened as he continued. 'I do however wish to speak to Lord Eltharion, so convey my request for an audience to him forthwith.'

Caelir hid a smile as the captain of the gate attempted to reassert some of his authority by straightening his uniform and saying, 'I shall convey your requests to the Warden, but must ask as to the identities of your companions. All must be made known to the city guard before being admitted to Tor Yvresse.'

'Very well,' said Anurion, turning and gesturing vaguely towards Kyrielle and Caelir. 'This is Kyrielle Greenkin, my daughter, and this is her companion, Caelir of Ellyrion. The rest of our company are my household guards. Do you require me to identify them all?'

The officer shook his head and said, 'No, my lord, that shall not be necessary.'

Anurion squared his shoulders and urged his mount onwards as the officer rejoined his men and turned them about smartly. The line of archers above vanished from sight and the spearmen marched back within the city walls.

Caelir and Kyrielle followed Anurion, their armoured guards riding alongside them.

Caelir nodded respectfully to the captain of the gate as he passed him, hoping to restore a measure of the dignity Anurion's tirade had stripped from him. The officer returned the gesture gratefully and Caelir turned from him to savour his first sight of the fabled palaces and mansions of Tor Yvresse.

The light grew as they neared the end of the tunnel through the thick walls and Caelir felt himself holding his breath as he caught sight of domed roofs, silver arches and wide, tree-lined boulevards.

At last he emerged into the thoroughfares of Tor Yvresse and any disappointment he had felt when drawing close to the city was washed away in a rush of sensation as he saw its towering majesty up close. Elegant mansions, worked with great skill from the rock of Yvresse rose up in sweeping curves, the eye drawn around the graceful colonnades and gilded beauty of the multitude of marble statues that graced each roofline.

Beautiful elves in finery that would not have looked out of place in the palaces of Lothern walked the streets, glancing up with wary interest as they emerged into the wide esplanade before the gateway. Tall and clean limbed, these elves were ruggedly handsome, the equal of their land, and – he noticed – each was armed, either with sword or bow.

For all the finery and fearsome aspect of the inhabitants of Tor Yvresse, Caelir could not help but notice that the streets were nowhere near as busy as he would have expected them to be. Their route carried them along a wide, tree-lined boulevard, the marble-fronted mansions ghostly in their emptiness and the towers that rose above him on the hills seeming to stare down at him with bleak, forlorn gazes.

'This place is empty…' he said, feeling that to raise his voice above a whisper would somehow be wrong.

'Many died fighting the Goblin King,' said Anurion, 'and Tor Yvresse wears its grief like a cloak. These deaths hang heavily and the sombre mood of Eltharion carries over into his people. The celebrations and cheers that greeted his victory are stilled and now the city knows neither joy or life.'

Now that Anurion had spoken of it, Caelir could feel the ghosts of the war against the Goblin King in his bones; the distant clash of elf-forged steel against crude blades hammered out in the depths of forgotten caves and the anguished cries of those who saw their ancestral homes burned down around them whispered at the edge of hearing.

The sorrow he had felt in Athel Tamarha was a keen blade that pierced his heart, but this… this was a deeper ache, a constant hurt for the inhabitants of Tor Yvresse, for they had endured only to see the glory of their city fade.

Throughout the city, they saw daily life continue, but the more Caelir saw of it, the more it seemed that people were simply going through the motions. It was as though a part of them had died along with those who fell in battle and were just taking their time in lying down.

The physical splendour of the city was undimmed and much had been rebuilt, but where hands and magic had once raised architecture of sublime magnificence with joy, these new edifices were hollow replacements, more akin to monuments to the dead than celebrations of life.

Caelir found the city unbearably sad, like a weight on his soul and he initiated no conversations with Kyrielle, nor did he answer queries put to him beyond monosyllabic answers.

Eventually Anurion called a halt to their journey through the empty city and Caelir looked up to see a great tower, mightier and higher than any other around it. The mountains reared up behind the tower, but a trick of perspective seemed to extend it far beyond the magic-wreathed peaks and Caelir found himself dizzy with vertigo as his eyes travelled its full height.

A web of light seemed to pulse within the pale blue marble of the tower, its length pierced by not so much as a single window except at its summit, where a series of grim garrets and a lonely balcony stared over the city.

At the base of the tower, a single door, plain and unadorned, led within and Caelir found himself strangely reluctant to venture within this haunted, forsaken tower. This was a tower where the blackest magic had been unleashed and a duel that had sealed the fate of its inhabitant had been fought.

As their mounts halted before the tower, the door opened and a slender warrior shrouded in a plain tunic of black and armoured in gleaming plate stepped from the interior. His hair was pale to the point of being silver and his cheeks were sunken, but it was his eyes that chilled Caelir to the very depths of his soul.

Cold, dead eyes that held a wealth of bitterness that shocked Caelir with its intensity.

The elf crossed his arms and said, 'What business brings you to Tor Yvresse?'

The edge to his voice was like the last whisper of life in the mouth of a corpse and Caelir could see that Anurion and Kyrielle were as shocked as he at the warrior's terrible appearance.

Anurion collected himself and said, 'I am Anurion the–'

'I know who you are,' said the warrior. 'That is not what I asked.'

Caelir awaited the explosion of temper from the archmage, but it never came.

'Of course,' said Anurion, 'my apologies. We seek an audience with the Warden of Tor Yvresse to request passage across the mountains to reach the Tower of Hoeth.'

'I am the Warden of Tor Yvresse,' said the warrior. 'I am Eltharion.'

THE INTERIOR OF the Aquila Spire was pleasantly cool, a fresh westerly breeze blowing in through the narrow window that looked out over the descending slopes of the pass that led to the plains of Ellyrion. The scent of ripened corn was on the wind and Cerion thought wistfully of the times he had ridden those plains with the Ellyrian Reavers many years ago as he tried to lift himself from his gloomy thoughts.

Glorien's reports were spread out on his desk, and Cerion had despaired as he read his subordinate's take on the information he had already heard, first-hand, from the taciturn Shadow Warriors as they had returned from patrolling the mountains.

Their leader, Alanrias, had spoken of an ill-omened aspect to the mountains, a warning which Cerion took seriously, for the Shadow Warriors of Nagarythe had a bleak kinship with the darkness that lurked in the hearts of the Asur. When they spoke of such things it was with a degree of authority that could not be ignored.

No mention of this was made in Glorien's report, only the fact that the scout patrols had found no living thing in the mountains... expressed with a patronising air of superiority in the dismissal of their claims of impending threat.

He rested his elbows on the desk and rubbed the heels of his palms against his temple, hoping against hope that he could somehow circumvent Glorien's family influence to have a more suitable warrior appointed to be his second in command. The thought of retiring and leaving the Eagle Gate in Glorien's hands sent a chill down his spine.

Cerion put aside the reports, rising from behind his desk and making his way to the opposite side of the room and a fine, ellemyn-wood drinks cabinet. He opened the exquisitely crafted lattice doors and lifted out a crystal decanter of silvery Sapherian wine made from grapes grown on a strain of vine created by Anurion the Green.

Though it was still early, Cerion decided he needed the drink anyway and poured himself a stiff measure of the potent wine into a polished copper goblet. The breeze blowing in from the east was pleasant on his neck and he raised the glass to his face, enjoying the astringent scent of the wine.

As he raised the goblet to his face, the breeze behind him suddenly died and a shadow passed across the reflective surface of the wine. Cerion spun and hurled the goblet towards the narrow window, where a lithe shadow crouched on the sill.

His throw was wild and the goblet smashed into the stone of the wall, but it was enough of a distraction. The dark figure rolled into the room from the window, a dark blade flashing into its hand. Cerion's sword leapt from its sheath and he stabbed the point towards the rolling shape.

Faster than he would have believed possible, the dark warrior scissored to his feet, arching his back to avoid his thrust, and landed nimbly on his feet before him. A blade slashed towards Cerion's neck and he threw himself backwards, only just avoiding losing his head. His sword came up to block another blow, but before he could do more than bring the blade back down, his attacker had another weapon in his hand.

'Intruder!' he bellowed at the top of his voice, hoping that someone would be near the bottom of the steps to hear his cries. 'Intruder! Guards!'

'Guards won't save you, old man,' said the black-clad assassin and Cerion was not surprised to hear the dark, sibilant tones of the druchii issue from his attacker's mouth.

'Maybe not,' he said, backing towards the door, 'but

they'll see you dead with me.'

The assassin did not reply, but leapt forwards once more, the twin blades spinning in his hands as though he were a blade acrobat. Cerion blocked the first blow, but could not stop the second, and the assassin plunged the blade up into his armpit, dark enchantments laid upon its edge parting the links of ithilmar as easily as an arrow parts the air.

Cerion screamed in agony as the sword tore through his lungs and heart, blood pumping enthusiastically from the gaping wound as the assassin tore the blade free. He staggered backwards, the door to the Aquila Spire slamming open as he fell against it.

The assassin bounded forward and held him upright, stabbing him again and again. The blades tore into him with agonising fire, pain filled his senses, and he stared into the cruel eyes of his killer, horrified at the hate and the pleasure the druchii was taking from inflicting such pain. He wanted to fall, the strength pouring from his limbs as surely as the blood was gushing from his ruined body. His eyes dimmed, but he could feel hands keeping him from falling.

He felt fresh air on his skin and the sensation of brightness. His feet were unsteady and gore made the stairs slippery as he was dragged into the light.

With the last of his strength Cerion opened his eyes to see the wall of the Eagle Gate spread out before him, his warriors staring in open-mouthed horror at the sight above them. An archer took aim and swordsmen sprinted along the wall towards the stairs.

'Know this, old man,' said the assassin, leaning in to whisper in his ear. 'Soon all this will be in ruins and your land will burn.'

146 *Graham McNeill*

Cerion tried to spit a last defiant oath, but his words were no more than hoarse whispers. He felt the assassin's grip shift.

Something clattered against the stonework of the tower and he saw the splintered fragments of a white shafted arrow twirl away from him.

Then the world spun about him as he was hurled from the top of the steps.

AT FIRST, ALATHENAR had not known what to think when he heard the cry echoing from the mountains and had looked up from his freshly stringed bow in confusion. Smoothly rising to his feet, he saw that others were similarly alarmed by the sudden cry of pain. Without thinking, he nocked an arrow to his bow and leaned through the embrasure on the wall seeking a target.

Then the cry had come again and he spun towards the Aquila Spire as his keen hearing pinpointed its source. The door to the tower slammed open and he lowered his bow as he saw Lord Goldwing framed in the gloom of the tower.

Then he saw the blood streaming from his body and the shadowy form behind him.

'Assassins!' he cried and sighted along the length of his arrow.

His arrow all but leapt from his bow as he loosed, but his target was already in motion and he cried out as the commander of the Eagle Gate was hurled down the stairs cut in the rock. The bloody body tumbled downwards, end over end, and Alathenar heard the sickening sound of bones breaking.

Lord Goldwing's attacker vanished into the Aquila Spire and Alathenar swept up his quiver before taking to his heels after him. Anger and grief lent his stride speed and he sprinted past armoured swordsmen who hurried towards the tower. They halted at the bottom of the stairs, kneeling in horror beside the broken body of their beloved commander, but Alathenar already knew there was nothing to be done for him. He vaulted the warriors at the foot of the stairs, bounding upwards towards the Aquila Spire.

He reached the top of the stairs, the upper landing slick with blood, and he dived through the door, rolling as he landed and rising with an arrow pulled taut to his cheek.

The chamber was empty, though the stink of viscera and violence was fresh in his nostrils. Quickly, Alathenar scanned the room and found it empty. He slung his bow over his back and drew his sword as he saw a dented goblet in a pool of bitter wine below the chamber's only window. Carefully he edged towards the opening, his blade extended before him.

Behind him he could hear shouting voices and he knew that the assassin was long gone from this place of murder. Swiftly he swung himself through the window and caught his breath as he found himself on a narrow stone sill, hundreds of feet above jagged rocks that would kill him as surely as the assassin's blade.

He looked above him as he heard warriors pushing into the chamber behind him, spying a scuff mark on the eaves of the tower's roof. So the assassin had come over the mountains and lowered himself inside.

'He's gone over the mountains!' he shouted into the tower, before sheathing his sword and taking a deep breath. Alathenar bunched his legs beneath him and leapt straight up, grabbing hold of the edge of the roof. He swung himself up and over in one swift motion, clambering up the ridged parapet of the conical roof.

He leaned his back against the tower's finial and lifted his bow over his head. Hooking the quiver to his belt, Alathenar spared a glance back down to the wall of the fortress, seeing shouting warriors who pointed over at the cliffs of the pass. He followed their extended arms in time to see the shadowy form of the assassin as he bounded from the rocks and made his escape.

Arrows flashed through the air, but the assassin possessed some dark sense for them and either ducked back into cover or effortlessly dodged them.

Alathenar selected the finest, truest shaft from his quiver and kissed the arrowhead before nocking it to his bow and taking careful aim.

His target was at the extreme edge of his range, but he had his new bowstring and he silently offered a prayer to the Everqueen that her handmaids did indeed possess some magic. The assassin wove a ragged pattern through the rocks and Alathenar cursed as he quickly realised that there was no way he could predict his movements to aim ahead of him.

Suddenly he smiled as he saw a narrow cleft in the rock ahead of the fleeing figure and saw that his weaving course was leading him unerringly towards it. He took a breath and held it as he gauged the range to the cleft and how quickly the weaving assassin would take to reach it.

'Kurnous guide my aim,' he said.

Alathenar let out his breath and at the end of his exhalation loosed the arrow from his bow. He watched as the blue-fletched shaft arced into the morning sunlight, reaching the zenith of its flight before dropping in an almost leisurely arc.

'Yes!' he said as his arrow slashed down and punched through the assassin's shoulder. The dark shape stumbled and fell, but even as Alathenar watched, he picked himself up and made off once more.

Alathenar pulled another arrow from the quiver, already knowing that he could not hope to hit the assassin before he was out of sight. Sure enough, the figure disappeared from view before he could loose.

He lowered his bow and wept angry tears as he looked down to see the warriors of the Eagle Gate cover the face of Cerion Goldwing with a white cloak that slowly turned to red.

Alathenar the Archer let out a terrible cry of loss and anger.

And high above the mountains, it was heard.

FROM THE TOP of the Warden's Tower it was possible to survey the entire city of Tor Yvresse and Caelir soon appreciated the scale of the destruction wrought by the invasion of the Goblin King. Despite the work of the city's inhabitants, their domain still bore the scars of war, ruined mansions, fire blackened stretches of wall and abandoned parks where nature had been left to run riot.

He watched the inhabitants of the city going about their business, guessing that the city had originally been built to house at least twice the number of folk it currently sheltered. He and Kyrielle stood on the tallest balcony that overlooked the city, higher even than the tower palaces built upon the city's nine hills. Wind whipped the sea beyond the harbour into tall, foam-topped waves of blue and snapped the mournful banners upon their flagpoles, but not a breath of it touched them in the tower.

Upon meeting Eltharion, the Warden of Tor Yvresse had bid them dismount and leave their guards before following him within his tower. Its interior was as bleak as the exterior was imposing, bare walls and simple furnishings speaking of an occupant who cared nothing for beauty or ornamentation and whose ascetic tastes would make those of a Sword Master's seem vulgar.

Eltharion had said nothing more beyond his introduction and beckoned them to follow him upstairs to his chambers. Caelir inwardly groaned at the sight of so many stairs, having seen how tall the tower was from the outside, but barely had his feet set foot on the first than it seemed he was stepping onto a landing at the very top.

Looking back down the centre of the tower, he saw the ground hundreds of feet below.

Upon reaching the top of the tower, Eltharion and Anurion had retired to speak in private while he and Kyrielle had been left to their own devices in the tower's receiving chamber. Some effort had been made to make the interior of the tower less foreboding, but it was a token effort and only made the rest of their surroundings more depressing.

Food and wine had been set out for them, and so they had sated their thirst and hunger before moving out to the balcony to admire the view and await the Warden's decision.

'This isn't what I expected at all,' said Caelir.

'Tor Yvresse?'

'Yes. I remember the tales told of the city and the

return of Eltharion, but I expected a city of great heroes. I did not think to find it so… deathly.'

'As my father said, a great many elves died in the war, but our children are few and it is a sad fact that fewer and fewer of us are being born every year.'

'Why would that be?'

Kyrielle shrugged. 'I do not know. Some say that our time on this world is now a guttering flame and that soon it will be over. All things have their time in the sun. Perhaps the world is now done with our kind.'

'What? Surely you don't believe that?'

'How else would you explain our fading?'

'Perhaps the power of the elves *does* wane, but our time will come again, I know it.'

'Are you so sure? How many empires of men have risen and fallen in the turning of the world?'

'Men are fireflies, their lives flicker and burn for but a moment,' said Caelir. 'They live their lives as though in a race, never building anything of permanence. How can you compare the Asur with such barbarians?'

'We are not so dissimilar, my dear Caelir. Perhaps we are on the same path, but are simply taking longer to walk it.'

Caelir turned to Kyrielle and placed his hand on her shoulder. 'This doesn't sound like you, what is the matter?'

Kyrielle said, 'Nothing is wrong with me, silly boy. I think it is just being in Tor Yvresse. There are evil ghosts of memory here and they stir the darkest thoughts in me. I will be fine.'

'I have felt them too, Kyrielle, but we cannot let the evil of the past blight our lives in the here and now. The Goblin King was defeated and Tor Yvresse saved, surely that is cause for celebration?'

'Of course it is, but with every invasion, every battle, we are lessened. Every year the druchii grow bolder and so long as the Isle of the Dead draws the magical energy of the world to Ulthuan, creatures of Chaos will forever be drawn to our fair isle. We are clinging to life by our fingernails, Caelir.'

'Maybe so,' said Caelir, 'but is that reason to give up and let go? Maybe we are a fading race, I don't know, but if that is true I will still fight to the end to hold on to what we have. I do not know what will happen in the future, but I will not meekly accept despair into my heart. So long as I draw breath I will fight to protect my home and my people.'

Kyrielle smiled at him and he felt his spirits rise until he caught sight of the pledge ring on the hand resting on her shoulder. A fleeting image of a beautiful elf maid flashed behind his eyes, her eyes sad and her hair a flowing river of gold.

'What's wrong?' said Kyrielle, seeing the shadow pass over his features.

'Nothing,' said Caelir, taking his hand from her shoulder and turning away.

He was saved from further questions when he heard footsteps approaching from the tower. Anurion the Green stood before them, his features giving nothing away as to the outcome of his discussions with Eltharion.

'Well?' said Kyrielle. 'Does he grant us leave to travel over the mountains?'

'Not yet. He wishes to speak to Caelir first.'

'Me? What for?' said Caelir, suddenly nervous about meeting such a dark yet heroic figure as Eltharion the Grim.

Anurion said, 'Because I believe he thinks you a mystery and Eltharion is not one who enjoys mysteries as much as I. He has been told all that I know of you and he wishes to speak to you himself. When he asks questions, be truthful in all things. Do you understand me, boy?'

'I understand you, yes,' said Caelir. 'I am not a fool, but I still do not see why he wishes to speak with me.'

'Listen to me, Caelir, and listen well. Eltharion is the Warden of Tor Yvresse and none pass over the mountains to the Inner Kingdoms without his leave. If he wishes to speak to you then you do not refuse him.'

Caelir nodded and made his way across the receiving chamber towards the leaf-shaped archway that led to Eltharion's private chambers. The doors were shut and he knocked softly, unwilling to simply barge in.

'Enter,' said a cold voice and an icy dread settled on him as he obeyed.

PAZHEK LET LOOSE a string of the foulest curses he knew as he stumbled on yet another rock and fell to his knees. Where before the mountains had risen to meet his tread and hasten him on his way, now every rock was loose beneath him and every patch of scrub tangled his foot at every turn.

His shoulder ached abominably, the arrowhead still lodged painfully beneath his shoulder blade. He still couldn't believe that he had been hit, for he had employed all the techniques of evasion taught to the Adepts of Khaine and had been beyond the furthest extent of bowshot...

Or so he had believed.

He had bound the wound as best he was able and taken

an infusion of weirdroot to dull the pain before retracing his steps through the mountains. The Shadow Warriors would even now be on his trail and he was under no illusions as to the likelihood of his escape now that he was leaving a trail of his own blood behind him. But he would lead them a merry dance through the mountains and when they came for him he would kill and maim as many as he could before they brought him down.

He had applied a coating of poison to his blades, a mixture of manbane and black lotus, a concoction that would drive its victims mad with pain and delusions of their worst nightmares.

Let them come, he thought, I will give them cause to remember the name of Pazhek.

He smiled as he thought of the death of Cerion Gold-wing. Though it was not an elegant death it had been a very visible and bloody one that the garrison of the Eagle Gate would not soon forget.

A shadow flashed over the ground and he spun, swords raised before him.

He saw nothing, no sign of pursuit, but knew that such things were meaningless, for his enemies would not come upon him directly, but with guile and cunning. He turned and carried onwards, his breath heaving in his lungs, all stealth forsaken in favour of speed.

If he could somehow reach the coast and find a place of concealment then he could await the time when his people would come for him.

Another shadow crossed the ground and he stopped, breathless and desperate as he backed against the cliff. Once again he saw nothing and as a screeching cry echoed from the mountainsides, he suddenly realised his error.

Pazhek looked up in time to see a great, golden shape plunge from the skies.

Its wings extended with a boom of deceleration and hooked talons slashed towards him.

He cried out and tried to raise his blades, but the mighty eagle was faster, its extended talons snapping closed over his arms and lifting him into the air. Pazhek screamed as the ground fell away, dropping his swords as the eagle crushed the bones in his wrists.

'Assassin,' said the giant bird of prey as each beat of its wings carried them higher and higher. 'I am Elasir, Lord of the Eagles, and you have spilled the blood of a friend to my kind.'

Pazhek could not answer, the agony of the bird's razor talons grinding his bones and slicing his flesh too great to bear. He twisted in its grip, the ground spinning thousands of feet below him as he fought in vain against the strength of his captor.

'And for that you must pay,' said the eagle, releasing its grip.

CAELIR PUSHED OPEN the door and stepped into a vaulted chamber of cold light and distant echoes. Where the rest of the tower was bleak and displayed none of the character of he who dwelled here, this room gave dark insight into the mind of Eltharion.

Racks of weapons and framed maps of Ulthuan, Naggaroth and all the known world lined the walls. Alongside them were grim trophies set on wooden plaques and mounted around the circumference of the room, the heads of vicious monsters, orcs and men.

The golden sunlight of Ulthuan streamed in through a great aperture formed in the roof, below which an elaborate saddle-like arrangement of leather straps and buckles was hung upon a wooden frame. The illumination did not warm the chamber or reach the farthest corners, as though its occupant did not desire to feel the light on his skin.

Eltharion paced beneath the opening in the roof, the sunlight only serving to highlight the pallid cast of his flesh and the shadows beneath his cheekbones. His expression was grim, as Caelir had expected, and he turned to face him with barely a glimmer of interest in his icy, sapphire eyes.

'So you are the one washed upon the shores of my land?' said Eltharion.

'I am,' said Caelir, bowing respectfully. 'It is an honour to meet you, my lord.'

Eltharion ignored the compliment and said, 'Anurion tells me your memories have been magically locked within you. Why would someone do such a thing?'

'I have no idea, my lord. I wish I did.'

'I do not believe you,' said Eltharion and Caelir was surprised at his directness.

'It is the truth, my lord. Why would I lie about it?'

'I do not know, and that is enough to give me pause,' said Eltharion, walking towards him with his hooded eyes fixed upon him. Caelir had to fight the urge to back away from the Warden of Tor Yvresse, such was the weight of his intimidation.

'I do not like the unknown, Caelir,' said Eltharion. 'The unknown is dangerous and cloaks itself in mystery to better advance its cause. I sense a dark purpose to you, but cannot fathom what danger a callow youth such as yourself might present.'

'Callow? I am a warrior and have killed our enemies before now.'

'How do you know? You have no memory.'

'I… just know that I am no enemy of Ulthuan,' said Caelir.

'I wish I could be sure of that, but I do not trust you.'

'Then do you trust an archmage of Saphery?'

Eltharion laughed, but there was no humour to it, simply a bark of amusement that came from the exposure of another's ignorance. 'One might as well trust the sea or the faith of a woman.'

'But Anurion the Green vouches for me.'

'That he does, though even he does not fully trust you.'

'Why do you believe I am a threat?'

'It does not matter why I believe it, simply that I do. Someone went to a great deal of trouble to take away your memories and I cannot believe they did so for the benefit of Ulthuan.'

'Perhaps it was because I knew something of benefit to Ulthuan that my memories were stolen,' said Caelir.

'Then why not just kill you?'

'I do not know,' said Caelir, growing weary of having no answers to explain himself with. 'All I know is that I am a true son of Ellyrion and would rather die than harm so much as a single hair on the head of any of my kin!'

Eltharion stepped forward and placed his hands either side of Caelir's head, looking directly into his eyes with a gaze that frightened him with its intensity.

'I believe that you think you are telling the truth,' said Eltharion. 'Only time will tell if that is enough.'

'I *am* telling the truth.'

Eltharion released his grip and turned away as a mighty screech came from beyond the tower and a powerful beat of wings sent a rushing downdraught of air gusting through the chamber. Parchments fluttered like autumnal leaves scattered by the wind.

A shadow suddenly blocked the light from the aperture in the roof. Caelir looked up in amazement to see a mighty, winged creature drop through and land gracefully within the confines of the tower. Its head and forequarters were like those of a powerful eagle, its hooked beak and clawed forelegs terrifyingly muscled. Behind its feathered wings, the creature's body was furred and massively powerful, its hindquarters those of a mighty lion. Its pelt was the colour of copper, with dark stripes and spots dotting its fur like the great cats said to stalk the jungles of Lustria and the Southlands.

Caelir stared awestruck as the mighty griffon paced the breadth of the tower, its head cocked to one side as it glared angrily at him.

'Stormwing,' said Eltharion by way of introduction.

Caelir bowed to the powerful beast, the intelligence glittering in its eyes plain to see. 'It is an honour.'

Eltharion turned to lift the saddle-like arrangement from the wooden frame and Caelir now realised that it was exactly that – a saddle. The Warden of Tor Yvresse threw the saddle over the griffon's back and said, 'You are heading to the White Tower?'

'We are,' said Caelir, still awed at the magnificent creature before him.

'Then I will allow you to travel to Saphery, for I desire you out of my city. But you will not travel alone.'

'No?'

'I will send you on your way with a company of my finest rangers,' said Eltharion. 'They will take you through the secret ways of the mountains and escort you to the White Tower.'

Caelir smiled and said, 'You have my thanks, my lord.'

As Eltharion finished buckling the complex saddle to Stormwing he said, 'I do not do this as a favour to you, I do it to ensure you go where you say you are going.'

'I still thank you for it.'

'Your thanks are irrelevant to me,' said Eltharion. 'Be at the west gate at sunset and do not return, Caelir of Ellyrion. You are not welcome in Tor Yvresse.'

CHAPTER EIGHT

SAPHERY

As the sun began to set, the mountains cast long shadows over Tor Yvresse and the city felt even more empty than it had during the day. When Caelir, Anurion and Kyrielle emerged from the tower of Eltharion, a sombre darkness, more palpable than the gloom that engulfed the city during the day, hung over its populace.

Caelir looked up as the plaintive cry of Eltharion's griffon echoed from the heights of the tower and he saw the master of the city circling high above.

'He trusts no one, does he?' said Caelir as they mounted their horses and set off towards the western gate.

'Few have given him cause to, Caelir,' said Anurion. 'When Tor Yvresse was under attack, the other cities were too wrapped up in their own affairs to send aid. By the time most realised the seriousness of what the goblin shaman was attempting it was too late. Either

Eltharion would stop them or Ulthuan would fall.'

'He has allowed us to pass through the mountains,' said Kyrielle, urging her mount to catch up to Caelir. 'That must count for something...'

Behind her, the guards that had accompanied them from her father's palace rode alongside Anurion, their relief at leaving Tor Yvresse clear even in the gloom.

'Only to see us gone from his city,' said Caelir.

'Did Eltharion give you any indication of who would lead us to Saphery?' said Anurion.

'He told me his rangers would show us a secret way through the mountains.'

Anurion nodded and said, 'It is said that there are ways through the Annulii that even the wisest mages do not know, but I had never thought to travel them.'

The sound of their horses' hooves echoed in the empty streets of Tor Yvresse and it took them no time at all to reach the western wall of the city. It towered above them, its defences no less impressive on the side facing the Inner Kingdoms of Ulthuan than those facing the hostile world.

Mighty towers and colossal bastions spread out to either side of them, but Caelir could see that such defences would be of little consequence if a great horde came at them, for there was a paltry strength of warriors manning the wall.

Only now did the precarious nature of Tor Yvresse truly become apparent as he saw how few souls remained alive to defend their city. The Shifting Isles protected the eastern approaches to Ulthuan and it was clear that Eltharion relied on them to keep his city safe, for there were precious few warriors to do so.

Finally understanding a measure of the warden's

hostility, Caelir looked up once more at the circling form of Eltharion and said, 'I wish you well, my lord. Isha watch over you.'

Even as the words left his mouth, a number of ghostly shapes detached from the shadows and swiftly surrounded their company. They wore conical, face-concealing helmets of burnished bronze and silver, with dark cloaks that rendered them nearly invisible in the darkening twilight.

One of the warriors swept back his cloak to reveal the natural, rugged attire of a ranger, his physique tough and wolf-lean.

'You are to follow us,' said the shadow-cloaked warrior.

'Who are you?' said Anurion.

'We are servants of the warden,' came the answer. 'That is all you need know.'

Without another word, the warrior turned and set off in the direction of the city gate, which swung open noiselessly as he approached.

Caelir leaned over to whisper in Kyrielle's ear. 'Talkative types, these rangers.'

Their leader turned to face him and said, 'We speak when we have something of worth to say. Others could learn from us.'

Both Caelir and Kyrielle started in surprise, having thought the ranger far beyond the limits of hearing. She smiled nervously and Caelir shrugged as he rode towards the ranger.

Together with their mounted guard, they passed through the gate and followed the road down one of the nine hills of Tor Yvresse in a gentle curve towards the Annulii.

'Is it wise to set off into the mountains in the dark?' said Kyrielle.

The ranger nodded and Caelir could see that he found such discussions tiresome. 'We will be your eyes and there are some paths that can only be taken in darkness.'

Caelir already knew the skill of Eltharion's rangers was second only to that of the Shadow Warriors of Naga-rythe, having known they had observed their approach to Tor Yvresse without once revealing themselves. Even so, the idea of leading such a company into the mountains in darkness seemed an excessive display of hubris.

A faint glow permeated the night, the aura of raw magic sweeping through the mountains, and the further they travelled along the road, the stronger the taste of it became.

Their journey took them along twisting paths, which, though they led upwards, seemed to bring the mountains no closer. Though darkness had fallen on the world, a mist of magical energy lingered on the trees and ground like a light dusting of snow and Caelir could feel the power that resided in every fragment of Ulthuan as though it sprang from the very rocks themselves.

Tor Yvresse receded behind them, the lights of its shuttered mansions and towers a lonely, isolated beacon of light in the darkness behind them.

'How much further must we ride?' said Anurion. 'Lord Eltharion claimed you would show us a way through the mountains.'

'And so we shall,' said the nameless ranger. 'Be patient.'

At last the rangers led them into a narrow defile between two jutting fangs of rock that wound downwards into a dark hollow in which stood a tall, glistening stone at the confluence of three gurgling streams. Spiral patterns and ancient, faded runes had been carved into the rock and Caelir could see the faint image of a carved gateway against a far cliff.

Anurion and Kyrielle gasped as they followed the rangers down into the hollow and even Caelir could sense the reservoir of magic that collected in this place.

'A watchstone...' said Anurion.

Caelir had heard of the watchstones from Kyrielle, powerful menhirs that crossed Ulthuan from shore to shore and directed the energy of the vortex contained within the Annulii ever inward towards the Isle of the Dead on lines of magical energy.

Many of the island's mages built their homes atop these lines and great barrows of the dead were erected on auspicious points where these lines intersected. The souls of the dead were thus eternally bound to Ulthuan that they might guard the land they loved and escape the terrible prospect of being devoured by the gods of Chaos.

In other kingdoms such watchstones were a common sight, crossing the landscape in a web of mystical design, but in Yvresse their location was a closely guarded secret. After the catastrophe of the Goblin King's invasion, geomancers from Saphery had divined where else the toppled stones might still be positioned to perform the task for which they had been raised and secreted them in the hidden places where none but those who knew the secret paths could discover them.

The rangers led them to the base of the hollow, waiting until everyone had reached the bottom before kneeling at the watchstone and singing a strange, lilting melody. The words were unknown to Caelir, the mystical cadences felt in the soul as much as heard. Each word slipped though the darkness and the landscape around responded, the trees sighing and the rocks stirring themselves from their slumbers to hear such beauty.

Caelir watched the rangers with a mixture of awe and fear as he felt the world around him... *change*, as though the landscape around them shifted beneath their horses' feet in response to the song.

Looking into the night sky, he could see the stars spread out before him, their luminance rippling in the sky through the magical haze washing from the mountains.

He returned his attention to the rangers and their strange, singsong chant as a glittering mist gathered at the lip of the hollow and rolled down the slope towards them.

'Anurion?' he said. 'What's happening?'

'Be silent,' said the archmage. 'Do not disturb them. They are calling on the power of the watchstone and it would be perilous to interrupt.'

The mist now filled the hollow and Caelir felt its cold touch as it rose around them. The horses whinnied in fear as strange shapes appeared in the mist, revenants of long dead elves and fragmentary images of times and places as yet unknown to the living.

The mist gathered about them, coiling around them like a living thing, questing around their bodies and cocooning them in a moist, clammy embrace.

Caelir lost sight of his companions, his sight closed off by the thick mist. Icy fear slid through his veins and he twisted in the saddle as he suddenly felt very alone, the isolation more terrifying than the ominous shapes that drifted just beyond sight.

'Kyrielle? Anurion?'

The faint outline of something dark moved through the mist and Caelir reached for his sword as it approached, determined that no spirit of the mist would take him.

The breath rushed from him as the figure resolved from the mist and he saw that it was one of Eltharion's rangers, his eyes dark and glittering with magic.

The ranger reached up to take the reins of his horse and Caelir silently allowed the warrior to lead his horse, sensing that to speak now would be unutterably dangerous.

As the ranger led his horse towards the cliff, the foggy silence remained unbroken, even the sound of hooves on rock muffled by the smothering blanket of mist. Caelir saw the sheer cliff of white rock ahead of him, but where before it had been naught but the image of a gateway, now it yawned open, black and terrible.

Sinister moans and a breath of hot, vibrant air blew from it, rich with potent energies, and Caelir felt nothing but terror at the idea of venturing through such a dread portal.

'Where does that lead?' he said, every word an effort.

'Into the river of magic,' said the ranger.

BEYOND THE GATEWAY was darkness, but not darkness empty of wonders, rather one filled with magic and miracles. No sooner had the ranger led Caelir through than his senses were assaulted by a great, terrible weight of things, monstrously powerful things, lurking just at the edge of perception.

He could see nothing, but the power lurking in this place supplied the fuel and his imagination the tools to render all manner of terrors and dreamscapes before him. The darkness retreated in the face of such freshly realised potential: vast expanses of dark mountains ruled over by glistening towers of red meat, marching swords and spears atop great riding beasts, powerful armies destroying one another in a verdant field of blue flowers and a thousand other such visions, each more vivid and bizarre than the last.

Of his companions he saw no sign, the steps of his horse mechanical and automatic as it walked through this nightmare realm of infinite potential. Its ears were pressed flat against its skull in fear, but whether it saw the same things as he or fashioned its own skewed reality, he could not say.

His course took him along the edge of a great river, filled not with water, but the roiling bodies of the dead. A million corpses, bloated and stinking, flowed past him, their faces at once familiar and unknown to him. Caelir recoiled as the stench of the dead assailed him, the sight of so many dead sickening and unbearable.

The river vanished as the power of the magic around him dredged the depths of his mind for yet more things to make real. A cold wind that penetrated his flesh and chilled his very bones blew through him and a cavalcade of tortures paraded before him, though these were no bloody dismemberments, but sensual pleasures designed to break the spirit from within: degradations and humiliations heaped upon one another until the soul could take no more.

Caelir closed his eyes and begged the visions conjured into his mind by the power of the magic coursing through the mountains to withdraw, but such magic was raw and elemental, devoid of conscience and mercy and the visions neither relented nor retreated.

How long he remained beneath the mountains, a moment or an eternity, he could not say. In this place of magic, there was no time, no dimensions and no sense of a place in the world. Faces appeared, elves of both sexes; places, tall cities of white towers and a hateful dark city of great iron towers that echoed to the dreadful sounds of screams and the hammering of industry.

Fires burned in this city and something in this last vision possessed some kernel of truth the others did not, and Caelir focused his attention on the rampant flames and screeches of some great, unseen monster. He saw specks of white amid the darkness and his heart leapt to see Reavers mounted on bright Ellyrian steeds spreading destruction throughout the dark city, casting down what the evil masters of the city had built.

Was this a memory or a fantasy culled from unremembered boyhood dreams?

He fought to hold onto this last image, his attention fixed on two riders, one atop a gleaming black steed, the other atop a grey. They were achingly familiar, but before he could do more than register their presence, he felt the intensity of the visions fade and he had a powerful sensation of having emerged from the rushing waters of the most powerful river imaginable.

Caelir took a great, gulping breath as strands of raw magic slid from his mind and the darkness of the mountains reasserted itself. Reality settled upon him in the click of trace and harness, the gasps of his companions and the clatter of their horses' hooves on rock.

'No, show me...' he said, twisting in the saddle to look behind him, though on an instinctual level he knew that such a term was meaningless in this conduit of magic beneath the mountains.

'Show you what?' said Anurion, riding behind him and looking exhilarated to have touched such primal energies and lived to tell the tale.

Caelir shook his head, the significance of the vision already fading from his mind as though a smothering blanket had been pulled over it. 'I don't know. I thought I saw something familiar, but it's gone now. I don't remember it.'

He turned away from the archmage and saw that the ranger still led his horse, his guide so oblivious or inured to the nightmares they had just faced that they no longer affected him.

Their company travelled along a narrow passageway cleft in the mountainside, a warm, yellow glow coming from somewhere up ahead that blew away the last of the cobwebs that entangled Caelir's thoughts after the journey through the darkness.

The rock of the narrow passageway glistened with what he at first took to be moisture, but, when he reached out to touch it, turned out to be a dewy residue of magic. Glimmering beads of light clung to his fingers and he smiled as he realised they must be close to Saphery, the horrors unleashed within his mind only moments before now quite forgotten.

Caelir emerged into the bright sunshine, shielding his eyes as the ranger led him out onto a wide shelf of rock that jutted from the cliff of the mountains. The air smelled sweet and columns of green trees grew tall around him, stark against the summer skies above.

Kyrielle sat on her horse at the edge of the plateau, her cheeks flushed with the pleasure of seeing her homeland once more. Her father's mounted guards milled around and their faces were bright and open with anticipation, such was the power of this homecoming.

A boulder-lined path curled down the mountains, leading to a fertile land of golden fields and blue, coiling rivers. Caelir looked over his shoulder and saw the ramparts of the Annulii Mountains towering above him, their shimmering peaks wreathed in a haze of magic.

'We have crossed the mountains already?' he said, amazed that they should have covered such distance in the blink of an eye. Their journey had begun in darkness, but he judged it to be early morning here, though it felt as if only moments had passed since they had left the hollow of the watchstone.

'You have,' said the ranger who had first spoken to them in Tor Yvresse.

'How?' said Caelir. 'A journey like that should have taken us several days at least.'

'Lord Eltharion wished you to reach Saphery sooner,' said the ranger, raising his arm and pointing to Caelir's left. 'And the White Tower awaits.'

Caelir followed the ranger's pointing finger and his eyes widened as he saw the Tower of Hoeth spearing half a mile into the sky, a sharp white needle of stone thrusting upwards and surrounded by light. Though the sun had yet to reach its zenith, the brilliance of the tower outshone its radiance.

'I hope for your sake you truly are a seeker of knowledge,' said the ranger, reaching up to place a hand on Caelir's arm and looking over to the tower. Though his helmet concealed much of the ranger's face, Caelir saw that his expression of concern was sincere.

'What do you mean?'

'The White Tower is unforgiving with those who knowingly approach with deceit in their hearts or who seek power for its own sake.'

'I appreciate the warning, but I spoke the truth to Lord Eltharion.'

The ranger nodded and released his arm. 'I wish you good fortune, Caelir of Ellyrion.'

'Come on!' cried Kyrielle. 'Let's go. It won't take long to get to the tower now.'

'Yes, come on, boy,' said Anurion, the wings of his pegasus spreading wide in anticipation of taking to the air. 'No slacking off now that we're almost there.'

Caelir smiled, amused at the galvanising energy that filled the natives of Saphery now that they had returned to their homeland. Would returning to Ellyrion produce a similar rush of infectious enthusiasm in his own heart?

He hoped so.

Caelir watched Kyrielle gallop down the road and Anurion take to the air, the guards following after the archmage's daughter.

He turned to thank the ranger for bringing them here so swiftly, but his words died when he saw they had vanished and the cleft in the rock from which they had emerged had disappeared.

A cold wind blew from the high peaks and Caelir pulled his cloak tighter as he felt a stirring of ancient magic, more powerful than anything left in the world, sweep over him like the breath of a terrible, slumbering monster kept imprisoned by the forgotten glamours of a distant age.

Caelir turned from the now sinister mountain, very aware that he was alone in this strange land, and set off down the path after Kyrielle and her warrior escort.

The Tower of Hoeth loomed ahead of him, stark and cold, and Caelir wondered what destiny awaited him within its walls.

He did not look back at the mountains as he rode, anxious to be kept safe by the presence of those who called this land home.

Yes, Ulthuan was an enchanted isle, full of wonders and miracles, but every now and then it taught those who dwelt upon it that magic was the most dangerous force in the world.

It was a lesson Caelir vowed not to forget.

CAIRN AURIEL WAS the name of the harbour and Eldain could remember no finer sight as the sharp prow of the *Dragonkin* sliced the clear waters of evening towards it. Together with Rhianna, he stood at the sloop's prow as they sailed past the glowing beacon of a silver lighthouse that lit the natural harbour cut into the high cliffs on the western coast of Saphery.

Structures of grace and simplicity surrounded a naturally sheltered bay of pale sand: white towers, golden domes and columned arcades were artfully arranged in an orderly and elegant manner around the fringes of the cliffs. Laughter and music drifted through the darkness and Eldain felt his heart sing in response to the sounds of life and joy. He put his arm around Rhianna and drew her close.

'I had forgotten how much I had missed Saphery,' he said. 'It has been too long since I have travelled here.'

'We were always welcome at my father's villa,' Rhianna said.

'I know, but after the expedition to Naggaroth...'

Rhianna returned his embrace and he felt as though the great weight of guilt upon his shoulders might someday be lifted by the healing magic of Ulthuan and the love of this wonderful companion beside him.

'It will be good to set foot on dry land,' said Rhianna. 'Though I feel the magic throughout Ulthuan, I feel it most strongly in Saphery.'

Eldain smiled at the sound of her enthusiasm and turned his head to call out to Captain Bellaeir. 'My thanks, captain. You have sailed us true.'

Seated at the vessel's tiller beneath a glowing lantern, Bellaeir waved and returned to his steering of the ship.

As they drew closer, Eldain marvelled at the construction of the harbour buildings, their slender marble quays projecting into the bay and floating just above the smooth surface of the water. Now that he knew to look for it, he saw the ripple of magic around the settlement, clinging to tall watchtowers, shimmering over the placid waters and carrying the sound of its inhabitants to them.

The crew of the sloop moved to attend to the task of bringing their ship into the harbour, but their efforts were unnecessary, for magical currents drew the ship in safely and brought it to a smooth halt against one of the quays.

Laughing, the crew disembarked and tied their ship to silver bollards, though Eldain suspected that the ship would remain exactly where it was without such restraints. He turned to retrieve his belongings, watching as Yvraine rose from her position in the centre of the sloop and bowed to the captain before smoothly vaulting onto the quay, her sword impeding her not at all.

Eldain marvelled at her liquid movement, knowing that, save on the back of the horse, he could never match her preternatural grace. Ever since they had sailed past the Isle of the Dead, the Sword Master had kept her own counsel, her silences broken only by the occasional affirmation of her wellbeing.

Now that she set foot on Saphery once more, Eldain could see a lightness to her spirit he had not known she possessed in all the days he had known her.

'Someone is glad to be back,' he said to Rhianna as she joined him.

She looked up with an indulgent smile and said, 'I can understand how she feels. Imagine how *you* will feel when you return to Ellyrion.'

'True. Even though Saphery is not Ellyrion, it will be good to ride Lotharin once again. The smooth waters of the inner ocean do not compare to riding a fine Ellyrian steed.'

As he gathered up the last of his possessions, the crew lowered a ramp from the side of the *Dragonkin* to the quayside and Eldain all but bounded over to the hold where their horses had spent the bulk of the sea journey.

Lotharin cantered from the hold first, his black coat shimmering in the glow of the lighthouse, closely followed by Rhianna's horse, Orsien – a fine, silver gelding from Saphery with dappled flanks and a haughty intelligence in his pale green eyes. Behind these two magnificent steeds came Irenya, a dun mare that had belonged to one of Ellyr-charoi's retainers, but who had been left riderless when her rider had perished on the same expedition that had seen Caelir lost. Yvraine had ridden Irenya from Eldain's villa and though the Sword Master had not enjoyed the ride to Tor Elyr, the horse had rejoiced in the chance to bear a rider once more.

Eldain let his horse nuzzle him and ran his hands down its neck, whispering in its ears and speaking in a manner unknown beyond the plains of Ellyrion. The horse whinnied excitedly and Eldain laughed at its pleasure in being able to bear him onwards.

He led Lotharin and Irenya from the *Dragonkin*, glad
to feel solid ground beneath him, even if it was supported by magic. Rhianna led Orsien and when their
mounts and belongings were disembarked, Eldain saw
Bellaeir approach from the vessel's stern.

'Lord Eldain, do you wish me to await your return?'
said the captain.

'Yes,' said Eldain, 'though I cannot say how long we
will remain in Saphery.'

Bellaeir shrugged. 'We can rest here in Cairn Auriel for
a spell, my lord. We are not required at the muster of
Lothern, for a ship the size of the *Dragonkin* would be
of little use in a battle.'

'I will send word when our situation becomes clearer,
captain,' said Eldain. 'In the meantime, payment will be
lodged at the counting house and you may take what
you are owed until we return.'

'That will be most satisfactory, my lord,' said Bellaeir
with a smile. 'If you are looking for accommodation for
the night, you could do worse than the Light of Korhadris. The food is plentiful and the wines are of the finest
vintage known to elfkind.'

Eldain waved his thanks to the captain and turned
away, following his horse as it led the way to the
harbour town of Cairn Auriel. He caught up with
Rhianna and Yvraine as they awaited him at the end
of the quay.

With the glow of the lighthouse now behind him, he
saw a distant spike of white light on the horizon.

'I thought the Tower of Hoeth was supposed to be
hard to find,' said Eldain.

'You have no idea,' said Yvraine.

* * *

CAPTAIN BELLAEIR'S RECOMMENDATION that they stay at the Light of Korhadris proved to be an inspired choice, for their welcome was hearty and the menu extensive. Set amid white cliffs, Cairn Auriel spread outwards in radiating streets from the horseshoe shaped bay, fanning upwards on the slopes of the coastline towards the land of Saphery itself.

The proprietor of the establishment was a jovial elf of advancing years who bid them welcome and immediately set about seeing to their comfort with utmost vigour. The interior of his hostelry was elegant and, though somewhat ostentatious for Eldain's tastes, apparently typical of Sapherian vernacular.

Few other patrons were present and the three of them made no effort to socialise with the well-dressed travellers they saw at other tables. Softly glowing orbs of magical energy hung in the air, casting a warm, homely light throughout the public areas and Eldain felt his skin tingle with the presence of so much magic in the air.

'Is it not a little frivolous to employ magic for such mundane things as lighting?' he asked.

Rhianna laughed. 'You are in Saphery now, Eldain. Magic is all around you.'

'I suppose,' he said. 'I had forgotten how different your land is from mine.'

'Well we're here now and it's good to be back. Don't you agree, Yvraine?'

The Sword Master sat a little way from them, close enough to be included in their company, yet far enough away to appear distant. Eldain noted Yvraine had the same revitalised look he could see in Rhianna's eyes and was not surprised to hear an edge of anticipation in her voice when she spoke.

'Yes, it is good to be home. Though I will be happier when we reach the White Tower.'

'How far is it from here?' asked Eldain.

'That depends,' said Yvraine.

'Depends? On what?'

'On whether the tower deems us worthy of approaching it.'

'I thought we were invited? By Rhianna's father.'

'We have been,' nodded Yvraine, 'but the magical wards that protect the tower will not relax its guard for something as prosaic as an invitation. Only the true seeker of knowledge can approach the tower safely.'

'These wards,' said Eldain. 'What are they?'

'Spells woven in the time of Bel-Korhadris, the builder of the tower. A maze of illusions and magical snares that entrap those who come seeking power or whose hearts are poisoned by evil.'

Eldain shifted uncomfortably in his chair and said, 'And what happens to such people?'

Yvraine shrugged. 'Some find that no matter which direction they walk, their footsteps will always carry them away from the tower.'

'And others?'

'Others are never seen again.'

'They die?'

'I do not think that even the Loremasters know for certain, but it seems likely.'

Eldain felt a tightness in his chest as he thought of Caelir and wondered if the White Tower would find that black spot in his heart and if it would judge him harshly when the time came.

Surely the acquisition of love, no matter how it was attained, could not be held as evil? He looked over at

Rhianna and smiled, enjoying the play of shadows cast
by the magical lights on her beautiful features.

Sensing his scrutiny, she turned to face him and
returned his smile.

He reached out and took her hand as the proprietor
returned with platters of silver-skinned fish, steaming
vegetables and a decanter of a robust, aromatic wine.

They smiled their thanks and ate the remainder of
their meal in silence, enjoying the homely atmosphere
and the sensation common to all travellers enjoying one
another's company in unfamiliar, exciting locales.

At the conclusion of the meal, Yvraine excused herself
and retired to meditate and complete her daily regime of
martial exercises. When she had left, Eldain and Rhianna climbed a curving set of stairs to the establishment's
upper mezzanine, where their own chambers were
located. A perfumed breeze sighed into their room, rippling the gossamer-thin curtains and carrying the salty
tang of the ocean. Together, they stepped through an
archway onto an elegantly crafted balcony constructed
of willowy timbers that overlooked the bay.

As they made their way to the rail, Rhianna's arm
naturally slipped through Eldain's and they sipped their
wine as they stared out into the peace of the ocean.

Like a great black mirror, the waters reflected the stars
above and a perfect image of the heavens spread before
them like a velvet cloth sprinkled with diamond dust.

A few ships plied the open waters, guide lights shimmering at their mastheads and bowsprits the only sign
of their passage across the sea. The lights of Cairn Auriel
linked together in a golden web, as though the streets
ran with molten fire, and Eldain thought the scene
unbearably beautiful.

The sense of contentment he felt while looking out over the ocean was a soothing balm on his soul and the cares he had felt loosening since their departure from Ellyr-charoi now seemed as though they belonged to someone else.

'What if we never went back?' he said suddenly.

'What? Never went back where?' said Rhianna.

'To Ellyr-charoi. You said it yourself – we've been cooped up there too long. A weight of grief hangs over it now, too much for us to bear for very much longer, I think. If we remain there we will become ghosts ourselves.'

Rhianna looked up at him and he could see the idea appealed to her.

'You really mean that? You'd leave?'

'For you I would,' he said. 'Since we left to travel to Saphery, I have felt the cares of the last few years fall away and I have realised that my grief was dragging you down with me. If we are to start living our lives then I believe it must be away from Ellyr-charoi.'

'Where would we go?'

'Anywhere you like,' promised Eldain. 'Eataine, Saphery, Avelorn... Anywhere we could start afresh, you, me and... who knows, perhaps even a family.'

'A family?' said Rhianna, tears gathering in the corners of her eyes. 'Us?'

'Yes. If Isha wills it.'

Rhianna buried her head against Eldain's shoulder and he could hear her cry softly, but unlike the tears he knew she had shed in Ellyr-charoi, these were wept in joy.

'You do not know how long I have wanted you to say these words, Eldain,' said Rhianna. 'I didn't dare hope our lives would ever be lifted from Caelir's shadow.'

He smiled and pulled her close, feeling no pain at the mention of his dead brother's name, no heartsick flinch or wave of black guilt, merely an acknowledgement that his brother was gone and that Rhianna was now his.

'I know, and for that I am truly sorry. I think a lingering taint of the Land of Chill remained in my heart ever since I returned from the raid on the druchii. It poisoned me, but it is gone now, my love. I am yours now, heart and soul.'

He leaned down to kiss Rhianna and she raised her face to his. They kissed and there was no restraint and none of the reserve that had marked their expressions of love in the few times they had shared the marriage bed.

By unspoken agreement, they drained the last of their wine and withdrew from the balcony to the bedchamber. In the pale luminescence of magical light, they undressed and slipped beneath silken sheets with the excitement of lovers on the verge of new and undiscovered pleasures.

Starlight streamed in through the archway, shimmering their skin and bathing their lovemaking in pure silver light. They explored each other's flesh as though it were an undiscovered country, learning more of each other in one night than they had in all the years since they had met.

The magic of their union poured into the air of Saphery and it in turn returned their passions, magical winds swooping and dancing around the room and the softly glowing lights that floated above the bed flaring with incandescent fire.

They laughed and cried together and Rhianna held Eldain tightly as they finally lay in one another's arms;

lovers, friends and, at last, devoted husband and loving wife.

As the world turned and starlight gave way to sunlight, Eldain awoke with a smile upon his face and his body singing with the promise of great things to come.

CHAPTER NINE

TOWER

HAND IN HAND, Eldain and Rhianna made their way downstairs to find Yvraine waiting for them at the breakfast table. The Sword Master smiled at the sight of them and said, 'You both look… refreshed.'

'I am refreshed,' said Eldain, sitting beside Yvraine and cutting several slices of bread from a freshly baked loaf. 'I feel more alive than ever before. How are you this morning? Did you finally get to meditate properly now that you're back on dry land?'

'I did,' said Yvraine, looking over at Rhianna and blushing as she understood the nature of their new-found happiness. 'I slept very well.'

Eldain passed a plate of bread to Rhianna and wolfed down a number of honeyed oatcakes before draining a glass of fresh aoilym juice. His appetite sated, he ventured outside to the stables where their horses had spent the night, pleased to find that the ostler knew his

trade and that the steeds had been well cared for. Each
had been groomed and fed fine Sapherian grain imbued
with the magic of the land itself. Though an Ellyrian
groom would have already run the horses out before
now, Eldain's mood was too light to find fault with the
care the horses had received.

He thanked the ostler and walked the horses around
the paddock cut into the side of the cliff, allowing them to
shake out the night's torpor and prepare for the ride ahead.
If what Yvraine had said was true, and he had no cause to
doubt her, then it could be an indeterminate time until
they reached the White Tower.

By the time the horses had thrown off the lethargy
of the night and were ready for the day's exertions, he
could sense the anticipation they felt at the prospect of
exploring Saphery and led them around to the front of
the Light of Korhadris.

The streets of Cairn Auriel were busy and a number of
passers-by stopped to admire the horses. Eldain spent a
pleasant few moments conversing with each person as
they commented on the beauty of the Ellyrian steeds,
engaging in small talk he would have found intolerable
only a few short weeks ago.

Yvraine and Rhianna emerged from the hostelry looking refreshed and eager to continue on their way. They
mounted their steeds and Eldain checked the work of
the ostler one last time before vaulting onto Lotharin's
back.

He turned to Yvraine and said, 'This is your country
now, Mistress Hawkblade. Lead on.'

The Sword Master pointed to a road that climbed a
steep, zigzagging route up the cliffs between tall trellises of
gold and silver lined with summer blossoms.

'That way,' she said. 'Once we are at the top of the cliff, we will be able to see the White Tower. We will ride towards it and if we are welcome we should arrive there sometime this evening.'

'Then let's hope we'll be welcome,' said Eldain, urging Lotharin onwards with a gentle pressure from his knees. 'Seekers after truth, you say?'

Yvraine nodded. 'If you would be a real seeker after truth, it is necessary that at least once in your life you have experienced doubt.'

'Oh, that I have in plentiful supply,' said Eldain.

Soon the white buildings of the coastal settlement were behind them and they joined the road that climbed the sheer cliffs towards the flatlands of Saphery. Lesser steeds than those of elven stock would have balked at the climb, but to horses from Ellyrion, the climb was no more arduous than a straight road.

When he was halfway up the cliffside path, Eldain looked back down onto the settlement, relishing the dizzying sensation of height. The path was barely wide enough for his horse and a sheer drop of hundreds of feet awaited him should he fall, but Eldain had no fear of Lotharin losing his footing.

Rhianna looked comfortable enough, but Yvraine held on for dear life, her face pale and her knuckles white as she gripped Irenya's reins in terror.

'Do not hold on so tight, Mistress Hawkblade,' said Eldain. 'Let Irenya walk the path. Don't try and guide her.'

'Easier said than done,' said Yvraine, her eyes flicking back and forth from the path to the drop at her side. 'I told you, I prefer to trust my own two feet.'

'You're riding an Ellyrian steed, Mistress Hawkblade.

She'd sooner let a druchii on her back than allow you to fall.'

'I will take your word for it, but I have no head for heights.'

'You will be fine,' said Eldain. 'Just don't look down.'

Yvraine's head snapped up and she glared at him for giving such elementary advice, but it kept her attention focused on him rather than the drop. The climb to the top of the cliffs took almost an hour, by which time the sun had risen and cast a long golden glow across the cliffs.

Eldain's steed crested the top of the cliffs and he ran a hand through his unbound hair as he stared in wonder at the land of Saphery. Though he had travelled here on numerous occasions, the magical wonder of this kingdom still left him speechless.

Sweeping plains, as rich and welcoming as any in Ellyrion, stretched out in undulating waves, golden and green and reaching all the way to the ring of the Annulii Mountains in the distance. A rippling haze of magic hung over the land and glorious forests dotted the landscape, alive with birdsong and the lazy droning of insects. The air was heavy with the smell of magically ripened crops, which immediately conjured images within Eldain's mind of endless summers and days spent collecting the fresh harvest.

A temple of Ladrielle, its walls fashioned from the same white stone as the cliffs, rose from the edge of a field, its tumbled walls deliberately arranged so as to resemble a noble's folly, its statues artfully arranged to give the impression that they harvested the sheaves of corn themselves.

In the far distance, the White Tower dominated

the landscape, reaching into the azure skies to such a height that its construction would have been impossible without the magic of the elves to raise its magnificence towards the heavens.

'It looks as though we can just ride up to it,' said Eldain.

'And we will,' said Yvraine, riding past him, her relief at having reached the top of the cliffs apparent. 'Whether we get there or not is another matter entirely.'

'That's not very reassuring.'

'She's just teasing,' said Rhianna as she passed him.

'For all our sakes, I hope so.'

Without needing to be told, Lotharin set off after his fellow mounts and his longer strides soon caught up to Rhianna's steed.

'I still wonder why your father sent for us both,' he said as he rode alongside Rhianna.

'So do I, but I just don't know. Yvraine said it was an urgent matter.'

'Do you have any idea why he would want us to come to the White Tower instead of his villa? Perhaps his divinations have shown him that we are in danger?'

Rhianna shook her head, her eyes unconsciously darting towards the far south of Saphery, where the Silverfawn villa lay beyond an outthrust haunch of the mountains. Rhianna had grown to womanhood within its tall, fiery walls and the alliance between her family and that of Eldain's had been sealed with bonds of friendship and loyalty stronger than ithilmar.

Eldain had visited Rhianna's home with his father and brother on several occasions, but the Tower of Hoeth had never been more than a faint glow over the horizon. To now lay his eyes upon such a magnificent symbol of elven mastery over the physical world was intoxicating.

Rhianna's father was a mage of great skill and renown, famed for his mastery of the magic of fire and celestial divination, but the energies required to create such potent architecture was beyond the ability of all but the Loremasters, and Eldain doubted even they could recreate such a feat of arcane engineering.

'It is impossible to be sure with father,' said Rhianna. 'But if we were in any danger surely he would have come to us instead of asking us to travel to him.'

'Then perhaps his foretelling has revealed something.'

'Possibly, but we will have to wait and see, won't we?'

'I suppose so,' said Eldain, frowning as he caught sight of movement in the waving crops.

He looked closer, seeing a tiny, thin-limbed creature of glowing light weaving in and out of the crops, its every footstep leaving an imprint where a budding shoot of fresh corn pushed its way clear of the ground. The closer he looked, the more of the tiny creatures he saw, each one dancing to an unheard tune through the sheaves of corn.

'They are *uleishi*,' said Rhianna, guessing what he was looking at. 'Magical creatures who tend to the crops and ensure the harvest is bountiful.'

'I've never seen such a thing.'

'They mostly keep to Saphery,' said Rhianna. 'It's said that they were created as a side effect of the spells used in the creation of the White Tower. Isn't that right, Yvraine?'

Yvraine nodded and said, 'Yes, they are mostly harmless little things, but they love mischief and it is common for them to steal into a house and bang pots or mess the place up if they are not happy with the care the crops are receiving.'

'So why don't the mages get rid of them? Surely they have the power.'

'Probably,' agreed Yvraine, 'but it's said that if the *uleishi* were ever to leave Ulthuan then its fate is sealed.'

'What do they do?' asked Eldain.

'No one knows, but no one wants to take the chance of finding out what happens if they ever stop.'

Eldain watched the glowing little sprites capering through the long grasses until they were lost from sight and fresh wonders demanded his attention.

Rivers bearing water so clear it was almost invisible flowed through Saphery and though the sun was high and cast pleasant warmth over them, shining mists occasionally rose from the ground, gathering in miniature tornadoes that swept across the landscape, leaving no damage in their wake, but a glistening trail of moisture and crystal laughter.

Herds of animals so strange he had not a name for them could be seen on the horizon with every turn of the head, creatures that must surely be of magical origin, but which attracted no undue attention from Rhianna and Yvraine. He saw more of the magical sprites, a pack of them following his course for several miles, darting between Lotharin's legs until they grew bored with the lack of sport and vanished in a cloud of giggling light.

As they crossed one of the wide, shallow rivers that wound sedately from the Annulii to the Inner Sea, Eldain caught sight of a commotion upstream and watched as a host of translucent, blue-skinned nymphs with hair of foaming spume cavorted in the water, splashing and teasing one another. Realising they were observed, the nymphs disappeared beneath the surface of the river and Eldain saw them racing downstream towards him, their giggling features alive with amorous mischief.

He urged Lotharin from the water as the nymphs passed behind him and their playful laughter carried on downriver.

'Is everything in this land magic?' he said to himself.

As though in answer to that very question, a chill wind stole upon him and he blinked as a glittering phalanx of ghostly Silver Helms rose up from the ground, sunlight reflecting blindingly from the polished plates of their *ithiltaen* helms. If Rhianna or Yvraine saw them too, they gave no sign and though these wraiths appeared to have no hostile intent, Eldain found their presence far from reassuring.

'Who are these warriors?' whispered Eldain. Each time he attempted to focus on one of the silent riders, the warrior would vanish, as ephemeral as morning mist, only to reappear moments later.

'We ride along one of the lines of power,' was Rhianna's explanation for this spectral army's presence and Eldain tried to be reassured by that. Eldain had lived all his life in Ellyrion and though it too was bathed in eternal summer and power flowed through the land, it was a power that was part of the natural cycle of things and which did not manifest itself in such overt, disturbing ways.

Well, disturbing to him at least.

At last it seemed that the route they must travel to the White Tower differed from the course of the long dead Silver Helms and they faded from sight without a sound. Though their presence had been unsettling at first, Eldain felt a strange reassurance in the knowledge of their existence. He had no doubt that should he have intended any harm to Saphery, then the wrath of these spirits would have been turned upon him without mercy.

He bade the silent warriors a wordless farewell and turned his attention to the looming shape of the White Tower ahead of them.

By the position of the sun, Eldain judged that they had been travelling for at least four hours, yet the tower appeared no nearer. In fact it seemed farther away if anything.

Perhaps the magic of Saphery was distorting his perceptions or perhaps the sheer size of the tower was creating an optical illusion of distance.

The three riders journeyed in companionable silence, allowing the quiet of Saphery to lull them into the peaceful rhythm of contented travellers. Eldain felt his eyes grow heavy and blinked rapidly as he felt the gentle brush of a presence within his mind. The touch was not invasive and, curiously, he felt no threat or alarm at its arrival.

He sensed a familiarity in the touch, as though whatever power seeped into his mind was that of a friend, an old and trusted companion with whom uncounted dangers had been faced, adventures shared and terrors overcome.

Eldain looked over to Rhianna and saw the same slack smile on her face as he was sure was upon his. Yvraine alone looked untouched by whatever was occurring, her stoic, sharp features concentrating on the tower ahead…

With a start, Eldain realised he could no longer see the tower in the distance.

He spun in the saddle, but no matter which direction he looked, all he could see were the verdant fields of

Saphery, dust devils of corn ears billowing above the fields of gold. He looked up towards the sun, but it was directly above him and no shadows were cast to give him an idea of which direction they rode.

Soaring white peaks rose up on every horizon, as though they were trapped within a great plain surrounded by a ring of mountains, but a distant part of Eldain's mind knew that such a thing was impossible…

Though he could feel the reassuring sway of his horse beneath him and knew that it was as surefooted a mount as any rider could wish for, Eldain wondered where it was taking him, for he could see no landmarks and no sign of the Tower of Hoeth.

The Tower of Hoeth…

Was this the tower's defences rising up to ensnare him? 'Yvraine?' he said.

'Yes,' said Yvraine, guessing his question before it was even asked. 'The tower has sensed our desire to approach and is judging our intent.'

Panic began to rise in Eldain's chest, but even as it grew, he felt the soothing touch of the presence within his mind. Now knowing what it was, he relaxed into its embrace and allowed it to roam freely within his skull, the contentment and peace that had come to him over the last week or so of travel overshadowing all other thoughts and memories.

Eldain smiled as he felt the presence withdraw from him and his vision swam as illusions he had not previously been aware of faded from his eyes and the reality of Saphery arose once again.

Like a sleeper gradually realising that he has woken in a strange place, Eldain looked about himself as though seeing his surroundings for the first time.

The White Tower loomed large in his vision, its colossal verticality staggering now that he saw it without the camouflage of illusions. Though it was still a mile or so away, Eldain could now make out details upon its white walls: arched windows, crimson banners and golden, rune-etched carvings that wove their way up the entire length of the tower.

But something closer than the tower captured his attention more fully…

A castle of white and gold that floated in the air above them.

THE MOST MAGNIFICENT structures Caelir could remember having seen before now were the island castles of Tor Elyr and the towering statues of the Phoenix King and Everqueen in Lothern, but even their soaring majesty had paled at the sight of the home of the Loremasters. A millennium had passed between the breaking of the ground and its completion over two thousand years ago and the idea of a single structure taking so long to complete had seemed ludicrous to Caelir when he had seen the tower from the mountains.

But within moments of their arrival at the tower, he appreciated that it had in fact been a mighty achievement to raise such a heartbreakingly wondrous creation in so short a span of time. Craftsmen had laboured for centuries to create the intricate carvings that ran from the tower's base to its far distant spire and the magic employed in its creation imbued the tower with strength far greater than that of stone and mortar.

The Tower of Hoeth sat within a sweeping emerald forest, rising up from a colossal crag of shimmering black rock. Flocks of white birds circled the tower's topmost spire and countless waterfalls plunged from the black rock to foaming white pools arranged in tumbling tiers at its base.

The air was spliced with the colours of a million rainbows and Caelir could not remember a more perfect sight.

He and Kyrielle rode side by side, having delighted in the wonders of Saphery as they rode from the mountains to the tower. Over the course of their short journey through the tower's magical wards, Caelir had seen many unexpected, incredible things and many more that conformed exactly to his expectations of a land steeped in magic: a flying castle that drifted overhead, swirling troupes of wind-borne dancers and spectral dragons riding on streamers of light.

Though each sight was astonishing and filled him with wonder, he could not shake the nagging feeling that he had seen such sights before and that he had visited this land in the past.

Anurion flew high above, the outstretched wings of his pegasus throwing a cruciform shadow upon the earth, and their guards formed a ring of silver blades around them.

Through all the sights they had seen, he had expected a bewildering array of illusions and magical defences, but had seen nothing that might have led him to believe the tower was defended at all.

Kyrielle had laughed when he had told her this, reassuring him that the tower's wards had clearly judged him to be a seeker of knowledge and permitted his passage.

Caelir looked up as a shadow passed over them and Anurion's pegasus landed in a flurry of scattered leaves before the edge of the forest. A crackling nimbus of power played over the mage and his mount, rippling breaths of magic fluttering his robes and slipping through his steed's mane like an invisible hand.

Anurion spoke quickly to his warriors and dismissed them with a gesture. As one, the armoured riders dismounted and began forming an impromptu camp. Clearly they were not to accompany them towards the tower.

The archmage turned to Caelir and said, 'Loremaster Teclis is expecting us, boy. We should not keep him waiting. Hurry your pace.'

In all the times Caelir had spoken to Anurion before now, he had found the mage, by turns, bizarre and eccentric, short tempered and cantankerous, but never frightening. That now changed as the power gathered at the White Tower surged through Anurion's veins.

'Of course,' said Caelir.

Anurion turned his pegasus without another word and led them into the trees, the leaves and branches of which shivered though there was no wind to stir them. The trees pulsed with the energy of living things empowered beyond their natural growth cycles and Caelir could feel the pleasure Anurion and Kyrielle took in being surrounded by such fecundity.

A sudden caw made Caelir look up and he smiled as the birds that circled the tower now descended towards the forest in a great host. White-feathered choristers perched on every tree branch to welcome the archmage with song and gave the forest a gloriously festive aspect.

Their route climbed through the forest, passing numerous streams and wondrous groves where Sword Masters – alone and in groups – trained with their great blades, sparring, performing incredible feats of balance or meditating while spinning their swords around them with a speed Caelir could never hope to match.

Each warrior broke from his or her routine as Anurion passed, bowing in respect before acknowledging Caelir and Kyrielle's presence.

'Your father is well known here,' he said.

'He is indeed, though he does not travel to the White Tower often.'

'No? Why not?'

'You've seen his villa, remember? My father so loves to tinker and create, but there are those who think his work frivolous. Inevitably, father will get into an argument and leave, swearing never to return.'

Caelir could well imagine the temper of Anurion the Green getting the better of him, but shuddered to think of the consequences of arguments between those who wielded the awesome power of magic.

At last their course brought them to the summit of the black rock and Anurion climbed from the back of his pegasus and indicated that they do likewise. Caelir slid from the back of his horse and helped Kyrielle from hers as Anurion waited for them to join him at the base of the tower.

Caelir and Kyrielle approached the fabulous structure, their gaze inexorably drawn up the carved length of the tower. The pale stone utilised in its construction was suffused with incredible power and Caelir could feel the energies coursing beneath his feet and into the tower.

He had experienced a similar sensation at the foot of Eltharion's tower, but, as magnificent as was the warden's demesne, it could not compare to the sheer power and dominance of the Loremasters' domain.

'Come on, come on,' said Anurion, moving between

them and marching them towards the tower.

'How do we get in?' asked Caelir. 'There is no door.'

'Don't be foolish, boy, of course there is.'

'Where?'

Anurion stared at him as though he had asked the most idiotic question imaginable, and Caelir braced himself for an explosion of temper from the archmage.

Instead, the mage pursed his lips and brought a hand to his own forehead as though he could not believe his own thoughtlessness.

'Of course... you are not a mage, nor are you seeking to become a Sword Master.'

'No,' said Caelir, 'I just want answers.'

'Indeed you do, boy,' said Anurion, positioning him before the base of the tower. 'In that case you will need to make your own way in.'

'How do I do that?'

'Those who come as suppliants must make their own door,' said Anurion. 'Simply speak your purpose in coming here. The tower will judge the truth of your words and thus your worthiness to enter.'

Feeling slightly foolish, Caelir squared his shoulders and faced the carved face of the tower. He was no orator, so opted for the plain, unvarnished truth.

'My name is Caelir and I come to the Tower of Hoeth to seek answers.'

No door was forthcoming and the wall remained solid before him.

'Be more specific, silly,' advised Kyrielle.

'I'm talking to a wall,' said Caelir. 'It's hard to think of what would convince it to let me pass through.'

He sighed and closed his eyes, thinking back to all he had learned in his time with Anurion and Kyrielle: the truth of his name, the dagger that could not be drawn, the threat to Ellyrion from the druchii and the black gaps in his memory he hoped Teclis could restore.

Satisfied he knew what he would say, he opened his eyes to see the wall rippling like the surface of a bowl of milk, the magic bound in its creation now fluid and malleable. As he watched, the stone of the tower faded to form a golden portal ringed with silver symbols cut directly into the rock.

'Well done, boy,' said Anurion, striding confidently through the opening and into what looked to be a great, vaulted chamber devoid of furnishings and occupants.

'But I didn't say anything,' said Caelir.

'You think in a place like this you need words?' smiled Kyrielle as she followed her father into the tower.

'Apparently not,' he said.

'Well, come on then,' said Kyrielle, beckoning him inside.

'Do we just leave the horses here?'

'Of course,' said Kyrielle, pointing over his shoulder.

A handsome Sword Master emerged from the trees and bowed to the three mounts before whispering unheard words and beckoning them to join him in the forest. Their mounts followed the warrior and Caelir smiled as he recognised the skills of one born in Ellyrion.

Satisfied the horses would be well cared for, he turned and made his way within the tower in case the door vanished as suddenly as it had appeared.

As he stepped through the portal, he felt a sudden *shift*, as though a magical current had been passed through his body. It wasn't unpleasant, but it was unexpected. He pulled up short and spun on the spot to see what had happened.

The door behind him had vanished and in its place was one of the many arched openings formed in the face of the tower. Caelir's breath caught in his throat as he looked through the opening and saw the land of Saphery spread out before him like a relief map, its landscape and rivers rendered miniscule by height.

Thousands of feet below him, Caelir saw the forest the tower had been built within and the edges of the black rock it stood upon.

With one step he had travelled the entire height of the tower and he backed away from the precipitous drop as a voice said, 'Welcome, Caelir of Ellyrion.'

He turned to see Anurion and Kyrielle beside a slightly built elf in the vestments of a Loremaster. A cerulean cloak edged in gold anthemion hung from his narrow shoulders and thin strands of dark hair spilled from beneath a golden helmet with a sculpted crescent moon upon it. A sheathed longsword hung at his waist, looking incongruous as part of the apparel of a mage, and he held a golden staff topped with an image of the goddess, Lileath in the other hand...

Caelir realised who he now stood before and dropped to his knees in awe.

He had seen magnificently lifelike paintings of Teclis and his twin brother, Prince Tyrion, before – who of the Asur had not? – but none of them had come close to capturing the intensity of the Loremaster's stare. His sallow features were caustic and dark, his eyes hooded and heavy with the burden of ancient knowledge. His prudent gaze reminded Caelir of Eltharion, and he wondered if all great heroes were cursed with such pain.

But where Prince Tyrion was said to be robust, warlike and gregarious, Teclis was his dark mirror, cursed since birth with frailty that could only be kept at bay with potions and the power of the staff he bore. Where Tyrion was a warrior of epic renown, no greater mage than Teclis had ever been named Loremaster and his incredible powers were as legendary as the martial skill of his brother.

Together, they were the greatest living heroes of the Asur, for they had defeated the most terrible invasion of Ulthuan since the time of Chaos and Aenarion.

And now he was Caelir's only hope.

'My lord Teclis,' he said. 'I need your help.'

THE BREATH WAS stolen from Eldain's lungs as he saw the palatial castle in the sky, its white walls and tapering towers built upon an island of pink stone that drifted against the wind like a rebellious cloud. Sunlight sparkled upon speartips and helmets, and Eldain watched as a warrior leaned over the parapet and waved to him. The sheer ordinariness of the gesture flew in the face of the incredible strangeness of the moment.

'There's a castle…' he said, pointing into the sky.

Rhianna waved back at the warrior on the castle walls and said, 'Yes. That is the mansion of Hothar the Fey. He is a good friend to my father, though he can be a little… eccentric.'

'Eccentric? He lives in a floating palace,' said Eldain, aware that he sounded like a rustic woodsman from Chrace, but not caring.

'Yes, but it's not the strangest dwelling in Saphery,' pointed out Yvraine.

'It's not?'

'No,' said Yvraine and Eldain could sense the amusement of his female companions. 'The Loremasters say

that when Ulvenian Minaith returned from Athel Loren
he raised a magical villa of the seasons to remind him
of the forest kingdom.'

'A villa of the seasons? What does that mean?'

'I have never seen it, but it is said that every so often
it consumes itself and reforms from the essence of one
of the seasons.'

'Really?' said Eldain, unsure whether or not he was
being teased.

'Yes, but I don't think the Loremasters approved.'

'Why not?'

'I think they thought it a waste of power to create
something of such rustic appearance. I once heard the
Loremaster say that Ulvenian had merged his power with
that of the spellsingers of Athel Loren to create his palace.'

'So what does it look like?' asked Eldain, keeping his
eyes fixed on the castle above him.

'Sometimes it appears on the coast as a huge palace
shaped from drifts of snow and pillars of ice,' said
Rhianna. 'Other times it might be formed entirely of
autumn leaves and once I heard it manifested as corn
sheaves and beams of sunlight as solid as marble.'

Though it sounded ridiculous, Eldain could well
believe his wife's words having now seen this castle of
stone and glass floating in the air and enveloping him
in its cold shadow.

The base of the great castle was easily twice as large
as Ellyr-charoi, though Eldain guessed that without the
constraints of the natural topography, it could be as
large as its owner's magical power could support.

He watched as the aerial villa altered course and
began to slide away from the Tower of Hoeth, drifting
without urgency or apparent purpose. Guided as it was

by the whims of a mage whose epithet was 'the Fey', he doubted there was *any* purpose to its course.

As incredible as the floating castle was, it was simply another of the many wonders Saphery had to offer. Reluctantly, he tore his eyes from the domain of Hothar the Fey and concentrated on riding towards the Tower of Hoeth.

Now that they were closer and the veiling illusions had been stripped away, Eldain could see the tower perched upon a great black rock that reared up from a sprawling forest. The trees were filled with white birds and Eldain felt a growing sense of anticipation at the thought of experiencing a measure of the wonders the Tower of Hoeth had to offer.

'How long until we reach the tower?' said Rhianna.

'Not long,' said Yvraine.

'You are looking forward to returning.'

Yvraine nodded. 'It pains me to be away. I lived and trained here for years. It is my home.'

Eldain sensed the quiet regret in her voice and said, 'Will you be able to stay long?'

'If it is the will of the Loremaster, but I do not think it likely.'

'Then where will you go next?'

'Wherever the Loremasters bid me,' said Yvraine and would be drawn no more.

No more was said, and Eldain, Rhianna and Yvraine entered the forest of the tower, each relishing the prospect of their arrival for different reasons, but all unaware that a unique destiny awaited them.

A destiny that would bind their lives to the doom or salvation of Ulthuan.

CHAPTER TEN

CHAOS

THE MOMENT STRETCHED. Caelir looked up into the pale eyes of Teclis, seeking any indication that he would help. The Loremaster stroked his thin jaw and regarded Caelir with the same academic interest as Anurion had, as though he were a particularly complete specimen of great rarity.

'Anurion tells me that your memory has been magically locked within you. Is this true?'

'It is, my lord,' confirmed Caelir, unwilling to speak more than necessary in case he made a fool of himself before this legendary hero of Ulthuan.

Teclis approached him and a warm aura preceded him, bathing Caelir in resonant magic that seeped from the Loremaster like sweat on the skin of a human. The power inherent in Teclis, even when he conjured no spell or summoned no magic, was palpable and just being near him made every sense in Caelir's body feel sharper, more *attuned*.

'Who would do such a thing?' wondered Teclis, reaching out to touch Caelir's forehead, then thinking better of it as a frown creased his thin face. The Loremaster closed his eyes and Caelir felt a surge of magical energy pass through him.

Suddenly Teclis's eyes flew open and Caelir thought he detected the hint of a curious smile tug at the corner of his mouth.

'You are a strange one, Caelir of Ellyrion,' said Teclis. 'I sense no evil to you, but there is a part of you I cannot yet reach. Something buried deep inside and cloaked in veil upon veil of magic. Someone has gone to great lengths to hide it and I would know what it was and why.'

'I would ask you to do whatever you can, my lord,' said Caelir.

'Oh, I shall,' promised Teclis. 'But you may not like what I find.'

'I don't care, I just want my memories back.'

'Memories can be painful, Caelir,' warned Teclis. 'I have travelled far in this world; from forgotten Cathay to the jungles of Lustria and even the blasted wastes of the north. And there are many sights I would gladly burn from my memories if I could. You must be sure that this is what you want, because there will be no turning back once we begin.'

'Anurion told me the same thing, my lord, and I give you the same answer. Whatever it takes and whatever befalls me, I am willing to take the risk and accept the consequences of what happens.'

Teclis gave a derisive laugh and turned away from him, making a circuit of the chamber as he spoke. 'Do not be so willing to accept consequences you know nothing about, Caelir. None of us can know what will happen when I delve within your mind, but such a dark mystery should not be left unsolved, eh?'

As Teclis walked and Caelir recovered from his awe, he took in his surroundings in more detail, seeing that the top of the tower was a spartan place of meditation and serenity. The floor was a gleaming blue marble save for a circular pattern of an eight-spoked wheel at its centre marked in a mosaic of shimmering onyx. Eight narrow windows pierced the tower at regular intervals, each at the terminus of one of the wheel's spokes, and aside from a slender silver stand upon which sat a golden ewer, the chamber was devoid of furniture.

Teclis completed his circuit of the wheel and stood at the opposite side of the circle to him. The Loremaster's expression softened and he said, 'All my life I have sought out the truth behind the world and you intrigue me, Caelir of Ellyrion. Step into the centre of the circle.'

Caelir obeyed and joined Anurion and Kyrielle within the eight-spoked wheel, feeling a tremor of magic stirring within him as he did so. Kyrielle took his hand and gave it a squeeze of reassurance as her father concentrated on Teclis.

Teclis rapped his golden staff on the marble floor and a door worked seamlessly into the wall of the chamber opened in response. A procession of robed mages entered and Caelir blinked as he realised the impossibility of such a thing.

He turned his head as he looked through each of the windows in turn, seeing only the blue of sky or the magic-wreathed peaks of the Annulii through them. He looked back at the door in amazement, for surely such a door would open into the air...

But in this most sacred place of magic, he supposed that nothing should surprise him.

Behind the mages came four Sword Masters in long, shimmering coats of ithilmar mail and tall plumed helmets. Each warrior carried an elven greatsword, bearing the lethal blade as easily as Caelir might carry the lightest of bows.

The newly arrived mages were young and wore plain, unadorned robes of blue and cream. They walked unhurriedly around the circumference of the chamber until one stood at each window. Eight of them surrounded him and he could already feel a build up of power within the chamber, as though a charge of magical energy were even now being drawn up the length of the tower, gathering strength as it went from the mystical carvings worked into the walls.

The Sword Masters took up position behind Teclis, spinning their blades as smoothly as beams of light until they rested, point down, on the floor. They clenched their fists across the pommel stones and Caelir wondered what danger might require the presence of such formidable warriors.

'I am going to help you, Caelir,' said Teclis, entering the circle as the mages at its cardinal points lowered themselves into cross-legged postures in one smooth movement. 'Together we are going to find out what you know. Are you ready?'

'I am ready,' said Caelir, and Teclis nodded.

A shimmering nimbus of light built around the crescent moon on Teclis's staff and a depthless resonance saturated his voice. To Caelir it seemed as though the Loremaster's physique had swelled, the magic flowing into his frail body only barely contained within his frame.

The mages around the circumference of the circle began to chant and Caelir recognised songs of rebirth and cantrips of restoration he had heard Kyrielle mutter during his time in her father's winter palace.

Shimmering will-o'-the-wisps reflected in the blades of the Sword Masters and Caelir swallowed as he understood the magnitude of the power being wielded here.

He held on tightly to Kyrielle's hand as he felt something stir within him, something awakened by the unique aura of the Loremaster's magic. Was this his memories struggling to the surface, unlocked by Teclis's power?

Teclis advanced towards him, the moon goddess on his staff blazing with white light, though Caelir could feel no heat from it as the Loremaster lowered it towards him. Words of power spilled from Teclis and the walls of the chamber seemed to pulse with the rhythm of a heartbeat in time with his speech.

The mages around the circle rose to their feet, their arms describing complex symbols, and Caelir felt the power of Teclis's magic reach inside him, plumbing depths to which Anurion the Green's magic had not dared descend.

But the magic employed here was an order of magnitude greater than that which Anurion could wield, for Teclis was the most powerful and learned mage in the world. Even the greatest archmages of Ulthuan counted themselves fortunate if granted the opportunity to sit at his feet and learn the mystic arts.

Like a vital tonic introduced to his blood, the magic of Teclis thundered through Caelir's body and he could feel a colossal surge of magical power build within the chamber as the barrier between Teclis and what lay within him was stripped away. He wanted to fall to the floor, but his limbs were locked rigid, his grip on Kyrielle's hand unbreakable.

He shuddered as layers were stripped away and he felt his body respond to the Loremaster's magic. Teclis loomed above him, his blazing staff and fiery eyes terrifying in their determination to uncover whatever secrets he concealed…

Caelir closed his eyes to shut out the awful hunger for knowledge he saw in Teclis's eyes, turning his gaze inwards to see what secret history was now being revealed. He heard voices raised in concern, but could make no sense of them, the words meaningless as he looked deep into the pit of his stolen memories and being.

As though he looked into the depths of a forgotten chasm, he saw a formless shape rushing towards him, all restraint and barriers to its return now stripped away by the awesome power of Teclis. Hope surged bright and hot and his eyes opened wide, pearls of light streaming down his cheeks like glittering tears of starlight.

He saw Teclis before him, crackling arcs of magic playing about his head and his robes billowing as though he stood within a mighty hurricane. The Loremaster's feet had left the floor and swirls of light and howls of wind kept him aloft as chain lightning leapt from the outstretched hands of the mages around the circle.

'It's working!' shouted Caelir. 'I can feel it!'

He turned to Kyrielle and a hot jolt of fear seized him as he saw her face twisted in an agonised grimace of pain. Anurion was screaming, but Caelir could not hear the words as Teclis brought his staff up and searing blasts of lightning erupted from the edges of the circle.

Caelir struggled to understand what was happening,

suddenly aware of a monstrous power building in him that had nothing to do with that employed by Teclis.

No, this had been inside him all along; dormant, concealed and lying in wait…

The magical wards placed within him had not been entrapping his memories, but something far older and infinitely more malicious.

Too late, he recognised the danger of the trap and the ancient cunning that had gone into its concealment.

Too late, he realised that this hellish energy had been waiting within him for exactly this moment, its architects knowing that only the power of the greatest mages of Ulthuan could unlock the wards they had placed around its infernal strength.

He could see their scheming eyes: dark, violent and filled with thousands of years of hatred for him and all his kind. Monstrous, diabolical laughter bubbled inside him and dark magic surged from its living host, erupting with the force of a million thunderbolts.

Purple-edged lightning roared from his eyes and ripped into Teclis, hurling him against the chamber's wall and savaging him with forked tongues of daemonic wrath.

Raw magic, unfettered by the rigid control of a mage, exploded through the chamber in a whirlwind of howling madness, tearing open great rents in the fabric of reality. Gibbering laughter and bellows of rage-filled hunger echoed as the denizens of the nightmare realms beyond the physical sensed the breach in the walls between worlds…

Caelir screamed as the chamber exploded in a firestorm of magic.

* * *

YVRAINE LED THE way through the forest, passing bright conversation with the Sword Masters they encountered and Eldain could hardly credit the change that had come over her. Gone was the tight-lipped ascetic who gave little of herself away in her mannerisms or words, and in her place was a warm, likeable elven maiden who spoke with wit and vitality.

He shared a look with Rhianna and said, 'Homecoming suits her.'

Rhianna smiled, then the smile vanished and she cried out, her face a clenched fist of pain.

The scream cut through the air with its primal urgency and heads everywhere turned towards her. The birds took to the air in a frantic cloud of white feathers and the forest, which had seconds ago been welcoming and abundant, was suddenly shrouded in fear.

Eldain dropped from Lotharin's back as Rhianna toppled from the saddle, her hands slack and lifeless, and runnels of blood streaking her cheeks where they seeped from her eyes. He caught her before she hit the ground and held her close as she wept terrified tears.

'Rhianna!' he cried. 'What is it? What's wrong?'

She did not answer him, her attention fixed upon some terrible sight beyond him.

He twisted to look over his shoulder and his eyes were drawn to the top of the Tower of Hoeth, where dark thunderheads of magic swirled and red lightning seethed like whips of blood.

'Isha's mercy! Rhianna, what *is* that?'

Rhianna shook in his embrace, wrapping her arms around him in fear and pain.

'Evil…' she gasped. 'Dark magic!'

Eldain looked back at the shuddering tower as

Sword Masters ran towards it, their gleaming blades unsheathed. Yvraine remained at his side, staring in horror at a number of objects falling from the topmost spire of the tower.

They were little more than flaming dots at the moment, and he frowned as he tried to make sense out of what he was seeing.

'Oh no...' wept Yvraine.

Horrified, he saw that the falling objects were screaming figures.

Robed acolytes of the tower or mages, he couldn't tell, for unnatural black fire consumed them as they plunged to their deaths. Trails of smoke followed them down, alongside sparkling balls of magical light that exploded like the liquid fire some human ships were wont to use in battle.

Flames leapt into existence as one of the magical fireballs slammed into the ground before him, streamers of dirty light leaping back into the air and causing Lotharin to rear up and cleave the air with his hooves.

Eldain pulled Rhianna to her feet as the flames of magic devoured the trees and monstrous laughter, rich with spiteful glee, came from within.

'Yvraine!' cried Eldain as a darting, multi-coloured creature – part hound, part dragon – emerged from the light, as though passing through a gateway from some nightmarish realm of fire.

The Sword Master spun on the spot, her sword already in her hands as the beast leapt at Eldain, wings of magical fire spread out behind it. Its face was a fanged horror of flames and bone, its skull that of a dead thing. Talons the length of Eldain's forearms and wreathed in rainbow light slashed for Yvraine, but she somersaulted over the beast and struck downwards with her sword as she passed overhead.

The beast roared in pain, trailing scads of fire from a glittering wound in its back.

Even before she landed, Yvraine twisted in mid-air and slashed her blade across its wings.

More Sword Masters rushed to help her, but for all her youth, Yvraine displayed no fear in the face of such a terrible foe. Once again she closed with the creature of fire, rolling beneath a lethal slash of its claws and vaulting from a low branch to spin above the creature as it reared up to its full height.

Her boots slammed into its searing breast and her sword spun a silver arc as she beheaded it with a looping slash of her blade. Even as it fell, she surged backwards, twisting in mid-air to land before it once more, her sword raised before her as though she had never moved.

Eldain watched as more and more of the glittering fireballs rained down from the ruin of the tower's top and dozens of vile monsters were birthed from the protoplasmic magic. Horrors of unknown dimensions, twisted monsters and unspeakable abominations ran riot, slaughtering anything in their path as they thrashed in rage at the agony of their existence.

He longed to draw his blade and rush to fight alongside Yvraine and the Sword Masters, but he could not abandon Rhianna, her body still weak at the presence of so much dark magic.

He dragged Rhianna from the path through the trees as a fine rain of shimmering droplets fell from above and Eldain shuddered, feeling as though someone had just walked across his grave at the rawness of magic in the air.

'The magic…' said Rhianna. 'Oh no…'

'What about it?'

'The tower… it sits at a confluence of power… a focus for the magic around it, but something has broken the spells that keep it under control!'

Even as he formed the thought, he could taste a greasy, ashen taste in the air.

Not magic… but *sorcery*… the dark arts.

Screams and shouts echoed through the forest, blood-curdling cries of pain and anger. Elven greatswords clove unnatural flesh, formed from the essence of magic, and though the Sword Masters were amongst the greatest warriors of Ulthuan, even they were only mortal.

Elven blood was being spilled.

The howling winds that engulfed the top of the tower spiralled down its length, whipping cords of lightning slamming into the ground and hurling bodies and vitrified chunks of rock high into the air with its force. Shrieking spectres of magic swooped and spun through the air like spiteful zephyrs, gathering up anyone in their path and tearing apart with claws of glittering ice.

Eldain wrapped his arms around Rhianna as the base of the tower shuddered beneath the assault, the golden carvings worked into its structure blazing with incandescent power as they fought to contain the outpouring of uncontrolled magic.

'We have to help,' said Eldain. 'We have to do something.'

Rhianna nodded, wiping the blood from her face and said, 'If we are to get to the tower we need Yvraine. Remember what I told you on the *Dragonkin*?'

'Yes,' said Eldain, watching as Yvraine fought back to back with another Sword Master, their blows flowing like a ballet, spinning in and out of each other's killing zone as they wove a shimmering steel path towards them. To fight with such skill was unbelievable and Eldain immediately cast aside any doubts he might once have harboured to her ability.

He was a fair swordsman, but no more than that.

But this...

This was skill that bordered on the sublime, unmatched by any of the other Sword Masters that fought around them. Eldain's practiced eye could see the natural grace she possessed with the sword that elevated her skill beyond that of her brethren to another level entirely.

Eldain saw Yvraine deliver the deathblow to another creature of fire with a blindingly swift series of blows that even he could not follow. The Sword Master's eyes sought them out and he waved to her as she ran towards them.

'Are you all right?' demanded Yvraine. 'Is either of you hurt?'

'No,' said Rhianna. 'We're fine.'

Yvraine nodded in relief and Eldain could see the conflicting desires raging within her: to rush into battle beside her fellow Sword Masters or to protect those who had been entrusted to her care.

Eldain took her arm and said, 'We need you with us. I can't look after Rhianna and fight off those creatures as well. Your mission was to bring us safely to Rhianna's father and it's not finished yet.'

For a moment, he thought Yvraine was going to leave them anyway, but she nodded and said, 'You are right of course. Come on, we cannot stay here, it is too exposed.'

Between them they picked their way through the trees, flashes of magical light and spurts of fire erupting from all around them as the Sword Masters and mages of the tower fought the rampant creations of uncontrolled magic.

Eldain saw a cabal of mages hurling bolts of blue-white light at a shrieking horror of tentacles and jaws; a Sword Master beheading a hydra-like creature formed from a dizzyingly bright spectrum of light and the trees of the forest writhing with unnatural life as the magic of the earth spasmed in pain.

A mage screamed as he was torn apart by a toothed whirlwind of magic. A Sword Master was turned inside out, his organs hanging wetly from his ravaged skeleton for an agonised second before he collapsed. Everywhere was chaos…the rampant vortex of magic spawning new and ever more bizarre creatures with every cascade of power from the storm raging at the tower's top.

'What in the name of Asuryan is going on up there?' he shouted over the noise.

IN THE TOPMOST chamber of the tower, Caelir screamed as the reservoir of dark magic hidden from sight and knowledge within him poured into the world. The top of the chamber was gone, blasted away by a howling geyser of dark light, and a roiling sky of unnatural clouds seethed above him. The mages that had once surrounded the circle were gone, burned and cast to their deaths far below, and only two Sword Masters had survived to protect their master against the onslaught.

Teclis's body lay in a crumpled heap beside a ruined stub of blackened stone, all that had prevented him from falling to his death. His robes were a smouldering ruin, flickering black flames guttering on his chest and arms, and his flesh seared raw. The Loremaster barely clung to consciousness, the shrieking maelstrom of unleashed magic wracking his body with paralysing agony.

Manically shrieking pillars of sinuous fire sought to devour him, but the Sword Masters fought with sweeping silver blows of their greatswords to fend them off. But for their skill, the Loremaster might even now be dead. Anurion lay pinned to the floor, his face a mask of blood and terror as he stared at Caelir in horror.

Caelir felt as though the dark power flowing through him must soon consume him and he welcomed the oblivion, knowing it would finally end this pain. His limbs were locked rigid, but even as the latest wave of pain washed over him, he could feel its power begin to ebb. He looked over at Kyrielle as he heard her shrill voice rising in panic and fear.

He sobbed as he saw the dark magic ravaging her beautiful features, invisible tendrils thrashing within her flesh and draining it of life. Her pale, alabaster skin dried like ancient parchment, fine lines around her eyes and mouth deepening to become gaping cracks that bled like tears. Kyrielle's mouth opened impossibly wide, bones cracking in her jaw as the colour drained from her lustrous auburn hair and became thin and ancient, like that of a corpse.

'No... please no...' he cried, desperately trying to release her hand.

But neither his desire to save her or any power he possessed could force his hand to loosen its grip. He wept as the magic consumed her, helpless to prevent these malignant energies from using her body until she was spent. Her skin peeled away from her face, the muscles beneath atrophying to dust and falling from her bones.

Even as he screamed her name, her bones could no longer support her wasted frame and the wondrous, beautiful girl that had been Kyrielle Greenkin was gone. At last his grip was released and she fell to the floor, a shattered husk of drained, desiccated flesh housed in a green dress.

Caelir felt control return to his limbs and dropped to the floor, hot tears of pain and grief streaming from his eyes. Pain burned within him, but at least it was physical pain and therefore finite. His body would heal and the fire in his bones would fade, but the ache in his soul... that would live with him forever.

Through tear-gummed eyes he saw the wretched bones that were all that remained of Kyrielle and he screamed her name, remembering the bright, beautiful soul who had pulled him from the ocean and saved him from her father's carnivorous plant. She was dead and he had killed her as surely as if he had strangled her with his bare hands.

He stood as he felt the agony of her death, the fear and confusion that must have been her last thoughts. Caelir looked over to where Anurion lay, rendered immobile by grief or hostile magic, and said, 'I am so sorry. I didn't know...'

Caelir turned and walked to the edge of the tower as an all-consuming sensation of loss and regret flooded him. Already the dark clouds around the top of the tower were receding as the wards worked into the fabric of the tower began to regain control of the magic.

Thousands of feet below him, Caelir could see the anarchy surrounding the tower. Spots of fire lit the forest in dozens of places and smoke rose heavenward as trees that had stood for thousands of years were burned to ashes in the magical fires. He saw knots of Sword Masters fighting a legion of glittering monsters and could practically taste the blood that had been shed in defence of the tower.

Tears burned a guilty path down his face. So much death, and all of it his fault...

He had brought this evil here and that it had been others who placed it within him mattered not at all. So consumed by his need for answers was he that he had been blinded to the evil that lurked within him. Eltharion had been right not to trust him and only Teclis's obsessive thirst for knowledge had prevented him from seeing the nature of the trap.

He heard a voice call his name and turned to see Teclis, supported by the two Sword Masters and horribly burned, struggle towards him.

Caelir turned and looked down at the distant ground.

'No!' cried Teclis, guessing his intention.

'I am sorry,' Caelir said and stepped from the tower.

ELDAIN DREW HIS sword as they finally reached the tower, its white walls blazing with inner fire and the golden carvings blinding to look upon. He, Rhianna and Yvraine had fought their way through to the tower in stuttering fits and starts, the Sword Master cutting them a path through the magical creatures with lightning quick slashes of her sword.

Rhianna had regained her composure, each step taken that brought them closer to the tower reinvigorating her with the pure magic that flowed from it. Fierce battles raged on, with the Sword Masters linking up and fighting in disciplined phalanxes instead of the isolated struggles the initial attacks had forced upon them.

Yet even with such methodical precision, more and more of the horrific creatures were emerging from the slithering pools of magical energy shed by those that were slain. For every beast killed, more would rise to fight again and slowly, step by step, the Sword Masters were being forced back against the tower.

Eldain moved to stand alongside Yvraine, prepared to fight back to back with her as he had seen other warriors do, but she waved him away.

'No, you cannot fight so close to me.'

'Why not?'

'You are not a Sword Master and are not attuned to our way of fighting. Without that knowledge, my blade would cut you down or yours would wound me. Fight alongside me, but not as my sword brother.'

Remembering how Yvraine's blade and that of her fellow Sword Master had woven around one another, Eldain nodded, now understanding what a lethal mistake it would be to fight so close to her.

He moved away from her as yet more of the Sword Masters drew back to the tower. A host of shimmering monsters, formed from every nightmare imaginable, closed in and though the elven warriors displayed no fear, it was clear they could not fight off such numbers.

A hundred blades rose in unison as the beasts of magic surged forwards and battle was joined within a sword length of the White Tower. The Sword Masters were skilled beyond mortal comprehension and their weapons moved faster than thought, dazzling light cloven asunder with each precisely aimed blow. Though the odds were against them, not a single backwards step was being taken, but every second of the battle saw another elven warrior torn apart.

Eldain fought with all the skill he could muster, his sword cleaving through the jelly-like, immaterial flesh of the monsters. He ducked a sweeping tentacle of light, hacking through the limb with an upward sweep of his blade and bringing it back in time to block a razored claw aimed at his head.

Beside him, Rhianna fought with talents of her own. While she could wield a blade with no little ability, it was in the magical arts where her true skills lay. She conjured blazing walls of blue fire within the shambling ranks of the monsters that consumed them in shrieking waves. And where such flames arose, each creature was utterly destroyed, no residue of its ending creating others in its wake. Streaking tongues of flame leapt from her outstretched hands, but Eldain could see that she could not sustain such a tremendous expenditure of power for long.

Even as he despaired of winning this fight, a cascade of magical fire rained down upon the monsters. Explosions of white light exploded with retina-searing brightness as the mages within the tower finally unleashed their own powers in defence of their home.

Eldain cried in exultation as he saw that the tide of battle had turned.

The skill and sacrifices of the Sword Masters had bought the mages time to wrestle the rampaging energies of the tower back under control and now the full might of Sapherian magic was brought to bear.

He dropped his sword and turned towards Rhianna as she sagged against the tower, drained beyond endurance by the might of the magic she had unleashed.

'It's over,' he said. 'The battle's over.'

She smiled gratefully, her flesh pale and waxen.

'Thank Isha… I have no more to give.'

'Don't worry, it was enough.'

Rhianna shivered and Eldain felt as though the sensation travelled from her and into his own flesh. Eldain looked into her eyes and a shared moment of recognition passed between them, but recognition of what he could not say.

The noise of battle receded, as though an invisible fog had descended to deaden the senses. He looked back at Rhianna and knew she was experiencing the same thing.

'What…' he began, but stopped as he saw the look of wide-eyed shock upon her face.

He followed the direction of her gaze and his heart was seized in a clammy fist.

Standing amid the dying army of magical creatures was a bewildered looking elf, his features the mirror of Eldain's own.

'It can't be…' he said.

Caelir.

INSTEAD OF THIN air, his foot stepped onto solid ground.

Caelir felt the same shift in reality he'd experienced when he'd first set foot in the Tower of Hoeth; that same sense of magic changing things because it could. Once again he'd travelled the length of the tower, but this time he had not wished it to. This time he had wished for the rush of air past his falling body as everything ended peacefully.

But as the magic of Ulthuan rushed in to fill the void so recently gouged in his soul by the outpouring of dark magic hidden within him, all thoughts of oblivion fled from his mind and a wracking sob burst from his chest. He realised how close he had come to an inglorious death and the thought horrified him beyond belief.

No… if he was to atone for this monstrous debacle, then he would need to live. He would need to survive and finally discover what had been done to him and why.

Caelir stood, fresh resolve filling him as he took stock of his surroundings. He stood at the base of the Tower of Hoeth, at the edge of the charred remains of the forest he and Kyrielle had ridden through with Anurion…

Kyrielle!

He closed his eyes as the image of her terror flashed across his mind, her once perfect features melting down to the bone as the dark magic consumed her. The grief was still raw and bleeding and it took an effort of will to force it down to a level where he could still function. He would mourn her properly later, but for now he had to keep moving.

A host of armoured Sword Masters fought creatures the magic had summoned, cutting them down with deadly grace and skill. Flashing spears of fire were hurled from the tower and white flames leapt from the ground in rushing walls to burn them.

The battle for the tower was almost won, and though the shimmering army of monsters was doomed, they fought on with no regard for their ultimate fate. Caelir had little doubt as to his fate should the Sword Masters take him prisoner; their brethren had been killed and the Loremaster wounded almost unto death, so he turned and ran for the forest.

He heard a shout behind him and saw a figure break from the ranks of the Sword Masters and come running towards him. She wore long, flowing robes and her honey gold hair trailed behind her like the banner of an Ellyrian Reaver. She was beautiful but haunted, and Caelir could not bear the pain he saw there.

He reached the forest, zigzagging between fire blackened trees that wept sap and leaping fallen bodies. Caelir heard more shouts behind him, but paid them no heed in his desperation to escape. He skidded to a halt in a clearing that remained untouched by the fire, seeing a trio of magnificent steeds standing together by the body of a fallen Sword Master. The ground glistened with blood and the residue of magic like morning dew and Caelir instantly saw that two of the steeds were unmistakably of Ellyrian stock.

Caelir almost laughed in relief to see such a welcome sight and made his way towards them. They whinnied with pleasure to see him and the Ellyrion mounts came up and nuzzled him affectionately. The familiarity of the steeds was like a touchstone to him and he wept to see such reminders of a homeland he could not recall.

One of the steeds was jet black, normally considered unlucky to the riders of Ellyrion, but it was a fine and strong beast. Its companion was smaller and less muscled, but no less majestic. The third horse was a silver Sapherian mount and it too sought to welcome him, behaviour not normally expected from such haughty beasts.

He sensed a strange familiarity to these horses, as though he knew them from an earlier life, but there was no connection, no remembrance of their names or personalities.

'Would you bear me away from this place, friend?' said Caelir, running his hands down the flanks of the black horse.

The horse bobbed its head and Caelir said, 'Thank you.'

He vaulted onto the horse's back and gathered up its reins as he heard running footsteps drawing near to him.

Through the trees he could see the maiden he had seen earlier and another pang of familiarity stabbed home. Before her ran a warrior with a bared blade, his features partially obscured by the play of shadows through the smoke and trees.

Like the elf maid there was a familiarity to them, but...

Then the light shifted and Caelir cried out as he saw that the warrior's features were his own...

'Wait!' shouted his doppelganger, but Caelir was not about to obey any such commands.

He turned the horse with the pressure of his knees and rode off for the northern horizon.

Like Anurion before him, Teclis had been unable to lift the curse of his forgotten memory, but Caelir remembered that Anurion had spoken of another powerful individual who might help him discover the truth of his life.

The Everqueen.

BOOK THREE
INVASION

CHAPTER ELEVEN

LANDING

WAVES LASHED THE jagged, rocky coastline, relentless walls of cold black water funnelling between the broken islands that lay west of Ulthuan to hammer the sunken ruins of Tor Anroc. What had once been a glorious fastness was now little more than skeletal remains, its high towers smashed and its walls sundered by an ancient, but still bitterly remembered act of spite.

The lord of Tor Anroc and his sons were gone, lost to history and the remembrances of ancient taletellers. None now spoke of them, for their destiny was too heartbreaking to hear without one's thoughts becoming moribund.

Only broken stubs of lost towers remained, jutting from the storm-lashed waters like the fingers of a drowning victim. With each passing year more succumbed to the erosion of the sea and collapsed below the waves.

A sullen grey sky pressed down on the tower, the day

almost ended and the sun descending to the far horizon as a chill disc of white. Ghostly winds blew over the watchtower of Tor Anroc, a tall spire of dark rock raised upon the ruins of the sunken city.

From the tallest peak of the watchtower, Coriael Swiftheart looked over the bleak greyness of the western horizon. A shimmering, misty haze hung over the ocean, but such sights were not uncommon around Ulthuan and did not trouble him.

His armour caught the last of the sunlight and he shivered as another gust of biting wind whipped around the heights of the tower. Coriael listened to the noise of the ocean, imagining the sound to be the forgotten roars of dragons, and he recalled tales of ages past told to him by his grandsire by the fireside of their home in Tiranoc.

He had thrilled to stories of skies thick with the sinuous bodies of dragons as the magnificent warriors of Caledor had ridden them into battle. But as the volcanic fire of the mountains had cooled and the magic of the world lessened, the dragons slumbered for longer and longer, no longer rising at the clarion call of the Dragonhorn.

Coriael wished he could have lived in those days of splendour, when Tor Anroc still stood proud and strong. He longed for the heady glory of fighting in the glittering host of Ulthuan against its many enemies instead of watching the flat emptiness of the western ocean.

He gripped the haft of his spear, standing a little taller as he imagined himself standing proud in a line of spearmen, their courage unbending and their blades gleaming in the sunlight. Such was not the case, however, and though he understood the necessity of what he and his fellow warriors did here, it did not sit well with his hunger for glory to be stranded on this desolate and forgotten island as a mere watchman.

Far below him, a hundred other warriors of Tiranoc garrisoned the watchtower, guardians of the magical beacon that would give warning of any hostile force approaching the isle of the Asur. In addition to these citizen soldiers, a group of Shadow Warriors had arrived the previous evening, an occurrence greeted with some trepidation, for only rarely did these cruel guardians of Ulthuan's coast choose to fraternise with the soldiers of the Phoenix King.

Right now, Coriael would have preferred it to be even rarer, for his companion upon the ramparts of the watchtower was a cold-eyed Nagarythe named Vaulath.

The Shadow Warrior wore no woollen tunic, but seemed not to feel the cold despite having only the protection of a thin shirt of dulled mail and a grey cloak that blended with the stonework of the tower. His longbow was fashioned from a wood so dark as to be almost black, the intricate embossing worked in deeply tinted copper.

'Still dreaming of being a great hero?' said Vaulath and Coriael knew he had read his thoughts in his posture.

'No harm in dreaming is there?'

'I suppose not. So long as you realise that's all it is, a dream.'

'What do you mean?' said Coriael.

Vaulath shook his head and said, 'I can't see the likes of you fighting in a battle line.'

'Why not?'

'Too much of a daydreamer. You'll be killed in the first charge, too busy thinking of the glory you want to win to defend yourself against the first enemy that tries to gut you.'

'How do *you* know?' snapped Coriael. 'You don't even know me.'

'I don't need to. I can see it plain as day. You haven't suffered the way we Nagarythe have. You still think war is about glory and honour.'

'And so it is!'

Vaulath laughed, though the cruel edge to it robbed it of any humour. 'You are a young fool if you think that. War has nothing to do with such notions. It is all about killing and death. It is about killing your enemy before he even knows you are there. Striking him down from the shadows as quickly as possible by whatever means necessary. And once he is defeated you hang his body from the gibbet tree by his entrails so that his friends will learn not to come back!'

Coriael recoiled before Vaulath's words, shocked at the vitriol if not the sentiment, for the Nagarythe were known to be cruel warriors. But to hear such words from one of the Asur was chilling, more akin to something he would have expected from the mouth of a druchii.

'You are wrong,' said Coriael. 'The great heroes of Ulthuan would never stoop to such barbarity.'

'Think you not? Where was the glory when Tethlis the Slayer's Silver Helms drove the druchii from the cliffs of the Blighted Isle to break on the rocks below? You think Tyrion allowed notions of honour to stay his hand when he slew the Witch King's assassin on the Finuval Plain? No, the Everqueen's champion slew his opponent as quickly as he was able.'

The night closed in as Vaulath's venomous words spat forth and Coriael dearly wished he could have passed this watch with another of his fellow warriors of Tiranoc instead of this caustic Nagarythe.

Disgusted, he turned away and leaned on the parapet, seeking to find something in the darkness to distract him from Vaulath's gloomy pronouncements. The Shadow Warrior said nothing more, apparently content he had made his point and dashed Coriael's dreams of glory.

Aside from the booming crash of the water and white patches of surf, he could see little of interest, though that did not surprise him. Dark clouds loomed on the horizon, drawing nearer with every second, and a storm was likely brewing far out to sea.

A sliver of darkness shifted below him, the light of the rising moon casting long shadows over the rock, and he stared over the edge of the parapet in puzzlement.

'Did you see that?' said Vaulath, his whispered voice audible even over the crashing waves.

'I saw something,' nodded Coriael.

'Look again.'

Coriael leaned further over the parapet, squinting against the darkness in an attempt to spot the shadow once again. He heard the soft creak of Vaulath's bow being drawn and turned to ask what he saw when he heard a series of soft clicks and excruciating fire exploded in his shoulder.

He screamed in pain as Vaulath loosed a black-fletched shaft, falling to the stone floor of the tower as he heard an answering cry of pain from the base of the tower. Coriael rolled onto his back and dropped his spear, staring in shock at a pair of iron crossbow bolts jutting from his flesh. Blood streamed down his cream tunic and he felt a nauseous panic swell within him as he imagined that the barbed heads might be poisoned.

A clang of bolts smacked against the stonework of the tower and he looked up as Vaulath ducked behind a tapered merlon. Anger began to overwhelm his pain as he realised the Shadow Warrior had used him as bait to lure whoever was below into loosing and making himself a target.

'Still alive?' said Vaulath.

'No thanks to you!' spat Coriael. 'I could have been killed!'

'Maybe, but I killed the one that hit you,' replied Vaulath. 'Still think there's honour in war?'

Coriael didn't deign to answer that question and pushed himself to his knees, gritting his teeth in pain. He reached up to pluck one of the bolts from his shoulder, but Vaulath shook his head. 'Leave it. You'll bleed to death.'

He glared at the Shadow Warrior, looking over his shoulder as he saw the storm clouds he had noticed earlier drawing closer with unnatural speed.

'What's happening?' he said.

'We are under attack, what do you think is happening?' said Vaulath. 'Go below and light the beacon. If they have come with numbers then we will need help soon to live through the night.'

'Who are they?'

'Druchii. Who else?'

Coriael nodded, frightened, yet also exhilarated enough that he was now involved in a fight to protect Ulthuan that the pain of his wounds receded for a moment.

From below he heard shouts and the clash of weapons, but over and above that he heard a dreadful sound like a torn sail in the wind, a leathery ripping that set his soul to thinking of dark caves and mountain lairs filled with gnawed and bloody bones.

Vaulath heard it too and looked up as a thrashing blanket of living darkness blotted out the sky. But this darkness had little to do with the setting of the sun save that it was the shroud that hid the vile creatures within it from the sight of all that was good and pure.

With a speed that amazed Coriael, Vaulath loosed arrow after arrow into the seething cloud of flapping wings and screeching cries that filled the air.

'Go!' shouted the Shadow Warrior as he drew and loosed with terrifying speed.

A flare of purple fire from below lit up the sky and Coriael cried out as he saw thousands of hideous creatures circling in the air above the tower, their bodies a dreadful amalgam of female anatomy and that of a grotesque daemonic bat. In the flickering spears of purple lightning, he saw faces little better than those of wild animals, hunger-driven and horrible to look upon. Their wings were composed of an ugly stretched sinewy fabric, their claws and horns formed from diseased and yellowed bone.

Fear lent his limbs speed and he scrambled over to the stairs cut into the floor that led to the chamber of the beacon. He heard more piercing shrieks as more of Vaulath's arrows found homes in unclean flesh.

The tower shook as though from a mighty blow and Coriael gasped in pain as the impact threw him against the stonework. He dropped into the stairwell as he heard Vaulath's bow clatter to the floor, and the stink of unclean flesh filled his nostrils. The noise of the creatures' flapping wings grew as the cloud of monsters descended to the tower and engulfed its top in a flurry of screeching bodies.

Coriael looked behind him, but could no longer see

the Shadow Warrior. He heard the warrior scream in hatred as his sword clove the flesh of the flying beasts. The scent of blood and howls of triumphant bloodlust tore at his senses as he pushed down the stairs that curved towards the beacon chamber. He tried not to imagine the horror of being torn to pieces by these abominable creatures.

Deafening shrieks echoed behind him, the flickering light of torches throwing the madly jerking shadows of his pursuers against the white inner walls of the stair-well. He stumbled onwards, snatching a torch from its sconce with his good arm as he reached the landing.

A white timbered door blocked further progress and he staggered against it.

'Lady Isha, in whose grace I trust, I bid thee open!'

The timbers of the door pulsed with a soft light and he heard the click of the latch as the magic that barred the passage of enemies withdrew. He pushed open the door as a screeching cry of triumph and the clicking of bone claws scratching on stone echoed from behind him.

Coriael threw himself through the door and turned to hurl his weight against it, leaning his back against the door to push it shut. Before the door could close, a body slammed against the other side of it and he cried out as the shock jarred his injured shoulder. He pushed against the creatures on the other side of the door, the timber shuddering beneath their assault as iron-hard claws tore at the wood.

Shrieks of pain echoed in the corridor as the purity of the magic burned their flesh and he fought against the pain of his wound as he doubled his efforts to press the door shut. The glowing blue orb of the warning bea-con pulsed in readiness in front of him, but while the door remained unbarred, it might as well have been on Ulthuan for all the good it did him.

A gnarled hand of hard flesh hooked around the edge of the door, the bloody claws tearing across his chest.

Coriael flinched in pain and his weight on the door eased a fraction...

Arms corded with sinewy muscle forced their way through the wider gap, and with the extra leverage the door was hurled open. Coriael sprawled on the floor, wracked with pain, but knowing he had one last duty to perform before these depraved monsters killed him.

He crawled towards the warning beacon, but even as he reached for it a heavy weight pinned him to the ground as the winged monsters landed on him.

Coriael screamed as clawed hands tore into him.

His world ended in pain as fanged mouths fastened upon his flesh.

MOONLIGHT SPILLED OVER the peaks of the Annulii, bathing the rocky headlands and sandy bays of northern Tiranoc in silver as the fullness of night drew its veil over the world. The shimmering haze Coriael Swiftheart had seen in the twilight faded and as the sea reflected the light of the moon, a vast fleet of ships emerged from the haze.

Sleek, dark-hulled Raven ships with hooked rams and black sails carried hundreds of dark elf warriors and great wooden longships with high dragon prows bore the warriors of Issyk Kul. Hundreds of ships sailed into a sheltered bay known as Carin Anroc that thrust inland at the border between Tiranoc and the Shadowlands.

With the watchtower of Tor Anroc neutralised, stealth and cunning were sacrificed for speed. Though the warning beacon had been silenced, it would not take long for the defenders of Ulthuan to become aware of the invaders in their midst.

The first dark elf ships slid up the shingled bay and armoured warriors leapt into the shallows. They rushed ashore, blades bared and their cruel eyes eager for bloodshed. Ship after ship slid up the beach and scores of warriors assembled before the whips and shouted orders of their leaders.

Cloaked warriors led dark steeds from the holds of their vessels and rode out to watch for any enemy scouts as phalanxes of warriors clad in long mail shirts – called *dalakoi* – and golden breastplates waded through the surf. These warriors bore the feared *draich*, a mighty executioner's weapon, and a pall of dread came before them as they marched onto the beach.

Heavy hulled ships lowered ramps of thick timber and a host of dark armoured knights rode green skinned reptilian beasts onto the beach. Far larger than the mounts of their cloaked brethren, these scaly skinned creatures were muscular and vicious and their powerful jaws were filled with jagged fangs. The knights carried barbed lances that glittered in the moonlight and the thick, growling heads of their mounts swung back and forth as they tasted the air for blood.

Disassembled machines worked from gracefully curved spars of ebony and gold were lifted from the holds of other vessels, together with barrel-loads of deadly missiles – long bolts that more resembled heavy, iron lances and hundreds of smaller, lighter darts.

A black shape wheeled in the air high above the assembling army, a beast of darkness that bore the mistress of this host through the night. Its outward form resembled a powerful winged horse, and its sleek outline was like the essence of night bound into physical shape. Its burning, predatory eyes glowed red in the darkness and a jagged thrust of bone jutted from its skull.

Morathi straddled the night-hunting pegasus with her wicked lance held high for all to see. Against the blackness of her mount, her skin was like marble, smooth and pale and beautiful. A corslet of gleaming black leather and plate protected and exposed her flesh in equal measure and she was attended by a darkly glittering host of malevolent spirits that gathered about her in a cloak of woven mist.

Pledges of lust and adoration arose from the warriors below at the sight of her, but Morathi ignored them, soaring high on the magical energies blowing from the Annulii Mountains and smiling as she contemplated the undoing of her enemies.

Issyk Kul, her ally for the time being, landed his own ships further along from those of the Hag Sorceress, marching through the waters and onto the sand with his many bladed sword raised. Behind him a naked familiar led a towering steed with red flesh and heaving flanks that glistened with blood and exposed musculature. A silver saddle was sewn onto its back and its sapphire eyes blazed with ecstasy as the saltwater bathed its exposed viscera in fire.

Morathi watched as Kul vaulted into the metal saddle of the fleshy steed and raised his sword high above his head. He threw back his head and issued a long, whooping howl as he swung his sword like a madman.

At this signal, scores of men dropped into the sea from the longboats. These were leather-tough men of the far Northern Wastes, their hard flesh sculpted by the rigours

of battle and slaughter. Warriors in dark armour, furred
cloaks and horned helms marched ashore, their curved
swords and mighty axes hungry for slaughter and degra-
dation in their god's name.

Beasts with shaggy, horned heads loped alongside
these warriors, their anatomies hugely muscled and
furred by the fusion of man and beast. Snorting monsters with curling horns sprouting from their skulls
bullied smaller, red furred beasts ahead of them with
bellowed grunts and thumps of spiked clubs.

Great ramps were hurled from the sides of larger vessels and a dozen warriors clambered over the sides, each
group hauling a chained abomination behind them.

Howling roars echoed through the night as huge, mis-
shapen masses of flesh were dragged onto the land, their
many gnashing mouths snapping shut at anything that
came close. The beasts shambled forwards on grossly
swollen and twisted limbs with weeping sores clustered
in pockets of flab and sinew at the joints. Their bloated
bodies were thick with heavy cartilage and clawed limbs,
too many for any natural creature, and none possessed
any obvious head or primary means of discerning the
world around them.

Whatever manner of creatures they had once been,
each was now a monster spawned by the mutating
power of Chaos, little more than a terrifying living
engine of destruction and slaughter. Other ships began
disgorging yet more of these deformed monsters, hor-
rifyingly distorted and warped creatures that defied
understanding or description. Monstrous hulks of distended flesh, their bodies were horrors of thrashing
claws, fused heads, elastic limbs and spurting tentacles.

It was impossible to know whether their hideous

wails were of rage or pain, but whatever the reason for
their ululations, the winds blowing from the sea carried
them far inland.

Issyk Kul rode his loathsome steed along the length of
the beach, howling like a rabid wolf as his army came
ashore. His horse reared, like a great heroic statue of
pink marble come to life, and the blood that ran down
Kul's arms from the barbed hilt of his sword was like oil
in the moonlight.

Such silver radiance from the heavens was both a help
and a hindrance, for though it made the night landing
easier, it also made the many ships and hundreds of
warriors easier to spot.

Time was of the essence and it was with cruel effi-
ciency that the forces of Morathi and Issyk Kul pushed
from the beaches and up the craggy slopes to the land
of the elves.

The invasion of Ulthuan had begun.

THIS HIGH ABOVE the Annulii, the winds were charged with
magical energy, bearing the three eagles aloft with only
the barest minimum of effort. Warm air from the Inner
Kingdoms rose from the eastern flanks of the mountains
and met the cold barrier of wind blowing inwards from
the sea. Mingled with the waves of raw, powerful magic,
the resultant thermals made racing through the skies an
exhilarating experience, though the mighty birds of prey
appeared to care little for the sensation.

The eagles flew abreast of one another, though the
bird in the centre of their formation was clearly the
mightiest of the three, his feathers a stunning mixture
of gold and brown except for his regal head, which was
covered with feathers of purest white. This was Elasir,

Lord of the Eagles, and greatest of his race.

His kind had soared the magical currents of the world before the rise of the race of men, and the Phoenix King himself knew the eagle's proud countenance. Even the Loremasters of Saphery took heed when the eagles spoke.

Elasir angled his flight, dipping his left wing a fraction and descending as he followed the curve of the mountains. Together with his brothers, Aeris and Irian, eagles as regal and proud as he, Elasir flew southwards with powerful beats of his sweeping wings, anxious to return to the eyries around the Eagle Gate as soon as possible.

After slaying the druchii assassin, Elasir had flown north to Avelorn to take counsel from the birds and beasts of the forest realm, for their knowledge of hidden things was great. Elasir had told the counsel of the death of Cerion Goldwing and the doves had promised to carry the news of his passing throughout Ulthuan. Then the ravens had spoken of grim omens and the scarlet pheasants of the Everqueen had pronounced prophecies of great doom upon Ulthuan before urging Elasir to return home with all speed.

The sadness of Cerion Goldwing's death still sat heavily upon Elasir and the slaying of his assassin had done little to ease it. Revenge was a motive beneath the Lord of the Eagles, but natural justice had been served by the druchii's death and for that reason it had given him pleasure. The commander of the Eagle Gate had been a friend to his kind and had always displayed the proper respect their ancient lineage demanded.

Yes, Cerion Goldwing would be missed, for he had been a warrior of honour and humility.

A sudden shift in the currents of magic brought an

acrid scent to the mighty eagle and Elasir cocked his head as he sensed a rank odour of hate carried on the wind.

Brothers, do you sense what I sense? asked Elasir, his words forming within their minds.

We do, they said in unison.

Druchii, added Aeris.

Corrupted ones, said Irian.

Elasir could taste the foulness of the air, knowing now that the birds of Avelorn had spoken true.

Come, brothers, we must know the nature of this threat and carry warning to the Asur.

And kill the corrupted, said Irian.

Yes, kill them. Tear their flesh and pluck out their eyes! cried Aeris.

Elasir felt the same hatred for these terrible foes as keenly as his brothers, but could already sense that the threat below was too great for them to defeat on their own. He dipped his wings and pulled them in close to his body as he swooped down through the air and angled his course westwards.

The Eagle Gate would have to wait.

ELOIEN REDCLOAK REINED in his grey mare as she tossed her mane with unease, ears pressed flat against her skull. He knew his mount well enough to know that she had senses superior to his own and that if she believed something was amiss, she was usually right.

Something was abroad this night and he raised a fist to halt his patrol of ten Ellyrion horsemen, their exquisite skill the envy of all save the knights of the Silver Helms.

Steep fangs of stone rose around them and knifeback

ridges of wind-eroded rock surrounded them. The moon
was almost directly overhead and few shadows were
cast, which would make spotting any movement easier,
though the undulating terrain made it difficult to see
much beyond a hundred feet or so. With a gentle pressure of his knees, he directed his mount forwards, her
hooves making no sound as they traversed the stony
ground.

He did not yet know the source of his steed's unease,
but lifted his bow from its leather sling and nocked an
arrow to the string. His warriors followed his example
and Eloien scanned the landscape around them, letting
his own senses spread out into the night as he sought to
pinpoint the source of his mount's unease.

Further ahead, the ground rose up in a gentle slope
before falling away sharply in a great cliff that dropped
to the sea and he slid silently from his saddle. Eloien
slithered forward on his stomach, not wishing to silhou-
ette himself against the skyline, and peered through the
scrubby grass at the cliff's edge.

'Asuryan's fire!' he hissed, shock overcoming his natural caution.

On the beaches far below, a fleet of invasion mustered, the coast thick with boats of a shallow enough
draught to be drawn up the sand. Warriors in dark
armour formed up into disciplined regiments on the
beach and the breath hissed from him as he saw druchii
banners raised alongside those of foolish humans who
gave praise to the Dark Gods.

He slipped quietly back down the slope to where his
reavers awaited him, their faces tense as they sought to read
his expression. Without a word, he climbed back into the
saddle and settled his cloak over his horse's rump.

Fallion Truespear, his clarion and closest friend said, 'Well? What did you see?'

'Druchii,' said Eloien. 'And corrupt men.'

'Druchii?' said Fallion. 'Then let us take the fight to them, Eloien!'

He shook his head. 'No, these are no mere raiders, this is an army of invasion.'

The awful nature of the threat spread through the troop of reavers and Eloien let it sink in for a moment before saying, 'We ride for the Eagle Gate to take warning to its castellan.'

Fallion opened his mouth to reply, but before he could speak, an iron bolt flashed through the air and punched through the back of his helmet. The clarion toppled from the saddle and Eloien realised with sick horror that his mount's unease had been at something far closer than the enemy warriors on the beach.

He spun his horse as a volley of crossbow bolts slashed from the darkness and unseen shadows detached from the rocks around them. Screams of elves and horses sounded as iron bolts hammered into them. A shaft buried itself in his horse's neck and pitched him from the saddle as her legs buckled beneath her.

He leapt free of the dying beast and landed lightly on his feet with his bow drawn and an arrow ready to loose. A druchii shadow melted from the darkness and leapt towards him, a curved blade slashing for his groin.

Eloien let fly with his arrow and the attacker fell with a goose-feathered shaft buried in his throat. He dropped to one knee and loosed another shaft at a leaping figure that sprang from the rocks. The arrow punched low into the figure's stomach and the warrior doubled up in mid-air before crashing to the ground in a tangle of limbs.

He spun, searching for fresh targets and brought down another three of their attackers before a crossbow bolt ricocheted from the boulder beside him and slashed through his bowstring.

The clash of blades rang clear in the darkness and Eloien saw that his few remaining warriors would soon be overwhelmed. More than a dozen of the druchii – though it was hard to be sure, so seamlessly did they blend with the shades of night – still fought and at least five of his reavers were dead.

A hooded killer came at him with his blade bared and Eloien stepped to meet him, swinging the useless bowstave in a hard upward arc. The blow connected and as his attacker reeled, Eloien spun around him and drew his sword in one smooth motion. Silver ithilmar flashed and an arc of blood jetted from the druchii's opened throat.

More bolts flashed and Eloien's anger boiled within him as he heard the screams of horses. The druchii were targeting their mounts to prevent word of their landing from escaping.

Three more druchii killers ran towards him and Eloien relaxed into a fighting crouch, blade outwards and left arm cocked behind him. He swayed aside from the first attacker's blow, spinning and chopping the hard edge of his palm against the druchii's throat.

His foe collapsed, clutching his shattered windpipe as Eloien blocked the sweeping sword blade of his second attacker. A blade whistled over his head as he dropped to the ground and scythed his leg out in a wide arc.

The two druchii fell, their legs chopped out from under them. Eloien leapt forward, driving his sword through the chest of the first, but before he could turn to dispatch the second, searing pain exploded within him as a cold blade plunged into his back.

Eloien staggered and fell forward onto one knee, bright stars of pain bursting before his eyes. He turned as blood poured down his back and managed to block the druchii's next blow, but knew he could not block another. He raised his sword, the blade feeling as though weighted with iron bars. The sound of fighting diminished and he knew his warriors were dead.

Cruciform shadows flashed over the moonlit ground as he looked up into the faces of his killers. Perhaps a dozen of the cruel-eyed druchii remained standing, their blades bloody and their ivory skinned faces twisted with hatred.

He struggled to hold onto his sword as the hooded druchii that had stabbed him advanced slowly towards him, malicious intent writ large on his features.

A screeching cry ripped the darkness and to Eloien it sounded like salvation.

The druchii looked up in panic…

But before they could move, the eagles were amongst them.

Three died without knowing what had killed them, ripped in two by powerful claws or sheared to the bone by the snap of a powerful beak. Eloien laughed, despite the pain, as the great eagles tore through the druchii, killing with the swift economy of seasoned hunters.

The druchii scattered, but the eagles were too swift, tearing limbs from bodies or crushing skulls with massive beats of their wings. In the centre of the slaughter, Eloien saw a magnificent eagle with a golden-feathered body and a head of purest white.

Eloien had seen charging Silver Helms, the thunderous might of a host of Tiranoc Chariots and the glittering host of the Phoenix King's army arrayed in all its glory, but he had never seen a sight more welcome or awesome as this mighty eagle as it slew the druchii.

Even as he formed the thought, he saw the warrior that had been on the verge of killing him level his ebony crossbow at the eagle.

'No!' cried Eloien.

With the last of his strength, he hurled his sword at the druchii, the point burying itself between his shoulder blades. The druchii screamed foully and dropped to his knees, clawing at the blade jutting from his back. He toppled and Eloien slumped onto his side, relieved beyond words that he had prevented the cloaked warrior from harming the eagle.

Dimly he thought he could hear the sound of hooves on rock and through his dimming eyes he saw a host of dark riders galloping towards the battle.

He struggled to rise, but had no strength left and could only watch as the druchii riders drew near.

Then Eloien gasped as he felt strong claws grip his body and lift him upwards.

The ground fell away and cold wind rushed past his face as the angry cries of the druchii below faded with distance. Eloien looked up and saw the white-headed eagle as it bore him into the skies of Ulthuan.

Rest, warrior, said a noble voice in his head. *I have you now.*

Eloien closed his eyes as the eagles carried him to safety.

Chapter Twelve

Memories

In the aftermath of the battle around the Tower of Hoeth, Eldain found little time to process the fact of Caelir's survival. With the re-establishment of the binding spells that channelled the magic of Saphery through the tower and into the wards, peace had once more settled on the land of magic.

Fires still smouldered and dark scars cut through the forest where it had burned trees to the ground with its magical potency. The Sword Masters gathered the bodies of the slain and covered each warrior with their own bloodstained cloaks. Tears and songs of lament echoed through the violated forest as each new body was discovered and Eldain helped wherever he could.

He kept himself busy to avoid lingering on what he had seen, unable to believe that his younger brother was in fact alive. Together, he and Yvraine carried the body of a Sword Master towards the tower while Rhianna sat at the edge of the forest where Caelir had vanished. Her head was bowed and Eldain could not begin to imagine what she was feeling.

'You should go to her,' said Yvraine.

'And say what?' demanded Eldain.

'You do not need to say anything.'

He nodded and helped her lay the body they carried next to the others.

A chill entered Eldain's soul as he appreciated the true cost of the battle.

So many dead…

Row upon row of dead Sword Masters and mages, so many it was inconceivable. The Sword Masters were amongst the greatest warriors of Ulthuan and to see so many of them dead shocked Eldain to his very core.

'Excuse me,' he said and turned away, making his way towards Rhianna, his steps leaden.

His wife's outline seemed shrunken, as though part of her had fled on the back of Lotharin with Caelir. He wondered if Caelir's choice of steed had been deliberate or was it simply that the fates had decided to mock Eldain by having his brother escape on the back of his betrayer's horse?

He knelt beside her and put his hand on her shoulder.

'Rhianna?'

'He is alive, Eldain,' she said without turning. 'How can that be?'

'I do not know,' replied Eldain, unsure of what answer she sought.

She turned to face him and he saw tears in her eyes.

'You told me he was dead, Eldain,' she said. He searched for any accusation in her tone, but found none, simply a need for answers. Answers he could not give.

He knew he had to speak and said, 'I... I thought he was. It happened so fast. We rode out of Clar Karond and his horse was killed beneath him. I rode back for him, but he was hit by druchii crossbow bolts and he fell.'

'But did you see him die?'

Eldain shook his head and closed his eyes, reliving that bloody night as they had charged through the dock-yards of Clar Karond and burned scores of druchii ships at their moorings. Flames clawed at the sky and smoke blotted out the moon as fire raced through the docks. He remembered Caelir's hand reaching up to him, the glint of firelight on the pledge ring Rhianna had given him.

'The druchii were everywhere,' he said. 'I saw Caelir fall with druchii bolts in him. I wanted to go to him, but if I had stayed they would have killed me also.'

Rhianna heard the pain in his voice and the haunted memories of that night. She reached up to take his hand in hers and the force of the guilt that rose in him made him want to snatch it away from her.

For the grief he saw in her eyes was not just for herself; it included him.

An overwhelming urge to confess his crime arose within him, but he resisted the urge to tell her the truth. As much as the guilt weighed heavily upon him, he still desired what his betrayal had won him and he hated himself for such weakness.

He had not ridden back for Caelir, but had abandoned him to the druchii...

He had as good as murdered Caelir to win back the woman he loved.

The woman his brother had stolen from him.

Such self-deceit had kept the worst of the guilt at bay, but confronted with the reality of his crime he found he could not justify what he had done, no matter how many times he told himself that he had acted out of love.

He looked up as he heard footsteps approach, half expecting to see Caelir coming towards him to claim his vengeance with a bared blade.

Instead he saw a tall mage with long golden hair bound by a silver circlet inset with a gem at the forehead. His robes were a cobalt blue and he wore a wide belt of gold and gems at his waist. Behind the mage stood Yvraine, her greatsword once again sheathed over her back.

Eldain nodded in recognition and rose to his feet before the mage.

'It gladdens my heart to see you, Eldain,' said the mage.

He bowed and said, 'You honour me, Master Silverfawn.'

The mage turned to Rhianna as she rose to her feet and fresh tears ran down her cheeks.

'Father,' said Rhianna.

ONCE CLEAR OF the forest, Caelir pushed hard for the north, aware that even now there might be pursuers hunting him. After the initial mad dash of escape, he had taken more care to disguise his route, but there was little need; the black steed he rode was as surefooted and eager as any he could remember riding and left virtually no sign of their passing.

His path took him through the rocky lowlands of the

Annulii foothills, along narrow paths and craggy defiles shaggy with gorse and flowering plants of all colours and descriptions. This close to the mountains, even the undergrowth was ripe with magical energies and Caelir could see why Anurion was fascinated by such fecund growth.

Anurion…

Tears fell from Caelir's face once again as he thought back to the terrible, bloody events at the Tower of Hoeth.

Kyrielle Greenkin was dead and he had killed her.

If not by his own hand then by dragging her into the disaster that was his life.

The image of her melting features as the life had been sucked from her would haunt his dreams for as long as he lived and he knew he could never make amends for depriving the world of her bright spirit.

The gardens of Anurion the Green would flourish a little less brightly without her and he vowed to plant a flower in her memory when he reached his destination.

Avelorn.

The realm of the Everqueen was his only hope now, for her magic was bound up in Ulthuan's magical cycle of healing and renewal. When the Everqueen laughed, the sun shone brighter and when she wept thunder rolled across the heavens.

What Teclis's magic had unleashed, hers must surely undo.

Time passed, though he could not say how much, for he had no right to look up and gaze at the face of the sun. The mountains rolled past on his right and clouds gathered over the Sea of Dreams on his left and though it was surely beyond the horizon, it seemed as though he could see a thin line of emerald green forest ahead of him.

He rode as though the arrow of Morai-heg herself were aimed at his heart, wanting to put as much distance between himself and the White Tower as possible.

The carnage itself was terrible, but that had not been the worst of it.

The sight of the elf warrior who could have been his twin had shocked him to the core, for who could he have been? Was he even real? Was Caelir? Could 'Caelir' be some evil doppelganger of this brave hero who fought to defend the Loremaster's tower?

Might Caelir be some creation of magic designed to infiltrate the secret sanctums of the Asur and unleash destruction? As much as the idea horrified him and the evidence bore it out, he did not think it likely, for there were too many images burned in his mind that were too real, too resonant to be anything other than genuine memories.

Who then was this warrior? His brother…?

Just thinking the thought made it seem real and the more he turned the idea over in his head, the more likely it became. Though it seemed the most likely explanation, it did not explain the terrible fear and anger that welled up within him as he thought of this warrior being his brother. Why should the thought of a brother cause such conflicting emotions within him?

And the woman…

He had no conscious knowledge of her, but he had seen her face when he had spoken to Kyrielle and felt the first stirrings of attraction towards her. He looked at the silver pledge ring that glinted on his finger. Was she the maiden who had given him this token of love?

Such thoughts were too painful and he pushed them aside as he concentrated on the ride ahead. He had a long journey ahead and still had one last obstacle to overcome before then.

The battlefield of Finuval Plain.

MITHERION SILVERFAWN'S CHAMBERS within the Tower of Hoeth had escaped the destruction unleashed at the top of the tower. Filled with long benches strewn with astrolabes, lens grinders and all manner of instruments for celestial observation, it resembled a workshop more than a place of mystical study. Thick tomes of magic lay open, apparently at random, throughout the laboratory and a hundred or more scrolls were strewn about the room alongside dozens of inkwells.

Charts of astronomical movements and phenomena hung like war banners from the walls, each a mass of spirals and looping orbital patterns.

Though not at the summit of the tower, a great glass ceiling rippled above them like the surface of a lake. Though impressive, Eldain realised it could not possibly be a window, for it showed a star-filled night sky.

Mitherion made his way towards a long bench upon which sat a silver object that resembled a globe made from hundreds of thin loops of silver wire bound together with scores of brass-rimmed lenses. The object floated above a shallow concave disc of gold and spun gently on its axis as lenses slid through the silver wires, apparently at random.

Eldain and Rhianna followed him into the chamber, and Eldain could not help but sense a distance between them now that she knew Caelir was alive. The touch she had given him beyond the walls of the tower had not been repeated and though he ached to reach out and hold her, he suspected the gesture would not be returned.

'Father,' said Rhianna. 'What happened here?'

'I wish I knew,' said Mitherion.

'Does it have something to do with why you summoned us here?' asked Eldain, lifting a pile of books aside to find a place to sit.

Mitherion nodded as he checked the silver globe device and said, 'Perhaps. I am not sure, but your arriving here just as disaster strikes does seem rather auspicious.'

'Auspicious? We were almost killed.'

'True,' said Mitherion, wagging his finger at Eldain. 'But you are still alive. And the poor unfortunate who arrived with Anurion the Green claimed his name was Caelir. Rather a coincidence wouldn't you say? But it could not have been the Caelir that I once knew.'

Eldain stood and began to pace through the disorder of Mitherion's chambers. 'We saw him. Outside the tower. It was him.'

'Caelir Éadaoin. Your brother,' said Mitherion, glancing at his daughter. 'You are sure?'

'It was him, father,' nodded Rhianna. 'I saw him with my own eyes.'

'But how could he be alive? I understood he died on Naggaroth.'

'So did we all,' said Rhianna and Eldain winced at the unspoken, nascent accusation.

Mitherion returned his attention to the silver globe and adjusted several of the lenses before concentrating on an open book that lay beside him.

'Most curious…'

'What is?' asked Eldain.

'Caelir's appearance, if he is your brother, may indeed have something to do with our current troubles.'

'In what way?' said Rhianna, moving to stand beside her father.

'In every reading of the stars, I saw symbols that spoke of a figure without a name or a face, a phantom if you will. I did not know to whom this referred, but Caelir would seem to fit this description, arriving as he did with no memory save his name.'

'He has no memory?' said Eldain.

'So Anurion said. Apparently he attempted to restore it, but was unsuccessful. Hence why he brought him to see the Loremaster Teclis. A mistake, in retrospect...'

'And what happened?' said Rhianna. 'Did Caelir see Teclis?'

'He did,' nodded Mitherion. 'Another mistake I feel, but then the Loremaster does so love to seek answers where ignorance might be preferable. I do not know what happened between Teclis and Caelir, but whatever it was, it unleashed terrible dark magic and upset the balance of power flowing through the tower. And, well, you saw what happened...'

They let the moment hang in silence as they thought of the dead laid out below bloody cloaks at the base of the tower.

'Does this have anything to do with why you summoned us here?' said Eldain.

'It may have everything to do with that,' said Mitherion, rising and pulling yet more books from sagging shelves.

'And why was that?' said Eldain, his frustration turning to anger.

Mitherion opened the books, revealing page after page of scribbled notes, cosmological diagrams and calculations beyond understanding. 'These are divinations I took over the night skies to the far north of the Old World.'

'The Northern Wastes!' said Rhianna. 'Father, you know that is dangerous.'

'I know, but I had seen much darkness in your futures. Both of your futures and I had to know more.'

'And what did you see?' asked Eldain.

'I saw terrible danger descending on Ellyr-charoi. Death, destruction and the fire of war.'

'Then why send for us?' snapped Eldain. 'Why not warn us? If our home is in danger then we should be there to defend it.'

'Against this danger there is no defence.' said Mitherion. 'And if I had told you Ellyr-charoi was in danger what would you have done?'

'We would have stayed,' finished Rhianna.

'Exactly.'

Eldain wanted to argue, but he knew they were right. He sighed. 'What is this danger?'

Mitherion said, 'That I do not know, but the currents of magic speak of dark times ahead, Eldain. Whatever fate is to come, both you and Rhianna are bound to it. The druchii attack our ships and the ravens of Avelorn bring news of omens seen throughout the land. Something evil is coming, of that I have no doubt.'

'You are wrong, Mitherion Silverfawn,' said a cracked voice behind them.

Eldain and Rhianna turned and gasped as they saw the terribly wounded elf borne on a litter between four Sword Masters.

The flesh of Teclis's face was raw and burned, poultice-dipped bandages wrapping his skin and covering his thin chest and neck. His robes had been burned from him and he now wore a simple gown of white.

'The evil you speak of,' said Teclis. 'It is already here.'

THE CONCLAVE GATHERED in the ruins of the uppermost chamber of the Tower of Hoeth. The scent of discharged magic was carried on a strong wind, but the enchantments of the tower prevented its force from disturbing those who gathered to hear the Loremaster's words.

Only blackened stubs remained of the upper walls of the tower and the clouds displaced by the wind in the clear sky gave Eldain a giddy sense of flying since he was unable to see the ground.

Seated on his padded litter, Teclis convened them and was attended by his Sword Masters. The Loremaster's voice was weak and Eldain could see the effort of will it took him to address them.

The tales spoken of Teclis told of how sickly he had been as a youth and Eldain marvelled that he was able to remain upright after the grievous hurt done to him. Dark magic had ravaged his body, melting the flesh from his bones and he now resembled a skeleton draped in loose flesh and robed to appear in some mannish freak show.

Despite the Loremaster's terrible appearance, to stand in such illustrious company was an honour and a terror for Eldain and he kept his gaze lowered, humbled and not a little frightened at the presence of so many powerful individuals. What fate might Teclis pronounce upon him? Did he know of what Eldain had done on Naggaroth?

258 Graham McNeill

Might this be some ritual pantomime to humiliate and punish him?

Rhianna stood on his right, a subtle distance between them, and Mitherion Silverfawn had a fatherly arm around her shoulders. Yvraine stood to his left and her robes were still smeared with the blood of her fellows.

A stooped mage in a tattered green robe stood beside Teclis and Eldain wondered what horrors he had recently endured, for his face was a mask of anguish. Other mages, whose names Eldain did not know, gathered around Teclis, though they kept a discreet distance from their green-robed fellow, as though they wished not to be associated with his sorrow.

Looking at the assembled company, Eldain could see that no one here appeared at ease, for a lingering current of dark magic still hung in the air, a greasy, ashen taste in the back of the throat that tasted like biting on metal.

Teclis rapped his staff on the ground and all eyes turned to him.

'We have suffered a grievous hurt this day,' said Teclis, in what Eldain felt was a gross understatement.

Murmurs of assent circled the room as Teclis continued. 'One thought lost to us returns, but instead of joyful reunion, he brings death and treachery. I speak of the one named Caelir and his apparent return from the dead.'

Startled gasps greeted this pronouncement, for none had considered that the dread sorcery of undeath might have played a part in today's terror.

Teclis stilled such fears. 'Be at ease, my friends. It is not of necromancy that I speak, but perhaps Lord Éadaoin would elaborate on the tale of Caelir?'

Eldain felt all heads turn towards him and looked

up to see the sunken eyes of Teclis staring at him with a look of pity. His mouth felt dry and he knew he was expected to speak, but no words would form in his mind that were not those of his confession.

'Lord Éadaoin,' said Teclis, seeing his hesitation. 'If you please?'

Eldain nodded and cleared his throat, taking a deep breath before continuing. 'Yes, my lord, of course.'

He looked around the room, picturing the scene as he and Caelir had boarded the ship that was to carry them to their destiny on Naggaroth.

'We set sail from Lothern with a fair wind at our back,' said Eldain, and he went on to tell of how he and Caelir, together with a company of the finest Ellyrion Reavers, had sailed across the Great Ocean to Naggaroth to avenge the death of their father. He spoke eloquently of the chill that descended as they approached the blasted coast of the land of the druchii and the pall it cast over the company.

Eldain's voice grew stronger as he spoke of the evil, sulphurous river they had sailed along to get as close to the druchii city of Clar Karond as possible, whereupon they had continued on horseback. He spoke with pride as he told of how the skills of the Reavers had been tested to the utmost as they evaded patrols and fought the gloom of the soul that the druchii's homeland pressed upon them.

Eventually, they had reached the outskirts of Clar Karond and laid eyes upon the target of their raid, the shipyards where slaves toiled to construct the ships of the druchii fleet. No finer raiding force existed than the Ellyrion Reavers, and Eldain's voice surged as he spoke of how he and his warriors had run riot through the

shipyards, burning ships with enchanted arrows provided by Mitherion Silverfawn.

Eldain vividly described how he and Caelir had
toppled a mighty craft built onto the back of a great
sea drake and he could feel the emotions of those
around him swell with this tale of heroism and valour.
So caught up was he in the telling that Eldain could
almost convince himself that such had been how events
had eventually played out, but his voice faltered as he
described how the raiding force, having done as much
damage as it could do without being overwhelmed, had
ridden away.

He hesitated as he reached the crux of his tale, and
he licked his lips as he pondered his next words. 'When
Caelir and I rode through the gates of the shipyards, we
were met by a hail of crossbow bolts. Caelir was hit and
his horse was killed. He fell…'

Eldain's voice cracked as he pictured what happened
next and he saw that his audience believed it to be
anguish at the thought of his brother's 'death'.

'He ran to me, but… another bolt hit him and he…
he went down. I… couldn't reach him. I tried, but the
druchii were all around and I…'

'You would have died trying to save him,' said Teclis.

'Yes,' nodded Eldain, tears of guilt streaming down
his cheeks. The fact that they were mistaken for tears of
grief made them harder to bear, but he choked back his
self-loathing and continued.

'There was nothing I could do and, Isha help me, I
rode away… I left him there. I thought he was dead,
but…'

'It would have been better for all of us if he *had* died
that day,' said the mage in the ragged green robe beside

Teclis. The Loremaster reached out and placed a withered hand on the mage's arm, the sorrow etched on his gaunt face matching that of his companion.

'Anurion the Green speaks a sad truth,' said Teclis, 'for it is clear now that Caelir did not die that day, but was taken alive by the druchii. A fate none gathered here can imagine.'

'I curse the day Caelir came to my household,' wept Anurion and Eldain felt the mage's sorrow cut lines of fire across his soul. 'My dear daughter would still be alive...'

Eldain shuddered as he felt the echo of a departed soul, heard her screams and felt the agony of her final moments. He saw from the reactions of those around him that they too sensed her passing.

The sadness of her death was like a poison in the air, though none turned away from it.

No one spoke for many minutes until Rhianna said, 'How did Caelir come to reach the Tower of Hoeth? Did he escape from the dungeons of Naggaroth? Is such a thing even possible?'

Teclis shook his head. 'No, none have escaped from such captivity.'

'Then how?' said Rhianna, shaking her head.

'Anurion tells me that his daughter found Caelir washed upon the beaches of Yvresse, bereft of his memory and muttering my name.'

'How could such a thing happen?' whispered Eldain.

'I do not know,' said Teclis, 'but it seems clear that the druchii must have hurled Caelir into the ocean of the Shifting Isles, knowing the waters would bring a true son of Ulthuan home. Master Anurion's daughter, Kyrielle, discovered him and nursed him in the home of her father. Caelir returned to health, and when Anurion's magic could not unlock his memory, he was brought to me.'

Mitherion leaned in close to Eldain and whispered, 'You see? Auspicious. Two brothers, divided by loss reunited at almost the exact moment…'

Eldain did not answer as Teclis continued. 'When Caelir stood before me I looked into his mind, but I saw no evil in him. I have given thought as to why this should be so and I believe that the goodness of his soul blinded me to the darkness placed within him.'

'Who could have placed such darkness within him?' demanded Anurion.

'There is only one amongst the druchii I know of with the power to rob someone of their memory and so cunningly conceal such a deadly trap,' said Teclis.

'The Hag Sorceress…' said Anurion, clutching at a delicate silver pendant at his breast.

Teclis nodded. 'Yes, Morathi.'

At the mention of she who had once been Aenarion's consort, a visible shudder went through the assembly, for her mastery of the black arts was the terror of those who stood against the druchii. No other being had opened the gates to the Chaos hells and emerged as powerful as she. Vile, unnatural blood rites kept her as youthful as the day she left the shores of Ulthuan over five thousand years ago, and even the strongest willed hero had been reduced to a brainless fool by her bewitching allure.

'It is my belief that Caelir was taken by the Hag Sorceress,' said Teclis, 'where his mind was broken by unnatural tortures.'

'No,' spat Anurion. 'I examined him thoroughly

before I attempted to unlock his memories. I saw no evidence of torture.'

'There are other forms of torture than those that are inflicted upon the body, Anurion. The Hag Sorceress has ways of reaching into the farthest depths of a mind to wring out its worst fears, its darkest desires and its secret lusts. There are ways to break a mind that leave no mark.'

Eldain fought against fresh tears as he tried to imagine the torments Caelir must have endured at the hands of the druchii. Better that he had cut his throat in his sleep than allow him to suffer such pain.

'Morathi is unmatched in her mastery of the darkest pleasures,' said Teclis. 'There is not one amongst us who could resist her wiles, not even me. We should not hate Caelir, my friends, we must pity him and we must help him, for it is clear to me that he did not do this thing knowingly or willingly. He will be frightened and desperate for answers, but his ultimate destiny is beyond my powers to see.

'We must find him and undo what has been done to him, for I fear that he has yet a part to play in events to come. I feel the touch of the druchii somewhere upon our shores and a Black Ark lurks on our southern coast. The destruction unleashed here is but the first stage in a grander scheme, my friends, one that aims to destroy us all.'

'So how do we find Caelir?' asked Eldain. 'He is my brother and if anyone is to hunt him it should be me.'

'Indeed it should, Lord Éadaoin,' agreed Teclis. 'As Master Silverfawn says, it is more than coincidence that you arrive here on the same day as your brother. Fate has delivered you to us and it is clear there is a bond between you and Caelir that goes beyond that of brotherhood. But you shall not hunt alone.'

Teclis turned to Rhianna, his shadowed eyes narrowing as he spoke. 'Amongst the confusion of Caelir's mind, I saw one thing brighter than all others. I saw your face, Lady Rhianna. Clearer than any other thought in his head, though even he is not fully aware of it.'

Rhianna held her head high as she said, 'Caelir and I were once betrothed.'

Teclis nodded, as though he had expected her answer. 'Yes, and that is why you must accompany Eldain. Together you must find Caelir and save him.'

'Caelir rides an Ellyrion steed,' pointed out Eldain. 'He will leave no sign of his passing. He could be anywhere by now.'

'How will we find him?' said Rhianna. 'Can your magic locate him, my lord?'

'No,' said Teclis. 'The key to finding Caelir lies with you, Rhianna, daughter of Mitherion. I cannot probe the forbidden mysteries of a daughter of Ulthuan, but the priestess of the Mother Goddess can.

'You must travel to the shrine of the Earth Mother within the Gaen Vale. She will tell you what you need to know.'

CHAPTER THIRTEEN

ARMIES

NO SUNLIGHT WARMED the Finuval Plain, though it lay within the Inner Kingdoms and would normally be spared harsh winters and perpetually bathed in balmy summers. A shadow passed over Caelir's soul as he rode from the entangling forests and beheld the plain where Prince Tyrion had led the desperate armies of the Asur to victory against the host of the Witch King.

Outwardly, the plain resembled the flatlands of Ellyrion or the rest of Saphery, but there was a distinct chill in the air, the memory of lives lost reaching from the past and touching the present.

Though he could have been little more than a babe in arms, Caelir still remembered the tales of this place, though, frustratingly, not the teller...

Two hundred years ago, the Witch King had led an invasion that cut a bloody swathe through Avelorn and threatened to completely overrun Ulthuan. The

Everqueen had been thought lost, though Prince Tyrion had rescued her from the clutches of assassins and kept her safe while the armies of the Phoenix King fought for the survival of the Asur.

This had been the darkest hour of Ulthuan since the days of Aenarion, but Tyrion had returned with the Everqueen to fight the final battle against the druchii and their infernal allies on the Finuval Plain.

The slaughter of that day still resonated across the bleak moor of Finuval, nature and history combining to create a melancholy mood that drove most right thinking people to seek other places to dwell. Civilisation had chosen not to take root here, save for wisps of smoke from the occasional remote village huddled in the twisting trails of sharply rising hills or upon the high cliffs of the coastline.

The path he followed curled around rounded hills smoothed by eons of wind and water, while clouds raced across the barren hillsides, their shadows swathing vast areas of the plain in darkness before swiftly moving on. Caelir's route narrowed as the ground dropped into the Finuval Plain, becoming a long, tight valley flanked by massive crags that loomed overhead like grim sentinels.

He rode down through three squat peaks separated by rocky ravines. He splashed through water dancing over stones as it sought to find the quickest way down the mountains in impromptu waterfalls. A few hardy trees clung to the streambeds, under the cliffs or any other place even vaguely protected from the biting wind that blew off the plain.

His mood soured in sympathy with the broken terrain and the long dead spirits of the battle fought here many years ago. He shivered in the darkness of the ravine, the long shadows draining his body and spirit of any warmth.

At last the rocky shingle of the ravine gave way to earth beneath his horse's hooves and the ground began to level out as he left the crags leading down to the plain behind.

Before him, the Finuval Plain stretched out in an endless vista of broken moorland and withered heath. There would be no hiding in this place and all he could do would be to cross the ancient battlefield as quickly as he was able and hope any pursuers would be similarly discomfited by the melancholy that seeped from every square yard of this place.

He rode onwards, the black steed making good time though he had not stopped to feed or water it for some time. The horse had welcomed him as a rider, as though they shared some kinship he was not aware of, and he was grateful for such a blessing.

Though apparently deserted, it was soon clear to Caelir that others still travelled the Finuval Plain. He saw recent hoofprints and the long trails of what looked to be the wheel ruts of a caravan or wagon, though he had no idea as to who might choose to travel this way.

The morning receded into the afternoon and as the day wore on, Caelir saw more and more relics of the great battle fought here. Broken speartips and snapped sword blades jutted from the ground, and here and there he caught sight of a splintered shield. He saw no bones, for those of his people would have been gathered up and those of the druchii would have been burned.

He kept his thoughts focused on the journey ahead,

letting his horse find its own path across the windswept plain, the ghosts and echoes of the battle leeching any thoughts of his own from his mind as surely as though he were drunk on dreamwine. He tried to remember the warrior he believed was his brother, but found himself becoming inexplicably angry every time he summoned his face.

Each thought of anger was dispelled as soon as he thought of the golden haired elf maid who had accompanied him. He wished he could remember her, for she was a balm on his soul and he would often catch himself indulging in daydreams where they rode the mountains, her atop a steed with glittering silver flanks and he upon a grey mare…

He shook off such dreams, knowing they could never come to pass, miserable and angry in equal measure.

As night fell and a hunter's moon rose above the mountains, he drew near a bare, rounded hillock in the midst of the battlefield. A collection of barrow mounds had been raised around the circumference of its base and each was topped by a tapering menhir carved with spiralling, runic patterns.

Elven hands had clearly fashioned these mausoleums in ages past, for there was a grace and symmetry to each that was beyond the skill of the lesser races. Darkness framed by marble pilasters and lintels led inside, but Caelir felt no compulsion to venture within, for the echoes of the dead were strong here and they jealously guarded their final resting places.

A low mist hugged the ground and Caelir wrapped his cloak tighter about himself as he contemplated riding through the night. Though his horse had valiantly borne him from the White Tower without complaint, he knew that it would need rest soon or else he risked riding it into the ground.

He looked for somewhere to rest, but could see nowhere that would offer more shelter from the wind than the spaces between the barrows at the base of the hillock. As much as he did not relish the prospect of spending the night in such close proximity to these monuments of battle, he felt no threat from the dead gathered here, for they were defenders of Ulthuan and they watched over this land.

Caelir made a quick circuit of the round hillock before dismounting and hobbling his horse next to a mausoleum with a graceful arched entrance. A cold wind gusted from within like a sigh and he bowed respectfully before finding a patch of dry, flat earth upon which to lay his saddle blanket.

He wrapped himself tightly in his cloak and settled down to sleep.

WHEN HE AWOKE, he saw stars above him, but not the stars beneath which he had fallen asleep. The mist that had been gathering when he had stopped for the night was thicker than before, but only now did he see that it was no ordinary mist.

Elves moved within it, ghostly warriors in armour of times past limned in silver light who marched around the hillock in grim procession. He rose to his feet, amazed at how refreshed he felt and turned to look up at the hillock.

And gasped in horror as he saw his still sleeping form curled on the ground.

Caelir lifted his hands to his face as he saw the same spectral light that outlined the ghosts emanating from his own flesh. In panic he reached down to his body, but his fingertips simply vanished within as though he were no more than an apparition.

'Am I dead?' he asked himself, but as he saw the rhythmic rise and fall of his sleeping form, he slowly came to the realisation that he was still alive.

Caelir watched the marching warriors for a time, their ranks swelling as an endless tide of sentinels emerged from the arched entrances to the barrows. He wondered what purpose this moonlit vigil served and glanced up at the top of the hillock, where he saw a shadow where no shadow ought to be, a sliver of darkness against the moon.

A figure stood there, etched against the night as though an evil memory had been caught in time and now raged at its captivity at the hands of these ghostly warriors.

Though no more solid than smoke and memory, the shape wore the suggestion of armour, as though this were a revenant of the battle fought here long ago. It raged biliously, and Caelir took a step towards the shape, something in its armoured darkness familiar and repulsive.

It towered above the battlefield, green orbs of malice staring out from behind the cruel curves of its mighty, horned helmet and Caelir felt his legs go weak as he realised that he looked upon the black imprint on time left by the Witch King of Naggaroth.

His pulse quickened, though how such a thing could be possible in ghost form he didn't know. This figure of evil had lurked in the darkest nightmares of the Asur for thousands of years, yet few had laid eyes upon him and lived to tell of it.

With sudden, awful certainty, Caelir knew that he could count himself amongst their number. Though he had no memory of the event, he knew he had stared into those eyes and had felt his soul shrivel beneath their awful gaze.

'What did you do to me?' he shouted, dropping to his knees. 'Tell me!'

The shadow at the top of the hillock did not answer him or even acknowledge his presence, for it was merely an echo, a phantom of that bloody day when the fate of Ulthuan had been decided in blood and magic upon the Finuval Plain.

Caelir lay down on the glittering grass of the hillock and wept silver tears.

And the spectral guardians continued to circle.

THE AQUILA SPIRE was now clean and pristine, the very model of a noble commander's quarters, though Glorien had taken the sensible precaution of having the Eagle Gate's mages cast a warding spell upon the open window. A precaution the late Cerion Goldwing would have been well advised to implement, he thought wryly.

The blood of his former commander had been washed away and Cerion's personal keepsakes sent back to his family in Eataine, together with a detailed letter in which Glorien had outlined the unfortunate events that had led to his death, together with several suggestions he had made previously on how such a tragedy could have been prevented.

That he had made no such suggestions was immaterial, but they would enhance his reputation as a warrior of vision and sense; and if his time at the court of Lothern had taught Glorien Truecrown anything, it was that reputation and perception was everything.

The Eagle Gate was his now and with the elderly Cerion out of the way, albeit in a bloodier way than he would have preferred, he was free to run this fortress the way it ought to be run. A neat row of bookshelves now occupied the far wall, stacked high with treatises on the art of war by great heroes of Ulthuan. Mentheus of Caledor's great texts, *Heart of Khaine* and *Honour and Duty*, sat next to *In Service of the Phoenix* and *The Way of Kurnous* by Caradryel of Yvresse. Other, lesser works, gathered over his years of advancement, had been read and devoured, each with its own specific instructions on how the military might of the Asur must be properly commanded.

Heart of Khaine sat open before him and the words of General Mentheus filled him with the glories of ancient times in the long wars against the druchii. Now that this fortress was his, he would organise and run things the way the books told him they should be done, not in the slapdash, ad hoc way that Cerion had advocated with his talk of hearts and minds.

No, a garrison of high elf warriors respected discipline and he would ensure they received it in abundance. Glorien snapped shut the book and returned it to the bookshelf before turning to the armour rack beside him.

He already wore his mail shirt beneath his tunic; the assassin's attack had made him cautious if nothing else, and lifted his gleaming silver helmet. The glorious, conical helm was a masterpiece of elven craftsmanship and cost more than the combined pay of every soldier stationed at the Eagle Gate. Its ithilmar surface was decorated in embossed filigree and the edges lined with fluted gold piping. Nothing so crude as a visor would obscure his features, for how would those around him see his face?

A carved golden flame rose above the forehead of the helmet, and Glorien longed to add wings to its side, white feathered wings that would proclaim his courage to all who looked upon him. Only the High Helm of a troop of Silver Helms was permitted to adorn his helmet with such things – a petty regulation that only served those who chose a more prosaic, obvious route to glory by riding a horse straight at the enemy.

He slipped the helm over his head and checked his appearance in the full-length mirror that sat opposite his desk.

The warrior reflected in the silvered glass was every inch the perfect commander, the very image of Aenarion himself. Long hair spilled from beneath his helmet and his patrician features were exquisitely framed by the curve of his helmet's cheek plates. An elegantly cut tunic, fashioned by the most sought after tailors of Lothern perfectly fit his slender frame and he wore wyvern skin boots, crafted from the hide of a beast slain by his father's hunters.

Satisfied with his appearance, he turned as a knock came at the door to the chamber.

'Yes?' he asked.

'Lord Truecrown,' said the voice of Menethis, his adjutant. 'It is time for your dawn inspection.'

'Of course it is,' he said, straightening his tunic and opening the door.

Menethis stood to one side as Glorien emerged from the Aquila Spire to take a deep breath of crisp mountain air and survey his command.

Dawn's first light was easing over the eastern horizon and the stark whiteness of the Eagle Gate glittered with armoured warriors holding spears and bows at precisely the right angle. Bolt throwers on the parapets of the high towers were manned by crews standing to attention and blue banners fluttered in a bitingly cold wind from the west.

As much as Glorien knew this assignment to the Eagle Gate would advance his career, he looked forward to his next posting when the garrison was rotated to another command and where he would not have to suffer the chill blowing in from the ocean.

'A fine sight, eh, Menethis?' said Glorien, setting off down the steps and pulling a pair of kidskin gloves from his belt.

'Yes, my lord,' said Menethis, quickly catching up to him. 'Though if I might make an observation regarding your inspection?'

Glorien scowled and paused in his descent. As much as it chafed him to listen to the prattling of his underlings, the writings of Caradryel spoke of how a good leader should take counsel from those around him.

'Go ahead.'

'I wonder if it might improve the morale of the warriors to conduct such formal inspections with less regularity? Perhaps a weekly inspection would better serve our needs?'

'Weekly? And have the discipline of the garrison slide in between? Out of the question. Why would you even suggest such a thing?'

Menethis averted his eyes as he spoke, saying, 'It is tiring on the warriors, my lord.'

'Tiring?' snapped Glorien. 'Soldiering is *supposed* to be

tiring. It's not meant to be an easy life.'

'Yes, but we have only so many warriors, and to defend the wall as fully as you deem necessary allows no rest time in between the guard rotas. Each warrior has barely enough time to sleep, let alone maintain his weapons and armour to the high standards you demand.'

'You think my standards too high, Menethis?'

'No, my lord, but perhaps some leeway–'

'Leeway? Like Cerion Goldwing permitted?' demanded Glorien. 'I think not. Look where that got him, an assassin's blade between his ribs. No, it is thanks to such lax enforcement of discipline that soldiers like Alathenar think they can get away with leaving their bows unstringed while on duty. I was lenient in simply confining him to barracks. He deserved to be sent home in disgrace.'

'Alathenar *did* wound the assassin who murdered Lord Goldwing,' pointed out Menethis. 'No one else managed that.'

'Yes, the archer may have a decent eye, but that does not give him the right to flaunt regulations. And anyway, it was that eagle that caught the assassin,' said Cerion waving a dismissive hand as he remembered the gruesome sight of the druchii's corpse.

A magnificent white-headed eagle had flown back to the fortress and deposited the bloody remains of Cerion Goldwing's assassin upon the battlements, though quite what it had expected them to do with them, it had not said.

Before Glorien could speak to the creature, it had spread its wings and flown northwards, leaving them to deal with its kill.

Glorien understood that war was a bloody business

from his books, but to see such a gory mess had been highly unsettling to an elf of his refined sensibilities.

He shook his head and set off once again. 'No, Menethis, we will continue with dawn inspections and daily drilling. I will tolerate no laxness among my command and, tired or not, I demand the highest standards of readiness and competence from every warrior. Is that understood?'

'Yes, my lord,' said Menethis.

Glorien nodded, satisfied his orders were clear, and made his way along the length of the wall. His warriors stood to attention, each one a tall, proud and noble specimen of elven soldiery. He reached the Eagle Tower at the centre of the wall and climbed the curving steps cut into the back of the carven head.

He emerged onto a recessed battlement in the neck of the great carving where sat a trio of Eagle's Claw bolt throwers. These mighty weapons were the elite of his command, powerful weapons resembling a huge bow laid upon its side and mounted upon an elegantly crafted tripod carriage. As with so many martial creations of the Asur, the bolt throwers merged art and warfare, such that each weapon resembled a majestic eagle in flight, with the apex of the bow worked in gold to resemble the noble head of the birds of prey.

Each weapon could fire a single bolt capable of bringing down the most terrifying monsters or a hail of smaller shafts that would scythe through enemy warriors at a far greater speed than any group of archers could manage.

Individually, these weapons were fearsome, but grouped together they were utterly deadly. Nine more such machines were spread along the length of the wall, and Glorien nodded to himself as he saw that each weapon gleamed with fresh oil and that the golden windlass mechanisms were spotless.

The crews appeared tired but proud, and he rewarded them with a smile of appreciation. Their armour gleamed and their white tunics were crisp and pristine. Each carried a long spear, a weapon Glorien had decided was more in keeping with his idea of how such warriors should be armed.

He turned to make his way back down to the wall when one of the crewman next to him shouted in alarm, 'Target sighted!'

All three crews leapt into action, discarding their spears and seizing wooden 'combs' that contained enough bolts for several volleys. One crewman slotted the comb onto the groove rail on top of the weapon, while the other sighted it.

Glorien stood back and watched, pleased at the alacrity of the crews, but irritated that they had simply dropped their spears to the ground.

Within moments, all three weapons were ready to fire and Glorien awaited the distinctive, rippling *crack-twang* of bolts being loosed.

'Why aren't they unleashing?' he asked when the weapons didn't open up.

'There is no need,' said Menethis, pointing to the western horizon. 'Look!'

Glorien squinted into the dim light of morning and saw three shapes flying towards the Eagle Gate. At first he didn't recognise them for what they were, but when he noticed the distinctive white head on the lead bird, he saw they were eagles.

'One of them carries something,' observed Menethis.

Glorien sighed. 'Another bloody offering perhaps. I don't remember Cerion Goldwing being presented with everything these birds killed. Come on then, I suppose we ought to see what they've brought us this time.'

Menethis followed him as he made his way back down to the ramparts and the crews of the bolt throwers made their weapons safe once more.

By the time he had descended to the wall, the eagles were much closer and Glorien could see that the white-headed eagle carried another body. Exactly what it was, he couldn't yet see, but it appeared to be swaddled in a red cloak.

The warriors on the wall cheered as the eagles approached, for the sight of an eagle over a battlefield was an omen of victory and Glorien permitted them this brief moment of relaxation.

He marched to the centre of the battlements and watched as the trio of eagles circled lower and lower until they landed before him in a boom of outstretched wings. The eagle bearing the red-cloaked burden gently laid it at Glorien's feet and he saw that it was not some bloody trophy torn by claws or beak, but an elven warrior in the accoutrements of an Ellyrion Reaver.

The eagles stepped back as Menethis knelt by the warrior and unwrapped the blood-stiffened cloak from around him. Glorien's lip curled in distaste as he saw the paleness of the wounded elf's features.

'Is he alive?'

'Yes,' said Menethis, 'though he is badly hurt. We must get him to our healers if he is to live.'

The bloodied warrior's eyes flickered open at the sound of elven voices and he struggled to speak.

'What is your name, warrior?' said Glorien.

'Druchii...' hissed the warrior through bloodstained teeth, his voice barely a whisper.

'What did he say?'

'He said "druchii", my lord,' replied Menethis.

'What does he mean? Quickly, ask him!'

'He needs a healer!' protested Menethis.

'Ask him, damn you!'

Menethis turned to the wounded elf, but he spoke again without prompting. 'I... I am Eloien Redcloak of Ellyrion. My warriors... all dead. The druchii... landed at Cairn Anroc. An army of them. Druchii and corrupted men. Coming here...'

'How close are they?' demanded Glorien. 'When will they reach us?'

Eloien's eyes shut, but as he slipped into unconsciousness he said, 'By... tomorrow...'

Glorien felt a cold in his bones that had nothing to do with the winds blowing over the walls of the fortress as the bird that had borne the wounded Eloien Redcloak threw back its head and let out a deafening screech.

The druchii are coming, he thought. By tomorrow.

Isha preserve us...

Chapter Fourteen

Companions

WARM SUNLIGHT FILLED the pavilion, but the warrior within cared little for the delicate aromas carried on the cooling breeze. He stood naked but for a white loincloth as two of the beauteous handmaidens of the Everqueen oiled his flesh before scraping him clean with ironwood knives.

His muscles were hard as stone and perfectly sculpted, the perfection of his form marred only by the many scars that crossed his body. All these old wounds were to the fore and it was clear that this warrior had faced every enemy head on and had never once retreated from a fight.

Long blond hair streamed from his temples and the maidens bound it into braids with iron cords to prevent an enemy blade from cutting it and depriving him of his strength in the midst of war. Not that there were any skilled enough to perform such a feat, for this was Prince

Tyrion of Avelorn, greatest warrior of the age.

He raised his arms and a long shirt of white was slipped over his muscled arms and shoulders, before being secured at the front with silver ties and buttons. Swiftly the handmaidens dressed Tyrion in soft leggings of pale blue before retreating to the corners of the pavilion as he sat a thin diadem of gold upon his brow.

Tyrion's face was thunderous and at odds with the sounds of music and laughter that drifted in through the rolled sides of the pavilion. A burning pain filled his thoughts and his limbs ached as though he had been fighting continuously for a week.

Though his training and practice sessions with the Everqueen's handmaidens had been as rigorous as ever he knew that this pain within him had a very different origin.

Teclis…

Ever since their youth, he and his twin brother had shared a bond that not even the wisest of the Loremasters could explain. What one felt, the other felt and now he experienced a measure of his brother's pain as though inflicted upon his own body. Over impossible gulfs, each twin knew how fared the other and Tyrion knew some dreadful evil had befallen Teclis with every fibre of his being.

He closed his eyes and let the sound of the forest wash over him, hoping the gentle rhythms of his queen's realm would soothe the troubles and pain that weighed heavily upon him.

He opened his eyes and stared at the suit of magnificent golden armour hanging on a wooden rack across the pavilion from him. No finer suit of armour had ever been forged, by elven craft or dwarven skill, and the sunlight seemed to flicker with an inner flame within its burnished plates.

Forged within Vaul's Anvil, the Dragon Armour of Aenarion had been worn by his legendary forefather, the Phoenix King who had saved Ulthuan from the forces of Chaos in ancient times.

Tyrion's father had presented the armour to him before the great victory of Finuval Plain and he had worn it in every battle since, its siren song to war never far from his thoughts.

As wondrous as the armour was, Tyrion knew it was a relic of a time long passed, a time when the mad fury of Aenarion waxed mightily and the fiery soul of the elven race had burned brightly upon the face of the world.

Such times were lost now and each time he donned the armour, he felt that loss keenly.

'It calls to you, does it not?' said a voice behind him and he smiled at the soothing, feminine tone as the words flowed like honey into his mind.

'It does, my lady,' said Tyrion, turning and dropping to one knee before his queen. 'The curse of Aenarion lives on within his armour.'

The sun's glory flowed with her and the pavilion was filled with light that had no source yet seemed to carry all the goodness and warmth of summer. The scent of fresh blossoms came to him and Tyrion felt his pain diminish and the warlike call of the armour recede.

'It surely does,' agreed the Everqueen and warm rain pattered softly on the roof of the pavilion. 'His madness lives on and casts a shadow over us all, but please, my prince, stand. You of all people need not kneel before me.'

'I will always bend the knee to you, my lady,' said

Tyrion, looking into the face of the most beautiful woman imaginable, the blessed child of Isha and most beloved scion of Ulthuan.

'And I can never disobey you,' he said with a smile, rising smoothly to his feet.

The Everqueen of Ulthuan moved without effort, her every gesture graceful beyond measure and her every word like the sound of spring's first song. Her long gown clung to her shapely form and it filled his heart with love to have her near him.

Her name was Alarielle, the Everqueen of Ulthuan, and it was said her beauty could move even the immortal gods.

Just to have her address him was the most sublime pleasure, and to be her champion was an honour for which Tyrion knew he would never be worthy. Beyond her immaculate beauty, the Everqueen was bound to the land of Ulthuan like no other elf. Where she walked, new blooms followed in her wake. Where she sang, the world was a gentler place and when she cried, the heavens wept with her.

'You would leave without saying farewell?' she said.

Tyrion bowed his head. 'War is coming, my lady. I am needed elsewhere.'

'I know,' she said and the light dimmed as she spoke. 'I too have felt the tread of those who worship the Lord of Murder upon our land. They come with the followers of the Dark Gods to wreak great wrong against us.'

'Then it is even more imperative I leave now, my lady.'

'You go to your brother?'

'I do,' said Tyrion. 'I feel his pain and I must go to him.'

'Yes,' nodded the Everqueen. 'You must, but promise

me you will heed what he says, for your heart will be filled with anger and you will seek to avenge his hurt.'

'I will,' promised Tyrion as the two handmaidens lifted his armour from the rack and began buckling it to his body. Breastplate, greaves, vambrace, gorget and pauldrons; each was fitted to his form as though designed for him and him alone.

With each piece of armour placed upon his body, Tyrion felt the peace brought by the Everqueen diminish and the warlike spirit of his people surge through his veins. Lastly he lifted his mighty weapon, the runesword, Sunfang, a blade forged in elder days to be the bane of daemons.

Tyrion buckled on his sword belt and accepted the last piece of his armour, a fabulously ornate helm decorated with glittering gems and sweeping golden wings. He reached up and slid the helmet down over his head, feeling the fire of Aenarion's legacy overwhelm the last of his gentler qualities.

He turned to face the Everqueen and said, 'I am ready now.'

'May Asuryan watch over you, my champion,' said the Everqueen, moving aside to let him pass.

Tyrion marched from the pavilion into a clearing within the forest of his queen, a wondrous kingdom of dreams that nestled beneath a patchwork sky of deepest blue. Tall trees with great, arching canopies of emerald green surrounded him and the sound of crystal laughter drifted from beneath their enchanted boughs.

Darting sprites whipped through the undergrowth and glimmering lights ghosted in the deepest reaches of the forest. Magic was in the air, taken deep into the lungs with every breath, and Tyrion felt an ache in his heart that he must leave.

Music and song filled the air and beautiful elves of both sexes danced beneath a rain of petals, garlanded with flowers and laughing as though the cares of the world were unimportant and far distant.

For a moment Tyrion despised them. What did such revellers know of the blood he had shed and the sacrifices he had made to keep them safe? How dare they dance and sing as though the darkness of the world was not their concern?

He was gripping Sunfang's hilt when a gentle hand touched his and the rage fled from his body.

'Calm yourself, my prince,' said the Everqueen. 'Do not let the curse of your forefather lead you down the same path he once trod. You resisted the call of the Widowmaker once, you will do so again.'

Tyrion let out a deep breath and turned as he heard the whinny of horses approaching and the joyous note of a silver clarion. He saw a group of armoured knights on horseback, a silver assemblage of glorious warriors in gleaming ithilmar armour and shimmering white robes. Their silver helms were polished to a mirror sheen and they carried long white lances tipped with blades that shone like diamonds in the dappling sun.

Each rode a pale white horse, draped in cloth of blue and white and armoured in flexible ithilmar barding that caught the sunlight in a multitude of glittering sparks.

At the head of the knights rode Belarien, Tyrion's boon companion and most trusted lieutenant. Alone of the knights, his helmet was furnished with a set of feathered wings that swept back from the cheek plates, indicating that he was the leader of this warrior band.

Belarien led a magnificent white stallion sheathed in a caparison of deepest blue and armoured in a similar fashion to the other horses of the knights, though with a girth of gold and gems encircling his deep chest. But as Tyrion was above the knights, so too was his horse more magnificent than those of the Silver Helms.

This was Malhandir, a gift from the kingdom of Ellyrion and last of the bloodline of Korhandir, father of horses. No finer mount existed in the world and Tyrion felt a measure of his war-lust ease as he went to meet his steed.

Belarien handed him the reins and Tyrion climbed smoothly into the saddle as a crowd gathered to watch the knights depart. The Everqueen's handmaidens sang songs of glory and musicians played epic laments from elder days as the knights' guidon unfurled Tyrion's personal banner.

The knights cheered as the wind caught the long streamer of crimson silk, revealing an embroidered golden phoenix entwined with the Everqueen's silver dove.

Tyrion looked down from his horse and bowed his head towards the shimmering beauty of the Everqueen.

She smiled and a beam of yellow sunlight speared through the treetops to shine through the silken banner.

Tyrion felt his spirits soar, watching the phoenix ripple as though aflame.

'Knights of the Silver Helm!' he cried. 'We ride for Saphery!'

CAELIR RODE THROUGH the morning, pushing the black horse hard as he journeyed towards the northern horizon. Though the battle of Finuval Plain had spread throughout the northern reaches of Saphery, he had ridden through the heart of it at last and the melancholy gloom of the moor receded with each mile that passed beneath him.

He had woken upon the hillock where the Witch King himself had stood on that fateful day when Teclis had struck him down and banished him from Ulthuan once more. Whether Caelir had been in any danger from the dark shadow from the past, he did not know, but if he *had* been imperilled, the spirits of the fallen Asur had recognised him as one of their own and kept him safe.

The image of the Witch King still burned in his mind, but it was a phantom, fading like a dream as he travelled onwards. The further he rode from the battlefield, the more he felt the elven land come to life, as though the magic of Saphery was only now reclaiming land tainted by the tread of its enemies.

He crossed slender rivers that flowed crystalline through the landscape and Caelir quenched his thirst in their waters, though hunger still gnawed at his belly. A night's rest had refreshed his horse, and each time they stopped to rest, it ate heartily of the verdant grasses. His steed would have no problem reaching Avelorn, but he was going to need some nourishment before then.

Caelir reckoned upon reaching the realm of the Everqueen with perhaps another few days' ride and he could just make out the bright green limits of the northern forests.

He had seen yet more signs of travellers, the trails of wagons and horsemen riding side by side across the moor now a familiar sight, and had decided to follow them in the hope of obtaining some food. He had no coin with which to buy it, but he still had the strange dagger that could not be drawn. It was of little use to anyone, but perhaps one of the travellers would find it curious enough to trade for a little sustenance.

Some hours after midday, Caelir and his mount reached a shallow ford and waded through the water. He tilted his head back, enjoying the cold, crispness of the meltwater as it splashed on the rocks marking the crossing and filled the air with refreshing spray and glittering rainbows.

On the other side of the river, he saw deep tracks in the sodden earth of the riverbank and slid from his saddle to examine them. Whatever other memories he had forgotten, he had not lost his skills as a tracker and knew this trail was no more than a few hours old.

Caelir leapt back onto his horse and rode onwards, pushing harder than he would normally dare. Darkness would be upon him soon and he had no wish to spend another night alone upon the Finuval Plain, even far out on the fringes of the battlefield.

The sun dipped into the west and the sky deepened from shimmering blue to dusky purple. He had all but despaired of catching up to the travellers before him when he saw a series of twinkling lights ahead, shining silver and gold in the gloaming.

He slowed his pace as he saw that the lights were not moving and heard voices raised in song followed by enthusiastic clapping. Music soared and he heard unabashed laughter wrung from many throats.

As Caelir drew closer, he saw three brightly painted carriages drawn up in a curved line, each decorated with gleaming lacquer that shone in the light of oil burners suspended from tall staves arranged in a circle around a colourful rug. A crowd of elves sprawled languidly on the ground before the rug, its surface decorated with twisting symbols and patterns that drew the eye in confusing spirals.

A delicate elf maid with winsome features danced in the centre of the rug, spinning and leaping with joy as music flowed through her. She danced with her eyes closed, her limbs flowing fluidly around her and her body seeming to float in the air as though held aloft by the notes.

Caelir saw the musicians at the side of the wide rug and for a fleeting second he had the distinct impression that the music was playing *them*, its desire to be heard and enjoyed using their breath and fingers as a means to manifest its bounty.

The audience watched the performance with rapturous eyes and Caelir found he could not tear his eyes from the maiden's sensuous dance. Her skin gleamed in the torchlight and the gossamer thin fabric of her slip clung to her lithe, athletic form.

The music shifted in tempo, becoming faster and faster and driving the dancing girl to incredible heights of ecstasy. The audience whooped and cried as her form became a twisting blur of radiant skin and light.

Then suddenly it was over, the music died and the dancing girl made one final leap into the air. She twisted as she descended and landed gracefully in the centre of the rug, her head thrown back and her arms outstretched.

Applause exploded from the audience and Caelir found himself joining in, desperate to show his appreciation for this incredible performance.

The sound of clapping faded as the gathering became aware of his presence and he felt himself blush as open faces turned towards him with curious expressions.

Caelir slid from the back of his horse as a tall elf with lush features and long silver hair moved from the audience and came towards him. He extended his hand to Caelir.

'Welcome, dear boy, I am Narentir,' said the elf, his voice lyrical. 'Will you join us?'

'Caelir,' he replied. 'And yes, I will join you.'

'Most excellent,' said Narentir, guiding him towards the firelight. 'I take it you liked Lilani's performance then?'

Caelir nodded and the dancing girl threw him a coquettish grin before vacating the rug as other performers took her place.

'Very much,' said Caelir as Narentir handed him a silver goblet of smoky, aromatic wine. 'I have never seen anyone move like her.'

'I shouldn't think you have, she's a rare jewel is our Lilani.'

Smiling faces surrounded him as Narentir led him into the audience gathered about the rug. They were genuinely pleased to see him and Caelir felt the tension within his chest ease at the sincerity of the welcome.

He took a drink from the goblet and gasped in pleasure as it ran like liquid smoke down his throat. The wine was sweet, almost unbearably so, and its bouquet was that of a wild forest where creatures of legend still roamed free. Caelir smiled as it conjured visions of fabulous gardens, sun-dappled glades and the scent of honeysuckle and jasmine.

'You've never had dreamwine before, have you?' said Narentir as they sat beside the rug and the musicians began to play once more.

'Yes,' said Caelir, giddy from the taste, 'but this is good. Very good.'

'Be careful, though,' said Narentir. 'You shouldn't drink too much of it.'

'I have a strong stomach.'

'It's not your stomach you need worry about,' smiled Narentir as he took another drink.

'No?'

Narentir laughed. 'Do as you will, dear Caelir. Perhaps it will help your performance.'

'My performance? What performance?'

'Everyone takes their turn upon the rug.'

'But I'm not a singer and I can't dance,' said Caelir.

Narentir smiled. 'That doesn't matter. I'm sure you'll think of something.'

Caelir opened his mouth to protest, but the elves standing on the rug began their performance and all other sounds ceased as they sang ancient songs of love and rapture. He wanted to tell Narentir that he could not entertain them, but his enjoyment of the singers drew out a remembrance of the unknown talents Kyrielle had discovered within him.

Another sip of wine relaxed him and Caelir smiled contentedly as he settled back to listen to the performance. The singers' voices were exquisite, their music and lyrics swirling around the torchlit gathering like an unexpected, but wholly welcome guest.

Tears pricked Caelir's eyes as he felt his soul take flight in time with their achingly beautiful melodies.

THE RIDE BACK to Cairn Auriel was without the magic that had accompanied the ride towards the White Tower. It felt strange not to be riding Lotharin, though Irenya was a fine steed and bore him proudly on her back.

They rode in silence for much of the way, Rhianna lost in thought and Eldain unwilling to break the silence for fear of what might be said. Yvraine once again rode with them, Mitherion Silverfawn insisting that the young Sword Master accompany them, though now she rode a powerful Sapherian gelding.

After seeing her martial prowess in battle, Eldain wasn't inclined to gainsay the mage, and welcomed her presence. If war *were* coming to Ulthuan, there were worse things to have at your side than a Sword Master of Hoeth.

The land itself seemed to recognise the strained mood that had settled upon them and restrained its more outlandish excesses of enchantment. Magic still permeated every breath and whispering sprites gusted through the long grasses with wild abandon, but Eldain paid such sights no mind, too preoccupied with Caelir's survival and the absurd notion of hunting his own brother.

The subject of what would happen when they caught up with Caelir had arisen when they drew near the cliff top path that led down to Cairn Auriel.

'I wonder if he will remember us,' said Rhianna, breaking the silence of their journey.

'I don't know,' said Eldain. 'He didn't seem to back at the tower.'

'But maybe seeing us jogged his memory, brought something back.'

'Perhaps, but will it make any difference if he does remember us?'

'It will to me,' said Rhianna. 'I can't bear the thought of him forgetting us.'

'Us?'

'You. Me. His life. Can you imagine how that must feel, Eldain? Not remembering your childhood, your parents, your friends–'

'Your lovers?' interrupted Eldain and he hated the caustic tone he heard in his voice.

Rhianna sighed. 'Is that what you are afraid of? That if Caelir's memory returns and we get him back that I will leave you for him?'

'Wouldn't you? You were betrothed to him once.'

Rhianna rode close to Eldain and reached out to take his hand. 'Caelir is alive and for that I give thanks to Isha, but I have made a commitment to *you*, Eldain. You are my husband and I love you.'

Eldain felt his throat constrict and squeezed Rhianna's hand, wishing he could truly believe what she was saying. 'I'm sorry. I just… I just don't want to lose you. I lost you to him once before and… I don't think I could again.'

'You won't, Eldain,' promised Rhianna. 'I can't deny that seeing Caelir again brought back a lot of emotions, but much has changed since he and I were together. You and I are married. And there is blood on his hands.'

There is blood on his hands…

Eldain fought down the guilty nausea building in his stomach as Yvraine said, 'There is also the question of what happened to him in Naggaroth. The druchii held him in the dungeons of the Witch King for over a year. The Caelir you both knew may no longer exist.'

'What do you mean?'

'I have heard it said that the loyal slave learns to love the lash,' said the Sword Master. 'Your brother may yet be an enemy of Ulthuan.'

'What are you saying?' said Eldain, hearing a cold anger in Yvraine's voice.

'I am saying that when we find Caelir, we may have to kill him.'

'Kill him?'

Yvraine nodded. 'Who knows what else he has been sent back to do? What if the trap to catch the Loremaster was just the first of his missions of assassination?'

'I cannot kill my own brother,' said Eldain, forcing the words from his mouth when he saw Rhianna's look of horror at what Yvraine had just said.

'You may have to,' said Yvraine as she reached the cliff top path. 'But if you can't, I will.'

The Sword Master rode onto the path that led down the cliff to Cairn Auriel and Eldain and Rhianna shared a look of unease as they followed her. The idea that their hunt might end in blood had clearly not occurred to her, but in Eldain's mind it had been the only possible outcome.

As he watched Rhianna ride onto the path, cold resolve hardened in his heart and he knew he would have no hesitation in striking Caelir down should the fates decree they stand face to face once again.

He had come so far and gained so much that he could not bear the thought of losing everything again. The guilt would always be with him, but no burden was too great to keep Rhianna by his side, no deed unthinkable and no price too steep.

A small fleet of ships bobbed in the glittering blue water against the floating quays of Cairn Auriel and red tiled dwellings rose up in tiered layers from the sea. Eldain thought the scene unbearably sad, picturing druchii ships sailing into the bay and fanatical warriors of the Witch King butchering women and children as the streets ran red with blood.

He shook off such grim images and rode onto the path. The blooms garlanded around the trellises were now white flowers of spring and the fragrances were those of the dawn.

Eldain passed beneath the flowers and picked his way carefully down to the settlement.

CAPTAIN BELLAEIR WAS pleased to see them again, for it sat ill with him to have a crew idle when there were seas to cross and magical winds to be caught in the sails. His sailors had made friends with the other crews berthed in the harbour and news and rumours from across Ulthuan had quickly passed between them.

Yet more druchii ships had been spotted off the southern coasts of Ulthuan, but had apparently made no forays to shore. The skies above the Annulii were thick with birds crossing from one side of the island to the other and it was said that the magical currents roaring through the mountains were becoming more powerful.

More and more creatures were coming down from the mountains, drawn there by the dangerous currents of magic, and hunters from Chrace were fighting a near constant battle against unnatural monsters preying upon the inhabitants of the northern kingdoms.

Vaul's Anvil rumbled and smoked as though the smith god himself was displeased and one crew claimed to have been caught in a storm in the seas around Avelorn, a sure sign of dark times ahead. Most of the other crews had scoffed at such a tale, but upon seeing the battering the ship had taken and the blackened scars of lightning impacts, they had retreated to their own vessels to ponder this evil omen.

More worrying, however, was the news that the druchii had landed on the western coast of Ulthuan. No one seemed to know exactly where, but as Eldain recalled Mitherion Silverfawn's warning of terrible danger descending on Ellyr-charoi, he feared the druchii were even now marching upon one of the gateway fortresses that protected Ellyrion.

All across Ulthuan, citizen levies were being armed for war and portents of doom were being reported from Yvresse to Tiranoc. As they had ridden through Cairn Auriel, Eldain had felt the potent fear of its inhabitants upon the air like a contagion.

Captain Bellaeir had taken the liberty of purchasing supplies for the journey, though he had not liked the news of their destination.

'The Gaen Vale?' he said with a frown. 'Not a place for the likes of us.'

'No,' agreed Eldain, 'but we have no choice. The Loremaster himself has despatched us.'

Bellaeir nodded absently and looked out to sea. 'I have sailed the waters of the Inner Seas for many years, my lord. When Finubar the Seafarer became the Phoenix King I saw the ironwood ship carrying him to the Shrine of Asuryan and followed long enough to see the great flame. In my youth, I sailed as close as any have dared to the Isle of the Dead and I saw the day of my own passing.

'But in all my years as a seafarer, I have never once thought to venture near the Gaen Vale. The warrior women of the Mother Goddess jealously guard its shores and no male dares to set foot on that island. Any that try are never seen again.'

'Then you and I will be sure to remain on board the

Dragonkin while Rhianna and Yvraine go ashore,' said Eldain.

Bellaeir sighed and left Eldain standing at the quay, directing Rhianna and his crew in getting the horses on board safely. They were intelligent beasts and none of them relished the prospect of being cooped up in the cramped hold of the sloop for several days.

Eldain couldn't blame them and shrugged apologetically as Rhianna's horse caught his eye and glowered at him. He saw Yvraine standing with her arms wrapped around herself, watching the sailors leading the horses onto the ship. The wind blowing in off the sea tousled her platinum hair and she was clearly not looking forward to another sea journey.

He made his way across the quay to stand beside her and said, 'It seems you loathe travelling by sea as much as our mounts, Mistress Hawkblade.'

'Can you blame me?' she said.

'I know why the horses dislike it,' said Eldain. 'In Ellyrion they are used to the freedom of the steppes, but why do you hate it so?'

Yvraine shrugged. 'I do not like placing my fate in another's hands. I prefer to be master of my own destiny.'

'Can any of us claim that?' asked Eldain. 'Does the will of the gods not shape our future?'

'I do not know. Perhaps it does, but I make my own choices and live by my own code.'

'Does that code include killing my brother?'

Yvraine shielded her eyes from the low sun and said, 'If that is what it takes to keep Ulthuan safe. Do not think to stop me.'

'If Caelir threatens Ulthuan, I will wield the blade

myself,' said Eldain, surprised at the lack of feeling such an utterance caused within him.

'Then we understand one another,' said Yvraine, returning her attention to the horses.

'It would appear so.'

An awkward silence fell until eventually Yvraine said, 'Isha willing, your horses will soon know the freedom of the steppe again.'

'You sound as though you're not sure they will.'

'Perhaps I am not,' agreed Yvraine. 'You heard what Lord Teclis said. The druchii are abroad and war is coming. None of us may see our homelands again.'

'Are you worried you might not see Saphery again?'

'No,' said Yvraine, shaking her head. 'It is the fact that I am *leaving* Saphery when war is coming that disturbs me. I should be with my brethren defending the White Tower as I swore to do.'

Eldain smiled grimly. 'If Lord Teclis is right, then all of us will have to fight soon. I do not think it matters overmuch where we make our stand.'

'It matters to me.'

'Then for all our sakes I hope your blade fights where it is most needed,' said Eldain.

Chapter Fifteen

Confluence

THE MORNING SUN rose higher, long shadows of dawn retreating before the advancing day and illuminating the valley before the Eagle Gate. Since the eagles had brought the wounded reaver and news of the advancing enemy, Glorien Truecrown had done all his books had recommended before battle.

Three riders had set off on the fastest steeds to Tor Elyr to bear news and request reinforcement, and scouts had been despatched to watch for the arrival of the enemy. Arrows had been stockpiled on the walls and every weapon checked and rechecked. The few mages attached to the Eagle Gate had spent the night in meditation, gathering their strength and powers for the coming battle.

He had personally inspected every inch of the wall and gate for weakness and had been relieved to find nothing out of place. As sloppy as Glorien had considered Cerion Goldwing's leadership, he could find no fault with the defences.

At midmorning the Shadow Warrior, Alanrias, returned and Glorien met him at the gate.

The news was not good.

'They will be here in an hour, maybe less,' gasped the hooded scout, blood coating his grey cloak where an iron bolt had pierced him. 'We harried them from Cairn Anroc, but the druchii of the Blackspine Mountains are skilled hunters and many of us were slain. Dark riders range ahead of the army, fighting running battles with reaver bands from Ellyrion.'

'Where are these reaver bands now?' asked Glorien, seeing no horsemen behind the scout.

'Most are dead, though some will have escaped into the mountains.'

Glorien thanked Alanrias and sent him to the healers before returning to the walls with Menethis at his side, trying not to let the fear that threatened to overwhelm him show in his long strides and confident mien. Together, they walked the length of the wall and Glorien took heart from the steely determination he saw in every warrior's face. He dearly wished he felt the same confidence as these soldiers, for he had never yet faced an enemy in battle...

He attempted to converse with the warriors, as he had seen Cerion do on many occasions, but his words were awkward and stiff and he gave up after a few attempts. Instead, he took heart from the sheer solidity of the fortress, its sweeping white walls high and impregnable, its towers proud and inviolate. Hundreds of elven warriors manned the defences and he was as knowledgeable as any noble who had commanded its walls.

Caledor had built his fortresses well and never once had a guardian fortress fallen to an enemy. That thought alone gave Glorien hope.

That hope sank in his heart as the sun climbed higher and the enemy host came into view.

They marched along the centre of the valley, thousands of dark elf warriors in disciplined regiments, carrying long spears and serpent banners on poles topped with silver runes. Armoured warriors with executioners' blades slung over their shoulders advanced next to them in grim silence, banners scribed with the blasted rune of Khaine held proudly before them.

A ripple of horror passed along the wall as a trio of huge, black-scaled beasts with many serpentine heads was herded onwards by sweating beastmasters armed with long-tined goads. Acrid smoke seeped from the fanged mouths of the monsters and their roars echoed from the valley sides as they snapped and strained at the chains that bound them.

Glorien's eyes widened as he saw a group of prisoners herded before the monsters, their garb and fair hair marking them as warriors of Ellyrion.

'Oh no...' he whispered as one of the prisoners stumbled and was snatched up in the jaws of one of the hydra creatures. His screams carried in the cold air and Glorien watched in horror as the beast's many heads fought over the body, ripping it to shreds in a feeding frenzy.

Already blood was being spilled and the reptilian cavalry of the druchii snorted and clawed the ground as they caught its scent. The dark nobles who rode these beasts wore elaborate armour of ebony plate and carried tall lances, the dread symbols of their houses borne proudly on kite-shaped shields.

Flocks of winged creatures wheeled above the advancing army, leathery fiends of repulsive feminine aspect, filling the air with loathsome screeches.

Alongside the druchii, a horde of corrupt men marched with raucous cries while beating their axes and swords upon their shields. Whipped madmen capered before the horde, deviant slaves sewn into flesh suits fashioned from flayed elven skin.

Barbaric tribesmen bellowed and shouted, their bodies glistening with oil and gleaming with plates of metal fused to their flesh by unnatural magic. As brutal as these men were, Glorien felt his blood run cold as he saw the champions who commanded them, warriors who had sworn their souls to the Dark Gods and whose runes were carved into the meat of their bodies.

Each champion was surrounded by his own blood-thirsty band of followers: muscular beasts that walked on two legs, mutant horrors of indefinable form, outcast warriors touched by the warping power of Chaos and gibbering shamen uttering forbidden doggerel.

Thousands of warriors filled the valley and Glorien watched as the terrifying host halted just outside the extreme range of his bolt throwers.

'So many…' he said, his throat dry and his stomach knotting in fear.

Menethis said nothing, but pointed a trembling finger to the centre of the enemy horde.

Two figures rode towards the Eagle Gate, one an alluring woman atop a dark steed with sinewy wings of night, and the other a monstrously powerful man riding an enormous, skinless horse with its saddle and bridle fused to its exposed musculature.

'What should we do, my lord?' asked Menethis.

Glorien licked his lips and said. 'Nothing yet. Let me think.'

The two riders stopped and Glorien knew they were well within range of every one of his archers. He knew he could order them killed, but such a dishonourable act was beneath him. Men and druchii might behave without respect for the honourable conduct of war, but Glorien Truecrown was a noble of Ulthuan.

Instead, he took a deep breath and hoped his voice would not betray his awful fear.

'These lands are the sovereign territory of Finubar, Phoenix King of Ulthuan and lord of the Asur. Leave now or die!'

The silence of the valley was absolute, as though the mountains themselves awaited the response of the enemy leaders.

The druchii woman threw back her head and laughed, a bitter, dead sound, and the giant on the glistening steed shook his head, as though he could taste the fear in Glorien's voice.

Glorien flinched as the woman's dark steed spread its wings and leapt into the air, its red eyes like fiery gems and its breath a snorting cloud of evil vapours. Though she wore no saddle and held no reins, the woman showed no fear as the evil pegasus carried her through the air towards the fortress.

'Archers!' shouted Glorien. 'Stand ready!'

Six hundred bows creaked as every archer on the wall drew back his string and stood ready to loose. Glorien would not kill an enemy who came to parlay, but this reckless ride was something different altogether.

Now that she was closer, Glorien could see that this was no ordinary druchii female, but one of incredible dark beauty, her pale flesh slender and taut and her hair a thick mane of shimmering darkness. She gripped the flanks of her mount with her thighs and Glorien knew he had never seen a more powerfully erotic sight.

'My lord?' said Menethis. 'Shall I order the archers to loose?'

Glorien tried to answer, but he could not form the words, his soul ensnared by the unearthly allure of this dark femme. His lips moved, but made no sound and he was struck by the sheer absurdity of fighting this woman.

He felt a strong grip on his arm and shook it off as he continued to stare at this vision of dark beauty. Nor was he the only one so afflicted, for many of his warriors were similarly struck by the incredible power of this druchii's rapturous comeliness, easing their strings and staring in wonder at this druchii.

Druchii...

The word screamed in his mind and Glorien gasped in horror as the spell of the woman's beauty slipped from his mind.

This was no ordinary druchii...

He let out a great breath, as his body threw off the glamours of the sorceress and gripped the white stone of the merlon as his legs threatened to give out beneath him.

Glorien turned to his archers and shouted, 'Bring her down! Now!'

Barely half the archers loosed, the rest still enraptured by her evil charisma, and at such close range, Glorien would have expected every warrior to hit his target.

But as the volley of shafts flashed through the air, a crackling haze of magic bloomed around the woman and the arrows fell from the sky as withered, ashen flakes. In response, she aimed her barbed staff towards the fortress and uttered a dreadful chant in the foul language of the druchii.

Howling winds, like the freezing breath of Morai-heg, swept over the battlements and Glorien cried out as bone-numbing cold seized his limbs. The deathly chill of the utterdark burned through him and an icy mist drifted over the battlements.

He heard screams as warriors dropped to their knees in pain, and glittering webs of frost appeared on the stonework of the fortress. Slicks of dark ice formed underfoot as Glorien's every breath felt like daggers of frost in his lungs.

'I can taste your fear and it pleases me!' shrieked the druchii sorceress with malicious amusement. 'An eternity of agony in the Chaos hells awaits those who stand before my warriors. This I promise, for I am Morathi and you are all going to die!'

THE WARM GLOW of the torches surrounded him and the applause of the audience filled Caelir with confidence as he made his way to stand in the centre of the rug. Smiling faces wished him well and he dearly hoped that he would not disappoint this gathering with his performance.

Narentir had given him a silver harp and he plucked a few strings experimentally, hoping the skills he had discovered with Kyrielle had not deserted him. The thought of Anurion's daughter gave him pause, but instead of pain, the memory awakened only pleasant memories and he dearly wished she was here to see him play.

'Come along,' said Narentir, 'don't keep us waiting all night!'

Good-natured laughter washed over him and Caelir smiled as he saw Lilani lounging at the back of the audience, watching him with naked interest.

He closed his eyes and though he knew of many songs, he suddenly realised he didn't know how to play any of them and a hot jolt of fear seized him as his mind went blank.

Had his unremembered talent deserted him?

The thought of letting down his audience terrified him and though he knew it was the dreamwine talking, he felt as though it would be the greatest failure of his life were he to stand here useless and without the gift of music.

He ran his hands across the instrument once more and then, without conscious thought or effort, his fingers began to dance across the strings. Golden music leapt from the harp to fill the night and Caelir emptied his mind of fear, giving his unknown muse free rein over his hands.

Delighted laughter sparkled from the audience and they clapped in time with the melodies wrung from his instrument. Caelir laughed as the music poured from him, fuelled by the appreciation of his listeners, and he knew that he had been accepted as one of them.

Before he knew what he was doing, he began to sing, the words flowing as naturally as though taught from birth:

Isha be with thee in every forest,
Asuryan at every day revealed,
Grace be with thee through every stream
Headland, ridge and field.
Glory to thee forever,
Thou bright moon, Ladrielle;
Ever our glorious light.

Each sea and land,
Each moor and meadow,
Each lying down, each rising up,

In the trough of the waves,
On the crest of the billows,
Each step of the journey thou goest.

And then it was over, the words ended and the tune played out. He lowered the harp and let the moment hang, his breath hot in his throat and the excruciating desire to please still hammering in his chest.

Heartfelt cheers and applause greeted his song and Narentir rose from his seat at the edge of the rug. His face was smiling as he said, 'Well done, Caelir, well done,' and pulled him into an embrace.

'It was just a simple wayfarer's tune,' said Caelir, faintly embarrassed by the praise.

'True enough,' said Narentir, 'but you sang it honestly and played it well.'

Caelir smiled and felt the muse within him cry out for more, but he handed the harp back to Narentir as another performer made their way to the rug.

Hands clapped his back and kisses were planted on his cheeks as he returned to the fold of the audience. He felt their approval wash over him and smiled as he was handed yet another glass of dreamwine.

Caelir passed through the audience in a blur, painted faces and smiles and kisses passing in a whirl of excitement and the rush of performance. He drained his glass and another was immediately thrust into his hand.

He laughed with them and joined in their applause as more performers came to the rug. A hand slipped into his and he found himself face to face with Lilani, her dancer's physique pressed close to his and her wide eyes looking up into his.

'Your song was sad,' she said and her voice was as silken as her movements.

'It wasn't meant to be.'

'I meant beneath the words,' she said, leading him beyond the torchlight towards the grassy slopes of a low hill. 'Your heart is in pain, but I know ways to heal it.'

'How?' said Caelir as her hands slipped up and around his neck. Lilani pressed the curve of her body against his and without conscious thought he leaned down to kiss her. It was instinctive, and her boldness – which did not surprise him – felt like the most natural thing in the world. She tasted of dreamwine and berries, her lips soft and her skin cool beneath his hands.

With barely a shrug her robe and his clothes were discarded and they lay down in the silvered grass together as music and song and laughter drifted on the air.

But Caelir heard none of it, for there was only Lilani and the time they shared beneath the moon.

CAELIR OPENED HIS eyes and blinked rapidly in the light of the risen sun. For a moment, he wondered where he was, and then looked down to see the sleeping form of Lilani, her arm draped across his chest. Morning dew glistened on her skin and he smiled as the hazy memory of last night's pleasurable exertions returned to him.

'Ah, you're awake at last, dear boy,' said a voice and he looked up to see Narentir holding out a plate of bread and fruit to him.

Caelir slipped from Lilani's embrace and scooped up his clothes, feeling faintly ridiculous as he pulled them on before this stranger. He remembered hugging him last night and feeling as though they were as close as brothers, but without the effects of the dreamwine, he realised that he knew almost nothing about these people beyond their names.

His stomach growled, reminding him that it had been days since he had eaten, and he gratefully took the offered plate, wolfing down great mouthfuls.

'Thank you,' he said.

'You are most welcome,' replied Narentir. 'I trust you enjoyed yourself last night?'

'I did, yes,' said Caelir between bites of fruit. 'I have never performed before an audience before.'

'Oh I know, but I meant with Lilani.'

Caelir blushed, looking back at the sleeping dancer and unsure of how to respond.

Narentir laughed at his discomfort, though there was no malice to it, and said, 'Don't give it a moment's worry, my boy. Here, we do not restrain our desires with antiquated moral codes, for we are all travellers on the road of the senses.'

'The what? I don't understand,' said Caelir.

'Really?' smiled Narentir, slipping an arm around his shoulders and leading him towards the wagons, which Caelir now saw were lacquered in a riot of colours and patterns. 'I thought from both your performances last night, you were only too well acquainted with the life of the voluptuary.'

'Wait a minute…' said Caelir, as the import of Narentir's words sank in. 'You said *both* my performances?'

'Yes,' said Narentir, gesturing towards Lilani. 'Or did you think your singing was the only thing you had an audience for?'

Caelir blushed at the thought of having been observed, but there was no judgement or lasciviousness in Narentir's comment and he felt his embarrassment fade. Instead, he smiled and said, 'Then yes, I did enjoy myself. As you said, she is a rare jewel.'

'That's more like it,' said Narentir. 'That's the kind of attitude that will get you noticed in Avelorn. Now come on, sate your appetite and we shall be on our way.'

'Wait, you are heading to Avelorn?'

'Of course. Where did you think we were going?'

'I... I hadn't given it much thought, to be honest,' said Caelir. 'Everything happened so quickly, I didn't get a chance to think about it.'

'True enough, but isn't that just the most delightful way of living life?'

Narentir climbed onto the padded seat of the lead wagon and Caelir asked. 'What takes you to Avelorn?'

'What takes anyone to Avelorn, dear Caelir? Music, dancing, magic and love.'

Caelir smiled, bemused at Narentir's carefree attitude, but as he watched the revellers of last night rouse themselves from their slumbers and ready themselves for travel, he could not fault their enthusiasm in greeting the day. The group was made up of perhaps two dozen elves, and everywhere Caelir looked, he saw smiles and genuine affection for those around them.

Laughter and yet more music filled the air and to Caelir's eyes his surroundings seemed more vital, more alive than they had before, as though the land welcomed the travellers' joy and returned it tenfold.

He smiled as elves he had met only the previous night welcomed him with kisses and the familiarity of old friends. An arm slipped around his waist and he turned to see Lilani beside him.

'Good morning,' he said.

She smiled and Caelir felt a surge of wellbeing suffuse him. Perhaps she had indeed healed his heart as she had claimed she could.

'Do you travel with us?' she asked, slipping around him and planting a kiss on his lips.

Caelir looked at the love and friendship he saw in the elves around him and felt more at home than he could ever remember.

'I think I will be, yes. At least until we reach Avelorn.'

'Good,' she said, dancing around him with teasing grace. 'Because I think I'd like you to perform for me again soon.'

THE ISLAND OF the Gaen Vale came into view as a beautiful swathe of green, gold and sapphire. Glittering blue cliffs, shaggy with lush forests, rose from the sea and the scent of wild flowers and flowering plants were carried from its centre. Game roamed free within the low-lying forests and Eldain could see deer and pale horses running wild through the surf that skirted the western shores of the island.

The *Dragonkin* had sailed from Cairn Auriel with the first tide and Eldain had spent much of the journey sitting alone at the tiller with Captain Bellaeir, finding him a voluble conversationalist, so long as their discussions revolved around ships and sailing. The closer they had sailed to the Gaen Vale, the more excited Rhianna and Yvraine had become, their anticipation at setting foot on the hallowed soil of the Mother Goddess passing like a magical current between them.

Neither seemed inclined to discuss the island, as though doing so with a male would somehow defile the beauty of it for them.

He and Rhianna still slept together beneath the stars, but with each mile that brought them closer to the Gaen Vale, he felt the distance between them widening and prayed that it was simply the proximity of the island and not some deeper gulf opening between them.

On the morning of their third day of travel, Captain Bellaeir stood on the tiller step and pointed towards an outthrust spit of rock fringed with tall evergreens. As the ship swung around the peninsula, Eldain saw that it formed the edge of a natural bay and he gasped as he saw the wondrous landscape beyond.

'Lady Rhianna, yonder is the Bay of Cython!' cried Bellaeir.

Rhianna and Yvraine joined Eldain at the gunwale and linked their hands at the sight of the island's beauty.

Golden beaches and verdant forests spread out before them, with crystal waterfalls tumbling from rounded boulders into foaming pools that ran to the sea. Flocks of white birds circled overhead and the sound of silver bells sounded from somewhere out of sight. The waters of the ocean were unimaginably clear, the sandy sea bottom rippling beneath the ship like the bed of the freshest stream of Ellyrion.

Eldain thought the scene unbearably beautiful, but as he looked over at his wife, he saw that Rhianna and Yvraine were weeping openly.

'What's wrong?' he said.

Rhianna shook her head. 'You wouldn't understand.'

He shared a look with Bellaeir, but the captain simply shrugged and turned the tiller inwards towards the shoreline.

No sooner had the vessel's prow turned towards the island, than a silver shafted arrow streaked from the forest at the end of the peninsula and hammered into the mast. Eldain ducked as the arrow vibrated with the impact and Bellaeir swore, turning the *Dragonkin* away from the island.

'They're loosing arrows at us?' exclaimed Eldain, catching a glimpse of a naked archer at the edge of the trees. 'Why are they doing that?'

'It's us,' said Bellaeir. 'It's because there are males aboard. I should have realised.'

'Then how do we land?'

'You don't,' said Yvraine. 'Lady Rhianna and I will have to swim ashore.'

Eldain rounded upon the Sword Master and said, 'It's nearly half a mile.'

'The island will guide us.'

'We'll be fine, Eldain,' said Rhianna, smiling as she looked towards the island. 'Nothing bad will happen to us here.'

Captain Bellaeir weighed anchor and the two elf maids stripped down to their undergarments in preparation for their swim. Yvraine reluctantly passed her sword to Eldain and it was clear how much it pained her to venture into the unknown without her weapon.

'Be careful,' he said as Rhianna took a deep breath at the edge of the rail.

'I will be, Eldain,' she promised. 'This is a place of healing and renewal. Nothing bad can happen here.'

'I hope you are right.'

She leaned forward and gave him a soft kiss, then turned and dived into the water with the natural grace of a sea sprite. Yvraine followed her a moment later and together they swam through the clear waters of the Sea of Dusk towards the beach.

Eldain saw more of the archer women moving through the forests as they shadowed these new arrivals to their island.

He hoped that Rhianna was right.

Hopefully nothing bad could happen here.

RHIANNA SWAM WITH powerful strokes, the water blessedly cool and crystalline. The waves were small and the island quickly drew closer, as though the sea itself were helping to carry them inwards. Yvraine swam ahead of her, her more powerful, warrior's physique allowing her to pull ahead more easily.

She swam onwards, feeling the cares of the world melt away with every stroke. Ahead, Yvraine splashed through the gentle surf of the beach and Rhianna felt an irrational stab of jealousy that Yvraine would set foot on the island before her.

No sooner had the thought surfaced than it instantly washed from her mind as she realised how ridiculous it was. Yvraine was also a supplicant here by the simple virtue of her sex and a fellow devotee of the Mother Goddess. Competition between them was irrelevant. Such futile strife was the preserve of the race of males.

At last Rhianna reached the shallows and began wading ashore. She felt the welcome of the island in her very bones, as though it had been waiting for her for uncounted years, and she cursed that she had waited this long to journey to it.

Yvraine was waiting for her, her sodden undergarments plastered to her body, and they hugged as the island's joy filled them with love.

The ground beneath Rhianna's feet felt charged with the magic of creation and they made their way hand in hand up the beach, the warmth of the white gold sand between their toes delicious and warm. Gentle winds carried homely scents and a life-giving breath that seemed to reach out from the trees and draw them in.

'Which way do we go?' asked Yvraine.

'Just onwards,' said Rhianna. 'The island will show us the way.'

Yvraine nodded and followed as Rhianna set off towards the edge of the forest.

As she drew near the trees, Rhianna saw a narrow path winding upwards from the beach, its boundaries marked by gleaming white stones, and immediately knew that this would lead them to where they needed to go.

The warmth of the sun penetrated the leafy canopy and spears of light waved through the shadowy forest as they followed the path up through the forest. Though the path was long and the slope steep, Rhianna found the going easy, as though the ground itself rose to meet her every footfall. It took an effort of will not to abandon all restraint and sprint to the end of the path. She could see the same excitement on Yvraine's face as they passed between the ancient trees of the island.

The forest air was a tonic in her spirit, the cares of the world far behind her and insignificant in the face of the ancient power that lay beneath the earth here. The mages of Hoeth might wield power that could destroy whole armies, but not one amongst them could create life as this sacred place could. Who amongst the warriors of the world could match the awesome power of the Mother Goddess?

'Rhianna...' whispered Yvraine.

She stopped, though her feet ached to carry her onwards.

'What is it?' she said, turning to see Yvraine kneeling to examine the edge of the path.

'Look at this,' said the Sword Master, beckoning her over.

Rhianna tore her eyes from the inviting horizon and knelt beside Yvraine as the Sword Master dug rich, black loam from around one of the smooth white marker stones. Dark earth fell away as she lifted it from the ground, and Rhianna recoiled as she saw that Yvraine held a smooth, fleshless skull.

'Isha preserve us,' she said, now realising that all the white markers were similarly gruesome artefacts. 'Skulls? But why?'

Yvraine replaced the skull in the ground and said, 'I imagine that these belong to males who could not contain their curiosity.'

Rhianna felt a chill pass down her spine and the forest, which had previously been filled with light and promise, now seemed a darker and more dangerous place. For the first time, she understood that the energy she felt here was elemental and raw, the awesome power of creation without the discipline of intellect.

Perhaps Eldain had been right to counsel caution.

'We should move on,' said Yvraine.

'Yes,' agreed Rhianna, backing away from the buried skulls and making her way uphill along the dead centre of the path.

Their route curled uphill, weaving a circuitous route through shady arbours and golden clearings until, at last, they arrived at the edge of the forest and a rippling curtain of sunlight.

Rhianna closed her eyes and walked through the light, feeling warmth caress her skin with soothing, welcoming affection.

She opened her eyes and wept at the beauty before her.

Chapter Sixteen

Duty

Rhianna had lived amid the magical wonders of Saphery and ridden the enchanted plains of Ellyrion. She had seen the glory of Lothern and marvelled at the rugged splendour of Yvresse, but nothing could compare to the wonder of the Gaen Vale. The landscape spread out before her in a rolling patchwork of bountiful forests, fast-flowing rivers and wide groves of graceful statues and temples of purest white.

Music filled the air, but it was not the tunes of elves, but the melodies of the earth: birdsong, the rustle of wind in the branches of tall trees and the gurgle of life-giving waters as they flowed from a rocky peak at the centre of the island.

Together the sounds of the island formed a natural orchestra that played the symphony of creation in every breath. She felt Yvraine's hand take hers and she squeezed it tightly as they made their way into the depths of the island.

'I expected it to be wonderful,' she said, 'but this… this is incredible.'

'I know,' agreed Yvraine. 'I wish I had travelled here sooner.'

Rhianna nodded, only too aware that she had meant to travel here after her wedding to Caelir. She pictured Caelir's face as she had last seen it, terrified and running for his life, and a strangled sob burst from her as a host of emotions, which until now she had kept buried deep inside her, were dragged to the surface by the magic of the Gaen Vale.

Yvraine stopped and said, 'Rhianna? What is the matter?'

'Caelir,' she sobbed, sinking to her knees beside a pool of mirror-still water. 'I can't even imagine the torment he must have endured at the hands of the druchii. I thought he was dead and I married another. I should have waited… I should have waited!'

Yvraine held her tight and said, 'You were not to know, Rhianna. His own brother told you he was dead. What more could you have done?'

'I should have known,' said Rhianna. 'I should have felt he was still alive.'

More sobs shook her frame and she cried into Yvraine's shoulder.

'I had a duty to him and I failed…' she whispered.

'No, you didn't,' stated Yvraine without pity, but not unkindly. 'He was dead and you moved on. Now you have a duty to Eldain and your duty to him is to love him as you once loved Caelir.'

Rhianna looked up into Yvraine's face and felt her composure return at the Sword Master's words. She smiled through her tears and said, 'Thank you, Yvraine. I underestimated you.'

'How so?'

'I thought you just a warrior, but I see now there is more to you than that.'

Yvraine smiled. 'I learned more than how to fight from Master Dioneth: ethics, philosophy, history and many other skills. If the Sword Masters are to be the eyes and ears of the White Tower they must know how to see through deception to unearth the truth.'

'Then is there nothing you fear?'

Yvraine considered the question for a moment before saying, 'I fear to fail.'

'To fail? You?'

'Yes,' said Yvraine. 'My first mission was to bring you to Saphery, but when we reached the Tower of Hoeth and the beasts of magic attacked, I feared failing Master Silverfawn more than my own death.'

'I never knew...'

'Like you, I have a duty, but if I fail in mine, people die and that is a heavy burden for any shoulders.'

'And how do *you* cope with such a burden?'

Yvraine smiled. 'I strive to do my duty to the best of my ability and through doing so, I learn a little more about myself. All any of us can do is our best and let the gods take care of the rest.'

Rhianna found herself admiring the youthful Sword Master more and more, pleased that she had been right to defend her against Eldain's opinion that there was no wisdom in wielding a sword for the Loremasters.

She shook off her sadness and felt the healing touch of the Gaen Vale flow through her as she forgave herself for believing Caelir to be dead. A warm, golden light built behind her eyes and she said, 'Thank you.'

No sooner had the words left her than a shadow fell

across them and a skyclad elf maid carrying a moon-coloured longbow emerged from the undergrowth. Yvraine's hand instinctively reached for her greatsword before she realised where she was and that her weapon was still aboard the *Dragonkin*. Rhianna rose to her feet in surprise at the maiden's sudden appearance.

The elf maid's skin was unblemished and startlingly white, her blonde hair reaching down to the backs of her knees. Her features were thin, elliptical and Rhianna thought she was perhaps the most beautiful person she had ever seen.

'The oracle consents to see you,' said the maiden. 'You must follow me.'

ALATHENAR DREW AND loosed yet another arrow as the enemy horde came at them once again. The arrow thudded home between the neck plates of a warrior armoured in heavy plates of iron and he collapsed in a heap before the charge. Alathenar loosed arrow after arrow, his fingers and forearm raw from the volume of shafts he sent slashing into the enemy ranks. The day was less than four hours old, yet the defenders of the Eagle Gate had already seen off three separate attacks.

'Don't they ever stop?' he hissed as he loosed his last arrow and snatched up a fresh quiver from the ground.

'Apparently not,' said Eloien Redcloak, his shorter bow reaping a lesser, yet no less deadly tally than Alathenar's. The magic of the Eagle Gate's mages had saved the reaver's life, but Alathenar knew he should not be fighting, for his wound was not yet fully healed.

Despite this, Eloien had immediately taken his place on the wall and refused any notion of riding to Ellyrion; this enemy had killed his warriors and he had vowed to exact a measure of retribution for their murder.

Alathenar had liked his spirit and kept a wary eye
on the reaver, fighting back to back with him on several occasions. Both immediately recognised the warrior
spirit in the other and Alathenar could feel bonds of
friendship forming as they often did between warriors
in battle.

'Be ready with that sword of yours, Redcloak,' advised
Alathenar. 'We're not going to stop them before they get
to the walls.'

'Have no fear of that, archer. Just be sure to leave
enough for me.'

Alathenar wanted to believe the Ellyrian's words were
a jest made of bravado, but saw the grim set to his jaw
and knew that no levity remained within the reaver.

The welcome *crack-twang* of the bolt throwers unleashing was audible over the baying of the corrupted humans
as they charged the walls of the Eagle Gate again. A score
of the debased followers of the Dark Gods were mown
down like wheat before the scythe as the lethal hail of
darts thudded home.

The valley floor was carpeted with the dead and
wounded, bodies trampled underfoot as the howling
champions of Chaos drove their followers forward with
whips and threats. A tide of armoured warriors surged
towards the walls, armed with roped grapnels and long
ladders. Their raucous war chants rang from the sides of
the valley and Alathenar knew he had never heard voices
so filled with hate.

Blue-white rods of molten light leapt from the walls,
immolating a dozen tribal warriors in a searing explosion of winged flames, and volley after volley of deadly
accurate arrows sliced through armour and flesh as the

defenders sought to keep the enemy from the walls.

'Ladders!' shouted Alathenar as an iron-topped ladder thumped into the wall in front of him, sending sparks flaring from the stonework. He stepped away from the battlements as a gold banner was raised and a disciplined line of warriors armed with swords stepped forward, glittering weapon points aimed at the tapered embrasures.

A roaring warrior with a monstrous axe appeared and Alathenar sent an arrow through the eye slit of his helmet. The man screamed and toppled from the ladder, but even as he fell, another warrior clambered up and Alathenar's arrow thudded uselessly into his raised shield.

All along the length of the wall, struggling warriors in fur cloaks and dark helmets fought to gain a foothold on the ramparts and the bloodshed was horrendous. Artisan-fashioned steel met steppe-forged iron in a clash of brute strength and martial skill.

Eloien stepped in close to the parapet and stabbed his sabre through a bare-chested warrior with a skull-fronted helm. Another warrior appeared and Eloien clove his sword through his shoulder, hacking the arm from his body. The tribesman fell from sight and Eloien reared back as a monstrous creature with the head of a snarling bear hauled its bulk over the pale stone of the wall.

Alathenar loosed an arrow that ricocheted from the braying creature's skull as it reared above the ramparts and Eloien lunged forwards to stab his blade through the beast's jaws.

The monster howled and bit down, snapping the reaver's blade. Another arrow hammered home in its chest, penetrating barely a handspan before snapping against the stone of the wall.

Eloien rolled beneath a sweep of its massive clawed hand and with a muscular scramble the beast was on the ramparts. Blood drooled from its jaws and Alathenar saw that its fangs were so monstrous and distended that it could not possibly close its mouth.

Screeching wails of the winged she-creatures sounded above him, but he could only hope the great eagles who had brought warning to the fortress could defeat them. He put the aerial battle above the fort from his mind as the mighty beast unlimbered a great hammer from its back and swung it in a wide arc.

Elves were smashed asunder by the blow, broken and dead as they flew from the wall to land in the courtyard far below. Alathenar threw himself flat to avoid the huge hammer's head and Eloien pressed his back against the wall.

The reaver swept up a fallen sword and slashed it across the monster's hamstrings.

The thick sinewy cords were like wet rope and the blade scored across the backs of its legs without cutting them, but his attack had given the defenders on the wall an opening. Two warriors armed with spears charged from either side and plunged their long polearms into the beast's flanks.

It roared in pain and Alathenar rolled onto his back, holding his bow side-on and offering a prayer to Kurnous as he loosed a pair of shafts at the beast's head. Both shafts struck home and gushing blood jetted from its torn throat.

The straining spearmen used their weapons to push the monstrous beast from the wall and Alathenar rolled to his feet as the sounds of battle rushed in to fill his senses.

Desperate clashes between elves and men and creatures that defied description ran the length of the wall. Warriors with swords defended the ramparts, while archers filled the skies with shafts and brought down the disgusting winged creatures that harried the crews of the bolt throwers.

Spearmen periodically surged forward to hurl the enemy back and flames of magic leapt back and forth; the blinding white of elven magic and the dark, purple fire of druchii sorcery.

Mystic sigils of protection worked into the stone of the wall dissipated the worst of the enemy magic, but each rune smoked and hissed as the dark arts of the Hag Sorceress gradually burned through their strength.

Periodically the wall would shake as the horrifying beasts the corrupted humans had brought to the battlefield hammered the gate below. Such monstrous by-blows of the Dark Gods were virtually immune to pain and only a multitude of shafts could bring them down.

Ladders were cast down by straining warriors and magical fire, and grapnels were cut with single sword strokes, elven steel easily parting the crudely woven human ropes. Spearmen thrust forward in linked ranks, pushing the enemy back from the wall and the battlements became slippery with the blood and viscera of the dead.

'We have them now,' said Eloien, his chest heaving with the exertion of battle. 'They're fighting to live now, not to win.'

Alathenar nodded. 'Maybe so, but it's not over yet!'

He pointed further along the wall where a tribal war leader in a suit of dark armour had formed a fighting wedge and was pushing the defenders back with wide sweeps of a mighty greatsword. Dozens of warriors waited behind him and it would only be a matter of time until the enemy swept the defenders away.

Alathenar vaulted onto the saw-toothed ramparts to get a better view and nocked another arrow to his bow. He saw crossbowmen below taking aim and knew he did not have much time.

He waited until the warrior's sword was raised above his head and whispered, 'Guide my aim, Arenia my love,' and loosed a pair of shafts, one after the other. Both sliced through the mail at the warrior's armpit to punch through his ribs and pierce his heart.

Alathenar leapt down as a flurry of crossbow bolts clattered against the wall and the war leader fell to his knees, a jet of blood pouring from beneath his helmet.

The elven warriors he had kept at bay surged forwards, their speartips stabbing and driving the remainder of the enemy from the walls. The last of the ladders was cast down and archers moved to the walls to slay as many of the enemy as possible as they fell back to their camp.

A ragged cheer chased the corrupted ones away and elven warriors sagged against the stone of the ramparts as they realised they had won another respite.

'That was an incredible piece of archery,' said Eloien, cleaning his sword on the tunic of a dead tribesman.

Alathenar said. 'I have my true love's hair woven into the string.'

'Does that help?' asked Eloien, lowering himself to the ground with a wince of pain.

'I like to think so.'

He sat on the rampart as the reserve groups of warriors made their way up from the courtyard to take the place of those who had been fighting. The bodies of fallen

elves were carried away to the rear wall of the fortress
while those of the foe were hurled unceremoniously
over the walls. Buckets of water sluiced the worst of the
blood away and stretcher-bearers carried injured warriors to the infirmary and the surgeons' arts.

'Shall we get down from this wall and have some
water?' said Eloien.

'That sounds good,' agreed Alathenar. 'All too soon it
will be our turn to fight again.'

'And when will it be your glorious leader's turn?'
asked Eloien, nodding towards the imposing crag of the
tall tower at the end of the wall.

Alathenar did not reply, but privately had wondered
the same thing.

When *would* Glorien Truecrown leave his precious
books to come down from the Aquila Spire and fight
with his warriors?

THEIR GUIDE LED them through the wondrous valley
of the Gaen Vale and the natural beauty of the landscape enchanted Rhianna with every step she took. All
Ulthuan was a marvel of nature's genius, but here it was
allowed its reign unfettered by the handiwork of the
elves. Wild groves of apple trees and waterfalls filled the
air with pungent scents of good earth and fresh water,
and the magical creatures – unicorns, pegasus and
griffons – that roamed freely through the forests were
unafraid of them.

The deeper they journeyed into the high sided valley,
the more of its fey inhabitants they saw, dancers and
archers who practised their arts in groves so glorious
Rhianna felt her heart would burst at the splendour of
them.

White marble temples sat in overgrown arbours, priestesses of the Mother Goddess pouring wine and honey on the sacred places as they gave praise for the fertility of the land. Kneeling maidens of Ulthuan received instruction from the inhabitants of the island and everywhere Rhianna looked, she could see welcoming smiles of acceptance at their presence.

From somewhere she acquired a floral wreath and the sound of haunting earth music came from ahead, as if to draw them onwards, though the island had no need of such blandishments, for their approach was a willing one.

Their guide had said little since she had surprised them, though, in truth, neither she nor Yvraine had desired to talk, so caught up in the wonders of the isle were they. The elf maid's body was hard and toned through a lifetime of duty and Rhianna had to force herself to keep her eyes from lingering too long on the sway of her muscular back.

Their path led them up through an archway formed from the overhanging branches of looming trees. Through the gently waving canopy she could see the tall peak at the centre of the island, streams of mountain water pouring down its flanks like trails of tears.

A wide stream tumbled energetically over a cascade of pebbles worn smooth over thousands of years and Rhianna felt her pulse quicken as they emerged from the forest and she saw a dark cavern ahead.

The path curled up towards the flanks of the peak through a procession of votive statues and piles of offerings to the Mother Goddess. Sparkling mist clung to the rocky ground before the cavern and shimmering rainbows arced from the glistening stones.

Their guide halted while they were still a hundred yards or more from the entrance.

'I can go no further,' she said. 'You must travel on alone.'

Rhianna looked towards the cavern mouth, its yawning darkness wide and fearful now that she knew they faced it without the protection of one who dwelled amongst its wonders.

'The oracle is within?' asked Rhianna.

'She is,' confirmed the maid. 'Now go. It is perilous to waste her time.'

With that warning, the elf maid turned and vanished into the forest as effortlessly as she had appeared, leaving them alone and uncertain before the cavern temple of the Mother Goddess.

The mountain loomed over them, powerful and frightening now that they stood at its base and saw the raw, hard-edged ruggedness of it. From a distance it had appeared regal and majestic, but here, its stone was dark and threatening.

'We should move on,' said Yvraine, when Rhianna didn't move.

'Yes…' said Rhianna.

'Is something wrong?'

'I don't know… I just feel a little frightened now, but I am not sure why.'

Yvraine looked from Rhianna to the cave mouth and said, 'I understand what you mean. I thought everything on the island would be like what we've seen before, but…'

'But it's not, is it?' finished Rhianna.

'No,' agreed Yvraine. 'This is different. Dangerous. But we should have expected this.'

'How so?'

'So far we have only seen the beauty of the island, but for everything of beauty there is a balancing darkness: day and night, good and evil. For everything wondrous in nature, there is cruelty to match. Nature is a bloody world of death and rebirth. So it is here too.'

'Now I *really* don't want to go in.'

'It is perilous to waste her time,' said Yvraine, repeating the elf maid's warning. 'I do not think we have a choice.'

'No, I suppose not,' agreed Rhianna, setting off with fresh resolve towards the cave mouth.

They climbed the path and as they reached the darkness of the cave Rhianna smelled the aroma of dark, smoky wood, as though a fire smouldered deep within the mountain. She caught the aroma of white poppy, camphor and mandrake, and her vision blurred for a moment as she took a breath of the aromatic smoke deep into her lungs. Rhianna saw flickering lights ahead and as she stepped into the cave, she saw bowls of oil on the floor, blue flames dancing just above the rainbow-sheened liquid.

The cavern walls were adorned with a multitude of paintings of the moon, new-blooming roses and writhing serpents. She walked deeper into the cavern, walking with the oil bowls to either side of her. Her eyes adjusted to the gloom, but even so, there was a darkness here that her elven eyes could not penetrate. The oil lamps created no smoke, yet she felt a cloying thickness to the air as though spider webs ensnared her every step.

Momentary panic fluttered within her and she looked over her shoulder to check that Yvraine was still with her.

She was alone…

Yvraine was nowhere to be seen and even the light at the cave mouth was gone, as though a great door had come down to block off the outside world. Rhianna fought down her rising unease and forced herself to continue, following the route of the dancing blue flames as it led her deeper into the painted temple.

The deeper Rhianna went, the more she became aware of a soft tremor to the earth, like an infinitely slow heartbeat, powerful and yet impossibly distant. She could feel it in the earth and in the air, as though the pulse of the world was all around her, and its rhythmic cadence eased her spirits.

The passageway widened and Rhianna emerged into a smoky cavern, at the centre of which sat a thick stone with a carving of a knotted net across it. Pungent smoke drifted from the top of the stone and standing behind it was a hooded figure dressed in a long white robe and who carried a staff made from the branch of a willow tree.

'Welcome, Rhianna, daughter of Saphery,' said the figure and the voice was powerfully feminine. Rhianna tried to reply, but the thickness of the smoky air coiled in her throat and she could not form the words of a reply.

The woman beckoned her forwards and pointed to the stone. 'At the birth of the world, the Emperor of the Heavens sent a phoenix and a raven to fly across the world and meet at its centre. Upon the omphalos stone is where they met and through it, the oracles of the Mother Goddess can speak to the kingdom of heaven. Though whether they understand the reply is another matter.'

'Where is my friend?' said Rhianna, her voice muffled and weak. 'Where is Yvraine?'

'She is safe,' said the oracle. 'This is not her time to learn of the future. It is yours.'

'The future...?'

'Yes, for is that not why you journeyed here, child? To know of things hidden and things as yet unknown?'

Rhianna felt a mounting terror as her feet carried her towards the smoking stone at the centre of the cave. This wasn't what she had come for; she didn't want to know the future.

All she wanted was to find Caelir...

'They are one and the same, child,' said the oracle, her voice rising in power and authority as she spoke words of ancient power:

The New Moon is the white goddess of birth and growth;
The Full Moon, the red goddess of love and battle;
The Old Moon, the black goddess of death and divination.'

Powerless to resist, Rhianna placed her hands upon the stone and looked into its hollow core as the darkness of the cavern rose up around her. Her spirit felt as though it was being pulled down into the smoke and the hot breath of the gods engulfed her.

She screamed a wordless cry of anguish as images thundered through her, flashing swords and howling blood-hungry warriors, Caelir, Eldain and a wondrous forest kingdom of magic and beauty – not the natural magic of the Gaen Vale, but the artful enchantments of elves...

Fire swept over her and it seemed as though the cavern filled with roaring, searing flames that burned the paintings from the walls and seared the flesh from her bones. A whirling vortex of terrifyingly powerful energies swept over her and she was aware that she was no longer alone. A circle of mages surrounded her, their hands describing complex mystical symbols in the air and chanting words of ancient power.

Their bodies were wasted and gaunt and their eyes spoke of a suffering that never ended, an enduring agony that stretched from times forgotten to times unknown.

Amid the phantom mages she saw a laughing, raven-haired druchii princess, her beauty bathed in blood and her eyes full of an age's malice. She moved through the chanting mages like a dancer, spinning and leaping with a curved dagger in each hand. With each leap, a blade swept out to cut the throat of one of the mages and as each one died, the chaos around her surged in power.

'Stop it...' she cried. 'Please stop it!'

'No, child,' said a voice that sounded as though it came from a far distant time and place. 'Like all things a woman must suffer, this cannot be stopped. Only endured.'

The image of the murderous princess faded and Rhianna wept in relief as she saw the enchanted forest once again and the shimmering form of a woman so beautiful she could only be the Everqueen of Avelorn. The bright light enveloping her was a soothing balm upon her soul and she let out a great, shuddering breath.

No sooner had her racing heartbeat calmed when a black rain began to fall and Rhianna cried out as the dark waters stained the purity of the Everqueen's robes. Her face withered as the rain melted away everything that was good and pure of her, and as Rhianna watched, a bright red spot of blood appeared at her breast.

'No, please... no!' said Rhianna as the bloodstain spread like a blossoming rose.

As the Everqueen faded, the land sickened and died, the grasses turning black and the trees cracking and wilting as the life was drained from them.

With the last of her strength, the Everqueen looked up and her eyes locked to Rhianna's.

'Come to me, my child,' she said. 'He needs your help. Save him and you will save me!'

Rhianna closed her eyes and screamed as she saw a spreading bloodstain on her own chest. She felt the pain of a wound, the same sharp, piercing agony she had felt when the druchii crossbow bolt had pierced her shoulder so long ago, and her hands flew to her breast.

As her hands left the omphalos stone the pain vanished and her sight returned to normal. She slumped to the ground, her breathing ragged and her mind filled with the residue of what the oracle had shown her.

The darkened cave snapped back into view and she saw the oracle step around the stone to stand above her. Rhianna looked up, a glimmer of light shining beneath the woman's hood, and she screamed again as she saw her face transform.

In an instant, her face changed from that of a youthful elf maid to one of full womanhood and then to that of a deathly crone, ravaged and withered by time. Even as she watched, the cycle repeated itself over and over and Rhianna scrambled away, desperately pushing herself to her feet.

She turned from the oracle and fled the cavern temple of the Mother Goddess.

* * *

TYRION KNELT BY his twin's bed and held his hand, watching his thin chest rise and fall, each breath a victory for his magically ravaged body. When he and his Silver Helms had ridden into the forest surrounding the Tower of Hoeth, he had been shocked rigid by the devastation he had seen, unable to comprehend what power could unmake something so powerful as the Scholar King's tower.

He had ridden hard and without pause, but when he had seen the ruin of his brother, Tyrion wished he could have pushed Malhandir to even greater speeds. Even before his wounding, Teclis had been slight and reliant on the power of magic to sustain him, but now he was a shadow even of that.

'Do I really look so terrible? ' asked Teclis.

'No,' said Tyrion. 'I am just tired from the ride south. You are looking better.'

'Ah, Tyrion, my dear brother,' smiled Teclis. 'You have too good a heart to be much of a liar. I know how I must look and I know that it pains you that you cannot fight it.'

Mitherion Silverfawn had explained as best he could what had happened to Teclis and Tyrion had kept vigil by his twin's bed, holding his hand and praying to Isha to grant him the strength to survive.

'I will hunt down this Caelir and kill him,' promised Tyrion.

'No!' said Teclis, pushing himself onto his elbows with a grimace of pain. 'Promise me that you will do no such thing, my brother!'

'But he nearly killed you! And who knows what else the druchii will have him do?'

'He is as much a victim as I,' said Teclis. 'We must not

hate Caelir for what has been done to him. I need you to promise me that you will not harm Caelir if your paths should cross.'

'I cannot do that,' said Tyrion, rising to his feet. 'He is an enemy of Ulthuan and deserves only death.'

'No,' said Teclis, reaching up to grasp his arm. 'Please, Tyrion. Listen to me. You are a great warrior and your name carries great power. In the days of blood that are coming, your presence will be needed to steel the courage of all around you. If you give yourself over to this quest for vengeance, others will look for your leadership and they will falter when you do not provide it. You have a duty to Ulthuan and that duty does not include revenge!'

Tyrion looked at the urgency in his twin brother's face and took a deep, calming breath. He sat back down next to Teclis and said, 'I promised the Everqueen I would heed your counsel.'

'And you can never disobey her,' smiled Teclis.

'No,' said Tyrion. 'It is the curse of males to be forever in the thrall of beauty.'

'Some things are worth being in thrall to.'

'I know,' said Tyrion, his earlier anger forgotten. 'Very well, if you will not have me hunt Caelir, what would you have me do, sail to Ellyrion and lead the defenders of the Eagle Gate? Rumours from the west say that the Hag Sorceress herself leads the armies of the druchii.'

'She does,' said Teclis. 'I have felt her power on the winds of magic.'

'Then I will go to Ellyrion,' spat Tyrion, 'and cut the vile heart from her chest!'

'No, for there are warriors there with the seeds of greatness within them and Ellyrion must look to its own defence for now. The hammer of the druchii will land elsewhere, and it is there that your courage will be needed most.'

'Tell me, brother, where will this hammer strike?'

'In the south,' said Teclis. 'Upon Lothern.'

BOOK FOUR
AVELORN

CHAPTER SEVENTEEN

SEA OF BLOOD

OF ALL THE marvels of Lothern, the Glittering Lighthouse was one of the most famed and most magnificent. Rearing up from the sea atop a rocky isle to the south of Ulthuan, it was a great beacon filled with thousands of lamps that tradition held could never be extinguished. Mighty fortresses clustered at its base, each bastion equipped with scores of bolt throwers and garrisoned by hundreds of Sea Guard warriors.

Designed to protect the Emerald Gate that led to Lothern itself, the fortifications blended seamlessly with the cliffs and rocks of the island in a manner both lethal and aesthetically pleasing. The Emerald Gate itself was a mighty arched fortress that spanned the gap between the jagged fangs of rock that formed the mouth of the Straits of Lothern. A gleaming gate barred the sea route to Lothern, though such was the skill of the gate's designers that it could be opened smoothly and quickly when the need arose.

The fleets of the Asur roamed freely around the southern coasts of Ulthuan thanks to its protection, for should any vessel be threatened, it could flee to the coverage of the war machines mounted on the walls of the lighthouse and the Emerald Gate.

The first warning of the attack came as low, lightning-split thunderheads rolled in from the south and a dusky mist drew in around the lighthouse. Its dazzling halo of lanterns faded until it was visible as little more than a soft glow from the watchtowers of the Emerald Gate nearly a mile away.

A looming shape, like a mountain shorn from the land and set adrift on the sea, hove into view, the wreckage of a silver ship smashed against its flanks.

A host of smaller trumpet blasts sounded from the lighthouse and magical lights flared in the gathering night as the elven lookouts recognised the mountain as one of the feared Black Arks of the druchii.

Cries of alarm passed from bastion to bastion and warriors rushed to the ramparts and Eagle's Claw bolt throwers were loaded with deadly bolts. A host of enemy war machines known as Reapers, an evil corruption of the noble bolt throwers of the Asur, opened up from the ark and loosed hails of barbed iron darts from on high. Hundreds of shafts slashed through the air and, without protection from above, dozens of elven warriors were skewered and half a dozen bolt throwers were smashed to splintered ruin.

Coruscating fireballs of dark magic streaked from the crooked towers of the ark and exploded against the tower of the lighthouse. Streaming like horizontal rain, the purple fire of druchii sorcerers hammered the marble bastions of the island, searing flesh from the living and melting stone like wax.

Great rents were torn open in the fortress walls of the island and many brave warriors died as they were carried to their deaths by the collapsing walls. The Black Ark crashed against the island of the Glittering Lighthouse with the force of continents colliding, and a host of timber boarding ramps slammed down on the rock. Hundreds of druchii warriors stormed from the interior of the colossal black fortress, their sword blades reflecting the light of the beacon above them.

Fierce battle was joined as the Sea Guard of Lord Aislin rushed to plug the gaps torn in their defences by the druchii magic. Screams and the clash of blades echoed over the sea.

For all the carnage wreaked by the druchii, the defenders of Lothern recovered quickly from their surprise and fought back with all the skill and ferocity of their race. Hundreds of war machines opened up on the Black Ark and druchii were swept from their rocky battlements by a rain of lethal darts.

Magical bolts of white fire conjured by the lighthouse's mages erupted across the face of the Black Ark and the rock vitrified into glistening glass wherever it touched. The fighting on the Glittering Lighthouse waxed fierce as Lord Aislin's soldiers fought face to face with their ancestral enemies and neither side was in the mood to offer quarter.

The Emerald Gate groaned as the huge bronze valves to either side of the huge, arched fortress began to turn and, though it seemed impossible for such immense portals to move at all, they smoothly swept open to reveal the Straits of Lothern and a shimmering fleet of ships.

The elven fleet slipped easily through the bottle green waters, surging into the open ocean to engage the enemy. Hundreds of ships sailed through the gate, white sails bright in the evening sun and decks glittering with armed warriors. Such a fleet was more than capable of destroying a Black Ark and the warriors of the Emerald Gate held their fire as they watched the ships of the elven fleet sail out to do battle.

But as the mist parted before the lighthouse, it soon became apparent that the Black Ark had not come to make war on Lothern alone.

CAPTAIN FINLAIN WATCHED with trepidation as the mist parted before *Finubar's Pride* and he saw the full scale of the approaching druchii fleet. A tightening of his jaw was the only outward sign of his concern, for he did not want his unease to pass to the crew. Though it was hard to be certain, Finlain estimated that nearly three hundred ships cut through the waters towards the Emerald Gate. Raven warships armed with fearsome Reaper bolt throwers and hooked boarding ramps led the advancing fleet in a wedge formation with the point aimed straight for his ship.

Behind the leading warships came a host of wide galleys with high sides and a multitude of decks. No doubt these ships were packed with druchii warriors and Finlain longed to get in amongst these lumbering vessels, where his newly mounted Eagle's Claw would wreak fearsome havoc. But Lord Aislin's plan had another role for *Finubar's Pride*…

A host of fighting ships followed behind the druchii troop galleys in line abreast, but his lookouts high on the mainmast had already reported that too wide a gap had opened between the galleys and this last line of ships to make it a truly effective rearguard.

Thunder boomed overhead and a flash of lightning briefly painted the sky in blue. The first spots of rain fell and Finlain could feel the swell beneath his ship gathering in strength.

Finlain smiled and Meruval the navigator said, 'What can you possibly find amusing in all this?'

'The druchii are fearsome warriors, but they are no sailors,' replied Finlain.

'How so?'

'These vessels are clearly new, yes? Normally they make war upon the sea from these damned floating fortresses, but they've yet to learn how to fight properly on a ship of war.'

'And we'll teach them a lesson in how it's done, is that it?' said Meruval, angling the *Finubar's* tiller a fraction to keep her in line.

'Indeed we shall,' said Finlain.

He glanced left and right, satisfied that his fellow captains were following Lord Aislin's hastily assembled battle plan. For all its ad hoc nature, Finlain had to admire the admiral's instinctive grasp of what the druchii attempted and how it might be countered.

The elven ships sailed into the worsening weather to meet the druchii, manoeuvring perfectly into line abreast with the ships on the flanks sailing slightly ahead of the centre. As the distance closed between the two fleets, Finlain spared a glance to his left where the sounds of furious battle carried over the seas from the fighting on the slopes of the Glittering Lighthouse.

'Asuryan grant you strength, my brothers,' he whispered, knowing that, for the moment, the warriors there

were on their own. Flaring explosions of magical light
and the tinny shriek of swords seemed pitifully quiet for
what must surely be a desperate struggle to the death.

He shook off thoughts of that battle and focused on
the bloodshed and horror in which his own ship and
warriors were soon to be embroiled. The decks of *Finubar's Pride* were crammed with Sea Guard in glittering
hauberks of ithilmar mail and her sails snapped and
billowed in the blustery winds.

'They're coming on fast,' said Meruval.

'Good,' nodded Finlain. 'Their hatred will drive them
on faster than any storm wind.'

His experienced eye watched the advancing wedge of
druchii ships surge forward as their crews tacked into
the wind with more skill than he would have expected
and he cautioned himself against underestimating the
druchii sailors.

The threatening wedge of dark ships was pulling
ahead of the main body of galleys, no doubt hoping
to punch through the thinner line of elven ships and
scatter them before turning to savage them like a pack
of wolves.

You'll think you're about to get your wish, he thought as
he nodded to Meruval.

Closer now, the druchii ships resembled the long,
dark birds for which they were named. Their prows
were hooked and a boarding ramp with heated iron
spikes stood ready to hammer into the deck of its prey.
The glow of the lighthouse shimmered on hundreds of
blades and Finlain shuddered as he imagined these warriors penetrating the defences of Lothern.

The druchii ships were almost upon them and Finlain
knew he had to judge the next moment with exacting

precision. Too soon and the druchii would realise his intent, too late and they would be overwhelmed and destroyed.

White foam broke against the sleek hulls of the Raven ships, sending high sprays of dark water over their decks, and Finlain could see Reaper crews preparing to loose their deadly volleys of black darts.

He turned to Meruval and said, 'Now, my friend.'

The navigator swung the tiller around and *Finubar's Pride* heeled violently to port. Either side of her, the entire centre of the elven fleet seemed to pirouette upon the sea. Crewmen raced to haul lines and swing the sails around to catch the same winds the druchii flew upon and the deck became a flurry of activity.

Finubar's Pride plunged into a trough of green water, a rush of the sea pouring in over her deck at such a violent manoeuvre, but Finlain wasn't worried about that. Within moments, his ship was aimed straight back at the Emerald Gate, the sails booming as they filled with strong southerly winds and a hard rain began to fall.

Like colts freed from the stable, *Finubar's Pride* and a hundred other ships raced back towards Ulthuan with the Raven ships right behind them.

'Well done!' cried Finlain as he heard the ratcheting *whoosh* of the Reaper bolt throwers loosing. He looked over his shoulder and saw the long, wickedly sharp bolts arcing through the rain towards them and then splash into the sea less than a spear length behind them.

The druchii ships surged after them, hatred driving them after the fleeing elven ships.

'Well, they're definitely coming…' said Meruval.

Finubar nodded, watching with grim satisfaction as the elven ships on the flanks of what had once been their line surged forwards into the newly formed gap between the pursuing Raven ships and troop galleys that was widening by the second.

'They're reacting exactly as Lord Aislin predicted,' said Meruval.

'Let's hope they continue to do so,' said Finlain.

AVELORN. MAGICAL KINGDOM of the Everqueen and most ancient of the elven realms.

Every tale Caelir could remember of the enchanted forest realm had spectacularly failed to capture the beauty and sense of wonder he felt in every breath he took of the heavenly fragrances that hung heavy in the air. Everywhere were wonders for the senses; sights to beguile, scents to savour and sounds to revel in.

Music and song followed the company through the forest, some of Caelir's own creation and some of the forest itself. An air of barely suppressed excitement had seized the group as they crossed the river at the outskirts of the forest and Caelir had felt a potent sense of the ancient magic that lurked beneath the bewitching glamours of this land.

The air gossiped with news of their passing and tales of their songs, and each time they had crested a rolling hill or entered a different season of the forest, its inhabitants were ready to greet them with wine and requests for entertainment.

The journey northwards had been one of excitement and awakening for Caelir, and he had relaxed into a routine of talking and laughing with his fellow travellers during the day then enjoying the luxury of hot food and a soft bedroll at night. The rugged splendour of the Finuval Plain had eventually given way to the forested outskirts of Avelorn and Caelir had performed for the travelling company several times upon the rug, discovering yet more talents he had not previously been aware of. He recited long forgotten epics of Aenarion, played haunting laments from the time of Morvael and sang arias from the creation operas of Tazelle with Lilani.

The presence of such beauty kept the cares of the world at bay, and the blood and death that had surrounded Caelir since his awakening seemed to recede into the hindmost part of his thoughts.

Days passed in a blur of song and wonder and each time Caelir had thought his capacity for amazement exhausted, he would see yet another marvel to render him speechless with delight. In sun-dappled glades he saw elf maids clad in shimmering gowns of mist on the backs of unicorns; great, golden feathered eagles soared above the forest canopy and as they had descended into a shadowed dell, he heard the creaking, heavy footfalls of what Lilani told him was one of the ancient forest's treemen.

The dancer was a lover of rare vigour and nor was she shy in telling others of *his* prowess. On nights when the dreamwine flowed and ardent performances fired the blood of the company, they would take other lovers in the heat of passion and petty concerns such as jealousy and morality became irrelevant when art of such beauty and meaning was in the air.

Such behaviour was at odds with the disciplined life of the Asur Caelir remembered, but he could not find it in himself to think of it as wrong.

He had spoken of this as the company penetrated deeper into the Everqueen's forest, and in answer, Narentir had spoken to him of the group's philosophies.

They sat together on the padded seats of one of the wagons as Lilani rode beside them on Caelir's black steed and listened with wry amusement to their conversation.

'It's really quite simple, my dear boy,' said Narentir. 'To deny yourself the pleasures of the senses is to deny your soul its nourishment. Why would the gods have given us this capacity for sensual pleasure and enjoyment if not to use it?'

'I don't know,' he said. 'I don't think I'm much of a philosopher.'

'Nonsense, dear heart,' said Narentir, putting his arm around Caelir. 'Life is hard and every year it gets harder. Norse raiders attack from the sea and every day new horrors are unleashed upon the world. But none of that concerns us.'

'It doesn't?'

'No, for we are not heroes or warriors, are we? We are dancers, poets, musicians and singers. What possible use could we be in times of crisis? Folk such as us do not fight wars; we celebrate those who do in songs and poems. Without people like us, there would be nothing worth living for. A bland and tasteless world it would be without songs and singers to give them voice. So why let the cares of the world hang from our shoulders when there are elves like that golden fellow we saw with the splendid silver knights to bear them for us?'

Caelir remembered the armoured warrior with the winged helmet as he had ridden by them several days ago, and the strange feeling of accomplishment that had swept through him when they had ridden past still lingered in his memory. Only later had he realised that the warrior had been none other than Prince Tyrion and he wished he had savoured the sight of such a legendary figure.

'But surely everyone has to contribute to the greater good,' protested Caelir, dragging his thoughts back to the present. 'The citizen levies, for example.'

Narentir shook his head. 'Dear boy, can you see me as a soldier?'

'Maybe not now, but you must have spent some time in the levy.'

'I did, I did, that's true. I spent a loathsome summer in the ranks of the Eataine Levy and I was a terrible warrior. More dangerous to my comrades than the enemy I shouldn't wonder. Each of us has a place in the world, Caelir, and to try and fit where one does not belong is wasteful. When I realised this fact, I gave myself over to absolute pleasure and gathered like-minded souls about me to seek gratification in all things.

'Of course some small minded types disapproved of wantons such as us, declaring we were little better than the Cult of Pleasure.'

Caelir's eyes widened at the mention of the dark sect begun by the Hag Sorceress many thousands of years ago. Its devotees had indulged their every sordid whim and desire, plumbing depths of insanity never imagined, and evil stories of their excesses were still told as cautionary tales to the young.

'I see you've heard the name, dear boy, but we are nothing like those terrible monsters, merely poor players who wish to wring each moment dry of sensation and indulge in our passion for the arts. I ask you, do we look like the sort to engage in blood sacrifices?'

Caelir laughed and said, 'No, you certainly don't.'

'Thank you,' smiled Narentir. 'And since we clearly were unwanted in Lothern, we decided to make for the one place on Ulthuan I knew we would be welcome.'

'And what do you plan to do now that you are here?'

'Do, my dear Caelir?' said Narentir. 'I do not intend to *do* anything at all, I simply intend to *be*. To sing songs and tell wonderful tales, to make love beneath the stars and to become part of the Everqueen's court.'

'And become one of her consorts…' said Lilani.

Narentir laughed and said, 'Perhaps even that, my dear, perhaps even that. For this is Avelorn and who can guess what miracles are possible beneath its boughs?'

THE DRUCHII GALLEYS were monstrous ships, high sided and dark hulled, constructed in the hellish shipyards of Clar Karond. The vessels ran low in the water, such was the weight of warriors they carried, and displayed none of the usual grace of elven hands, even druchii ones, for they had been constructed with the bloody toil of slaves. These were simply hulks, fashioned to bear troops to another land and not to bring them back.

The Eagle ships that had sailed on the flanks of the elven line were wolves in a herd of slumbering sheep, their speed and manoeuvrability enabling them to slash through the lines of ships and attack with virtual impunity. Druchii crossbowmen shot iron darts from behind shield-lined gunwales, but the Eagle ships danced across the waves beyond their range.

Heavy silver bolts from Eagle's Claw bolt throwers smashed through the timbers of the troop galleys, wreaking havoc in the decks below as they speared dozens of warriors at a time. Hails of smaller bolts swept the decks of the druchii ships and they ran red with rivers of blood.

Elven mages hurled rippling sheets of fire from the forecastles of the Eagle ships and the tarred wood of the hulks burst into flame. The gathering storm clouds reflected the light of battle as a hateful orange glow and only the rain saved many of the hulks from instant immolation. The druchii ships attempted to sail close to one another for protection, but against the speed and skill of the elven captains there was nothing they could do but suffer the hails of blue-fletched arrows and lethal bolts that punched through their hulls and slaughtered their warriors.

The Eagle ships wove between the wallowing troop galleys like predators of the wild, denying them any respite from the killing. Flames leapt from ship to ship as flaming sheets of sail were caught on hot updraughts and set light to other ships.

Timber groaned and split as a druchii hulk broke apart and spilled its complement of warriors into the sea. Druchii screamed as they fell into the dark, flame-lit waters, splashing frantically as their armour dragged them to the bottom of the ocean.

The eastern flank of Lord Aislin's fleet drove many of the ungainly transports towards the cliffs of Ulthuan, where they would be dashed to destruction against undersea rocks.

The rearguard of the druchii fleet, seeing the horrifying carnage wreaked amongst the galleys, surged forwards and suddenly the Eagle ships were faced with a foe that had teeth and could fight back.

The Raven ships were larger than those of the Asur, but no less manoeuvrable, and the battle degenerated into a bloody duel of deadly missiles as the two fleets darted between burning galleys and hunted one another in billowing clouds of smoke and ocean spray.

Thus far, the Eagle ships had had the best of the battle,

but the Raven ships were not the simple prey the transport galleys had been.

Druchii sorcerers froze the water around the elven ships, whereupon they were ripped apart by hails of bolts or boarded by screaming warriors. Vicious boarding actions erupted as druchii assault ramps hammered against the hulls of trapped Eagle ships, and warriors fought to the death on the heaving, blood-slick decks of their vessels.

Sorcerous fire blasted great chunks from Eagle ships and sent them to watery graves as the sea poured inside their pristine hulls. The attacking rearguard reaped a fearsome tally of Eagle ships, but they were still outnumbered and without the added strength their vanguard provided, the Eagle ships could still win the fight.

EVEN THROUGH THE rain, Captain Finlain could see the walls of flame from behind the pursuing Raven ships. Lord Aislin's flanking ships would even now be running amok amongst the slower, heavier transport galleys and druchii warriors would be dying.

The thought made him grin.

Their feigned retreat had drawn the wedge of the druchii ships forward and he knew it was time to turn and fight. The flanking ships would need their support if this battle were to be won.

But first the druchii ships at his stern needed to be sunk.

'How many do you think?' he shouted over to Meruval.

The navigator threw a glance over his shoulder and said, 'Perhaps sixty or so.'

Finlain nodded, agreeing with Meruval's assessment.

Sixty armed warships was not a force to underestimate, but he had more ships and the best mariners in the world at his command.

And soon he would have the element of surprise when they turned on their pursuers…

The rain and wind were growing in power and intensity, but he had sailed the oceans of the world for long enough to know how to make use of such things.

'Meruval, prepare to turn about!' he cried over the howling winds. 'It's our turn to earn glory and honour!'

'Glory and honour, yes sir!' returned Meruval as Finlain marched between the eager warriors lining his deck. Their tunics were plastered to their armour by the rain and their silver speartips glittered with diamonds of moisture.

He nodded to these warriors as he passed, confident that they would smash this druchii fleet and send it to the bottom of the ocean, along with every one of their crews. They were almost within range of the mighty bolt throwers on the Emerald Gate and when they were, he would turn the ships of the elven fleet to face their pursuers as swiftly as they had turned away from them.

Caught between a suddenly resurgent foe and the lethal bolts of the Emerald Gate, the destruction of the druchii would be swift and merciless.

Finlain looked up into the sky as he heard a booming crack of air and awaited the flicker of lightning a second later. The skies remained resolutely dark and his eyes narrowed in puzzlement, but he put it from his mind as Meruval shouted from the tiller. 'Captain! Come quickly!'

Hearing the alarm in Meruval's voice, Finlain sprinted across the deck and flew up the steps to the vessel's tiller. He looked over the stern of *Finubar's Pride* and saw with horror the druchii were turning to rejoin the battle raging between his flanking Eagle ships and the enemy rearguard.

'What are they doing?' he cried as the Raven ships surged away from his ships.

'Looks like they're not taking our bait,' said Meruval.

'Quick! Turn us about!' shouted Finlain.

The *Finubar's Pride* angled into the sea and her sleek prow cut through a wall of dark water as she began a sharp turn. The other captains in his line had seen the same thing he had and were also bringing their ships about.

A tail pursuit was far from the ideal way to fight a sea battle, but Finlain saw they had no choice. If the enemy vessels earmarked for destruction at his hands were able to add their strength to the battle raging further out to sea then all was lost.

Once again Finlain heard the booming crack of air above him, but as he looked up once more, he realised that this was no peal of thunder as he saw a monstrous dark shape flash through the low clouds overhead.

He ran to the side of *Finubar's Pride* as he saw the dark shape drop through the clouds upon the silver ship next to his.

A terrifying reptilian shape, massive and scaled in darkness, spread its mighty wings and seized the ship's mast in its taloned hind legs. Timber shattered with a splintering crack as the boat was wrenched upwards and its keel split apart under the strain.

Finlain's heart turned to a lump of ice as the colossal black dragon was illuminated in a flash of blue thunder. Its great horned head snapped down and a handful of flailing elves were scooped up in its fanged jaws. Blood sprayed from between its teeth as it bit down and Finlain forced himself to act.

'Ready the Eagle's Claw!' he shouted as his archers took aim at the terrifying beast that beat the air into a whirlwind with its wide wings.

A streaking bolt of violet lightning leapt from behind the dragon's colossal head and Finlain had a brief image of a giant in dark armour sitting between the spines of the roaring monster. Cold green eyes glittered behind the figure's helmet and Finlain knew there was only one denizen of Naggaroth who encapsulated such force of hate and malice.

This was no mere druchii princeling...

This was the Witch King himself.

The dragon beat its wings and flew towards another ship, mercifully not the *Finubar's Pride*, and its jaws opened wide as a streaming cloud of hissing vapours erupted from its gullet. Finlain could only watch in horror as the ship's crew fell screaming to the deck, the skin melting from their bones and their lungs burning in the dragon's corrosive breath.

Arrows slashed towards the great beast, but its dark hide was proof against such irritants, and its diabolical rider hurled deadly arcs of lightning that set ships aflame with every flick of his clawed hands. Ships burned with magical fire or were smashed to matchwood by the power of the dragon. To their credit, Finlain's crew were able to loose a silver bolt at the rampaging monster, but the unnatural power of its rider protected it and the bolt burned to ashes before it even struck home.

A few captains attempted to sail clear of the carnage and reach the flanking Eagle ships, but the dragon and its hateful rider thwarted every effort, smashing them to ruin and slaughtering their crew. Ship after ship splintered and broke apart under the assault and Finlain saw that nothing could stand against such raw, violent strength.

'We cannot fight this!' shouted Finlain. 'Meruval, get us back through the Emerald Gate.'

The Witch King and his roaring dragon made sport of Lord Aislin's fleet and the destruction they wrought on each of their victims allowed a precious few of the remaining ships to turn and sail back towards Ulthuan.

Along with a handful of Eagle ships, *Finubar's Pride* fled the slaughter that was turning the ocean red and Finlain knew that, without support, the Eagle ships still fighting further out would soon be at the bottom of the ocean.

Through the smoke and fires of battle, Finlain could hear the blood-soaked victory chants of the druchii as they fought through the fortress walls of the Glittering Lighthouse. The shimmering beacon atop the lighthouse flickered for a moment in the storm-wracked darkness, as though fighting to stay alight.

He closed his eyes in sorrow as the light guttered and died.

The *Finubar's Pride* sailed between the great arched walls of the Emerald Gate and he whispered, 'Forgive us…'

The first battle for Lothern had been lost.

Chapter Eighteen

Kinstrife

THE MOUTH OF the River Arduil was a gentle bow in the coastline of Avelorn, and Eldain felt his pulse quicken as Captain Bellaeir steered them around the forested headland that separated it from the Sea of Dusk. To walk in the enchanted realm of the Everqueen would be a new experience for Eldain, but even as he felt the breath of magic from the northern kingdom, he reminded himself that they were not travelling here as pilgrims.

Then as what? Rescuers? Assassins?

Eldain didn't know and nor did he know yet which he would prefer.

He looked over his shoulder to where Rhianna and Yvraine sat huddled in conversation beside the mast and suppressed a flash of annoyance. Since swimming back to the *Dragonkin*, neither woman had elaborated as to what had happened on the island of the Gaen Vale. Rhianna had simply told Bellaeir to sail for Avelorn.

The mood of the ship had lightened the further from the Gaen Vale they travelled and Rhianna had come to him one night as they sailed beneath the starlit sky with her arms open.

'You understand I am forbidden to speak of the island,' she had said.

'I understand,' he said, though, in truth, he did not.

'Can you tell me anything at all?'

'Just that we have to go to Avelorn.'

'Is that where Caelir is?'

'It's where he is going.'

'Why? Do you know?'

She pursed her lips and shook her head. 'Not for certain, but I am beginning to think that what happened at the Tower of Hoeth was just the beginning. Whatever Caelir was sent back to do is just beginning.'

'That's a reassuring thought.'

'It's not his fault,' said Rhianna. 'You heard what the Loremaster said. Caelir is as much a victim here as anyone else.'

He nodded, but had not answered, and took her in his arms as the ship sailed onwards.

'Save him and you save me…' she whispered in the darkness.

'What's that? A quote?'

'No, something I heard. Something important.'

'What does it mean?'

'I don't know yet.'

She burrowed deeper into his embrace as a chill gust blew in off the water and a red shooting star flashed south across the blackness of the sky. They stayed that way, like a statue of embracing lovers, as night turned to day and the sea transformed from a dark mirror of the heavens to a glorious green.

Morning brought the coast of Avelorn into view and the sight of land that he could actually walk upon raised Eldain's spirits immeasurably. He made his way from the vessel's prow to the tiller, where Captain Bellaeir sat enjoying the stiff breeze blowing from the kingdom of the Everqueen.

'Captain,' he said, resting his arm on the raised gunwale.

'My lord,' nodded the ship's master. 'Isha willing, I'll have you in Avelorn in a few hours.'

'That sounds good,' said Eldain. 'I mean no disrespect when I say this, but it will be good to set foot on land once more.'

Bellaeir nodded. 'Spoken like a true Ellyrian, my lord. But you are right, it will do us all good to be off the seas for a spell.'

The sentiment surprised Eldain and he said, 'Really? I thought you would be happy to spend your whole life at sea.'

'Normally I would be,' agreed Bellaeir, 'but there are dark currents stirring in the waters and they are full of sadness. I don't know where, but somewhere elves are dying at sea.'

Eldain heard the pain in Bellaeir's voice and decided not to press the point as the captain guided them towards the river's mouth.

Towering trees rose up from the edge of the land, sprawling forests that stretched eastwards as far as the eye could see in vivid splashes of green, russets and gold. Misty with distance, the blue crags of the Annulii were a far distant smudge on the horizon, a barrier between the kingdom of the Everqueen and war-torn Chrace.

The *Dragonkin* eased past the forested headlands and Eldain narrowed his eyes as he saw a froth of white water bubbling where the placid waters of the river met the sea.

'Water sprites,' said Bellaeir as he saw Eldain's expression. 'We call them *keylpi* and they are playful things mostly, but don't get too close to them.'

As the ship drew nearer, Eldain saw the suggestion of white horses with flowing manes cavorting in the depths of the bubbling water and fancied he could hear their whinnying neighs of amusement in the foam that surrounded them. The sprites moved alongside the ship and Eldain saw ghostly horses of shimmering light galloping beneath the surface, their manes flowing with the current and their tails a fan of white bubbles behind them.

The urge to ride such a beast was almost irresistible, and his Ellyrian soul ached to climb upon its back and ride the waves, but such creatures were said to be capricious entities, as likely to drag him to his death as they were to grant him an exhilarating ride.

Eldain could hear the stamping hooves of their own horses in the ship's hold and knew they must also be sensing the siren song of the magical water horses. He turned away from the *keylpi*, hearing their displeasure as a crash of water against the side of the ship. A wave splashed over the gunwale and Bellaeir laughed as Eldain was drenched in water.

'I told you not to get too close,' said Bellaeir.

Eldain shrugged and went below to change his clothes, and when he emerged the water sprites were far behind them. The *Dragonkin* had passed from the Sea of Dusk and into the River Arduil, the waterway that marked the border between Ellyrion and Avelorn.

To the west, golden plains basked beneath an indolent summer sky and a sudden stab of homesickness pierced Eldain as he pictured his home of Ellyr-charoi. He saw the white-walled villa nestling between the two waterfalls, the heights of the Hippocrene Tower, the Summer Courtyard and the sweet smelling pines that shawled the landscape around it.

He missed his home. He longed to see it once again and to share it with Rhianna before leaving it forever.

Eldain shook off these reminiscences and turned from the land of his birth to face the kingdom of Avelorn.

Shaggy with dense and sprawling forest, the sound of distant music drifted on the air and twinkling lights seemed to dance in the forest's depths. Colourful birds nested in the treetops and a sense of powerful magic threaded between the smooth trunks.

The forests of Ellyrion had a youthful splendour to them, but Avelorn was of an age beyond reckoning, its farthest depths home to creatures that had dwelled there even before the coming of the asur: eagles, treemen and slumbering things whose names had been forgotten.

The forest had an eternal quality to it, an ageless majesty that not even invasion and war could diminish. The druchii had tried to burn the old forest, setting fires amid groves that had been planted when the world was young, but even they had failed to diminish its grandeur.

Trees that had stood sentinel over the Everqueen's realm towered above them like grim watchtowers and Eldain felt a brooding hostility from the forest's edge, as though their shadows cast a grim warning to any who harboured evil thoughts in their heart.

Eldain shivered and the *Dragonkin* sailed on.

* * *

THE SOUNDS OF battle echoed within the Aquila Spire and Glorien Truecrown could not shut it out no matter how hard he tried. He concentrated on his books, desperate to find some clue as to how to defeat the foe that daily hurled itself at the walls of the Eagle Gate. The bloodshed was prodigious and hundreds of the followers of the Dark Gods were dying every day; pierced by arrows, hurled from the walls or cut down by graceful blows from swords and spears.

Thus far the druchii had not attacked, save by sending in the disgusting flying creatures that filled the air with their unmusical screeches and swooped on the crews of the bolt throwers. Morathi was content to batter the humans against the wall and her monstrous ally, the great tribal warleader with the standard revering the Dark Prince, seemed eager to let her.

Screaming tribesmen erected mounds of their fallen and made sport of the flesh before burning them in great funeral pyres and conducting their filthy worship in full view of the fortress. The sight of such unclean devotions had made Glorien sick and driven him to his books, his precious books, to seek a solution.

But he had found nothing, despite days of searching, and the brawling sound of battle from beyond the locked door and shuttered windows of the tower continued unabated.

Glorien had sent desperate petitions for more warriors to Tor Elyr, but his mages reported that a terrible sea battle had been lost at the gates of Lothern and all musters of the citizen levy were being sent to Eataine. Some *were* gathering in Ellyrion, but not enough and not with enough speed to take the pressure off the warriors fighting on the bloody ramparts.

Casualty lists spoke of a hundred dead warriors already, with almost twice that injured. Many of those would not live to fight again and those that might would not heal in time to make any difference. The healers worked day and night, but they were too few and the enemy was sending them victims too quickly.

A sharp rapping came at the tower's only door and Glorien flinched at the sound.

'My lord, I must speak with you,' said a voice he recognised as belonging to Menethis.

Glorien rose from behind the desk and said, 'Are you alone?'

'Yes, my lord. There is no one with me.'

'Very well,' said Glorien and unbarred the door.

Menethis entered with unseemly haste and Glorien caught a glimpse of the fighting behind him. Once again, a host of ladders had been thrown against the wall, a trail of dead and wounded bodies scattered over the ground before it. Arrows and bolts filled the air as flocks of winged beasts circled above the towers, and desperate combats surged and withdrew like a dark tide along the length of the ramparts.

Glorien slammed the door shut as soon as Menethis was inside, unwilling to look upon the fighting raging below.

'What is it, Menethis?' said Glorien. 'I am very busy here. I am looking for a way to win this fight and I cannot do it with constant interruptions.'

'My lord, the situation below is desperate.'

'You think I don't know that?' said Glorien, indicating the piles of books scattered on the desk. 'The answer is in here, I know it.'

'With respect, my lord, it is not,' said Menethis, taking his arm firmly and pointing at the shuttered window. 'It is out there on the walls with the warriors who are fighting and dying to defend this fortress.'

Glorien threw off his second in command's grip. 'Ah, yes... but I found a passage in the works of Aethis. Here, look, it's in *Theories of War*.' Glorien scanned down the page until he found the specific passage he was looking for and held it up before him. 'Here, listen to this. "Any competently commanded fortress can expect to withstand a siege for an indefinite period of time so long as its garrison is well supplied, courageous and the enemy has not more than a three to one superiority of numbers." So you see, Menethis, everything hinges on the courage of the warriors. Only they can let us down, since we are well supplied, yes?'

'That was written a long time ago, my lord and Aethis was no soldier, he was a poet and a singer who fancied himself as a great leader. He never fought in a single battle.'

Glorien said, 'I know all that, but he was a *thinker*, Menethis, a thinker. His ideas are astounding. I know that if I can just–'

'My lord, I beg you!' cried Menethis. 'You have to come out and fight with our warriors. Morale is practically nonexistent and it is only the likes of Alathenar and Eloien Redcloak that are holding us together. You need to be seen, my lord! You need to fight!'

'No, no...' said Glorien, returning to sit behind the desk and placing his hand upon the scattered tomes. 'My books tell me that if the commander of an army should fall, it is disastrous for morale. No, I'll not expose myself to such danger until the time is right!'

'That time is now, my lord,' said Menethis.

* * *

SOARING HIGH ABOVE the bloody fighting ⟨
Gate, Elasir and his two brothers swoope⟨
mountains as they sought out enemy warri⟨
The skies above the fortress were clear now, for they
had driven off the twisted harpy creatures, though the
golden feathers of all three were bloodied and torn. Elasir himself sported a ragged scar, red and angry, across
his white crown.

Though battles such as the one now being fought in
the mountains were not to their liking, they had nested
in the high eyries and lent what aid they could to the
defenders of the Eagle Gate. As battle raged they would
swoop low over the walls, tearing off heads and slashing
limbs with their claws and beaks.

Druchii crossbowmen tried to bring them down, but
the eagles were too swift for them to hit and the cry of
the eagles soon became the terror of the Asur's enemies.
At the sight of the diving eagles, men would scatter
in panic and druchii would desperately try to gather
enough crossbows to fill the sky with bolts.

Elasir turned and extended his wings, slowing his
flight as he spied a foe worthy of their strength.

Approaching the gate, he said, bringing his wings back
in and turning in a tight circle.

His brothers had also spotted the danger and angled
their course to match his, tucking their wings in close
to their bodies as they plummeted back down towards
the valley.

Drawing close to the gate was a monstrous hydra, a
many-headed monster with iridescent scales, roaring
and tearing the ground as a pack of straining druchii
drove it forward with barbed tridents and vile curses.
Its multiple heads writhed on long, sinuous necks, and

ulphurous smoke billowed from each set of snapping jaws. Long spines like blistered growths sprouted from its back and a viscous slime seeped from weeping sores along its flanks where heavy iron plates had been fastened to its body with long chains and barbed hooks.

Volleys of arrows bounced from its armour or stuck in its flesh, but the monster was impervious to such minor wounds. Shouted cries echoed from the walls as war machines were brought to bear.

The eagles dived towards the hydra as its heads snapped forwards at a shouted command enforced by a barbed goad. A tremendous stream of liquid flame erupted from every mouth and the ramparts were bathed in searing fire. Elven warriors screamed as the creature's blazing excretions set them alight and gobbets of blazing sputum drooled down the wall.

Heavy bolts from Asur war machines stabbed through the air towards the beast. Some ricocheted from the armoured plates while others penetrated its massive body with spurts of black ichor.

Elasir sensed the Chaos taint within its flesh and knew the beast would not stop until every last drop of blood had been wrung from its body. He let loose a terrifying cry and opened his wings with a great boom and swung his claws around beneath his body.

Crossbow bolts slashed the air, but none came close to the diving eagles.

The hydra's nearest head twisted in the air like a snake as it heard their cry. Its jaws opened wide, but Elasir was already upon it. His iron hard claws raked across its skull, ripping through flesh and tearing into its dark, soulless eyes.

The head bucked under the assault and tore free from

his claws in a wash of blood. The eagles surrounded the hydra in a flurry of beating wings and powerful claws, tearing at its heads with vicious slashes of their beaks. Flames bloomed and Elasir heard Irian cry in pain as his feathers caught light.

Druchii warriors flocked around the beast, and Elasir dropped to land on the nearest, tearing his head off with a casual flick of his beak. Blood fountained and the eagle launched himself at the others as they levelled crossbows of dark wood.

Some ran and lived. Others stood their ground and died.

Elasir leapt back into the air and with powerful beats of his wings he came upon the hydra from behind. His golden brothers still fought the madly twisting heads, two of which lay limp and dead while three others fought with manic energy and terrible fury.

The lord of the eagles lunged forwards and fastened his claws on the base of one of the necks still fighting. The hydra bucked as it felt him land on its body, but his claws were dug into its hide and it could not dislodge him. Elasir's beak slashed into the meat and bone of its neck, slicing through it with three swift blows.

Druchii warriors swarmed around the beast, but were forced to keep their distance by the madly thrashing mêlée. Bolts filled the air and Elasir felt one score across his chest. Aeris opened the throat of another head and Irian blinded the last with a vicious sweep of his razored beak.

Helpless, the creature trampled druchii and men underfoot as it thrashed in its death agonies. The beast was as good as finished, and its final, frenzied moments would see yet more of the enemy dead.

The time had come to leave.

Fly, my brothers, cried Elasir, spreading his wings and taking to the air as yet more druchii ran towards the battle with crossbows. Fast or not, the lord of the eagles knew that with so many bolts in the air, at least some were sure to hit their targets.

Leaving the dying hydra behind them, the three eagles flew to safety.

ALATHENAR SLUMPED AGAINST the parapet, drawing his thighs up to his chest and resting his forehead on his knees. His body ached from exertion and a score of cuts he could not remember receiving.

The valley seemed abruptly silent now that the clamour of fighting had faded. To Alathenar's ears, days had two states: one of screaming steel and one of just screaming. As the sun dipped into the west and long shadows crept into the courtyard of the fortress, the sounds transitioned from the former to the latter as wounded warriors were carried from the walls and the routine of clearing the enemy dead began.

He was too exhausted to move and simply nodded as a wounded elf with his arm missing below the elbow handed him fresh quivers from a pannier slung around his neck.

Victual bearers made their way along the wall and Alathenar gratefully took a battered silver goblet of cool water and a hunk of waybread. Only when sluicers came to clean the wall of blood did he force his battered frame upright and make his way to the courtyard.

Eloien Redcloak was already there and arguing with the fortress's master of horses, but gave up and walked away when he saw Alathenar descending the cut stairs.

'Still alive then?' said the reaver.

'Just about,' agreed Alathenar. 'What was that about?'

'The fool wants to run the horses down to Ellyrion, but I told him we need them here.'

'For when we have to abandon this place and run,' finished Alathenar.

'Just so.'

'So you are not hopeful that we'll hold.' It wasn't a question.

'Are you?' countered Eloien.

'We may yet.'

'Don't be naïve, my friend. Look at the faces around you. The warriors are exhausted, leaderless and, worse, they have no hope.'

They walked over to a bench carved into the base of the Eagle Tower and sat in companionable silence for a few restful minutes to gather their strength. So far, the enemy had displayed an unwillingness to attack at night, content with burning corpses and chanting praises to the Dark Gods, but both warriors knew it was just a matter of time until such a ruse was attempted.

Eloien glanced up at the tall spike of the Aquila Spire. Yellow light seeped from the edges of the shuttered windows.

'Do you think he is ever going to come out of there?' asked the reaver.

'I don't know. I wish Cerion still commanded.'

'He was a good warrior?'

'One of the best,' nodded Alathenar. 'Knew when to keep to the rules and when to bend them. He had the heart of a Chracian lion, though he took a druchii blade to the face and never got his looks back.'

Alathenar jerked his thumb at the rearing length of the

wall and said, 'He would have seen this rabble off in no time, but Glorien…'

'Is an idiot,' said Eloien, 'a noble born fool who wouldn't know which end of a sword to hold and will see us all dead before he comes out of that tower. We'd be better off without him. What about his second? I've seen him fighting, but what is he like as a leader?'

'Menethis? More of a follower than a leader, but his heart is good. Why?'

'No reason, I just wondered if we might not be better off with someone else in charge?'

'Someone like Menethis?'

'Maybe, but as you say, he's not really what you would call leadership material.'

'Then who were you thinking of?'

'Don't be obtuse, Alathenar,' said Eloien. 'I've seen the way the warriors look to you and take your lead in all things. I'm talking about you.'

'Me? No… I'm not a leader, don't talk nonsense.'

'Nonsense, my friend? Nonsense would be letting Glorien Truecrown's cowardice lead us to death. Nonsense would be sitting and doing nothing about it.'

'Be that as it may, Glorien is the commander of the Eagle Gate and there's nothing we can do about that.'

'Maybe, maybe not,' said Eloien nodding thoughtfully and leaning forward, resting his elbows on his knees as a warrior Alathenar had not previously noticed emerged from the shadows beside them.

From his intense features and the skilful way he had concealed himself, Alathenar knew him to be one of the Nagarythe, and a shiver of apprehension worked its way down his spine.

'This is Alanrias,' said Eloien by way of introduction.

'I know who he is,' said Alathenar as Eloien continued.

'It is time to face up to the truth of our situation, my friend. If Glorien Truecrown remains in command of the Eagle Gate, it will fall. You know that to be true, I can see it in your eyes.'

'So what are you suggesting?' asked Alathenar, his gaze shifting from Eloien to the Shadow Warrior.

'You *know* what we are suggesting,' hissed Alanrias.

'This is sedition,' said Alathenar, rising to his feet. 'I could be executed just for hearing this.'

Eloien rose with him and said. 'You know I'm right, Alathenar.'

He took a deep breath. 'I will think on what you have said.'

The coarse, braying note of a tribal horn sounded from beyond the wall, echoing from the valley sides and warriors began hurrying to the battlements.

'Don't think for too long,' advised Eloien.

THE STORM HAD passed and the sea at the gates of Lothern was calm once more.

Smashed timbers and the dead bodies as yet untouched by sharks floated on the surface in sad bobbing clumps of defeat. Barely a handful of elven vessels had managed to escape into the sanctuary of the Straits of Lothern, the rest now little more than wreckage and grief.

The defenders of the Emerald Gate could only watch in impotent horror as the druchii fleet landed its surviving troop galleys on the island of the Glittering Lighthouse, its beacon extinguished and its walls home to the victorious warriors of Naggaroth. The Eagle ships had destroyed a great many of the troop galleys, but the returning vanguard of the druchii fleet had attacked without mercy and the slaughter had been tremendous.

Not a single Eagle ship survived the night and the druchii now had control of the ocean before the gates of Lothern. Sleek and deadly Raven ships patrolled the sea around the island of the lighthouse, alert for any counterattack and taking care to remain beyond the range of the Emerald Gate's war machines. Hulking galleys hove to alongside the island of the lighthouse in grim procession and thousands of dark-cloaked warriors marched from the packed holds with their spears glinting.

As each vessel was emptied, it would sail around the southern coast of the island to join a growing line of wide-bodied ships anchored side-by-side to form a great bridge between the island of the lighthouse and Ulthuan. Thick hawsers were lashed between the galleys and anchored to the land at either end.

Atop the ruined peak of the lighthouse, the armoured form of the Witch King sat astride his mighty dragon, Seraphon, and watched the labours below with grim satisfaction. Hundreds of warriors garrisoned the captured fortifications of the island and thousands more were disembarking from the galleys in preparation of marching on Ulthuan itself.

The Witch King knew that attacking the Emerald Gate from the sea was as close to impossible as made no difference, but if the fortresses guarding the shoulder haunches of the arching fortress could be taken…

The great, black-scaled dragon leapt from the ruined lighthouse and spread its midnight wings as it swooped down over the island with a bellowing roar of challenge.

CHAPTER NINETEEN

AWAKENINGS

OF ALL THE music and beauty Caelir could remember, none came close to matching those of the court of the Everqueen. He reclined on soft, autumn leaves and watched Lilani dance to the music and song of Narentir. The sound of silver bells chimed in the distance and a crowd had gathered beneath colourful silken pavilions to watch Lilani's performance.

Her movements were sinuous and graceful, but Caelir saw a harsh, aggressive vigour to her movements now, the muscles bunching and swelling beneath her glittering skin. At first he had wondered why the softness had disappeared, but then saw one of the Everqueen's Handmaidens among the appreciative spectators.

Like Lilani, the Handmaiden was slender and taut, but unlike the dancer, she wore a form-fitting breastplate of gold and carried a long spear. A scarlet plume, the same colour as her cloak, swept down the back of her helmet and a bone coloured longbow was slung across her shoulder.

The Handmaidens of the Everqueen were not mere

courtiers, but warriors the equal of any elven knight with bow, spear or sword. Chosen from the best dancers, singer, poets and lovers of Ulthuan, the Handmaidens epitomised the pinnacle of achievement in elven society with their mastery of both the courtly and martial arts. Caelir cast an appreciative eye over the Handmaiden, taking in her long bare legs and the moulded physique of her breastplate.

Watching Lilani dance, he now understood her reasons for seeking out the court of the Everqueen and saw they were little different from Narentir's.

He smiled to himself as he closed his eyes and let the sensations of the forest wash over him. To perform in the court of the Everqueen! Such things were the dreams of every elf of Ulthuan.

Musicians and singers trained all their life to be worthy of playing in Avelorn and the youths of Ulthuan dreamed of becoming a consort of the Everqueen while the maids aspired to become one of her Handmaidens.

Life in Avelorn was like living in an eternal festival, decided Caelir. They had been here for a few days now and, at every turn, musicians delighted audiences, dancers made play in the forest and poets recited their latest works.

The days were magical and the nights scarcely less so.

Ghostly light filled the court at night and glittering sprites darted from tree to tree to light the wondrous folk of the forest as they created art and beauty with every breath. Gaily coloured pavilions were pitched randomly through the forest and all manner of elves from all across Ulthuan came to play and make merry in the forest of the Everqueen.

Despite himself, Caelir had been caught up in the

spirit of Avelorn and slipped into an easy routine of player and spectator. By day he would sing to steadily growing crowds of admirers and by night he would walk the moonlit paths of the forest with Lilani and make love beneath the stars on a bed of golden leaves.

Thus far Caelir had seen no sign of the ruler of Avelorn, but Narentir assured him that the Everqueen rarely ventured openly among the court until she knew whom she would choose to accompany her glorious cavalcade through the forest realm.

The urgency that had driven him to seek the Everqueen had all but vanished, his anguish smothered by the healing magic of Avelorn. The imperative to see her arose powerfully with every dawn, beating its fists against the walls of his mind, but the soothing balms of the forest's music and light soon eased his troubled brow and the day would go on as before.

The sound of rapturous applause signalled the end of Lilani's dance and Caelir opened his eyes to see her perched on the low branches of a sunwood tree, her chest heaving and her hair unbound and wild.

Caelir joined in with the applause as she bowed deeply to her audience and somersaulted from the tree. The gathered elves moved on swiftly, their butterfly interest already anticipating the delights the rest of the forest had to offer. Narentir went with them, surrounded by a gaggle of admirers and Caelir smiled to himself as Lilani danced over and lay down next to him.

'Did you see?' she asked breathlessly, draping herself across his chest. Her skin glowed golden and he leaned down to kiss her.

She tasted of wild berries and her breath was hot in his mouth.

'I did, you were exquisite as always.'

'Liar,' she said. 'You were asleep. I saw.'

'No, I was awake,' he said.

'Then why didn't you watch me?'

'You weren't performing for me,' he said. 'I saw the Handmaiden in the audience.'

'I think she was impressed. Perhaps she will speak of me to the Everqueen,' said Lilani, her words coming out in a rush. Caelir smiled at this youthful, insecure side of Lilani, finding it an entertaining change from the confident aloofness she usually affected.

Such insecurity was understandable, for, as Caelir was quickly learning, the forest of the Everqueen was a seething hotbed of ego and intrigue, where every performer vied for the favour of the Everqueen and the chance of a place at her side.

To be chosen as a consort or Handmaiden was the highest honour imaginable for a youth of Ulthuan, but those whose artistry failed to impress the fickle inhabitants of the forest soon found themselves objects of ridicule.

Only the previous day, Caelir, Lilani and Narentir had watched a pair of singers perform in a sun-dappled glade. He had thought their voices magnificent, soaring into the treetops and entwining like lovers as the notes fell back to earth in a rain of flowers. He had found himself alone in applauding them and quickly stopped as he felt disapproving stares upon him.

A tall noble in a long robe of shimmering teal had stepped from the audience and bowed to the singers. 'Congratulations,' he had said. 'The Keeper of Souls must weep to know that one of her own has fallen from the heavens to entertain us with song. Truly it is said that anything too prosaic to be said is sung instead.'

The crowd had dispersed with ringing laughter and Caelir saw the light of joy flee from the singers' eyes at the comment, though he had been mystified as to why.

'My dear boy,' explained Narentir later. 'In Avelorn excellence is the very *least* that is expected of a performer. And while the caterwauling of those two so-called singers might impress the rustics of Chrace, it was hardly of the standard required here.'

'But that noble congratulated them.'

Narentir shook his head. 'You must learn that many of the quips directed at a performer, while appearing to be congratulatory, conceal deadly barbs.'

'I don't understand.'

'That noble compared their singing to the wailing of Morai-heg's banshees,' said Lilani.

He realised he was being spoken to and shook off thoughts of the previous day.

'Can you feel that?' said Lilani. 'Something's happening...'

He looked up, seeing the same leafy canopy of brilliant green and radiant summer sky beyond it. White birds perched in the treetops and their song trilled pleasingly. Nearby performers smiled and hugged one another, their faces alight as a subtle vibration raced through the air, a burgeoning sense of anticipation and excitement left in the wake of its passing.

Caelir leaped to his feet as the vibration surged through him, inexplicably invigorated by this strange sensation sweeping the forest.

'What is this?' he cried.

His question was answered when Narentir danced back into the clearing and swept them both into a crushing

embrace, his eyes bright with tears of joy. 'Do you feel
it?' he wept.

'We do!' nodded Lilani.

Seeing Caelir's confusion, Narentir laughed and said,
'The Everqueen, dear boy. She walks among us at the
dawn!'

ASPERON KHITAIN DREW his sword, a weapon crafted in
the forges of Hag Graef and quenched in the blood of
slaves. His armour was the colour of bloodwine, fresh
from the vine and his long dark hair was bound in a
trailing scalp lock.

His warriors formed up around him, a hundred hardened fighters in long mail coats and lacquered breastplates
that gleamed like the oily waters of Clar Karond. Long,
plum-coloured cloaks hung from their shoulders and
those few who did not carry long, ebony hafted spears
helped carry scaling ladders.

As the glorious standard of House Khitain was raised
high, he felt a thrill of anticipation and knelt to take a
handful of the coarse, powdery stone of the ground he
stood upon.

To have sailed across the Great Ocean and set foot once
more on Ulthuan…

The mountains reared up above him and the sun
bathed everything in a warm glow that made his skin
itch. He remembered the last time he had fought in the
land of his ancestors, pillaging and killing through the
green forests of northern Ulthuan, hunting down the
queen witch through the blazing ruin of her realm. The
invasion had stalled when her protector had rescued her
and Asperon shivered as he recalled the fury of the golden
armoured warrior cutting down scores of the greatest

druchii warriors in their escape.

Such a blademaster came but once in an age and Asperon cut his palm open as an offering to Khaine, mixing the welling red liquid with the dust of Ulthuan. He stood and climbed onto a nearby boulder to better see the preparations for the assault on the Emerald Gate.

Thousands of druchii warriors had crossed the great bridge of galleys from the island of the lighthouse and now marched along the overgrown pathways that crisscrossed the coastline. Perhaps these had once been the route of the long dead builders of the lighthouse or a neglected patrol route, but Asperon did not care what purpose they might once have served. Now they allowed the army of the Witch King to march into the mountains and lay siege to the shoulders of the first sea gate of Lothern.

Forests of speartips and lances glittered and Asperon watched as great war machines were unloaded from the troop galleys and carried onto the mainland by sweating, straining slaves. A host was being assembled that would sweep over the Emerald Gate and allow them to push the Asur back along the Straits of Lothern.

As he watched, a red banner was unfurled upon the peak of the captured lighthouse and he grinned wolfishly as he leapt down to rejoin his warriors. The signal soon passed to every warrior in the army and a predatory hunger for slaughter swept through Asperon.

'Warriors of Naggaroth!' he cried, his noble voice easily carrying across the mountains to his soldiers. 'Today we bathe our blades in the blood of the Asur! We march on their fortress and we will not stop until the banner of House Khitain flies above its ruins!'

A hundred spear shafts hammered on the white rock

of the mountains and Asperon took his place within
the ranks of his warriors. A great chorus of horn blasts
sounded from the assembled army and echoed from
the mountains like the bloody fury of Khaine himself.

He raised his sword above his head and shouted,
'Onwards!'

With disciplined steps, he and his warriors set off up the
slopes of the mountains, their strides long and sure. The
ground was rough, but far easier than the rugged harsh-
ness of the Iron Mountains around Hag Graef where he
relentlessly drilled his soldiers. Compared to the harsh
climate and terrain his warriors trained on, this was easy
going.

Their mile-eating stride carried them swiftly up the
rocky slopes, the hard packed earth of the wide paths overgrown and partially obscured, but providing a swift route
up the mountains. The occasional flurry of arrows flashed
from above as cloaked scouts loosed shafts from hiding
and screams of pain swiftly followed.

The shock of the lighthouse's capture and the crushing
defeat of their fleet had paralysed the Asur into inaction
and the pathways through the mountains were only
lightly defended. Small groups of their own scouts darted
forwards and soon the rain of arrows halted and Asperon
heard sounds of vicious struggles from above.

At last he could see the crest of the ridgeline above him
and briefly halted their advance on the rocky plateau to
redress the ranks that had become ragged on the climb.
Ahead, a gentle slope led towards the eastern flank of the
Emerald Gate and Asperon felt his blood surge as he saw
what lay before them.

The thought that the Glittering Lighthouse might be
captured and the Emerald Gate be attacked from the sides

had clearly never entered the thoughts of its builders, for its defences had clearly been designed to face a frontal assault from the sea.

From what Asperon could see, the defensive architecture of the fortress's flanks consisted of little more than a hastily prepared defensive ditch and a turreted blockhouse. A wall of less than a hundred paces safeguarded the route onto the arched span of the fortress, but it was low and unprotected by outworks or high towers.

Yet more druchii warriors marched onto the plateau before the fortress and Asperon laughed as he saw the panic sweeping the silver armoured elves on the wall at the sight of such a host. He could taste their panic on the air and shouted, 'You see, the Asur's complacency and arrogance will reap them bloody ruin!'

More carnyx sounded, the skirling sound heralding the death they would inflict upon their enemies. He reopened the cut on his palm and reached up to smear his blood upon the standard of his house to offer those who would fight and die beneath it to Khaine.

A rumbling tremor of weapons clashing on shields echoed from the mountains and Asperon could see the desperate scramble on the wall ahead of him as archers and spearmen rushed to fill the ramparts.

The advance began as a steady trot, the druchii walking briskly with their spears raised, then became a jog as spears lowered and ranks of crossbowmen formed up behind them.

Asperon could see faces pale with fear and drank in that fear as the wall drew nearer. His heart thudded in his breast and his fingers flexed on the wire-wound grip of his sword.

He saw a sword with a silver blade chop downwards

and a singing volley of arrows arced from the wall in a white rain.

'Shields!' shouted Asperon and his warriors dropped to their knees and lifted their left arms above their heads. A whooshing *thwak* of displaced air sounded and a hundred arrows slammed into them, but most smacked harmlessly into his warriors' shields. A few screamed in pain as a lucky arrow found its mark, but most quickly rose to their feet unharmed.

Though they had sacrificed speed to stop and raise shields, he saw that they had suffered least amongst the advancing army, with many druchii corpses simply trampled by their charging comrades in their hunger to reach the wall.

Insane courage was all very well, but it was pointless if you reached the enemy with too few warriors to kill them.

A staccato ripple of crossbow strings filled the air with black bolts and Asperon laughed as he saw a dozen enemy warriors pitched from the walls. Blood stained their pristine tunics as they fell. More bolts slashed towards the blockhouse as they set off towards the ditch before the wall and gate. Blue-fletched shafts slashed down, though many fewer than before thanks to the relentless hammering of crossbows.

An arrow punched through the helm of the warrior next to him and blood spattered Asperon's face as the warrior fell. He licked the droplets from his lips as the druchii warriors ahead of his own hurled their ladders against the wall.

Swords flashed and blood was spilled as the Asur fought the warriors at the tops of the ladders. Screams and ringing steel cut the air and warriors toppled from the ramparts, skulls cloven or chests sliced open. The wall was not long and Asperon halted his warriors as he scanned its length, his experienced eye seeking out the weakest section of the defences against which to lead his warriors.

Then something unbelievable happened.

The gates of the blockhouse were opening.

Had they carried the wall so swiftly that some brave warriors were even now within?

'With me!' he shouted and sprinted for the gate. His warriors followed without hesitation and Asperon screamed with inchoate elation as he pictured being the first noble of Naggaroth to plant a standard in the Emerald Gate.

His euphoria turned to horror as he saw the column of knights with tall, gleaming helmets of silver galloping from the fortress. Dust billowed at their passing and Asperon felt his innards clamp in terror as he saw the warrior in golden armour that led them. He carried a blazing sword, like a sliver of the sun bound within a length of shimmering steel, and rode a white steed adorned with glittering scales of gem-encrusted barding.

Golden wings swept back from his helm and though he had never before laid eyes upon this warrior, he instinctively knew him, for his identity was a curse and the terror of the druchii.

Tyrion, Defender of Ulthuan...

Tall banners of white streamed behind the cavalry and their silver lances lowered in unison as they charged out. Elven soldiers armed with spears and long swords spread out behind the cavalry, cutting into the disorganised ranks of the druchii as they milled at the base of the wall.

'Halt!' shouted Asperon. 'Form a shield-wall!'

Even as he gave the order, he could see it was already too late.

His warriors were spread out, scattered as they raced to the opened gate, and easy prey for mounted warriors.

He snatched a shield from the warrior next to him and raised his sword as the pounding of hooves on stone swallowed them and the charge slammed home with a deafening thunderclap of splintering lances and screams.

Blood spurted as glittering lance blades spitted their ranks and the fiery sword of Tyrion clove warriors in two with golden sweeps that melted through armour and seared flesh. The charge of the Asur cavalry punched through the disordered ranks of Asperon's warriors and trampled them into the ground, leaving scores of broken bodies in their wake.

He picked himself up from the ground, blood pouring from a deep gash on his forehead and white agony flaring as splintered bone jutted from his elbow. His shield was useless and he heard the screams of warriors dying before the relentless slaughter of the Asur.

An ululating note sounded from a silver trumpet and the cavalry expertly wheeled on the spot as they prepared to charge once more. The golden warrior at the head of the silver knights aimed his sword at him, and Asperon welcomed the challenge of the gesture.

If he were to die this day, then what better way to end his days than in combat with the infamous Tyrion himself?

A beam of radiant sunfire leapt from Tyrion's blade and Asperon's flesh was burned from his body in a firestorm with the power of a star dragon's breath.

* * *

HOT, SULPHUROUS FUMES clung to the rocky walls of the underground passageway like gauzy curtains and wisps of hot steam drifted lazily from vents cut into the floor. A dim red glow, like cooling lava, seemed to come from the rocks themselves, and banked braziers added their own smoke and heat.

The sound of distant song came from somewhere far below and its musical cadences were unlike anything heard elsewhere on Ulthuan. The songs sung here were ancient beyond understanding, the rhythms and harkening melodies unknown in the world above save by those who dared to venture below the mountains of Caledor and learn the songs of awakening.

The songs of the dragons...

The mists parted like a smoky yellow curtain before a warrior who delved deep into the labyrinthine passages of the mountains, the songs of valour and tales of peril echoing within his soul like a lone voice in an empty temple.

His name was Prince Imrik, and of all the waking denizens of the caverns below the Dragonspine Mountains, none carried themselves with a fraction of the martial nobility and courage as did he. His countenance was fair, his long white hair bound with iron cords and his strength of purpose was like the furnace heat that stirred below the peak of Vaul's Anvil.

The blood of Caledor Dragontamer flowed in his veins and his lineage was of the proudest noble house of Ulthuan. In him, it was said, the strength of Tethlis the Slayer was reborn and the might of his sword arm was unmatched, save perhaps by that of Prince Tyrion.

Red light shimmered like fresh blood on Imrik's armour, an engraved suit of ithilmar mail that was as light and flexible as silk, yet was impervious to sword and fire. His cloak billowed in the heat of the passageway and the swiftness of his stride, for bleak news had come from Lothern and all the might of Ulthuan was being roused to war.

The passageway widened out into an impossibly deep cavern, though it was next to impossible to gauge its exact dimensions because hot, aromatic smoke obscured its farthest reaches. A distant rumble, like the breath of the world, vibrated the air at a frequency beyond the comprehension of most mortals, but to Imrik it was as clear as a note wrung from the great dragonhorn at his side.

It was the breath of slumbering dragons.

The songs of awakening grew louder as Imrik entered, and his soul took flight as he saw the multitude of scaled, draconic forms clustered around scalding vents that plunged into the deepest heart of the volcanic mountains.

Fire roared and seethed in the air, held aloft by the songs of the fire mages who sang to the slumbering dragons. He heard the songs in his heart and cast his gaze around the chamber to see if any of the mighty creatures were close to waking.

Powerfully muscled chests rose and fell in time with the chants of the mages, but the dragons' hearts beat a slow refrain, a beat that had slowed as the molten heat of the mountains had cooled and the magic of the world diminished.

Imrik knew there had been a time when the sight of dragons riding hot thermals rising from the Dragon-spine Mountains had been commonplace, but such a vision had not been seen in hundreds of years. In these threatening times, only the younger dragons commonly awoke, though even they were a shadow of the former glory of Caledor and its famed dragon riders.

Naysmiths at the court of Lothern bemoaned the slumber of the dragons as indicative of the slide into ruin of the Asur, but Imrik had never surrendered to such melancholy. Long had he studied the ways of dragons and no mortal could claim to know this most ancient of species better than he.

Imrik made his way around the circumference of the cavern, careful not to disturb the rites and chants of the singing fire mages. Many of these chants would have begun months, if not years, ago and none knew better than he the folly of interrupting a dragonsong.

He made his way to the centre of the cavern where a great brazier burned with a white gold light. Mages in scarlet robes and with long hair that fell like cascades of flame from their scalps surrounded the brazier, speaking with heated voices that crackled with a fire the equal of the conflagration before them.

The debate ceased as Imrik drew near, though he could see the golden light of Aqshy smouldering in their eyes. Ever were the hearts of those who studied the fire wind bellicose.

'My friends,' said Imrik. 'The Phoenix King sends for our aid. What should I tell him?'

'The dragons still slumber, my lord,' said a mage known as Lamellan.

'How many awake?'

'None save Minaithnir, my lord,' said Lamellan. 'His soul burns brightly and the hearts of the younger dragons stir with thoughts of war, but the dreams of the great dragons are too deep to reach. We summon the heat that burns at the heart of the world with songs of legendary times and glorious deeds, but the memories are cold, my lord…'

'The fire of the dragons is gone?' said Imrik. 'Is that what you are trying to say?'

'Not gone, my lord,' said Lamellan. 'But buried deep. It will be years before the ashes are wrought into flaming life. Too late for us now.'

'You are wrong,' said Imrik, pacing around the brazier and his pale eyes reflecting the fire that burned at its heart. 'The age of glory can never be forgotten, by elf nor dragon. By such means are the dragons of Caledor roused from sleep. The druchii once more set foot on our beloved homeland and the Phoenix King has sent missives pleading for our aid. Lothern is besieged and the Hag Sorceress herself leads an army at the Eagle Gate!'

'My lord,' protested Lamellan, 'you know as well as I that to reach the heart of these noble creatures takes great time and effort.'

'Time is the one thing Ulthuan does not have, my friend,' said Imrik. 'Our fair isle would have fallen into darkness long ago without the might of the dragons. They are as much a part of Ulthuan as the Asur, and I will not believe that they will fail to heed our call to arms in this time of woe.'

He could see his words were fanning the flame of Aqshy that burned in the hearts of the fire mages and stoked the warlike embers of their souls to greater effort.

'Ulthuan is under attack and requires all the martial power it can assemble. Go! Sing the songs of ancient days!

'The dragonriders of old must soar the skies again!'

Chapter Twenty

ANATHEMA

THE PYRES BURNED long into the night, illuminating the battered white wall of the Eagle Gate with hellish light and thick with the aroma of roasting meat. Warriors with plates of armour fused to their flesh by magic capered around the giant bonfires, their scarred bodies jerking as though they were not theirs to command.

And perhaps they are not, thought Issyk Kul as he watched the sensuous dances and orgiastic feasting. The flesh-suited madmen capered in time to the beat of Hung drums, and chants in praise of Shornaal soared with the sparks spat from the fires.

His own body was slathered in the blood of his latest kill, and the exquisite high he had achieved with his latest partner in violation had been sublime. The elves of Ulthuan were far superior subjects to the poor specimens who dwelt in the cold wastes of the far north. To those used to a life of misery and hardship, torture meant little, but to effete souls raised in a land of plenty and who had never known the brutality of life beyond their pampered existence, it was a nightmare that enhanced Kul's pleasure tenfold.

The defenders of the wall still held, though he knew it was simply a matter of time until they broke. And when that moment came, he and what remained of his followers would debase the remainder and make bloody ruin of this isle.

He turned from the wall and made his way through the campsite towards the neat lines of the druchii camp, shaking his head at such rigidly enforced order. The camp of his warriors was a battered and broken landscape dotted with piles of shattered weapons, excrement and dead or insensible bodies. Order was anathema to Kul and he allowed, and encouraged, his warriors to indulge every sordid desire, so long as they were able to fight upon the dawn.

A bloody procession of chanting zealots, chained to one another by flesh hooks piercing the meat of their arms, danced around him. He acknowledged their devotion to the Dark Prince by gathering up the chains that bound them all and jerking them savagely, ripping the iron hooks from their flesh and drawing shrieks of bliss and blood from their lips.

Kul dropped the chains and left his torn followers behind as he approached the sentry line of druchii warriors. Morathi kept her followers carefully segregated from his own, lest the entire army devolve into a heaving, bloody mass of perversion and slaughter.

The guards recognised him and stepped aside to let him pass and Kul could taste their fear of him. Mingled with that fear was a colossal arrogance and condescension, for these were warriors of a race that looked upon humanity from the perspective of those that had almost held the world in their grasp.

He resisted the urge to draw his sword and cut them down for such presumption and naïvety. The evidence of their foolishness was clear for all to see, for was not the surface of the world crawling with the maggots of humanity? Such arrogance was misplaced when you were forced to eke out an existence in the coldest, bleakest place imaginable.

Everywhere within the druchii camp he could see ordered ranks of flimsy tents that wouldn't last a night on the steppe, yet were thought to be fit to bring on campaign.

Druchii warriors gathered around campfires and the noise of low conversations buzzed in his ears like an insect trapped in a bottle. Only recently had warriors arrived that Kul thought the equal of Morathi, a troupe of long-limbed she-elves clad in gleaming leather and fragments of flexible armour. Wild-haired and sumptuous, he had thought them dancers or courtesans until he saw them slay armed prisoners in ritual combats of spectacular violence.

Those same warrior women now stood guard around Morathi's tent, a monstrous pavilion of purple and golden silk that billowed as though it had breath. A trio of the manic she-elves paced before the pavilion's entrance, scenting the blood that dried on his skin.

As he drew near, two peeled off to the side while one remained defiantly before him. The two circled him, moving slowly, but with exquisite grace as they ran fingers over his hard muscles and scraped blood from his flesh with their fingertips.

'Are you going to get out of my way?' said Kul to the she-elf before him.

'Maybe,' said the elf woman, exposing her teeth and

Kul fought the urge to break his fist against her jaw. 'Maybe we will demand a price for your passage.'

'What price?'

The she-elf thought for a moment and said, 'Send ten of your finest warriors to us.'

'Why?'

'So we can kill them, of course.'

'And why would I do such a thing?'

'They will be honoured with bloody deaths,' said the elf. 'And it would please us.'

Kul nodded, for he knew this was no negotiation, simply a price to be paid. 'I will send them to you in the morning. Kill them and give me their hearts when you are done.'

'Very well,' said the elf. 'When we have their blood, you may have their hearts.'

Without seeming to move, the she-elf slipped aside and the three of them bowed extravagantly to him. His business with them was over and he ignored their mocking obeisances as he entered Morathi's tent.

Inside, the luxury of the Hag Sorceress's domain had been transported from Naggaroth and reassembled here. Velveteen throws were draped over an ebony chaise longue and carved busts no doubt thought exquisite stood on black marble plinths. More of the insane she-elves lounged around the perimeter of the tent, sharpening knives, turning bloody trophies over in their hands or sipping goblets of ruby liquid.

Gold brocade hung from the ceiling and a low fire burned in the centre of the pavilion.

A great black cauldron of beaten iron hung on graceful black spars over the fire, the metallic reek of blood coming from the gently steaming red liquid that filled it to the brim.

As Kul watched, a thin hand emerged from the bubbling cauldron, pale and as unblemished as virgin marble. Arms followed, sculpted and smooth, and Kul felt arousal stir at the sight of this bloody birth.

A mane of black hair plastered red with blood rose from the cauldron and a pair of wide, staring eyes wept red tears as the Hag Sorceress emerged and lifted her head. The blood in the cauldron hissed as Morathi let it soak her breasts, hips and thighs. Her flesh was white and renewed, streaked with red as thick, gooey runnels ran down her naked, ivory body.

Stripped of her robes, Morathi was the single most desirable thing Kul had ever seen, a siren of death and sensation that commanded devotion in all things. Her flesh glowed with vigour and a bloom of youth that was surely impossible for one of such unimaginable age.

Not even the most powerful shamans Kul had slain had displayed such carnal devotion to Shornaal and he longed to rip her from the cauldron and violate her in every way imaginable.

He restrained his rabid impulses, knowing that this was not the time for such loss of control. The she-elf protectors would rip him to shreds before he came within striking distance of Morathi and he had no wish to end his days as fodder for their ritual sacrifices.

In any case, the Hag Sorceress had bigger plans than simple pleasures of the flesh, plans that would see the world dragged through the gates of hell and unleash the realm of the Dark Gods upon its surface.

The restraint of his desires was painful to a devotee of Shornaal and as Kul saw the knowledge of his frustration in her eyes, he felt the killing rage rise in him once more. He closed his eyes and recited the six secret names of his patron, gripping the hilt of his sword and concentrating on the pain as the blades and spikes cut into his palm.

When he opened them again, Morathi was reclining on a chaise longue and clad in a robe of crimson doupioni, its fine weave already staining with the blood on her limbs. One of the she-elves plaited her bloody hair, pulling sodden, matted lengths into long, drooping spikes.

'Your messenger said you had news,' said Issyk Kul.

Morathi flicked her eyes towards him and nodded slowly. 'My son makes war on the Asur at Lothern. His warriors lay siege to the Emerald Gate.'

'Then we must make haste to take this fortress,' said Kul.

'Must we?' said Morathi, her voice smooth and seductive, like a young maiden. 'But it seems like your warriors so enjoy to fight.'

'They relish the chance to fight and feel the bliss of pain,' agreed Kul. 'But they wish victory more. I need to know when your warriors will take to the field of battle.'

Morathi smiled and shook her head.

'My warriors will fight soon enough,' said the Hag Sorceress. 'When this dirty little siege is over. I leave such grubby battles to your northern tribes.'

'The battle would go swifter if you were to commit warriors to the fight,' pointed out Issyk Kul. 'You claimed time was of the essence.'

'And so it is, my dear Kul,' said Morathi, rising from her repose to stand before him. 'But such inelegant battles are ill-suited to our sensibilities. You knew the price for allowing you to join me was the blood of your warriors. Trust me, when the Eagle Gate is ours and Ulthuan is laid open before us, you will receive all that you desire.'

'All?'

'All,' said Morathi, allowing her robes to fall open and expose a slice of virgin skin.

Kul licked his lips as he pictured the rewards of success.

More was at stake than simply the attainment of the promise of ravaging Morathi's flesh – the fulfilment of what the weak fool, Archaon, had singularly failed to achieve.

Morathi spoke again. 'When will your warriors carry the wall?'

'Soon. Your race is a spent force in the world,' he said, enjoying the flare of anger he saw in her eyes. 'Even in the remote north, that fact is understood. I have warriors to lose by the hundred, but each enemy that falls in battle is an irreplaceable loss. We will simply batter them into defeat. For my warriors do not fear pain or death. They do.'

'Then be sure to give them what they fear,' said Morathi.

Kul smiled, exposing sharpened teeth and said, 'Never doubt it.'

CAELIR HAD NOT slept at all and neither, it seemed, had any other inhabitant of Avelorn. The news that the Everqueen would walk amongst the forest had banished all thoughts of rest and imparted a manic energy to the elves that had come to pay homage and hoped to become part of her court.

Though no one had seen them come, fresh pavilions with an ethereal quality of simple grace had appeared in the midst of the forest, ones that needed no cords or poles to support them and were held aloft by the soft winds that gusted around them.

Lights flitted around these pavilions and armoured elf maids in golden armour ringed them, though the presence of such warriors did not detract from the peace and tranquillity of the scene.

Lilani held his hand and Narentir stood behind them both with a paternal hand on their shoulders. Neither could keep the joy from their faces and Caelir suspected that his face was similarly stretched with an unrestrained smile. All through the assembled elves, over a hundred estimated Caelir, he could see the same unabashed love and radiant happiness that made him proud to be part of this gathering.

His mind was a mad whirl of thoughts and emotions, a jumble of ideas vying for supremacy in his consciousness. He would see the Everqueen, the most beautiful woman in the world, and his memory could be restored. He would play for her and who knew what might transpire in the wake of such a performance?

Caelir had dressed in clothes lent to him by Narentir, an elegant tunic of silks and satins that was thin and light, yet clung warmly to his skin. He carried the harp that had won him such acclaim within the forest and wore a belt of black, upon which was hung the dagger he had carried since being washed upon the beach of Yvresse – such a long time ago it seemed.

So much had happened since then and though he knew much of it had been terrible, the magic of Avelorn prevented the true horror of it intruding into his thoughts, as though the forest could not bear the thought of its inhabitants' anguish. Dimly he realised that such denial was unhealthy, but shook off such gloomy thoughts as a pale nimbus of light built from within the Everqueen's pavilion.

'She comes...' breathed Narentir and Caelir felt the hand on his shoulder tighten.

Caelir gripped the harp and ached to play a welcoming refrain upon its strings, but restrained himself, sensing that to spoil this moment with his own selfish desires would be gross and unwelcome.

The skin of the Everqueen's tent peeled back and a bright light, like sunlight on golden fields poured from inside. Amid the wondrous halo of shimmering brilliance, the ruler of Avelorn emerged – the most beauteous elf in creation and most wondrous ruler of Ulthuan.

The assembled elves dropped to their knees, overcome by wonder and emotion. Tears of joy spilled from every eye and even the skies shone with the reflected radiance of her smile.

Caelir wanted to join them in worship of this enchanted daughter of Isha.

Instead, he found himself gripping the hilt of his dagger.

THE FOREST OF Avelorn flashed past them as they rode for the court of the Everqueen. Eldain pushed Irenya hard, digging his heels into her flanks in a way he would never normally do. He risked a glance over at Rhianna, seeing the same anxious expression that had settled on her face as soon as they had set foot on dry land at the fork of the River Arduil.

It was stupid to be riding this fast through a forest, for a moment's inattention could cost a rider dear. A low branch or rabbit hole could be the end of a rider or mount, but Rhianna had insisted that they immediately ride into the depths of the forest.

'Save him and you save me...' she had whispered, repeating the phrase she had first uttered on the *Dragonkin* as they sailed towards Avelorn as a mantra.

The implications of the phrase were not lost on Eldain and a clammy hand had taken hold of his heart despite the wondrous beauty and sun of the Everqueen's northern realm. He knew the sights and sounds of the forest should beguile him, should entrance him with their incredible splendour, but his mind endlessly turned over the dreadful possibilities of what might be about to happen.

As much as the deaths he had witnessed recently pained him and weighed guiltily upon his soul, the thought that the Everqueen herself might be in danger eclipsed them all. The idea that it was he who had led to her being placed in danger had silenced any objections to riding at speed through the forest.

Yvraine rode behind him, her aversion to travelling by means other than walking forgotten as she shared a measure of Rhianna's fear that they might already be too late.

Eldain caught sight of her greatsword and knew that if Caelir dared hurt the Everqueen, he himself would gladly wield the blade that would end his life...

THE EVERQUEEN...

Caelir's hands began to tremble as the ruler of Avelorn walked amongst her people. Though no musician played, the forest provided an accompaniment of its own for her. Birds trilled musically, streams gurgled and the wind sighed through the excited branches of trees.

The land itself welcomed her.

Behind her came a Handmaiden bearing a banner of emerald leaves plucked from the branches of trees and woven with golden hair. The light of the forest was captured in the banner, but it was a willing captive, and it bore the heart of Avelorn in its rustling, living fabric.

Caelir saw fresh white flowers spring from the ground where the Everqueen walked and her radiance caused those already in bloom to turn their faces towards her. The forest came alive at her presence and the adoration in every face was heartfelt and pure.

None averted their gaze from the Everqueen, for she desired her subjects to know beauty, and she blessed them all with the healing light of her magic.

Without knowing how, he knew the dagger he gripped was now loose in its sheath and he could feel a terrible hunger from the blade, willing him to draw it. He fought its malign touch, pressing the quillons hard against the heavy scabbard.

I have to get out of here, he thought desperately, but the haunting majesty of the Everqueen held him fast. He could feel the puzzlement of those nearby and a number of faces tore their gaze from the Everqueen and regarded him with hostility at his lack of respect.

'Caelir!' whispered Lilani. 'What are you doing?'

'I don't know...' he hissed between clenched teeth as he fought the urge to draw the dagger from its heavy black scabbard. He remembered Kyrielle telling him that she had not liked holding the blade and her father saying that it had shed a great deal of blood.

The Everqueen moved amongst the people of the forest, smiling and radiant, reaching out here and there to touch the forehead of a kneeling elf. The foremost artistes, singers, musicians, poets, artisans and mages laughed as she selected them to become part of her court and their laughter was like the chiming of the clearest golden bells.

Caelir fought to move, to turn and run from the dark emanations slithering up his arm from the dagger, but his limbs were not his to command, his grip held fast to the metal hilt. More performers were chosen, and as each rose from their knees, the Handmaidens of the Everqueen led them into the forest.

The Everqueen came closer and Caelir's limbs twitched, as though two opposing forces waged silent war for control of his body.

Then she paused as she reached towards a gifted poet and tilted her head as though listening to a faraway sound. Her posture stiffened and the sunlight fled the sky, a forlorn gloom and unknown menace descending from the forest in an instant.

Caelir heard the roaring of a storm in his head.

He wanted to scream a warning.

The Everqueen looked up.

Their eyes met and a moment of awful knowledge passed between them.

'Caelir…' she said.

At the sound of his name from her divine lips, the chains slipped from around his memory and what had been locked away now rushed to the forefront of his mind.

It all came back.

Everything…

THE LINE OF warriors emerged from the trees as though they had been part of them but a moment ago. Spears levelled, ten elf maids in golden armour and plumed helmets barred their way forward and only Eldain's superlative horsemanship saved him from running straight into a line of lethal spear points.

Rhianna and Yvraine halted with somewhat less grace, but their horses saved them from running straight into the blades of the warrior women. Without waiting for them to demand his business, Eldain cried, 'Please, we have to get to the Everqueen. She is in danger!'

A warrior with long dark hair beneath her helmet put up her spear at his words. She took a step from the ranks of her warriors and said, 'You are wrong. The Handmaidens of the Everqueen protect her within the boundaries of Avelorn. She is quite safe.'

'No,' pressed Eldain, riding towards the elf maid. He heard the creak of bowstrings being pulled taut and knew he was a hair's breadth from dying. 'You don't understand the danger she is in. We have to reach her court.'

'What manner of danger do you mean?'

Rhianna rode alongside him and said, 'There is a young elf here under an enchantment of dark magic, though he does not know it. He will seek to harm the Everqueen.'

'What is this elf's name?' said the Handmaiden. Eldain could see her scepticism and wished he could penetrate her disbelief at what he knew must seem a fantastical claim.

'Caelir,' said Eldain. 'He is my brother.'

A ripple of recognition passed through the handmaidens and Eldain felt a sick dread settle in the pit of his stomach.

Caelir was already here...

'They speak the truth,' said Yvraine. 'I speak as a Sword Master of Hoeth and emissary of the White Tower. You must let us pass.'

The Handmaiden's eyes narrowed as she took in Yvraine's sword and martial bearing and reached an uncomfortable conclusion.

'Someone of that name is known to the forest,' she said before turning on her heel and issuing curt commands to the Handmaidens accompanying her. In seconds her warriors had vanished into the forest and she turned back to Eldain.

'Quickly then,' she said. 'Follow me.'

CAELIR REMEMBERED EVERYTHING in the space of a heartbeat...

The dockyards of Clar Karond were aflame, the magical arrows that had been a wedding gift from Rhianna's father proving their worth as fire tore through great stockpiles of timber and ships with hungry appetite. Smoke curled from the devastated shipyards in monstrous black pillars and the screams of the druchii were music to his ears.

Aedaris bore him with the grace of Korhandir himself, galloping through the twisting, nightmare streets of the druchii's dockyards with unerring skill and speed. Ellyrion Reavers rode in ones and twos ahead of him as they made their escape and Caelir laughed with the sheer joy of what they had accomplished.

Eldain rode ahead of him, the black flanks of Lotharin heaving as his brother's stronger mount stretched the gap between them. He rode past blazing timber stores and ruined piles of blackened lumber as spears stabbed for him and crossbow bolts slashed through the air.

He crouched low over his steed's neck, speed carrying them past the stunned druchii without a fight. Ahead, Eldain slashed his sword through the arm of a warrior guarding the gateway and hacked down another before riding clear.

A pair of druchii charged him, their spears aimed for his horse's chest, but Caelir hauled back on the reins and Aedaris danced around the spear thrusts. His horse reared and its lashing hooves crushed the chest of its closest enemy and Caelir split the skull of the other with a swift blow from his sword.

The blood sang in his veins with the thrill of the fight and he turned to ride after his brother. He heard the snap of cross-bow strings and cried in pain as an iron bolt slammed into his hip. Yet more bolts flashed through the air, hammering into Aederis's chest and flanks.

He felt himself falling as the horse collapsed, blood froth-ing from its mouth and its legs thrashing in agony. He hit the ground hard and rolled as the breath slammed from his chest. He saw druchii running towards him and scrambled to his feet, weeping tears of pain and loss as he saw that his beloved Aedaris was dead.

He ran with a stumbling gait towards his brother.

Eldain would save him!

More bolts flashed through the air, and he screamed as another missile buried itself in his shoulder. He stumbled, but kept running.

'Brother!' he yelled, holding his hand out towards Eldain.

Eldain looked at him and Caelir saw his gaze fall upon the silver pledge ring that glittered in the firelight – seeing a depth of bitterness that shocked him to the depths of his soul.

Eldain said, 'Goodbye, Caelir,' and turned his horse from him.

Caelir dropped to his knees in horror as he watched his brother ride away towards the hills, the pain of his wounds nothing compared to the ache of betrayal that stabbed his heart with the force of a lance.

He hung his head as he heard the druchii surround him, the last of his strength stolen from his body at Eldain's abandonment of him. His vision turned from grey to black and the world fled from him as he pitched forward onto his face.

Darkness.

Pain.

Sorrow.

Anger.

Hatred.

Light...

He remembered long months of black horror and longer days of cold terror. He remembered sweating agony as a nightmare figure in iron armour and with blazing green eyes had regarded him with dread fascination and words Caelir could not understand. A terrifying, sinuous woman with raven hair and the face of a seductress worked upon him day and night, subjecting him to degradations and dark pleasures that left him full of loathing and revulsion.

A dark tower of brazen iron that presided over a city of murder and death.

The screams of a city that bathed in blood and celebrated the vilest practices imaginable.

Nightly his violation continued, pleasured and tormented by the weakness of his flesh and tortures that left his body unmarked, but left nightmarish scars upon his mind. He was plunged deeper into the abyss of madness than any mortal should ever go until his sanity began to crack and buckle at the seams.

He screamed himself hoarse, forgetting his name and past, everything that made him Caelir, brother of Eldain and husband to be of Rhianna. His mind detached from his history and he was reduced to a frame of meat and bone without intellect, reason or memory as magical tendrils wormed their way into his mind to plant a seed.

Only emotion remained: anger, hatred and fear...

*And when there was nothing left of him but the last frag-
ment of his self, he was brought back, the building blocks of
his psyche rebuilt enough for him to function as a sentient
being. He resisted, unwilling to face the horrors he had just
lived through, but he felt the touch of magic as those memories
of pain, darkness and manipulation were closed off, hidden
beneath enchantments of such cunning that they could only
be released by secret commands or specific magic.*

*Dreadful nightmares plagued him as he lay weeping in his
cell, but as the magic took hold within his mind, he slept more
soundly, lost in the wilderness of his mind as new thoughts
and talents – music, art, poetry and song – were seeded within
him.*

*Still he was but a mass of emotion and selective memory,
and only as he had been held above a heaving ocean on the
deck of a black ship that pitched and rolled in a shimmering
fog had the last shreds of intellect and reason been returned
to him.*

*Then he was falling and cold liquid filled his lungs as he
hit the water and sank beneath the waves. He struggled to the
surface and coughed a heaving breath of saltwater.*

*A fragment of timber detritus bobbed next to him and he
gratefully seized it.*

*Thunderous booms echoed from the cliffs as surf crashed
against rock and exploded upwards in sprays of pure white.
The icy, emerald sea surged through channels between rocky
archipelagos in great swells, rising and falling in foam-topped
waves that finally washed onto the distant shores of a mist-
shrouded island…*

CAELIR LET LOOSE a howl of pain and betrayal as the
memories buried within him surfaced in a torrential
rush at the magic of the Everqueen. Time slowed and his

focus narrowed as he gripped the hilt of the dagger and saw the beautiful ruler of Avelorn reach for him with outstretched arms.

He saw the pleading look in her eyes and wept bitter tears to see her so anguished.

Her very presence was anathema to the thing at his side and the heavy scabbard of black metal disintegrated in the face of Isha's power to unmake the baubles of Chaos...

Where before he had held a sheathed weapon that could not be drawn, he now held a triangular sectioned blade of crimson iron that reeked with the blood of a thousand victims and the evil bound within it.

The ground beneath him blackened and the trees around him died in the blink of an eye as the power of its evil rotted them to the core. Birds dropped dead from the trees and the elves of Avelorn cried out as they felt the diabolical presence within the blade.

Caelir fought to resist the impulse to raise the weapon, but his limb was no longer his own.

The weapon smoked, dark tendrils of magic seeping from the blade as the daemonic power within fought to resist the Everqueen's purity.

Everything around him was moving as though in a dream, with glacial slowness and terrible inevitability. A trio of riders arrived at the edge of the clearing around the Everqueen's pavilion and Caelir felt as though a blazing fist had seized his heart.

One rider he did not recognise, an elf maid with a greatsword sheathed across her back.

But the others... oh, the others...

Rhianna.

Eldain.

Hot anger surged in him and the dagger in his hand fed upon it, drawing on the well of hatred that had been stoked within him to sustain its blasted existence in this realm of healing magic.

Caelir heard someone shout his name, the sound drawn out and slow.

He saw Eldain, now knowing him as his brother and not some monstrous doppelganger.

He saw the betrayal his own flesh and blood had visited upon him.

Caelir screamed as the smoking, daemonic weapon thrust itself into the Everqueen's chest.

The story continues in Sons of Ellyrion,
by the same author

ABOUT THE AUTHOR

Hailing from Scotland, **Graham McNeill** worked for over six years as a Games Developer in Games Workshop's Design Studio before taking the plunge to become a full-time writer. Graham's written a host of SF and Fantasy novels and comics, as well as a number of side projects that keep him busy and (mostly) out of trouble. His Horus Heresy novel, *A Thousand Sons*, was a New York Times bestseller and his Time of Legends novel, *Empire*, won the 2010 David Gemmell Legend Award.

Graham lives and works in Nottingham and you can keep up to date with where he'll be and what he's working on by visiting his website.

Join the ranks of the 4th Company at *www.graham-mcneill.com*

WILLIAM KING

WARHAMMER

BLOOD OF AENARION

A TYRION & TECLIS NOVEL

UK ISBN: 978-1-84970-090-0   US ISBN: 978-1-84970-091-7

OUT DECEMBER 2011

An extract from Blood of Aenarion
by William King

THE DUEL WAS about to begin. All sixty warriors were forming in a circle, presenting their blades, points towards the centre. The duel would take place within a ring of sharp steel. The warriors would strike down any contestant who tried to flee from the battle.

The formalities were already gone through. Larien was not willing to retract the insult. Tyrion felt that honour must be satisfied. The seconds had done their best to make sure the quarrel had been settled amicably. Duty was done. The fight could begin. Both participants stripped to the waist and took up their weapons.

'I shall kill you slowly and painfully,' said Larien, as they walked down into the depression and took their places in the flat space below.

'The way you think,' said Tyrion and smiled brightly.

Larien looked hard at him.

'Slowly and painfully,' Tyrion said, to make sure Larien got the point.

Things were not obviously going the way he expected. Tyrion's nonchalance had obviously surprised him. He had come expecting to kill a nervous boy. He had found someone more self-possessed than he was. Tyrion decided that in part this fight was to be won in the mind. He suspected that most individual combats were. It was as much about the attitude of the fighters as it was about skill.

'I am of the Blood of Aenarion,' said Tyrion, simply, as if he were explaining something to someone slow of mind. It was an attack designed to increase Larien's unease and make him less sure of himself.

'I will soon see what that looks like,' said Larien. 'I am guessing it is the same colour as anyone else's.'

It was a good response and Tyrion smiled at it as if hearing a joke he enjoyed particularly.

'Shall we begin?' he asked, looking from Korhien to Larien's chief second. The two of them nodded. They stepped back to take their places on the edge of the ring. They too presented their blades. There was no way out of the circle now. All of the gaps were closed. Anyone trying to get out would be impaled upon a blade.

Larien sprang forward as lithe as a tiger. Tyrion parried easily enough and stepped forward. Blade strokes blurred between the two of them for the moment. Tyrion kept his guard up and made a few ripostes. He was content simply to ride out the fury of the initial attack and take the measure of his opponent.

Larien was quick and he was strong and his technique was excellent.

Tyrion did not need Korhein's training to know this. Something in his mind was aware of it, in the same way as he was aware of the strength and weakness of a chess position. He doubted Larien had the same quickness of reflex as he himself possessed but he decided not to act on that assumption until he had more proof of it. Larien could, after all, easily be faking it, hoping to make him overconfident.

A few more passes of the blades told him this was not so. The elf's personality was reflected in his blade work. His swordplay was intricate and deceptive but the deception was in the technique. Larien relied on that and his natural strength to overcome his opponents. He was much better with a sword than most elves ever would be. He smiled at Tyrion, teeth gritted.

'I see what you mean about killing me slowly,' said Tyrion as they stepped apart. 'Are you trying to lull me to sleep?'

'No,' said Larien, springing forward. His blade was aimed high. An elf less quick than Tyrion might have had his head split. As it was Tyrion merely stepped backward, parrying as he went, noticing that the rain of blows Larien had unleashed did indeed have a rhythm, and one most likely intended to lull the opponent into parrying the pattern of it.

He found himself falling into the pattern almost automatically, as an elf might sometimes find himself tapping his fingers in time to a drumbeat. He could see the danger of what Iltharis had predicted happening. It came as no surprise when suddenly the blade was not where it should have been according to the pattern of strokes. Tyrion had already predicted where it would be and parried it. He brought his left fist crashing into Larien's face.

Cartilage broke under the impact. Larien went reeling back, blinded by pain and tears. Tyrion leaned forward to full extension, ramming his sword into Larien's stomach. He felt the impact all the way up his arm. There was a scraping sensation as his sword hit bone. Larien screamed like an animal being pole-axed. Blood gouted forth, covering Tyrion's sword and hands, spraying onto his naked chest. Some of it got in his mouth. He caught the coppery taste.

Part of his mind was aware that this should be horrific. It was certainly not beautiful or glorious. There was a stink of blood and entrails, of things that should normally be inside an elf's body but now were not.

He did not mind it, just as he did not mind the screaming, or the sight of the light dying in another elf's eyes. The main thing was that, at some point, the sword had left Larien's hand and was now lying on the ground. His own life was no longer in danger. He had wiped out an insult to his family's honour and he had forestalled an attack on his clan by their enemies.

He felt a twinge of sympathy for Larien's pain. Korhien had been right in one way. It was hard to watch another elf die, but that too was a problem easily solved. He struck again, aiming for the heart and silenced Larien's screams forever. He looked around at the other elves present. They stared at him in wonder and something else; it might have been horror.

'Unorthodox and inelegant,' said Iltharis. 'But effective.'